THE MIXED MARTIAL ARTIST

LANTA BROWN

First Edition - October 2019

Trade paperback ISBN 978-1-9162506-0-4
Hardback ISBN 978-1-9162506-1-1
Ebook ISBN 978-1-9162506-2-8

For all the fighters who dedicate their lives to competing inside the cage

Do not pray for an easy life, pray for the strength to endure a hard one

- Bruce Lee

CHAPTER 1

In the decaying gymnasium of a disused California high school — where teenagers once played basketball and made out beneath the bleachers — two adult women were trying to make a living by punching each other in the face. Juliette's opponent was smothering her, and with a knee pressed deep into her stomach, had her pinned to the canvas flooring. The crowd wailed and booed. A plastic cup swung up into the air and crashed down into the center of the cage, its frothy contents showering both combatants, the liquid glistening as it trickled over the naked skin of their limbs.

As Juliette fought to escape from underneath her foe, she caught a glimpse of her brother Earl's lumbering silhouette through the fishnet pattern of wires that made up the cage wall. She saw the glow of his eyes watching from the dark underside of his brow, as though he was some kind of circus master seeking to control her with his authoritative glare.

"Don't do this to me, Jules," Earl said as he paced to and fro with the hunched gait of an ape, his clenched fists jutting forth sporadically, in miniature, punch-like thrusts.

You could see by the way he filled his tracksuit that he was thickset, solid-shouldered, broad like a heavyweight boxer. However, the opened zipper of his track-jacket revealed he was carrying a paunch of excess weight around the stomach, muscle tone that had slid down his frame and settled about his waist, symptomatic of an athlete who had fallen into disrepair. The stage lights shone from high among the ceiling of the dimly-lit gymnasium, reflecting off the back of his track-jacket to reveal the moniker "Coach Earl Diaz" embroidered above a logo which appeared to be an illustration of a devil's face. Beneath this demonic emblem, a further line of text read, "Diablo School of MMA."

"Jules, you gotta get up," the increasingly red-faced Coach Earl Diaz cried from outside the caged enclosure. "On your feet," he demanded, "up, up, up." Sweat bled from the edges of his graying crop of hair, a zigzag of veins pulsed through the flushed skin of his temple like a cable running underneath his flesh.

The cacophony of pleas bombarded Juliette, an aural barrage of equal measure to the shower of fists and elbows raining down on her blood-soaked face. She felt as though she was suffocating, her opponent looming over her like a solid, immovable structure, the endless cries from her brother, the compulsion to perform to his expectations, the howl of the audience, the stifling atmosphere in the gymnasium as the baying crowd sucked all of the oxygen from the air. It was all pressure, pressure to perform, and it filled Juliette's body with a burning sense of urgency, a fire that coursed through her veins. Desperate to advance her position, she rolled onto her front, hiding her face from the relentless blows.

"Don't give up your back," Earl said. "Don't get caught like that." He took out a folded handkerchief from the pocket of his tracksuit, patted at the beads of sweat gathering on his forehead, and turned to his young assistant. "She knows better than that, Tommy," Earl insisted.

Tommy, a tall, narrowly-built man with a contrastingly bulbous sphere of loose Afro hair, opened his mouth to reply. "Coach, I'm telling you, we gotta start working the submissions," he began, but was quickly silenced by the realization Earl was focused solely on the action before him.

Juliette's slender frame was somewhat dwarfed by the muscular physique of her opponent. There appeared to be at least a weight class between the pair. The two Lycra-clad figures were intertwined on the floor; a ball of arms, legs, sweat, and hair, a struggling mass of taut flesh rolling back and forth, heaving for some sort of outcome. All the while, Juliette seemed to be working the hardest, fighting for survival against her visibly stronger adversary. Juliette wound up flat on her back with several strands of her opponent's golden hair hanging in her face. She could barely see through the blood in her eyes. She couldn't even be sure whose blood it was at this point. Adrenaline had rendered her numb to the pain of any wounds she may have suffered, and the dark, metallic taste running into her mouth gave no clue as to who this particular bodily fluid might belong to.

"Don't let her mount you," Earl shouted. But it was too late; Juliette's opponent had already achieved the ultimate, dominant position and was now straddling Juliette's prone body. "She's finished," Earl snapped to his fellow cornerman.

The golden-haired woman began to unleash an onslaught of punches from the mount position, her tightly-clenched fists encased in fingerless leather gloves. Juliette's bloodied face was contorted with panic. She flailed her arms wildly, like a drowning swimmer fighting to keep her head above water. The referee stepped closer to the two fighters, poised to intervene at any moment. The crowd fell almost completely silent in anticipation.

"He's gonna stop this," Earl said. "It's over."

Juliette raised her hands in defense, grabbing at the arms of the larger woman, trying desperately to neutralize the attack.

"Thirty seconds," Earl said, "hang in there, kid."

Juliette strained to single out her brother's voice among the commotion of the audience and the cries from her opponent's coaches. She could hear the opposing team's lead cornerwoman calling out direct and concise words of instruction. "Finish her off," the cornerwoman's voice demanded with a level of composure that made Juliette feel as though she was falling further behind in the fight. "She's got nothing

3

left," the woman said dismissively. And then, for just a split second amidst the flurry of punches bombarding Juliette like a stampede, she caught a fleeting glimpse of her opponent's lead cornerwoman through the wire-grid of the fence. The woman's head was entirely shaven, with only a dark covering of stubble indicating the pattern of her hairline. She stood with her shoulders pushed back, her arms folded and her chin raised as she proudly guided her student through battle. When her arms unfolded and her body turned about, she looked wide and powerful, every movement of her limbs suggesting infinite athletic capabilities. "Come on now, ref, put this old-timer out of her misery," the woman said, and the words burned Juliette to her very core, filling her with the fury she needed to make it through this ordeal, to prove she wasn't finished, to prove she was worth more than any of these people knew.

Juliette raised one arm and gave a thumbs-up signal through the onslaught to let the referee know she was able to continue. The crowd erupted with cheers at the courageous gesture.

Earl shook his head and wiped the sweat from his brow. The cheers of the crowd forced a reluctant smile onto the weathered skin of his face. "She's got balls," he said. "You gotta give her that. My little sister's got some serious balls."

The crowd continued to cry out in support of Juliette. Most of the audience was on their feet by now. "Dee-az! Dee-az! Dee-az!" they chanted, willing Juliette to survive until the end of the round. The referee stepped closer still, his posture almost a crouch, his hands outstretched, ready to intervene. Then came the short burst of the clapper, indicating there were only ten seconds remaining until the round was over.

"Hang in there, Jules," Earl pleaded.

A clean, solid forearm landed directly to Juliette's temple, slamming her head into the mat. The hollow thud of flesh against bone — like a slab of meat hitting a butcher's block — reverberated to the furthest corners of the arena, and the crowd gasped. This was exactly what the audience had come for. They were a bloodthirsty mob, eager to be horrified by the gladiatorial bout before them. Juliette was shell-shocked by the blow. Everything went dark for a moment. Her lifeless body hung limp against the canvas floor; her eyes turned a cadaverous shade of white as her pupils rolled up into her head. The golden-haired woman—displaying all the restraint of a wild animal—continued with her onslaught. Ironically, it was these consecutive blows, a series of hammer-fists landing to Juliette's lifeless body and bloodied face, that pulled her out of her semiconscious stupor.

As Juliette came around, her vision was blurred. She saw, through a haze, the referee pulling her opponent away from her. She was certain the fight was over, certain she'd been knocked out and the ref had stepped in to save her. Anonymous bodies flooded into the hexagonal cage, dark shapes hurrying around in Juliette's peripheral vision. Suddenly, an arm was around her waist. Her brother had appeared by her side and was helping her to her feet. Earl threw one of Juliette's arms over his shoulder, supporting her weight as he practically carried her to their corner. "I'm sorry," Juliette said through ragged breaths as she choked on her own blood. "I blew it."

"You got another round, kid," Earl explained. "It ain't over yet."

"Another round?" Juliette replied in a muffled tone through her mouthguard, saliva hanging from her swollen lips as she spoke. "But I was out cold."

"Saved by the bell," Tommy exclaimed eagerly.

"Hurry up with that stool, will you?" Earl demanded of his assistant.

Tommy placed a low stool against the wall of the cage, his loose Afro bouncing wildly with every hurried action. Earl tutted and fussed around with the positioning of the stool until his sister collapsed down onto it. Tommy held a bag of ice on the back of Juliette's neck and Earl wiped the blood from her face with a towel. Juliette's mouse-colored hair—tied close to her head in a series of plaits—was slick in places with a dark red mixture of blood and sweat. The pale skin of her sinewy body glistened all over with perspiration. Her chest heaved back and forth as she drew labored breaths through an open mouth.

Earl hunched over and looked his sister directly in the face. "We can't have another round like that," he said. "You took a beating in there, kid. If it goes on like that, I'm gonna have to throw the towel in. Do you hear me?"

"Don't you quit on me now," Juliette spluttered between deep inhalations. "Don't let him do it, Tommy." Her head hung loose on her neck as she turned from one cornerman to the next.

"She's too big," Earl insisted, "too young. You should have listened to me."

"I got this," Juliette replied. "I can take her."

"Jules, listen to me," Tommy began. The young man spoke rapidly to get his words in. "If she takes you down again, you need to forget trying to get back to your feet. I'm telling you, her wrestling's too much. We gotta start working the submissions off of your back. She's got no jiu-jitsu."

"Not now," Earl interrupted. "Don't confuse things."

"But, Coach, please."

Another man appeared at Earl's side, pressing a cotton bud into a cut which had opened on Juliette's eyebrow. "Out of the way," Earl snapped at his assistant. "Let the cutman work."

Juliette winced as the cutman rubbed a large globule of Vaseline into the wound. She struggled to focus her thoughts. A spotlight shone in her face from high above. Her vision was blurred through the one eye she was able to hold half-open. She caught glimpses of the crowd through the diamond-grid wires of the cage. Wild eyes bulged and peered in, faces burned red with anger as mouths hung open. Indistinguishable roars filled the air, a baying mob jostling for a better view, fists waving, drinks spilling.

"Stay with me," Earl said, and he struck Juliette open-handed across the cheek. "Focus kid, focus. You're two rounds down. You can't let this go to the judges."

"She's done," Juliette spat through heavy breaths, her words distorted by her swollen lips. "She's got nothing left."

Earl turned to look at Juliette's opponent. The muscle-bound young athlete was already up off her stool, bouncing from one foot to the next, shadowboxing in Juliette's direction, raring to go. Earl glanced over at his rival cornerwoman. The shaven-headed lead coach turned to face the crowd and raised her arms, encouraging their applause. The words "Team Zen" were printed in a circular formation on the back of her T-shirt, and when she spun back toward the cage, her name, "Shaolin," could be seen emblazoned over one side of her chest. Earl placed a hand on the waistband of his sister's shorts, pulling the tight fabric away from her abdomen in an attempt to aid her heavy breaths. "You don't have to go back out there," he said. "Nobody expected you to beat Oksana The Ox."

Juliette swept her brother's hand away from her shorts. "Nothing I do is ever good enough for you, is it?" she said, her eyes laden with moisture as her tear ducts fought to clear her vision. "I'm telling you, I can take her."

Small segments of the crowd could be heard cheering on Juliette's opponent. "Ox, Ox, Ox," they repeated, waving little homemade flags and signboards with bull-like emblems scrawled across them. As Juliette glanced around, it was immediately apparent that a larger number of the audience was holding up signs and posters in support of herself. "Jules Diamond Diaz," the posters read, complete with crudely-drawn diamond logos bearing a resemblance to those printed on the T-shirts Earl and Tommy were wearing underneath their open track-jackets. Juliette was reminded of all the reasons she loved her audience. The adoration seemed to satisfy a part of her that was otherwise forever empty, forever longing for some abstract sense of fulfillment she could never seem to appease. Feeding off of the crowd's energy, she struggled to her feet and poured the icy contents of a water bottle over her head. The crowd roared again, spurred on by her tenacity. "Always trying to control me," Juliette said, looking back at her brother.

"Just looking out for you, kid," Earl replied as he watched his sister take up her position opposite Oksana.

Juliette stood poised for action, like a sprinter at the starting line of a race. Her slight figure was almost entirely exposed to the audience, covered only by a crop-top-style sports bra and hot-pants which clung to her body like a second skin. Juliette's limbs were slim, defined, hardened with muscle tone. Her chest was modest, her hips narrow. The contrastingly thick-limbed, broad-shouldered Oksana smiled at Juliette from across the mat. It was a narrow-eyed, devilish smile that suggested Oksana was looking forward to exacting further punishment on her rival. Then, to add insult to injury, Oksana closed one eye in slow motion, offering Juliette a patronizing wink of encouragement.

"Been in this game far too long for that," Juliette said to herself through her mouthguard.

The referee stepped into the center of the hexagonal cage. "You ready?" he asked each fighter in turn. "Then let's fight," he said, directing both fighters into the center of the mat with a swift movement of his hands. Juliette hurried forward, eager to teach her younger opponent a lesson and to show her brother exactly what she was capable of.

"Patience, Jules," Earl said, "take your time." But it was too late. Oksana held out a stiff jab which sent Juliette stumbling to one knee. "Stay on your feet," Earl called out, before turning to his fellow cornerman. "She can't even see the jab out of that eye."

Oksana lunged at Juliette, taking full advantage of her stumble, tackling her to the ground. Juliette wound up on her back again, with Oksana bearing down on top of her. Earl turned his attention towards the cage-side seats to seek out the fight promoter: a mountainous, bald-headed man drowned in a huge fur coat. The sheer mass of the man's body — coupled with the bulk of his fur coat — gave him an animalistic appearance which distinguished him as somebody of importance, quite separate from the rest of the crowd. The dark skin of this bear-like man's facial features concealed his reactions to the bout, but the stage lights reflected off the plump flesh of his lips just enough to reveal an upturned smile, an unflinching expression of disapproval at Juliette's lackluster performance.

"Gotta get Caesar's attention," Earl told his young assistant. "The Ox is killing her in there." Earl held his towel aloft and flailed it wildly to indicate he was on the verge of thrusting it into the cage in an act of surrender.

"But, we said we wouldn't do it, Coach," Tommy insisted.

Earl refused to heed his assistant's words and continued to signal in the direction of Caesar, the fight promoter. Earl froze, waiting for Caesar's approval, but instead, the huge man's frown grew broader as the edges of his mouth sunk further down his chin, revealing a look of sheer disgust at Earl's suggestion.

"This ain't a fight," Earl said. "It's a beating."

Tommy took a deep breath to settle his nerves and stepped a little closer to the cage, emerging from his coach's shadow. "Hang in there, Jules," Tommy shouted, his hands cupped over his mouth so that his uncertain voice might travel further.

Earl practically growled with contempt at his assistant's outburst. He placed a hand on Tommy's shoulder and pulled the young man back so that he could muscle his own way to the edge of the cage. Earl opened his mouth to speak, but no words came out. As he watched Oksana smothering his sister in the center of the mat, he couldn't think of any single instruction or phrase of encouragement that might help Juliette advance her position.

"Coach, please," Tommy pleaded.

Earl glanced over his shoulder toward his assistant. He paused for a moment amidst all the chaos, looking the tall, spindly-limbed young man up and down. Tommy looked eager, his hands balled up into fists. Earl raised his handkerchief and dried the sweat from his forehead. He was far too proud to verbally acknowledge the fact he needed his young assistant's help. So instead, he nodded his head an almost undetectable amount and stepped aside.

Tommy hurried forward, his bobbing Afro exaggerating his swift movements as he craned his neck to get a better view of the action. "Don't let her mount you again, Jules," Tommy said. He spoke loudly, but with a calm sense of composure his superior coach seemed to lack. "Work the submissions from the bottom. She's got no jiu-jitsu."

Juliette struggled to free herself, twisting and jerking her body, bucking frantically like a rodeo bull in an attempt to shake off her larger opponent.

"Tie her arms up to neutralize her attacks," Tommy instructed.

Juliette found solace in Tommy's voice. His calm tone — unaffected by emotion — cut through all of the chaos, resonating directly, making Juliette feel as though she had an ally inside the cage. She grabbed Oksana's left arm with two hands and rolled to her side.

"Work the Kimura," Tommy shouted, instantly recognizing the opportunity.

"Not the Kimura," Earl interrupted. "The Ox is just too strong for that."

"Coach, please," Tommy pleaded.

Juliette tugged at Oksana's arm in an attempt to extend and rotate the muscular limb beyond its normal range of motion. Earl was right; Oksana was simply too strong, easily pulling her arm free from the submission attempt with a loud roar of exertion. Once free, Oksana began to punish Juliette for her efforts, slamming heavy knees down into her rib cage.

"For Christ's sake," Earl barked at his assistant, "we're not in the gym now, kid. This is the real world. You say the wrong thing out here and somebody's gonna get hurt. You understand me?"

"But, Coach, look," Tommy said, seemingly unaffected by the scolding he'd just received. "We've got them rattled."

"What the hell are you talking about, rattled?" Earl asked, reluctantly peeling his scornful gaze away from his young assistant. As Earl turned back toward the cage, he saw Oksana's lead coach, Shaolin, was up on her toes barking out instructions, attempting to stand up as tall as she could in the hope her fighter would take notice and heed her advice.

"Get out of there," Shaolin demanded. "Finish her on the feet," she called out, her flushed skin emphasizing her loss of composure. Oksana refused to listen to her coach. She was too caught up with the satisfaction of hurling her fists into Juliette's midsection. She continued to work away, leaning further forward over Juliette, exhaling louder with every blow. Juliette made no attempt to defend herself from the bombardment, noticing the way Oksana's upper body was stooping lower and lower with each consecutive punch.

"Clever girl," Earl said, "clever girl. Batten down the hatches, Tommy. The water's gonna be rough, but I think we're about to steer this old ship to victory."

"It's a trap! Get the hell out of there," came the cries from Oksana's corner.

"Out of the way," Earl said, barging past his assistant. "Triangle!" he shouted. "The triangle is there. Do it now, Jules, slap it on."

Juliette chose her moment wisely, like a snake waiting to strike with its venomous fangs. She grabbed hold of Oksana's hands and pulled her upper body closer. Juliette threw her legs up over Oksana's shoulders, timing the maneuver perfectly. She wrapped her left leg around the back of Oksana's neck, and then she hooked her right calf over her left foot, creating a sort of necktie that she could pull tighter and tighter like the aforementioned snake constricting its prey. Oksana was pulled down to her knees and the audience gasped in disbelief.

"That's it," Earl said. "Pull her head closer to you."

"I told you The Ox had no jiu-jitsu, Coach."

"Not now, Tommy."

As Oksana struggled to free herself from the triangle hold, her face began to redden. In an act of desperation, she lifted herself first to one knee, and then, with a roar of effort that filled the gymnasium, she unfolded her contorted body and rose to her feet, somehow managing to carry Juliette round her neck like a human scarf. Juliette hung upside down from Oksana's neck. Her legs burned under the strain, but she knew at such a late stage of the fight, this was her only chance of victory. Oksana stumbled across the cage, supporting Juliette's full body weight in a display of sheer strength.

"Hold on," Earl cried. "This is it, kid."

Juliette's eyes were closed tight as she bit down on her mouthguard. Even though she was hanging upside down, her eyes were shut, and her thoughts were operating on instincts alone, she knew, in those frantic moments, that Earl would be watching her, that his attention would be focused on her alone, and that he would have to think she was doing okay. He couldn't possibly be criticizing her or wanting to tell her the way it should be done, how he would do it, where she was going wrong. Her execution of this particular submission hold was undeniably flawless. She knew Earl would see that too. In those few seconds, all of the adrenaline, the nervous energy, the fire in her veins, all of it became inverted, transformed into pure exhilaration, a rush of fleeting ecstasy, the climax that made all of this worthwhile.

Oksana managed another few steps before dropping to one knee. Saliva bubbled and turned to foam on her lips. The entire audience seemed to be up on their toes, trying to get a better view into the cage. Oksana collapsed to the mat like some gargantuan beast succumbing to the effects of a tranquilizer dart. Her arms fell limp at her sides and her legs twitched wildly. The referee pounced upon the muddle of bodies. "Stop, stop, stop," he cried, and Juliette eased off, releasing the choke she'd been holding onto as though her life depended on it.

The crowd erupted in unison, leaping simultaneously from their feet into the air, spilling their drinks over each other with wild abandon. Juliette collapsed with exhaustion and rolled onto her back in the center of the cage. The referee was supporting Oksana's head, slapping her face in an attempt to resuscitate her. Juliette looked over to the mountainous Caesar. She saw he was nodding at her in approval, a hint of a congratulatory smile upon his lips. Shaolin was struggling against her fellow cornermen, desperate to gain access to the cage so she could be with her fallen comrade. Juliette looked deep into the crowd and noticed the countless bodies standing, thrusting their fists into the air, chanting her name in perfect timing, "Dee-az! Dee-az! Dee-az!" Finally, she looked over to her corner. Tommy was among the crowd, at one with them in their celebrations. Earl was frozen with relief, practically trembling, his eyes fixated on Juliette. It seemed like they were the only two people in the gymnasium. Juliette looked deep into her brother's eyes and she was certain they were wide open and unburdened, and she knew — at least for the time being — everything was okay between the two of them.

CHAPTER 2

The water turned a deep shade of red as it flowed over Juliette's skin. She felt the warm liquid running over her head, working its way deep into the tight plaits of her hair before cascading down her back, soothing her muscles, numbing her pain. As she opened her mouth, her bloodied saliva became one with the stream tumbling gently over her chest and down onto her thighs before reaching the aging, cracked surface of the cubicle floor.

"Where's the champ at?" a gruff voice called out from somewhere distant, reverberating off the walls beyond the shower cubicle. "Where's my girl?"

Juliette recognized her brother's voice immediately. His joyous tone was abrasive, an unwelcome contrast to the soothing tranquility of the warm shower.

"You coming out of there today, or what?" Earl persisted.

Juliette had been hypnotized by the warmth of the shower, standing motionless under its spell. Her body ached with every movement she could muster, so she remained still, wrapped up in the anesthetic blanket raining down on her.

"Let's go, kid," Earl said, his voice sounding closer now. "We got the after-party at Caesar's." He clapped his hands together several times, trying to spur his sister into action.

Juliette twisted the water control, squeaking the dial around to the off position. Her body became cold and rigid with pain as soon as the flow of water ceased. She kept her back to the cubicle door and reached behind herself to slide the lock open.

Earl swung the door wide and surveyed his sister's back through a fog of steam. Juliette's body—although laden with sinews and muscle tone—displayed all of the classic female attributes: the curve of the lower back, the dimples above the buttocks, the hourglass waste. Admittedly, these features may have been somewhat understated in Juliette's case, but her slender physique was far from anything that could be considered masculine.

"Come on now, champ," Earl said. "Let's take a look at the damage."

Juliette arched her back and gathered the tail ends of her plaits together, removing them to present the entirety of herself for her brother's inspection. She shivered and flinched as Earl's fingertips prodded at the ribs on her back, the bones of which protruded somewhat due to the low level of fat on her athletic physique.

Earl drew an audible breath at the sight of Juliette's reddened flesh. "Damn, kid, the Ox really messed you up in there," he said, running a comforting hand down to the small of his sister's back.

"I'll live," Juliette replied with a shrug.

"So what, you not talking to me now, champ?" Earl unfolded a large towel and held it out in front of himself.

"I ain't no champ anymore," Juliette said.

"You're my champ, kid. You won, didn't you?"

Juliette shivered as she wrapped the towel around herself. "So why did you quit on me out there then?" she asked, refusing to make eye contact with her brother.

"We're not gonna do this now, are we?" Earl said. "It's time to celebrate." He held his arms open to offer his sister a congratulatory embrace.

Juliette shrugged her shoulders indifferently.

"So what the hell was I supposed to do?" Earl asked. "You was getting your ass whooped out there, Jules. I had to do something."

"You know I've never tapped out, don't you?" Juliette replied. "Not once in all the fights I've been through. You've got no right to be throwing the towel in on me like that. And in front of a home crowd? You gotta be kidding me." Juliette turned away, drying the water from the shower while shielding herself from her brother's gaze. She grumbled with pain, her body aching as she shifted awkwardly within the folds of the towel.

"Here, let me help," Earl said.

"I'm fine," Juliette snapped.

Earl took a deep breath, exasperated with his sister's attitude. "Jules, now I gotta tell you…" He paused for a beat, bracing himself for the magnitude of what he was about to say. "As your coach, as your brother, I really don't know how much longer I can be doing this."

"What the hell are you talking about now?" Juliette asked, her voice sounding labored, as though she could barely muster the energy to speak. She winced with pain as she fastened the towel around her chest and lowered herself down onto one of the wooden benches that lined the walls of the locker room.

"I'm talking about watching you taking a beating from all these kids trying to make a name for themselves off of you."

Juliette closed her eyes in a display of indignation, allowing her head to fall back against the cold steel surface of a locker.

Earl gestured toward a mirror fixed to a post in the center of the room. "Take a look at your face," he said. "You got stitches all over your eyes, lips swollen, ribs bruised. You're a mess."

The mirror was positioned directly in Juliette's line of vision. Reluctantly, she studied her own reflection. Black thread held the cut above her eye together, the lid of which was inflated and closed up like a clamshell. Her forehead was reddened with sweeping grazes that made it look as though a vehicle's tire had plowed across her face. Her bottom lip was inflated and split open in one corner; her left ear swollen and misshapen like it had been chewed up and spat out. She hung her head, averting her gaze from the mirror. These types of injuries were nothing new for Juliette. She knew all about stitches, bruises, painkillers, scar tissue, and the amount of time it took to heel after a fight. But for some reason, under the harsh fluorescent lighting of the locker room, her war wounds seemed to speak volumes about the reality of her lackluster performance against Oksana.

Earl leaned forward and looked Juliette directly in the face.

Juliette's murky eyes shifted evasively in their sockets.

Earl persisted, attempting to catch his sister's attention as he spoke. "Listen to me, Jules, you got to know when it's time to call it a day."

"I'm still winning, aren't I?" Juliette replied, her voice an exhausted whisper.

"You're winning in the ring, kid. That much may be true. But the question is, are you winning in life?"

The door to the locker room swung open and Tommy stepped in carrying a swollen duffle bag. "You ready, Coach? Everyone's leaving."

"Give us a minute, will you?" Earl snapped. "We're talking business in here, okay?"

Tommy glanced at the floor, crestfallen at Earl's dismissive tone. "Your wife's been calling me," Tommy murmured, his head still bowed, the bulk of his hair covering much of his face. "Says she's been trying your phone for the last half hour."

"Margot?" Earl replied. "Well, spit it out, what the hell does she want?"

"Asking when you're gonna be done here, as far as I could make out."

Earl scratched at the back of his neck as he struggled to think of a solution. "Tell her we're not gonna make it tonight," he said, eventually. "Say we gotta take Jules to the hospital to get checked out. And don't you go giving her too many details. Make sure you sound convincing, okay?"

"Sure, Coach," Tommy replied, grateful that Earl had trusted him with such a task.

"And go wait in the car, or something," Earl said, tossing a set of keys in Tommy's direction.

Tommy's face lit up with a smile as he fumbled for the keys, "Can I drive the Mustang to Caesar's?"

Earl raised his eyebrows just enough to answer his assistant.

"I'll be outside," Tommy said. "Oh, and congrats on the win, Jules."

Juliette nodded and just about mustered a smile to thank the young man. "You know you did good out there tonight, right?" she said.

"Sure," Tommy beamed, smiling from ear to ear. "I knew The Ox had no jiu-jitsu," he said under his breath as he walked away.

Earl shook his head in disdain and sat down on the bench next to Juliette. The aging wooden surface creaked under the weight of his bulk. "At this point, Jules, you're about two, maybe three fights away from being punch-drunk. You know what I'm saying?" Earl fixed his eyes on the skin of Juliette's chest—just beyond the folds of her towel—where a small tattoo of the name "Shelby" was scrawled out in a script font. He placed his hand on Juliette's shoulder and ran his thumb back and forth over the tattoo. "You want Shelby to have to listen to her mom slurring her words? Is that really what you want?"

Juliette pushed her brother's hand away. "If you can't take it anymore, then maybe it's time you quit," she said, tightening her towel to cover her chest.

"Me quit? What the hell are you talking about?"

Juliette gestured in the direction of the locker room door. "I'm talking about the fact Tommy had to step up in there, because you gave up."

"That's bullshit. I was just giving the kid a chance, and he started talking about Kimura this and Kimura that. You know the Kimura's a strength-based move. How the hell are you gonna pull that off on someone who's as strong as The Ox?" Earl picked up a towel from the

18

bench and patted the sweat from his brow.

"You know I was just using that Kimura as a threat, to advance my position and get up off my back. You just don't want to admit Tommy did good tonight. Maybe it's time you start thinking about letting him take over."

"Take over," Earl grumbled. "Ain't nobody taking over, kid. As long as you're fighting, I'm cornering. That's the way it always has been, and that's the way it always will be."

Juliette hung her head to conceal the gratitude that was creeping onto her swollen lips.

"That's it now, champ," Earl said, "I knew that smile was in there somewhere."

"I'm still mad at you," Juliette said, forcing the grin from her mouth.

"All I'm saying is, how long do you think you got left in this game? You've gotta start making plans for when you get out. For your future, for Shelby's future."

Juliette leaned closer to Earl, finally bestowing the man with a few seconds of eye contact. She released her grip on the towel that was covering her chest, allowing it to slacken a little in an attempt to remind her brother that deep down, regardless of the barbaric physical acts she was capable of, she was still female, still his little sister. "I just need a couple more big fights. I can't just leave it at that."

Earl shook his head disapprovingly and raised his chin as if he were trying to avoid the sight of the loosened towel.

"To prove I can still do it," Juliette continued. "To prove that we can still do it, you and me, together."

"It's not your fault," Earl said, cutting her off abruptly. "You missed that boat, kid. Women's MMA wasn't even that big when you was on top of your game."

"I've got a few fights left in me yet." Juliette's tone was defiant. "A run at the title. Show these youngsters how it's supposed to be done."

19

"All I'm saying is…" Earl paused and took a deep breath. "All I'm saying is, I found this girl for us—"

"—No way. Not this again, Earl." Juliette fastened her slackened towel back into place.

"Hear me out," Earl insisted. "For once, just hear me out. This kid I've found, trust me, she's something else."

Juliette rolled her eyes, silenced by her brother's persistence.

"All I'm asking is, just take a look at her for me, just one time. You need something to focus on, a project, a protégé, and I'm telling you, this kid's perfect for you."

"That's just not me. I already told you, I ain't no mentor."

"Come on now, you know we'd make a great team. You and me, together. Put our gym on the map. Build up some of these kids. Really go places. With your jiu-jitsu, my wrestling, we could be huge."

"That's your dream, Earl. Not mine."

"You gotta recognize when it's time to pass the baton on. Just like I did with you. I made my sacrifices. I knew when it was time to get out. I was Earl Diablo Diaz, one of the early pioneers of the sport. But I gave all that up before the whole mixed martial arts scene even went mainstream. You see, kid, I missed my chance as well."

"Maybe I'm not ready to give up on myself just yet. Not for somebody else."

"You know what, kid? You're too stubborn. Just like Mom was."

Juliette shifted awkwardly among her towel and turned away from her brother.

Earl exhaled a large breath of frustration as he got up off the bench. "You got fifteen minutes," he said, tapping at his watch. "Get yourself dressed. We gotta be at Caesar's club. It's in the contract." With that, Earl turned to leave. As he approached the exit at the far end of the locker room, he turned back toward Juliette. "You gotta listen to your big brother some time," he said. "Just think about it. At least take a look at this kid for me, just once. Like I say, you're winning in the cage, yes.

But, are you winning out here, in life, where it matters?"

***

Juliette stood before the row of sinks in the locker room, studying her reflection in the mirror. She fastened the zipper of her track-jacket and tugged at the garment here and there to make herself look presentable. She raised her fists, her body taking on a boxer's stance. She rolled her shoulders, ducked and weaved. Her movements were somewhat stiff and awkward due to the fact she was still aching from the fight. She threw out a couple of punches, maintaining full eye contact with her reflection as she sparred with the air in front of her face. "Still got it," she said to herself, "you've still got it, Jules." She leaned over the sink, moving closer to the tarnished, fingerprinted surface of the mirror so she could assess the full extent of her facial injuries. The raw unsightliness of it all seemed quite in keeping with the decaying backdrop of the old locker room.

Juliette took a deep breath to compose herself. As she inhaled, her nostrils were filled with the scent of damp wood that had absorbed moisture over time, mold spores hanging in the humid air. She glanced down toward the cell phone she'd laid out next to the sink. The phone's screen was illuminated, displaying the name "Shelby" next to a green telephone icon. Juliette clasped her hands together and cracked her knuckles as though she was preparing for a physically demanding task. She nodded at herself in the mirror and tapped at the green telephone icon with her index finger. She pressed a second icon, which activated the phone's loudspeaker mode, filling the locker room with the synthetic drone of a dialing tone.

"Hey, Mom, where are you?" a voice called out from the phone, still positioned beside the sink.

Juliette's mind was filled with a vision of her teenage daughter in full ballet costume. She pictured the subtle curves of Shelby's lithe body vacuum-packed in a salmon pink leotard, her blonde hair tied back into a neat little bun on the back of her head. Juliette was always in awe of the flawless physical specimen she'd created, constantly enchanted by the graceful posture Shelby could achieve; the way she would extend up onto her toes, lengthening her slender legs, straightening her back and thrusting out her chest. Juliette imagined Shelby would be limbering up, going over her routines backstage, deep in concentration with all the other young performers, each of them dressed immaculately in their own close-fitting leotards and floating tutu skirts, their awkward, angular bodies stretched out via their ballet poses into more elegant silhouettes.

"Mom, are you there?" Shelby's voice called out from the phone, shattering Juliette's imagining and grounding her back within the dank surrounding of the locker room.

"Hey, Doll-face," Juliette said, forcing a smile in the mirror. "When you going on?"

"Fifteen minutes. Are you here?" Shelby asked, without taking a breath.

"Aren't you gonna ask how I did?" Juliette said.

"Did you win?"

"Of course I won," Juliette replied, feigning positivity. "I always win, don't I?"

"So did you make it? Where are you?"

Juliette imagined Shelby peering out from behind the stage curtains, her concerned little eyes surveying the faces of the audience as she frantically scanned the seats for her mother. And then her eyes would become heavy with disappointment, the exact same way Earl's always seemed to any time he looked in Juliette's direction.

"Listen, Doll-face," Juliette began, her expression straightening in the mirror. "They said I've got to go to the hospital. Nothing serious, just to get checked out." Juliette closed her eyes and winced as she uttered the lie to her daughter.

22

"But, Mom, you said you'd be here."

"I'm sorry, Doll. I'm gonna need a few stitches, and whatever—"

"—But, you could still make it for the second half. If you hurry."

"Auntie Margot's there, isn't she?" Juliette watched her reflection as her eyes filled with tears.

"But, Mom, you promised."

"We can watch the recording together tomorrow." Juliette tried to sound positive as the tears spilled from her eyes and rolled down her cheeks. "I'll be there to pick you up in the morning. But don't let Auntie Margot take you for junk food after the show tonight, okay? You know what that stuff will do to your figure." Juliette waited for a response, but was met with silence. "Shelby? You there, Doll?" Juliette broke eye contact with her reflection and looked down toward her phone. "Call ended," the screen read, coldly. She wiped the tears from her cheeks as she watched the illumination fade from the phone screen until it lost all color and turned an empty shade of black. Fighting back her tears, she unzipped her track-jacket and pulled herself free of the garment, allowing it to drop to the tiled floor so that her arms and shoulders were fully exposed, her upper body covered only by a tank top. Juliette clenched her fists and curled her arms up toward her chin, tensing her muscles so she could appreciate the view of her straining biceps in the mirror. She held her breath as she studied her physique.

She asked herself how any rational-minded person would ever have expected her to attend her daughter's performance in the first place. What was she supposed to do, turn up in her black tracksuit with gold piping, complete with the words "Jules Diamond Diaz" emblazoned garishly across the back? Or maybe she should have changed into something smarter first, so that her facial injuries were taken completely out of context and everyone would have suspected she was a victim of some kind of domestic abuse? Was she really supposed to sit among the mothers and fathers of Shelby's classmates with her loosened cornrows still wet from the shower, her head tilted back so she could just about see out of the one eye that had by now swollen almost completely to a close, her foot tapping manically at the floor as she went over the fight in her head, scrutinizing every mistake she'd made?

Juliette extended her arms down by her sides so she could inspect the definition of her triceps. A crudely drawn tattoo could be seen on one shoulder, just above her bicep. It was the basic outline of a diamond with several lines extending from its sides, indicating it was supposed to be shining or glimmering. She studied her physique, a perfect picture of health in her eyes, to remind herself of who she was, why she did this, how it all made her feel. She exhaled again, releasing herself from the bodybuilder-like pose. This is where Juliette belonged, here among the decay. This old high school gymnasium was a perfect example of the type of place Juliette plied her trade now in the twilight of her career. The lines of blackening grout that ran between the tiles on the walls of the locker room might as well have been the veins that decorated her sinewy arms. The dissipating steam had become her breath, the dented lockers her aging bones, and the shower cubicles the compartments of her imagination where all of her hopes and dreams seemed to wash away after every fight, no matter the outcome, win or lose.

Juliette drew stuttered breaths as she fought back the tears. She moved closer to the mirror and looked herself directly in the eye. She paused briefly before opening her mouth, her bottom lip trembling, swollen at one end. And then the words came out, "You're a cunt."

CHAPTER 3

Juliette sat alone at a small table in a semicircular booth toward the back of the club. She closed her eyes and dropped her head back onto the cerise velour cushioning that surrounded her. The room spun to a slow-motion soundtrack of driving bass lines and heavy beats. The bitter taste of alcohol lingered on her tongue. She allowed the liquid to sit in her mouth for a while before she swallowed, savoring its kick, a gentle burn she'd longed for throughout the grueling training schedule of the past few months. Juliette could feel the bass vibrating deep within the pit of her stomach, forcing her aching abdominal muscles to tighten. She tried to succumb to the rhythms, to relax, to give in to it all.

"Can I get you another drink?" a female voice said, just about cutting over the throb of the music.

Juliette opened her eyes. A young Asian woman, a drinks server, stood before her in a sheer nightgown. The vast majority of the server's flesh was visible through the transparent fabric; warm, olive skin reddened under the neon lights of the club. Juliette cast her eyes over the server's underwear-clad body, measuring the half-naked woman as though she were a potential opponent. Juliette couldn't help herself; she'd been obsessing over fight tactics for weeks, countless hours spent meticulously planning for every eventuality, culminating in the explosive brutal climax that was her fight with Oksana. She couldn't snap out of it now. It must have been the flashes of muscle tone in the server's thighs that had triggered the instinct; or perhaps it was the woman's bicep flexing under pressure as she balanced a tray on her upturned palm.

"Can I get you another drink?" the server repeated with a sharper tone this time.

Juliette pictured herself charging at the woman, knocking her off the towering heels she was balanced upon, taking her down to the carpeted floor of the club, wrestling with her underneath the twisting patterns cast onto their intertwined bodies by the revolving disco lights. Everybody in the club would be gathered around watching as the woman's underwear was torn from her body in the struggle.

"They're on the house," the server explained with a matter-of-fact expression which Juliette read as "make up your fucking mind."

Juliette raised her chin, nodding to accept the offer, and in turn, the server removed a bottle of beer from her tray and deposited it beside Juliette with all the finesse you would expect a stripper to expend on a customer from whom she stood to receive zero in tips. Juliette felt the cushioning of the seat compress underneath her. She rotated her upper body — still stiffened with pain — to see Earl sliding into the circular booth beside her.

"Gotta love it here in The Pink Tunnel," Earl said.

Juliette glanced around at the décor: the pink accents here and there, the heart-shaped seat backs and the red neon tube lights. The narrow, elongated space — like an oversized corridor — made Juliette feel uneasy, claustrophobic, even.

"This is the VIP lifestyle, right here," Earl said, leaning toward his sister so that he could speak into her cauliflower ear. He extended an arm across the top of the bench seat so that it ran along behind Juliette. "We're like royalty right now," he said. "You and me, up here on our thrones. King and Queen."

Juliette looked down at the single bottle of beer in front of her, and the small dish — half-filled with a variety of nuts — that sat by its side. "Royalty?" she said, mocking Earl's suggestion.

"You're never satisfied, kid," Earl remarked. "Take a look around." He swept one of his thick-fingered hands in front of himself, drawing Juliette's attention to the scene before them. The pair were seated in a raised area, a few steps higher than the rest of the club, a position that afforded them a clear view of the whole establishment and everything in it. From Juliette's vantage point, the narrow club was a sea of bustling heads, anonymous bodies tightly packed into the rectangular space. Caesar had sold tickets based on the premise of having several of the evening's fighters in attendance, and the place was full to capacity. Juliette looked over to the raised catwalk that ran along one wall of the club. The platform was adorned with a plethora of bare-fleshed young women, bodies writhing in slow-motion, dancers moving like felines on all fours, metallic thongs disappearing between ass cheeks, synthetically swollen breasts exposed underneath the glow of the neon lights. The entire spectacle was reflected by a wall of mirrors that ran along behind the catwalk, providing the audience with uninterrupted views of the women's shifting forms from every conceivable angle.

"Looks okay to me," Earl said as he sat back and took a swig from his beer. "Doesn't look as though Tommy's complaining either," he added, signaling with his bottle toward the bar, where his young assistant was perched upon a stool next to a few of the other fighters who'd competed that night.

A small crowd had gathered around the bar. The fighters appeared to be posing for photographs and exchanging stories with the club-goers. Juliette could hear the bursts of laughter wafting over every time there was a dip in the hypnotic thump of the music. She watched as the fighters attempted to reenact the highlights of their bouts, shadowboxing and prancing around like mime artists. Juliette had seen and heard it all before. She didn't have the energy for all of that machismo, the exaggerated versions of events that everybody had seen with their own eyes anyway. So instead, she chose to sit quietly, sequestered away in a secluded alcove, a portion of the club cordoned off with a rope barrier, out of bounds to the general public.

A synchronized wave of motion rippled through the bodies of the people packed onto the dance floor. Most of the club-goers turned at once, swiveling in unison to look toward the entrance at the far end of the oblong space.

"Here comes the freak show," Earl said, realizing exactly what had caught the attention of the other patrons.

The crowd swarmed toward the entrance lobby, their bodies heaving together, each of them eager to get the best possible view. Juliette sat up tall to see what was happening. A pair of doormen attempted to disperse the crowd, encouraging them to back away. Three figures appeared at the edge of the dance floor, a group of individuals who seemed to be of great interest to everybody else in the room. Juliette struggled to see the faces of these new arrivals amidst the commotion.

"What's all the fuss about?" she asked, intrigued by the level of excitement surrounding the trio.

"It's nothing," Earl said. "Just drink your beer and sit still."

Juliette stood to see over the crowd. "Who the hell is that over there?"

"Sit down, damn it," Earl said, pulling Juliette back onto the bench seat. "It's just Team-fucking-Zen making their grand entrance, that's all. Just ignore them and be cool, okay?"

The crowd separated to form a narrow pathway toward the bar. A single, shaven-headed figure emerged from the trio. Juliette quickly realized it was Shaolin striding out in front of her teammates, leading them through the parted crowd as though she was making her entrance to a fight. "Who does this clown think she is?" Juliette said.

"Let her have her moment of glory if that's what makes her happy," Earl said. "Try and remember you just choked out her number one student. That's all that really matters."

Shaolin proceeded at a slow pace, savoring the adoration of her onlookers. She walked with effortless grace, as though she commanded total control of every muscle in her body. Each movement of her limbs, no matter how subtle, was like an intentional expression of her capabilities as a martial artist. She ambled through the crowd with regal poise, like a male ballet dancer gliding across a stage.

"Funny how Oksana never bothered to show up," Earl said. "Probably too embarrassed to show her face after what you did to her."

"Do you think she sleeps with that damn strap?" Juliette asked, referring to the championship belt draped over Shaolin's shoulder, its shiny gold face flashing red as it reflected the glow of the club lights. "Don't see why everybody's so interested in these fools, anyway," Juliette said. "Not as if Shaolin was even fighting tonight."

"She's the champ, Jules. That's all anybody really cares about these days."

Juliette guzzled her beer, her eyes following Shaolin the whole time, the raised end of her bottle trembling enough to indicate the anger that festered inside of her.

"Would have been a real interesting fight, you and her," Earl said.

Juliette felt her spirits lifting. She straightened her posture and nodded in agreement with her brother.

"I mean, when you was in your prime, of course," Earl said, shattering Juliette's hope of receiving any kind of praise. "Obviously, she's at the peak of the sport right now," Earl continued. "But like I say, it would have been a hell of a fight once upon a time."

Juliette was aggravated by every aspect of Shaolin's appearance: the way her clothing was arranged over her body with an almost militaristic attention to detail, her breasts heaving through her T-shirt like powerful pectoral muscles, her high cheekbones and prominent nose making her look like something beyond a man or a woman, a hybrid creature that Juliette was certain she'd never be able to match up to.

Juliette hung her head, defeated by the spectacle. A strobe light kicked in and the club was flooded with intermittent flashes of complete darkness and brilliant white light. It was like somebody had activated a life-size flick-book, presenting Juliette with a series of freeze-frame images, each one a snapshot filled with a different combination of poses from the women on stage. Juliette studied the procession of dancers on the catwalk, admiring the variety of ways in which the women worked the crowd for tips, the expertise with which they clamped their bodies around the poles that extended toward the ceiling, climbing and descending with all the grace and poise of professional gymnasts.

"So what, you like girls now?" Earl asked. "You trying to get me excited or something?"

Juliette responded with an extended middle finger. "Just admiring their athleticism, that's all."

"Now, if you wanna talk about athletes," Earl said, clearing his throat, "you remember that kid I told you about? The fighter I wanted you to take a look at?"

"Didn't I already tell you I ain't no coach?"

Earl pointed his beer bottle towards the bar. "You see that little half-black chick on the stool over there?"

"Half what?"

"You know, like, maybe her daddy's black, her momma's white, or whatever."

Juliette sat up tall and craned her neck to see who her brother was referring to.

"Chick in the black baby-doll dress," Earl said. "Third stool from the right. Girl who's been trying to sell a private dance to that pumped up little frat boy over there. Stocky guy with all the useless gym muscles."

"That's the girl you want me to take a look at?" Juliette said, incredulously. "A stripper?"

"Weren't you the one telling me how these girls were athletes? And now you wanna get all precious on me because she gets paid to take her clothes off."

Juliette studied the young woman her brother had pointed out. The exposed skin of her arms and legs shimmered with an ever-changing palette of sepia tones underneath the glow of the club lights. Her dark hair hung loosely over her shoulders in a series of thinly-tied braids. Juliette noticed the woman's playful smile as she spoke to the stocky young man on the stool opposite her, the way her tongue toyed with the straw that protruded from her elaborately decorated cocktail, and the skill with which she drew the plastic stem back and forth across the surface of her black-painted lips. The stocky man was mesmerized by the girl's every move, the way she crossed and uncrossed her legs repeatedly, most likely in an attempt to captivate her prey with brief glimpses of her underwear through the mesh fabric of her baby-doll dress.

"Doesn't look like much of a fighter to me," Juliette said.

"Listen, Jules, let me tell you exactly how it went down." Earl glugged hard and fast on his beer to lubricate his mouth in preparation for what he was about to say. "So, this kid turns up at the gym a couple of weeks ago. Everybody's pairing off to work their wrestling on the mats, and this little chick walks in wearing what looks like yoga pants and a sports bra. Says her name's Amiyah. Tells us she's new in town and looking for somewhere to train."

Juliette stared past her brother, her face blank with disinterest.

Earl continued, determined to ignite some spark of enthusiasm within his sister. "The guys are all whispering and nudging each other, laughing quietly under their breath as if they're back in school, like they think this little girl is lost or something." Earl broke into laughter at the ridiculousness of the recollection.

Juliette struggled to focus on her brother's anecdote over the pounding of the music, the nearby laughter, and raised voices. She watched the movement of Earl's mouth, his lips forming words through a smile.

"So, I let this Amiyah kid train with Cody. I figured he's the smallest guy on our team, right?"

"You paired her off with that knucklehead Cody?"

"Hear me out," Earl said, shuffling toward Juliette until she was cornered. "I let them get into it. I go off, do my thing. Five minutes later, I hear this commotion coming from the other side of the gym. 'Come on Cody,' the guys are shouting. I turn around. I notice everyone's in a huddle like they're watching a playground scuffle. I go over and Tommy starts up. He's kind of excited, telling me how Cody can't take this chick down. Cody's bent double, his arms around her waist, and she's got the double underhooks sunk in, like this." Earl sensed Juliette's disinterest and repeated himself a little louder. "Like this," he barked, demonstrating the position from his chair, bending his arms at the elbows to illustrate the fact Amiyah was preventing Cody from taking her down by hooking her own arms underneath his. "All the guys are watching now. Cody's face is all red and screwed up with frustration. He's giving it all he's got, but this chick is just not going down."

Juliette tried to look away, to drink from her beer, to watch the strippers on stage, to focus on anything other than her brother, but Earl's solid physique, his broad shoulders, and his muscular arms through his T-shirt filled her entire field of vision. He was all she could see, his wide body twisted toward her, his thick arm behind her on the back of the chair whenever he wasn't gesticulating wildly along to his story. She flinched as he spat his words out, his cold saliva landing in tiny particles on her face.

"This kid was something else in these see-through little yoga pants," he said.

Juliette found his enthusiasm exhausting. She tried to remain calm, to ignore him, to avoid getting worked up by the story the way he wanted her to.

Earl took hold of Juliette's chin. The sudden firmness of his grip caught her off guard, sent a shockwave through her body, the way his thumb and forefinger directed her back toward him. "Listen, Jules," he said, "I'm telling you." Earl's hand was warm and comforting, but

Juliette's flesh was tender and sore from the bruising. As always, the physical interaction with her brother was bittersweet. "You should have seen it, kid. Who would have thought this little chick could have put up such a fight?"

Juliette toyed with the label on her beer bottle, determined to avoid any form of eye contact.

Earl straightened his posture, readjusting as if to signal a change of tactics. "You want to know what fascinated me the most?" he asked from his elevated position. "It was this kid's spirit as she avoided the takedown, the amount of heart she showed. It kind of reminded me of..." Earl paused. "Well, I guess it doesn't matter, you probably wouldn't be interested anyway."

Juliette waited for him to continue, but he never did. It was a battle of wills now, neither sibling wanting to show weakness by being the first to speak. The club seemed painfully quiet all of a sudden, despite the pounding of the music. Juliette's curiosity soon got the better of her. "It reminded you of what?" she asked, still tearing the label from her bottle, not wanting to show the full extent of her interest.

"Well, if you must know," Earl began, "the truth is, the potential this girl showed, I honestly can't remember being that impressed, that turned on, that excited by any fighter other than you."

Juliette tried to hold her lips straight, conscious they might be forming an appreciative smile.

"That's right, kid," Earl said, following Juliette's pupils as they darted evasively among her inflated eyelids. He placed a hand over one of his sister's on the surface of the table.

Juliette noticed the sheen of his knuckles where the skin had been damaged so repeatedly throughout his career as a fighter. Juliette's rigid posture unfastened, her mood becoming placated by the rare showing of affection from her brother. She ran her thumb over the smooth, familiar flesh of his knuckles.

Earl's mouth curled up into a grin as he watched Juliette's hand moving over his own. He knew he'd won her over. He pulled himself free of his sister's grip and shot up from the bench seat all at once. The table jostled. A beer bottle fell to its side, spilling its frothy contents until it was righted. "And what happens next," Earl said, continuing with his story, "Cody gets so frustrated that he can't complete the takedown, and his arms are all tied up in the clinch, so he starts throwing his shoulders up in this chick's face. And then, Amiyah pulls her arms straight out of those underhooks like pistons, and now they're both squaring up to each other." Earl threw his fists out in front of himself to reenact the altercation, his shoulders hunched, his head bobbing from side to side. "I don't know who swung first, but by now, these kids are really going at it. Before any of us can even react, it's a full-scale fistfight in there."

The strobe light kicked in again and Juliette watched Earl's performance flashing in freeze-frame slow motion, his huge fists pumping back and forth, sweat flicking from his face, thick veins throbbing in his neck, his whole body appearing flexed and erect. Everything about the man was so powerful, so square and so solid. Even his head appeared to be swollen with muscle through his short crop of hair. Juliette raised a hand about her chest to form a defensive barrier between herself and her brother.

Earl leaned forward to speak into his sister's ear. The redness of his face was exaggerated by the neon lights. The sandpaper texture of his stubble grated against Juliette's cheek, and the scent of cologne masking masculine perspiration rushed into her nostrils. She unzipped her track-jacket, suddenly feeling smothered in the humid atmosphere of the club.

"And, who do you suppose came out of this altercation on top?" Earl whispered into Juliette's ear, controlling the tone of his voice as he expertly delivered the climax to his story.

Juliette could only muster a shrug in response, exhausted by her brother's performance.

Earl crashed back down in his chair, his eyes narrowing to a squint. He folded his arms and studied his sister, taking a moment to enjoy her anticipation, her mouth slightly ajar, her lips trembling with suspense as she waited for his response. Eventually, Earl turned and nodded toward Amiyah. "It was her, Jules. She got the better of him."

"You're trying to tell me that little stripper over there got the better of Cody in a fistfight?"

"I probably wouldn't believe it if I hadn't witnessed it myself. She rung Cody's bell. She buckled his legs for a second. He did the dance, and then everybody piled in and pulled them apart."

Juliette looked over at Amiyah, her eyes darting over the young woman's slight frame.

"And then," Earl continued, "the chick walks calmly to her stuff, her sweater and whatever, picks it all up and says, 'Fuck this, I didn't expect to be dealing with a bunch of little boys.' Then she just walks straight up out of there like the whole thing never even happened."

Juliette exhaled long and hard, relieved at the climax of the story. Her eyes scanned the room to check whether anybody had noticed her losing her composure to her brother's words.

"From that moment, I knew we had to get her," Earl said, and he gathered a paper napkin from the table to pat the sweat on his brow.

"I don't know. Sounds kind of like she's a hothead to me. I haven't got time for no drama."

"Trust me, Cody got what he deserved," Earl said. "So anyway, I came in here last weekend and there she was, this same little chick on stage in her underwear. I couldn't believe my eyes. I tried to apologize, to make up for what happened, but she wouldn't speak to me. Said she'd have me thrown out if I didn't quit bothering her."

"So that's it?" Juliette said. "Now you want me to do your dirty work, huh?"

"I just don't see this working with anyone else. The guys can't handle her. We need you to take her under your wing."

Juliette pursed her swollen lips as she watched Amiya seducing her prey. "It's not for me. I got enough on my plate. I don't have time." As

Juliette spoke, she noticed the lights dimming in her peripheral vision. A wide, foreboding shadow loomed over the table before her.

"Jules, Earl," a deep voice rumbled from somewhere close by.

Juliette tilted her head back and blinked her eyes in an attempt to clarify her vision. She quickly deciphered the vast silhouette before her, the dark mass of a fur coat backlit like a solar eclipse by the neon lights.

"Congrats on the win, Jules," Caesar said. His voice was a drawl, a slurred and lethargic mumble, almost unintelligible. "Hell of a fight," he added. "Some folks are saying you got lucky in there, with the triangle and all. But, all I'm saying is, hell of a fight." A comparatively minuscule female companion clung to Caesar's arm like a spoiled child hanging on to its father.

"Caesar, Dolores," Earl said with a nod to greet the pair. He removed his arm from the back of the bench seat, conscious the limb stretched out behind his sister may have been perceived as a little over-familiar.

Caesar's blonde-haired companion, Dolores, widened her eyes judgmentally at the retraction of the outstretched limb. Dolores was a harsh-faced waif of a woman—seemingly beautiful from a distance but intense and hard-looking upon closer inspection. Her hair was a shock of white blonde with purposefully black roots, quite befitting the dark undercurrent of her personality.

"Wife not with you tonight, Earl?" Caesar mumbled sarcastically.

Earl smiled back, refusing to dignify the comment with a response.

"How about a private dance, Jules?" Caesar said. "You've earned it, take your pick."

"Thanks, but I don't see any guys dancing in here," Juliette replied.

Dolores raised her eyebrows as if to question Juliette's attraction to males.

"Ain't that kind of a club," Caesar said. "We got girls, every flavor. You want a dance or what?"

Juliette felt Earl's elbow nudging into her side. She knew precisely the message her brother was attempting to communicate, that he was prompting her to request a dance with Amiyah.

"Ain't gonna stand here all night," Caesar persisted.

"I'm good, thanks," Juliette replied.

"Suit yourself," Caesar said with a shrug of indifference. "Come see me on Monday if you wanna get paid, Earl." With that, Caesar reached out to a passing server and snatched a small white towel from over her arm. As he turned to depart, Caesar raised the towel above his head and swung it around before letting it go, tossing it into the center of the table. "You might need that, Earl," Caesar suggested with a grin, "in case things get a little too much for you in here and you wanna tap out."

Dolores threw her head back and opened her mouth wide. Her shrill laughter was indistinguishable from the synthesizers shrieking out of the club speakers.

"How about you and me get back in the cage one last time, big man?" Earl said. "For old time's sake?" His offer went unheard as Caesar and Dolores drifted away, disappearing among the jostling bodies of the lower level. "And you can wipe that grin off your face as well, Jules," Earl said. "Should have just taken the dance anyway. Wasn't like you were gonna have to pay for it."

"Not exactly my idea of fun," Juliette replied.

"Could have spoken to her one on one, but you blew it. Now look, poor kid's gotta deal with having that drunk-ass college boy all over her."

Juliette looked over to the stocky young man swaying back and forth with intoxication on his stool. Amiyah was running the tall heel of her shoe along the inside of the man's calf as he attempted to count the cash in his wallet.

"She's closing the deal," Earl said. "You gotta act now."

"You saw how she worked to sell that dance," Juliette said. "I'm not about to get in the way."

"Look at him over there," Earl began. "He's got the whole damn uniform on. The oxford shirt, the khaki slacks, the boat shoes. Kid looks like he just stepped straight off his daddy's yacht."

"And, what's your point?"

"What kind of respect do you think a rich kid like that's gonna have for a stripper coming out of a place like this?"

Juliette noticed the young man placing a hand on the exposed skin of Amiyah's thigh, and the way in which Amiyah swiftly but gently removed the hand, while simultaneously forcing a smile onto her lips. Juliette looked from Amiyah's mouth to her eyes and was instantly aware the smile was entirely false, and Amiyah's eyes were not casual or relaxed, but instead were intensely focused and alert.

Earl leaned towards Juliette, so close she could feel his face brushing against the wisps of hair that had broken free from her ponytail. "You gonna let him put his hands all over her like that," Earl whispered.

"Stop it, Earl." Juliette tried to maintain a steady, unaffected tone of voice in an effort to hide the fact she'd detected the sadness in Amiyah's eyes.

"You know he's probably gonna go in there and start waving his money around," Earl said. "Convince her to go back to his frat house, or whatever."

"Come on now," Juliette pleaded.

"And then what?" Earl asked, paying close attention to his sister's reactions. "You know his daddy's probably a lawyer, right?"

"Well, if she can punch like you say she can, then good luck to him."

"He's got to be at least twice her weight," Earl continued, "and, probably on steroids, judging by the size of the titties on him."

Juliette had known Earl long enough to recognize when she was being manipulated, but at the same time, she couldn't get the intensity of Amiya's eyes out of her thoughts.

"The clock's ticking," Earl said as he sat back and finished his beer.

Amiya took the young man by the hand and the pair climbed down from their stools. "This is on you, Jules," Earl said with a grin on his lips that suggested he already knew what his sister was going to do. "When they find her torn up, broken little body in the woods tomorrow, how are you gonna feel?"

"You're sick," Juliette said as she placed her hands on the table and pushed herself to her feet. "You know that, right? You're sick."

CHAPTER 4

Juliette waited anxiously, hands in pockets, hands out of pockets, arms folded, arms by her sides, her track-suited figure framed by a heart-shaped archway from which a beaded curtain hung toward the floor. She watched as Amiyah approached through the crowd. The young woman's brow was furrowed with determination as she swam among the sea of heads, battling against the current of jostling bodies in the narrow central gangway of the club. All the while, the lumbering frat boy—intoxicated with a mixture of high spirits and alcohol—was hindering Amiyah's progress as he clung to her hand and trailed several steps behind, his stocky build giving him the appearance of a cumbersome infant hanging onto its mother.

The heart-shaped archway behind Juliette was one of several that ran along the wall opposite the catwalk. Each sequential archway was an entrance to a small room, an alcove where dancers took clients to perform private shows. An unlit bulb mounted beside this particular archway had indicated to Juliette it was the only private room currently unoccupied. Upon realizing this, Juliette had decided to make her way over so she could lay in wait, hoping to intercept Amiyah once she arrived with her prey.

Earl was still seated in the booth, watching from the sidelines, studying Juliette's every move as though he was coaching her through a fight. His supportive presence bolstered Juliette with a sense of confidence, but at the same time, his observation brought with it a certain pressure to perform, to fulfill his expectations. Earl had been coaching Juliette for so long it had become almost second nature for her to endeavor to impress him, but it often seemed more than that somehow, as though she was striving to gain his approval in everything she did.

Juliette noticed Caesar was also watching from his position beside the bar. She read his blank expression as a confirmation that his offer of a free dance still stood. Dolores' overly made-up face bore a wide smile, a smug grin at the realization Juliette was waiting for a dance from another woman. Juliette took a step back from the crowds swarming in front of her; the revelers huddled together so they could shout into one another's ears, the couples with bodies interlocked, swaying in time to the music. Juliette's thoughts were still a little disjointed as she struggled to clear her mind of involuntary flashbacks to her fight. It seemed every ache and pain would trigger her brain to recall the punch or elbow that had caused it. She stared into space, her expression vacant, her vision blurred through a deliberate lack of concentration.

"You waiting for a bus, or what, sugar?" a female voice called out with the saliva-laden slap of a jaw chewing on bubblegum.

Juliette struggled to focus her gaze on the statuesque vision before her, the lithe silhouette with hands on hips, flashes of golden-brown skin visible through the net-like fabric of a baby-doll dress. Juliette felt a burning sensation somewhere inside as she ran her eyes over the striking figure balancing on stilt-like heels. She assumed the knots in her stomach were there as a result of her determination not to mess this whole thing up while operating under Earl's scrutiny.

Amiyah clicked her fingers to spur Juliette into action. "I'm gonna need that booth now, sugar," she said. "So, unless you're about to shake off that old tracksuit and dance for somebody, I'm gonna have to ask you to step aside." She finished her sentence by blowing out a large bubble of gum, which swelled and burst all over her darkly-painted lips.

"So what, you don't dance for girls?" Juliette asked, attempting to maintain her composure.

Amiyah's tongue emerged from her mouth and expertly retracted the exploded gum with nimble dexterity. She looked silently at Juliette, her big dark eyes narrowing to an inquisitive squint. Juliette squinted back at the young woman and tilted her head so she could see through her swollen eyelids. The two women were engaged in a showdown. The underwear-clad stripper with the semi-transparent dress draped over her body and the tracksuit-adorned fighter with the bruised faced, both individuals attempting to get the measure of each other like a pair of wild animals deciding whether to compete over territory.

Amiyah's tall heels exaggerated her perfectly average height and accentuated her svelte legs. She was a petite young woman with curvaceous lines around the hips that gave her figure doll-like proportions. The braids of her hair fell elegantly about her shoulders and she had a line of freckles running horizontally across the middle of her face that looked vaguely menacing, like a streak of war paint or battle camouflage.

The stocky young man at Amiyah's side extended his stout arm, revealing a large, bejeweled timepiece, which he proceeded to glance upon in an exaggerated manner. "We gonna do this or what?" he slurred at Amiyah before turning his out-of-focus gaze toward Juliette. "You already got lucky once tonight, Diamond Diaz," he said.

Juliette pictured herself tackling the squat little man to the ground, wrestling him into a submission hold and stretching his thick arm out across her body until the limb gave way and broke at the elbow. "What's the matter? Your mother never teach you it's supposed to be ladies first?" Juliette spoke calmly, her mind flooded with a vision of the little man rolling around on the floor clutching his broken arm and squealing like a stuck pig as he realized the splintered bone was protruding through his skin.

"Don't see no ladies in here," the man slurred, and he glanced around for somebody to laugh at his joke, the stench of alcohol heavy on his breath.

Amiyah checked her black-painted nails as if she was already bored with the confrontation. "I hope you both realize you're about to get yourselves thrown the hell out of here," she said.

The stocky man stood up tall and stuck out his chest to exaggerate his height and emphasize his muscles.

Juliette stared blankly at the man, unshaken. "Do you happen to know the funniest part about choking out a drunk person?" she asked casually.

Her question was met with silence.

"Well, do either of you know what it is?" She looked both to Amiyah and to the stocky man for an answer.

The pair exchanged glances, each waiting for the other party to solve the riddle.

"Well, let me tell you what it is," Juliette continued. "You see, if you apply the rear naked choke to somebody who's been drinking all night, when you've got them in that stranglehold and your arms are wrapped around their neck, at the very second that individual succumbs to the choke and they lose consciousness, they always, without fail, empty their bladder all over themselves." Juliette laughed quietly to herself. "It's hilarious. You gotta see it to believe it, really you do."

The stocky man's posture began to deflate and his eyes loosened with uncertainty.

"So, the million-dollar question is," Juliette said, "how much have you had to drink tonight, little man?"

The man thought for a moment and then looked to his watch again. "Ain't got time for this bullshit," he said. "You're lucky I've got somewhere else I need to be." With that, he turned on the spot and made his way into the crowd, ricocheting off the other club-goers as he struggled to maintain his balance.

"Well, thanks very much for that, sugar," Amiyah said, folding her arms across her chest. "You just lost me a paying customer."

"Seems like you had a lucky escape, to me."

"What makes you think I wanna dance for you anyway?"

Juliette nodded in the direction of the bar, where Caesar was propped up motionless, observing everything before him like a wise owl perched upon a branch. Caesar responded with a single nod and Amiyah's shoulders dropped as she came to realize her obligation to fulfill Juliette's request.

"All I can say is, you better have some deep pockets on that tracksuit," Amiyah said as she pulled the beaded curtain to one side.

"This one's on Caesar," Juliette replied.

"Well, don't be expecting too much out of me," Amiyah said, looking Juliette up and down disapprovingly. "I'm not busting my ass for no freebie." She led the way into the small rectangular booth, strutting toward a red leather couch at the far end of the space with the exaggerated gait of a catwalk model, her hips bouncing from one side to the other with every stride. Juliette attempted to analyze the body of the young woman before her, studying the curves of her calf muscles and the definition in her back through the sheer fabric of her dress. The lights were dimmed in the little room. Juliette decided she would need to get a closer look to fully assess Amiyah's athletic potential.

"So, what is this, a commiseration prize from Caesar for losing your fight?"

"I won tonight, thanks."

"Doesn't look much like you won to me," Amiyah said, her eyes darting to and fro across Juliette's face to illustrate her point.

"You should see the other girl."

"What is she, dead?"

"Give me a break, kid. It's been a long night." To Juliette's eyes, the young woman did not appear a great deal older than her teenage daughter. Although athletic, Amiyah's body had retained a level of softness, her flesh yet to be hardened by years of intense training the way Juliette's had been. "Are you even old enough to be in here?"

Juliette asked.

"I'm twenty-three, thank you," Amiyah replied. "But of course, we can pretend I'm a little younger if that's what you're into," she added, raising a suggestive eyebrow.

"I'm good, thanks."

"Suit yourself," Amiyah replied, with a tone that Juliette could have sworn suggested a hint of disappointment. "Sit down, relax." Amiya placed an outstretched palm in the center of Juliette's chest, directing her toward the couch. "This isn't a job interview."

Juliette fell back onto the leather seat, arching her spine and emitting a small groan of pain as she landed.

"If Caesar says I gotta dance for you, then I guess we might as well try and have some fun. Besides, it's not exactly every day I get to dance for a girl in here. So let me see if I can ease your pain a little, sugar." Amiyah raised a finger to her lips, requesting silence as she listened out for something. "DJ's about to play my song," she said.

The relentless thump of the music had been reduced to a tolerable volume by the walls of the small, booth-like room, as if somebody had fed the sound through a filter, taking the abrasive edge off the bass. Juliette realized she couldn't just come right out and reveal her true intentions; the fact she'd interrupted Amiyah's dance solely so she could attempt to persuade the young woman to come back to Earl's gym. So instead, she took a deep breath, removed her track-jacket, and sunk back into the cushioning of the couch.

The music slowed in tempo as one track blended into the next. "Damn, I love this song," Amiyah said, and she closed her eyes and smiled as if the sonic vibrations had injected her with intense sensations of pleasure. A bass-heavy rumble filled the little room. Electric blues guitar pulsated over a constant, driving rhythm. Passionate vocal outbursts wailed out sporadically. Amiyah raised her arms above her head and moved to the music in half time, her hips swaying with liquid fluidity on every other beat.

Juliette found herself unwittingly hypnotized as she observed the young woman losing herself to the music. Juliette tried to focus, to remain professional. She began to consider how Amiyah's fluid motions might translate into footwork and head movement within the cage. Surely if somebody can dance like this, they must be able to move well in a fight, she told herself.

Amiyah loosened her dress from one shoulder at a time, allowing the garment to fall to her waist. She turned her back on Juliette, expertly rolling her hips and bending forward so that her ass emerged from the sheer dress one rotund cheek after the other, causing the garment to drop to the floor. Amiya stepped out of her dress and stood almost entirely naked in a low-cut string-thong and a tiny lace bra that only just concealed the circles of her areolas.

"So, I guess you work out?" Juliette asked.

Amiyah laughed in response. "You like what you see?"

"I mean, you're in pretty good shape—"

"—Shush, now," Amiya whispered, and she placed a finger over Juliette's lips. "Relax, it's just you and me in here, sugar." She climbed onto the couch like a cat stalking its prey, straddling Juliette and kneeling over her lap.

Juliette sunk further back into the leather couch, desperate to escape the invasion of her personal space.

"You gonna look at me or what?" Amiya asked, and she moved her face closer to Juliette's in an attempt to make direct eye contact. She began to rotate her hips, gyrating her crotch over Juliette's lap. The young woman's underwear was nearly as see-through as her dress. Juliette tried to avert her eyes but Amiyah's hair hung like a shroud blocking Juliette's peripheral vision, forcing her to focus on the movements before her. She felt as though she was fighting the effects of a powerful sedative, with the soulful music filling her ears and Amiyah's scent—a faint, intoxicating musk of vanilla—flavoring the air.

"Is this how you like it?" Amiyah whispered into Juliette's ear. "Just imagine you're fucking me," she said, and she continued to sweep her crotch back and forth over Juliette's thighs.

Juliette swallowed nervously, stunned into silence by the suggestion.

"That's it," Amiyah said, "just let your mind run wild with all the things you'd like to do to me. I know you're an ass-girl, aren't you?"

"Sorry, I'm a what?"

"Come on, I noticed you checking out my ass when you followed me in," Amiyah said, turning around to sit in Juliette's lap. "You can't help what you're into." The young woman's teardrop-shaped derrière was almost entirely exposed, save for the thin string of her thong. She leaned back and whispered over her shoulder, "I'll let you see my asshole if that's what you want."

"Hang on now," Juliette interrupted, "we don't need to go that far."

"Don't be shy," Amiyah said, "but of course, it's gonna cost you a little extra if you want me to pull my thong aside." She leaned forward, bending over to provide Juliette with a better view. "Come on, sugar, let's play."

Juliette strained her eyes to follow the ribbon-like string of Amiyah's underwear as it traced a line between the bronze spheres of her ass cheeks, just about covering the dark, enticing center-point, before continuing down to the small pouch of fabric that encased her crotch. Juliette's stomach burned with nerves, forcing her to look away.

"All you gotta do is slip a little money under here," Amiyah said, as she lifted the waistband from over her hip, "and I'll show you everything."

Juliette paused, unable to move. Maybe she didn't want to offend Amiyah by rejecting her offer, or perhaps she'd been drawn into a near hypnotic state by the young woman's dancing, the muffled drone of the music, and the intimacy of the little booth.

Amiyah reached down and slipped a thumb under the string of her thong, teasing the cord of fabric away from her skin as if she was seconds away from pulling it aside.

"Wait a second," Juliette said, sitting up straight at the realization of what was about to happen, "you've got it wrong."

"What, that's not how you like it?"

"No, I mean, look, just sit down, please."

"What, you don't like me now?"

Juliette noticed Amiyah's dark eyes had widened, appearing uncertain and offended, the way they had when the stocky man attempted to put his hands on her. "I'm just here to talk, that's all," Juliette explained.

"You're a talker? But I thought you were getting into it?"

Juliette patted the leather cushioning of the couch. "Come on, sit down," she said. "Can't we just talk for a while?"

Amiya sat down beside Juliette and folded her svelte legs together.

"Listen, Amiyah, you know who I am, right?"

"I've seen some of your fights on the Internet. What of it?"

"And you know who my brother is?"

"You mean that asshole of a gorilla out there? What about him?"

"Yeah, the gorilla," Juliette confirmed. "He told me about what happened at the gym the other day."

"That little bitch had it coming. I'm not sorry for what I did."

"No, I don't want you to apologize, honey," Juliette said, trying to reassure the younger woman. "It's just, well, Earl kind of mentioned that you might have potential, as a fighter."

"So, let me get this straight. He sent you in here to talk about fighting? And, you had me shaking my ass like a fool for nothing?" Amiya seemed to withdraw into herself at the realization. She leaned forward over her crossed legs and folded her arms around her chest to cover herself up. "Are you even into girls?" she asked

"What does it matter? I wanted to speak to you," Juliette said, placing a comforting hand on the young woman's knee.

Amiyah drew a sharp intake of breath at the physical contact. Her body trembled momentarily, as though a cold shiver had passed through her. She looked down at Juliette's hand, and then into her eyes. "I never said you could touch."

Juliette removed her hand, avoiding Amiyah's gaze. The air seemed to thicken between them. "The thing is, Earl wanted to know if you'd be interested in trying out properly at Diablo MMA sometime."

"You mean like a test? You think I need to take a test to train with those losers?"

"Sort of like a test, yes. But more specifically, you'd be trying out to train with me."

"You're the one with all the bruises. Maybe it's you who needs to audition to train me."

Juliette emitted a single "huh" of a laugh. "I just went three rounds with The Ox, kid. Who did you ever fight?"

"Looks like The Ox has been using you as a punching bag for three rounds to me. Maybe it's time you thought about retiring. What are you now anyway, forty-five?"

"You can knock ten years off of that, thanks, sweetheart."

"Well, you look a hell of a lot older to me."

"That comes with having forty-four wins and five losses on your record. How many fights have you had?"

"A few," Amiyah replied defensively, with the tone of a child who couldn't think of a witty response. "Anyway, dance is over, I'm afraid. All the time I'm in here with you is time I could be out there, shaking my stuff for someone who actually appreciates it, making money, getting paid."

Juliette felt the opportunity slipping away from her, as though she was failing miserably at her task. Her competitive spirit wouldn't allow her to lose this easily. She thought about her brother waiting outside. She pictured the stern, disapproving expression that would be displayed upon his face if she went back to him with bad news. She tried to imagine what Earl would do in this situation. What words of advice would he shout from the sidelines? What kind of tactics would he want her to employ?

"Sounds like you're a little scared to me, kid," Juliette suggested.

"Scared of what, exactly? The pathetic little guy whose face I messed up?"

"It's okay, I see it a lot, girls feeling intimidated by all the testosterone flying around in the gym. Not everybody can deal with it like I can. Honestly, it's really nothing to be embarrassed about. Maybe you should stick to taking your clothes off, if that's your thing."

"I'm not intimidated by anybody, thanks," Amiyah replied, checking her short, but perfectly manicured nails as if she had no particular interest in the conversation. "And don't try that reverse psychology bullshit on me, okay? You've been hit in the head far too many times to act in any way convincing."

Juliette shrugged her shoulders to plead innocence. "If you're sure it's not for you, well, I suppose I'll just have to look for somebody else to coach then, won't I?" She placed her hands on the seat below her, lifting herself to indicate she was preparing to leave. "Plenty of kids out there who'd kill for the opportunity of free coaching from a jiu-jitsu black belt like me."

"Hold on a second. You never said anything about it being free."

"I guess you'd be my first real coaching assignment. You scratch my back, I'll scratch yours, or whatever."

"Well, in that case, if I don't have to pay anything, I suppose I might consider giving it a try. Just one time, of course. To see how it goes. That's if I haven't got anything better to do, obviously."

"Obviously," Juliette said, flashing her eyes around the booth judgmentally. "I mean, seems like your work here is far more important than training to become a professional athlete, right?"

"Yeah, well, maybe I gotta go get my nails done, my hair fixed, my eyebrows threaded, or any of the other infinity of things that are a whole lot more interesting than wasting my time with a has-been like you."

"I guess we'll see if you got the balls to show up at eight o'clock Monday morning then, won't we?"

"More like, we'll see if an old-timer like you still has what it takes to keep up with a young prospect like me." Amiyah gathered her dress from the floor. "But I really gotta go. You're costing me money now." She slipped the dress over her head and checked herself in a mirror mounted above the couch. "Love to say it was a pleasure, sugar," she said, turning to leave, her braided hair swinging dramatically as she swiveled on her tall heels.

"Oh, and Amiyah, honey," Juliette said, "I take it you're gonna wear something a little less revealing to the gym, right?"

Amiya raised an open hand to her pouting lips as though she was about to blow a kiss in Juliette's direction. But instead, she placed the kissed palm against the surface of her derrière. With that, the young woman was gone, disappearing through the beaded curtain, leaving Juliette alone in the little booth.

Juliette breathed a sigh of relief and struggled to her feet, her body aching as it unfolded. She pulled on her track-jacket, her hurried limbs becoming momentarily entangled in the garment as she spilled out through the beaded curtain, back into the main body of the club. She was filled with a rush of enthusiasm, certain Earl would be pleased with her performance. She looked over to the table where her brother had been seated, but quickly realized the semicircular booth was empty. She glanced over to the bar, wondering if Earl could have joined Tommy and the other fighters, but he was nowhere to be seen. She scanned the rest of the narrow club, checking the faces of the people in the central gangway to no avail.

From the corner of her eye, Juliette noticed Tommy at the bar waving a hand to catch her attention. She shrugged to ask what he wanted. Tommy signaled with an outstretched arm and Juliette looked to her right, following his instruction. She saw Earl was with the woman who'd brought her a drink earlier that evening. The server was leading Earl under one of the archways a few booths down. Juliette's enthusiasm faded as she watched her brother ducking through the beaded curtain with a smile on his face and his narrowed eyes transfixed by the fluid motion of the server's strides. Despite the fact Juliette was surrounded by people, she was suddenly overwhelmed by the emptiness of the realization she was entirely alone.

CHAPTER 5

Juliette exhaled a long breath of exertion. Her back was tight with pain as she climbed down from the high driving position of her vast black pickup truck. The intense glow of the morning sun highlighted every imperfection in the vehicle's bodywork, the surface of which was rippled with minor indentations and rust-dotted gouges, battle scars telling stories of advancing years and a general lack of upkeep. Juliette rotated her body ninety degrees so that her legs hung toward the floor. She slid awkwardly from the bench seat, lowering herself to the sidewalk like a clumsy child emerging from the branches of a tree. The glare of the sun forced her to squint through the bug-eyed sunglasses shielding her vision. She donned this specific eyewear after each fight with almost ritualistic regularity, the dark, opaque lenses hiding much of her facial bruising, the wide frames acting as a mask she could disappear behind.

Juliette glanced around to see if anybody had witnessed her graceless dismount. She straightened her leather jacket, tugging the garment back into position where it had ruffled forward as she'd tumbled out of her truck. The earthy smell of freshly-cut grass hung on the breeze, while the buzz of several nearby lawnmowers provided the sonic accompaniment, their varying tones echoing around the sprawling lawns of the suburban neighborhood. Juliette arched her back to stretch out some of the stiffness that was hindering her movement. She reached behind herself and squeezed a hand into the back of her jeans to rearrange the semi-thong underwear she'd chosen to wear on this rare day off of training. She often felt an awkward sense of self-consciousness when not clad exclusively in sportswear, fearing people might notice the way the clothing didn't quite sit as it should on her athletic frame. The tight jeans she was wearing seemed to cling to every part of her legs, a constant reminder of the denim's presence. She took a little time to adjust the fabric of her underwear and then to realign the waistband of her jeans.

"You okay there, sweetie?" a female voice called out from somewhere beyond the precisely trimmed hedgerow that stood before Juliette.

Juliette's body jolted; her heart raced at the realization somebody was so close by. "Margot?" she replied, raising a hand about her chest to steady her nerves.

"I could have sworn we said nine o'clock," Margot said, emerging from behind the rose bush with one hand at her hip and the other loosely clasping a pair of gardening shears. "Wasn't that what we agreed?" Margot's head tilted forward and her green eyes intensified, as though they were repeating the question themselves in a slightly sharper tone than her mouth had dared to employ.

Juliette noticed how the shears seemed to be angled in her general direction, and the way the long blades wafted through the air as Margot spoke, a sort of passive-aggressive gesticulation from her sister-in-law. "I got held up, I guess," Juliette shrugged, "getting gas and whatever." She studied Margot's attire. Her knee-high leather boots and beige chinos, her khaki shirt tucked neatly at the waist. She appeared to be dressed in clothing better suited to a safari than a spot of Sunday morning gardening.

"It's past ten o'clock. Did you forget or something?" Margot asked, waving the shears with a loose rotation of her wrist. She tossed her voluminous auburn locks from her shoulders as she spoke, a display of attitude that was juxtaposed awkwardly with her wide, ever-present grin, an exaggerated smile that never seemed to leave her ruby lips.

"Give me a break, Margot," Juliette said, ruffling a hand through her own lank, style-less hair, suddenly aware of the inadequacies of her own appearance in the presence of somebody so immaculately turned out. "It's not like we had an appointment, is it?"

"Try telling that to Shelby. She's the one who's been waiting for over an hour." Margot turned her attention to the rose bush as though it were of more interest to her than the conversation she was engaged in.

Juliette found herself fighting an overwhelming desire to kick the shears clean out of Margot's hand, and then to follow up by landing a swift and powerful elbow directly to her jaw. Juliette pictured the aftermath: Margot's hands clasped over her mouth, tears streaming down her cheeks as she tried to keep her broken teeth in place. Earl would run out of their perfect little white-painted bungalow onto the lawn, a mixture of panic and confusion on his face as he tried to work out what had happened, that disappointed look shooting from his eyes as always.

"So how did it go at the hospital anyway?" Margot asked, interrupting Juliette's fantasy.

"The hospital?"

"Yes, the hospital," Margot said, shaking her head. "You went there with Earl last night, didn't you?"

"Oh right, the hospital. So, you haven't spoken to Earl yet?"

"If you knew my husband anywhere near as well as I do, you'd realize there wasn't a rat's chance in hell he'd be out of bed this early on a Sunday morning."

"I know my own brother well enough, thanks," Juliette replied. "Obviously, I thought you might have seen him last night."

"I'm afraid I was well and truly out cold by whatever time he got done taking care of you. Some of us actually value our beauty sleep, you know?"

Juliette felt a burn of anger ignite within. Her subconscious quickly provided the perfect anecdote to her rage: a recollection of where Earl had been heading the last time she saw him, the way his eyes were all narrowed with lust as he'd followed the stripper into the booth. It was a moment Margot would never be aware of, a secret Juliette was keeping for her brother. Her temperament began to rebalance as she pictured the stripper gyrating in her brother's lap.

"So, what's the damage this time?" Margot asked. "Stitches? A concussion? Anything broken beyond repair?"

"I'm fine. I won last night, actually. Insurance says I have to get checked out, that's all."

"You know, it might have been nice if you'd explained that to Shelby, so she didn't have to go on stage worrying about you."

"Shelby knows how it works by now. She's gonna be fifteen this year. She's a smart kid."

"Well, aren't you gonna ask how her performance went?"

"I'm pretty sure she'll be dying to tell me all about it herself, thanks."

"Yes, good luck with that," Margot replied, widening her tooth-revealing grin.

Juliette felt the flame of anger rekindle within, shortly before a thunderous bang shattered the peaceful serenity of the morning, as if the force of Juliette's inner fury had somehow caused a nearby windowpane to shatter. Margot winced and shuddered like a malfunctioning robot. Juliette looked over toward the bungalow and saw Shelby slamming the front door a second time as though her first effort hadn't quite conveyed her mood accurately enough. The teenager stomped her way down the wooden steps of the veranda with her backpack slung over one shoulder, and then marched across the path that cut a line through the center of the lawn.

"How's my little ballerina this morning?" Juliette called out.

"Goodbye, Margot," Shelby said, ignoring her mother's greeting as she stormed by with her sandy blonde locks hanging forward to cover most of her face.

"Take care, sweetie" Margot replied. "You did great last night."

Juliette couldn't help but notice the exposed flesh of her daughter's legs as she made her way toward the truck. Shelby's naked thighs and calves appeared almost comically long as she hurried by in a tiny pair of denim shorts and a ruffled tube top that revealed her bronzed midriff and sun-kissed shoulders. Juliette struggled to recall ever having seen the close-fitting shorts before, or the tube top, for that matter. The unfamiliar garments left her feeling alienated somehow, like she hadn't been consulted. Juliette's eyes traced the back of her daughter's legs right up to the hems of her shorts. She couldn't quite tell where Shelby's thighs ended and her buttocks began, but either way, she was certain the shorts displayed a little too much of the teenager's flesh.

"Like I said," Margot began, with a magnificently porcelain smile, "good luck."

"Did you take her shopping?"

Margot placed an outstretched palm over her chest to protest her innocence, and then turned toward the bungalow, directing Juliette to the perpetrator. Earl's hulking figure waded clumsily onto the veranda, his muscular arms and shoulders emerging from an old faded tank top. Earl was accompanied by a small, blond-haired boy who clung to his back and peered over his solid shoulders like a baby monkey hitching a ride on its mother.

"Hey, Anderson," Juliette called out to the child.

"Hiya, Auntie Jules," the boy shouted back.

Juliette noticed Anderson was wearing his karate outfit. She saw the thick, white cotton sleeves of his gi top covering his arms as he clasped his hands together around his father's neck. The sight of the boy in his little uniform brought a smile to Juliette's face and she removed her dark glasses to get a better look.

"Gosh, your eyes are a mess," Margot said.

"It's nothing," Juliette replied, repositioning the glasses over the bridge of her nose.

"You want me to get you some ice?"

"I'm fine, really."

"I don't know why you insist on putting yourself through this all the time. You always had such a pretty face. I mean, it's hardly any wonder you don't have a boyfriend."

"Some guys actually like bruises. Trust me, you'd be surprised."

"I'm sure there are all kinds of wild perverts out there, but you really ought to slow down. You're getting too old for all this. Now, let me go get you some ice, I insist."

"Thanks for your concern, but we should really be going. And, you know, thanks for everything else, with Shelby."

"Oh, don't mention it, really. You should come over more often. Come for dinner sometime. You know we'd love to have you, both of you."

"I'm a little busy at the moment, but thanks," Juliette said, sidestepping to get away.

"Well, take care, won't you? Make sure you rest up now. And don't forget to put something cold on that swelling."

"Will do," Juliette replied, hurrying toward her truck. As she approached the vehicle, she saw Shelby had already climbed up into the passenger seat and had sat up tall, tying her golden hair into a ponytail while studying her reflection in the mirror on the back of the fold-down sun visor. Juliette laughed inwardly at her daughter's presumptuous, entitled attitude, the way Shelby thought herself to be some kind of a princess who deserved to be transported back and forth without even bestowing her chauffeur with so much as the common courtesy of a hello. Juliette took a deep breath, preparing herself for the ordeal that awaited. She opened the door to her vehicle and took hold of the handle above the window to pull herself up onto the bench seat. The air was warm and still inside the truck, almost stifling. The stagnation seemed to be magnified by a sense of tension that hung in the atmosphere between the two occupants. Juliette wound her window down a little to alleviate the pressure.

"So, you're not even going to say hi?" Juliette asked. "Come on, Doll, let's not fall out over this."

"Can we just go home, please?" Shelby said, peering over her spectacles to check her makeup in the little mirror, pursing and pouting her freshly-glossed lips.

"Look, I get why you're mad." Juliette said. "I'm sorry I didn't make it last night, okay? I messed up."

"It's fine." Shelby shrugged. "I had Margot and Anderson there with me. They seemed to have a great time."

"Well, I'm sorry, okay?"

Shelby shrugged again.

Juliette twisted her key in the ignition. The truck made a guttural crunching sound as though it was an old beast of a machine attempting to clear its mechanical throat.

"So embarrassing," Shelby uttered under her breath.

"Give the old girl a chance," Juliette said, turning the key again. She worked the ignition more forcefully this time and the truck rumbled into action. A satisfying vibration stirred up through the bench for a few seconds as the engine came to life. "That's my girl," Juliette said, with a hand on the dash to soothe the old vehicle. The truck's speakers began to rattle out a driving bass line, the aging stereo audibly straining even at a modest volume.

"Since when have you listened to anything like this?" Shelby asked.

"Must have heard it last night, I guess," Juliette explained, and she reached forward to lower the volume. "Another fighter's entrance music, I think," she said, trying desperately to sound convincing. She felt herself blushing slightly at the lie, but realized how difficult it would have been to recount to her daughter the memory of watching a stripper taking her clothes off to the song the previous evening. As she pulled the truck away from the curb, she watched in the rearview mirror, Margot,

Earl, and Anderson, the trio in front of their house waving in unison, perfectly in sync with one another, like the little wooden people that pop out of a cuckoo clock. Juliette couldn't quite make out their facial expressions at this distance, but her mind quickly filled in the blanks. She knew they'd all be smiling, grinning from ear to ear as they waved. Juliette was certain they'd all have happy little expressions to match the perfectly trimmed hedgerow, the white painted bungalow, the velveteen lawn of freshly-cut grass. She glanced around at the aging interior of her truck, the tarnished plastic surfaces, fragments of dead leaves and empty food wrappers in the foot-wells, the scent of old leather peeling from the seats. She wondered for a moment if it might have been kinder to have left Shelby behind with her brother and his wife.

Shelby was looking out the window, her head resting against the glass as she solemnly contemplated the suburban paradise she was leaving behind. Juliette marveled at the way the teenager's ponytail danced over her shoulders every time the truck passed over a bump or a pothole in the road. It never failed to amaze Juliette how perfect her daughter was in every way. Just to be in Shelby's presence was a breath of fresh air in all the suffocation of her existence. She paid attention to every last detail: the golden, doll-like skin of Shelby's exposed legs as they sat tangled over one another, the shape of her exquisite little face in profile, the way her glasses balanced over the cute little bump on the bridge of her nose. Juliette couldn't help but adore every single thing about Shelby, even on an occasion like today, when the girl was behaving so intentionally aloof. She took a moment to breathe in the bubblegum fragrance of her daughter's hair products and the fruit-infused scent of her lip gloss ringing out among the dank odors of the truck. It was all too much for Juliette to resist. She was desperate for interaction, unable to hold back from a further attempt at placating her daughter's seemingly impenetrable mood. "So, come on, Doll. You wanna tell me how the show went last night, or what?"

"I'm a little tired," Shelby replied, her voice distorted by an exaggerated yawn.

"I guess that means you don't want to go get ice cream then?"

"We had some last night, thanks. Margot makes it from scratch."

"She would, wouldn't she?"

"Margot says it's healthier that way."

"It's just Margot now, is it?"

"She said I was old enough to drop the Aunt."

"Is that right?"

"Besides, aren't you always telling me I need to watch my figure?"

"But it's our tradition," Juliette said. "We're celebrating, aren't we? We both nailed it last night."

"Well, don't blame me next time you can't make weight." Shelby leaned back in her chair and lifted her boot-adorned feet up onto the dash so that her bare legs were fully outstretched.

Juliette glanced from the side of her eyes, maintaining her focus on the road, refusing to comment on the fact her daughter's boots were pressed against the windshield.

"Do you think I'm getting fat?" Shelby asked, pinching little wads of skin from her stomach in an attempt to draw her mother's attention.

"You not a little cold in that outfit, Doll?"

"Since when do you care what I wear?"

Juliette rotated the air-conditioning dial to its maximum output. In turn, Shelby reached out and shut off the air vent closest to her, stemming the flow of cold air. Juliette glanced down at the goose-bumped skin of her daughter's legs. "Those shorts are practically underwear," she said.

"It's called fashion, actually. But I wouldn't expect you to understand that, of course." Shelby crossed her arms above her head to display the entirety of her outfit. "Uncle Earl picked them out, and as a matter of fact, I think he's got great taste."

"You're trying to tell me you managed to get Uncle Earl to go into a clothes store with you?"

"Sure, right after he picked me up from school on Friday. It was so much fun. We went to that new mall, the one by the freeway."

"Well, don't you go getting too used to that place. The prices in there are out of this world."

"He said I needed some new clothes now that I'm getting older. Said something about the ugly duckling turning into a swan."

"I guess that's one way to put it."

"Plus, they have those absolutely humongous dressing rooms with the couches, so Uncle Earl can come right on in there with me."

"You're kidding me, right?" Juliette asked, her attention drifting from the road.

"Mom, look where you're going."

"They let him come into the dressing room with you?"

"Of course, so he can pick my outfits and tell me which ones look best. We have these full-on little fashion shows, and Uncle Earl gives everything scores out of ten."

Juliette imagined her brother seated in a vast room of mirrors, charming the young sales assistants with tales of his exploits as a fighter while he waited for Shelby to emerge from one of the individual cubicles. She imagined Shelby proudly displaying her virtually naked body, her golden flesh covered only where it was absolutely necessary, the thin strands of her arms and legs emerging from her new little denim shorts and the strip of fabric that was supposed to be a top. She knew Earl must have looked the clothing over to assess the way it fit over Shelby's petite frame before giving it his nod of approval. She was certain he would have let Shelby wear the new outfit for the remainder of the day as he drove her around in his Mustang listening to music, the same way he used to drive around with Juliette when they were both teenagers.

"Mom, look out!" Shelby reached for the steering wheel and yanked it round toward herself. Juliette pressed the brake to the floor, causing the truck to lose its grip on the tarmac and swing around violently. A flash of white shot past the windscreen, a bright mass undefined among the panic. A horn sounded.

"Mom, what are you doing?"

The truck spun a full hundred and eighty degrees as it traveled across the intersection until the rear wing slammed into a streetlight. Juliette's head was thrown from side to side. She turned to see the vast white object she'd narrowly avoided—a cumbersome motor home— now hurtling along the road at a right angle to her truck. There was an ear-piercing screech as the ungainly vehicle's tires grated against the surface of the highway. The motor home wobbled awkwardly, its weight unbalanced, two wheels leaving the road momentarily before the giant thing mounted the curb and slid to a halt.

"It came out of nowhere," Juliette exclaimed, her heartbeat pounding in every part of her body.

"The fucking light was red," Shelby said, clinging desperately to the vehicle's interior.

"Hey, come on, no cursing. I'm sorry, I don't know what happened. I guess I must have got distracted."

"They're getting out," Shelby said.

Juliette watched the motor home as the driver's door swung open. A moccasin-clad foot emerged timidly, searching blindly for the floor. Shortly after, the ample-bodied male driver squeezed from the door and climbed down from the vehicle's cockpit. The portly man's gait was slow and uncertain, as though he was not entirely in control of his limbs. Juliette's mind immediately likened the man's disjointed movements to those of a fighter attempting to regain their balance after receiving a blow to the head.

"You think he's okay?" Shelby asked.

"He's just a little shook up, that's all. We should probably get out of here."

"But, he looks kind of old."

"Come on now, he's not that old, looks fit as a fiddle," Juliette said, forcing her truck into drive.

"Seriously, we can't just leave," Shelby said, placing her hand on her mother's wrist.

Juliette took a deep breath to calm her nerves. She noticed the man—somewhat advancing in years and noticeably swollen around the middle—had been joined by a woman of similar age and bodily proportions. The bulbous couple waddled about their vehicle with their hands on their hips as they surveyed the condition of the wheels on either side. Juliette released the brakes.

"Please, Mom, we can't just go."

"Calm down, will you? I'm just parking the damn truck. We're halfway across the intersection." Juliette settled her truck up on the grass shoulder and exited onto the road. "You stay right here," she told Shelby. She followed the long snaking skid marks, a record of the motor home's path of travel scrawled out onto the tarmac. The scent of burning rubber hung in the air. "I'm really sorry, truly I am," Juliette said upon arriving at the scene of her crime.

"You damn near killed us both," the man said, drawing in oxygen through his jowls.

Juliette realized the man was older than she had originally suspected. There was a level of formality to his attire—his neatly pressed shirt and slacks, his flat crop of hair and mustache combination—that made Juliette suspect he'd probably served in the military at some point. Upon surveying and reconsidering the bulk and softness of the man's physique, she thought it more likely he would have had a past as a scout leader rather than as a drill sergeant. "Are you both okay?" Juliette asked.

"You ran a red light. We oughta call the police on you," the old man's wife snapped, raising a hand to steady her bouffant hairdo as though she feared it might otherwise tumble from her head.

"But it was just an accident, surely you can see that?" Juliette pleaded.

"Well, accidents will get you killed or maimed when you're in charge of a motor vehicle," the old man said.

"Seems like nobody got hurt though, right?" Juliette insisted.

"These tires are brand-new," the old man said. "You've probably gone and taken half the damn tread clean off of them." He strained to lower his spherical body and ran a hand over the surface of one tire. "Looks like you buckled that street light pretty darn good as well. Don't suppose it'd make much difference to that old beater of yours, mind you."

"She's probably high," the old lady said. "We should call the police."

"There's no need for that, surely," Juliette said.

"Are you folks from over at the trailer park?" the old man asked.

Juliette noticed the man's gaze was focused beyond her, and that something else had caught his attention. She turned around to see Shelby approaching, the teenager hugging herself, her naked shoulders hunched, her whole body trembling.

"I thought I told you to stay in the truck."

"You know, lady, you really oughta be more careful, carrying precious cargo like that around with you," the old man said, his eyes scanning Shelby from head to toe.

"Close your mouth, Claude," the old lady said. "You're drooling."

Claude made a sort of grunting noise through heavy breaths in protest of his wife's suggestion.

Juliette noticed the man peering over the top of his driving glasses, his eyeballs dancing rapidly within their sagging orifices, as though he was desperate to take in as much of the spectacle as he could. Juliette realized she was probably duty bound — at this point — to land a slap to his slackened jaw, but she found herself caught a little off guard by a sudden swell of pride at such an open display of admiration for her daughter.

"You okay there, sweetheart?" Claude asked in Shelby's direction.

"You look a little rattled."

"She's just cold. Go back and wait in the truck."

"I'm fine."

"The little girl's high," the old lady said. "We gotta call the police. There's nothing of the poor thing. Her mom's probably got her hooked on meth, or worse."

"What the fuck? I'm not even high," Shelby insisted.

"No cursing, Shelby. How many times have I got to tell you?"

"Call the damn police, Claude. The child's out of control."

"Calm down now, Jean," Claude told his wife. "Just everybody calm down and hold onto your horses, okay."

"Look, please," Juliette began. She reached up and removed her sunglasses — quite purposefully — before continuing. "I've kind of got a lot going on at the moment," she said, waving a hand about the bruising to her eyes.

"Oh, my God," Jean gasped. "It is meth. I told you they was on meth. I saw a documentary on it, what it does to your face."

"Mom, what the fuck?" Shelby said, her mouth hanging open in disbelief as she surveyed the stitches, the swelling, the rawness of it all.

"I said no cursing."

"Well I'll be damned," Claude said, staring right into Juliette's face. "I didn't even recognize you there with those big old sunglasses on."

"You're trying to tell me you actually know these people, Claude?"

"Why, this is little Juliette Diaz," the old man explained to his wife. "Wild Billy Diaz's daughter."

Juliette straightened her back with pride. She flashed her eyes at Shelby, confident she had the situation under control now she'd been recognized.

Shelby sighed, unimpressed with her mother's fame.

The old lady shrugged her shoulders at her elderly husband, prompting him to offer further explanation.

"Juliette here's daddy was the greatest fighter ever to come out of this little old town," Claude said. "Ain't that right, sweetheart?"

"Well, I don't know if I'd say he was the greatest ever," Juliette said. "My own record's probably a little better than his ever was."

"But your daddy was a proper fighter. A good old traditional boxer. And, he fought for the heavyweight title as well. I watched it all on television. And let me tell you, that there was one hell of a fight, a real old-fashioned slugfest. So come on, how is the old boy these days, anyway? He still as light on his feet as he used to be?"

Juliette drew a deep breath through her teeth. "I guess I don't really see him all that much, if I'm honest," she said. "You know how it is with families and whatever."

"Well, why in the world would you not want to see your own daddy?" the old man asked, looking more intently at Juliette.

Shelby took her mother by the hand. "It's kind of a personal matter," she said.

"You mind your damn business, Claude," the old lady said.

Claude raised his chin. "All I'm saying is, you only get one daddy in life."

Shelby squeezed her mother's hand supportively.

"How's about a picture, then, at least?" Claude suggested. "The boys I play poker with sure as hell ain't gonna believe me when I tell them I ran into Wild Billy Diaz's little girl today."

"I don't know about all that," Juliette said. "I'm not really the posing type."

"Look now, what say we try and come to some kind of an agreement here? Considering how you ran us off the road back there and all."

"What kind of an agreement are we talking about, exactly?" Juliette asked.

"I think we both know I really oughta be taking your details and reporting you for all this. With the amount of tread I lost off those new tires of mine, and all. But listen, I'm a reasonable kind of guy, I'm willing to let all that slide if I can get just one little picture to show my buddies. Then I guess we can all forget about this sorry mess and be on our way. How's that sound?"

"Come on, Mom, it's just one picture. You did almost drive into these people."

Juliette fixed Shelby with a silencing glare.

"Can't you see the lady's face is all messed up?" Jean said to her husband. "Maybe she doesn't wanna be in your darn photo album."

"Just take the camera and point it, okay?" Claude waved Juliette toward him. "Come on, sweetheart, don't be shy now."

Juliette shuffled closer to the old man with her arms tightly folded across her chest. "Let's just get this over with," she said, wincing as the man threw one of his flabby arms over her shoulder.

"You as well, little girlie," the old man said to Shelby. "Scoot on in now."

"That wasn't part of the deal," Juliette protested.

"I don't mind," Shelby said, practically skipping into the frame next to her mother.

The old lady shook her head, disapprovingly.

"Hurry up now, Jean, we haven't got all day."

Jean took a series of photographs, each one capturing her husband's fat little mouth twisting up into a smile, Shelby blowing kisses and posing like a professional model, Juliette looking in every direction but toward the camera.

"Are we done yet?" Juliette asked, snatching Shelby's wrist to hold the girl still.

"See, that didn't hurt one bit now, did it?" the old man said.

"You've had your fun now," Jean said. "Let them be on their way."

"Well, ain't that something," Claude said, practically licking his lips as he studied the photographs on the screen of his camera.

Juliette took Shelby by the forearm and led her back toward the truck.

"You take care now, ladies," Claude called out. "Mind how you go."

"We will, Claude, we will," Shelby replied. "Don't you worry." She just about managed to shoot the old man a wink before Juliette packed her up into the passenger seat.

"What the hell is wrong with you?" Juliette snapped as she joined her daughter in the truck.

"Oh, come on, lighten up, will you?"

"Lighten up? Why the hell do you wanna go and encourage an old pervert like that?"

Shelby sighed. "You're just jealous because he wanted a picture of me more than he wanted one of you. I'm afraid you're just going to have to accept the fact you're not the only one these fans wanna take photos of anymore."

"It's not exactly a surprise he wanted a damn photo of you, seeing as how you're practically naked and all."

"Come on, everybody's happy. We're on our way, aren't we?" Shelby waved goodbye to the old couple as her mother pulled the truck off the grass and continued along the road.

"Yeah, everybody's happy now that old freak's got his pictures of you all dressed up like that."

Shelby folded her arms over her exposed midriff and crossed her legs together. "I don't see why you've gotta make such a fuss over my outfit. You wear less than this to fight in."

Juliette thought for a moment, noticing how self-conscious her daughter had suddenly become. "Fair point," she agreed. "But seriously, listen now, Doll-face. What I'm trying to say is, you look absolutely amazing in that outfit, I mean really you do. It's just I want you to realize there's plenty of weirdos in the world, like that old guy back there, who probably wanted to do things to your little body that are beyond your worst nightmares."

"That's disgusting," Shelby said, burying her face in her hands.

"It's like I always say: As a woman, you've got three weapons in life. Your looks. Your strength. And your mind. You just gotta work out when and how to use each of them, okay?"

"So now you're trying to turn this into some kind of a life lesson?"

"That's my job, I'm afraid."

"And anyways, I thought you said you never had any injuries."

"I'm still walking and talking, aren't I?"

"Seriously, Mom, your face is messed up."

"Enough with the dramatics, okay? You know how quickly I heal up."

"You can't keep doing this to yourself. You're too old. You're gonna end up all beat up and leathery like Uncle Earl."

"I am not, don't be silly," Juliette said, stretching to check her face in the rearview mirror. "He's fought some serious heavyweights in his time."

"Plus there's the other stuff," Shelby said, sinking lower into her side of the bench seat. "You know, like, with your brain."

"We're not gonna have all this again, are we? I told you before, female fighters don't hit anywhere near hard enough to do that kind of damage."

"Even football players get it. There's been studies. You can't keep taking punches to the head like this anymore. You're not young enough to absorb the punishment. At this rate, you're probably going to end up like a vegetable, lying there all day watching TV. And me and Uncle Earl will have to feed you liquidized meals through a straw, and Auntie Margot is gonna have to wipe your ass and change your diapers."

"Okay, okay, I get it, all right?" Juliette snapped. "Are you trying to cause another accident or something?"

"Oh, so that was my fault now, was it? I made you drive your truck into a post and nearly kill those people, did I?"

"Look, just calm down, will you? If you'd actually listen for just a minute, I've been wanting to tell you I've been thinking about it, okay?

And, well, maybe I've got an escape plan in the works."

Shelby sat up tall and turned to face her mother. "Are you serious? You're gonna stop fighting?"

"Settle down. I'm not making any promises, okay?"

"Well, what is it, what are you gonna do?" Shelby asked, bouncing in her seat with excitement.

"You'll see. I don't want to jinx it, okay? But don't you go getting all excited on me, because it might not work out. We just gotta see how it goes." Juliette pulled the truck off the main road and parked up in front of a row of stores. "But in the meantime, you can sit right here and try to figure it all out while I go in there and get me some damn ice cream."

"Fuck that," Shelby replied. "After what you just put me through, you seriously think I'm gonna miss out on ice cream?"

"But I thought you said you had some last night. Auntie Margot, sorry, I mean Margot's homemade stuff?"

"Are you kidding me, that stuff tastes like cat shit."

"I know it does, Doll-face," Juliette said. "I know it does."

CHAPTER 6

Juliette sat alone at the wheel of her truck. The engine breathed a labored growl as it propelled the vehicle through a maze of colorless factory buildings, a network of metallic structures churning smoke skyward, the foggy plumes undoubtedly indicative of the busied labor forces contained within. A shutter door rolled open deep in the midst of a vast cemented forecourt and several warehouse operatives clad in fluorescent jackets spilled out. Juliette slowed her truck and watched as the crew of workers descended upon a wooden pallet loaded with boxes, dismantling the stack with the autonomy of robots. She wondered briefly what it would be like to endure such an ordinary occupation, to work in a warehouse every day or to drive a vehicle delivering pallets of goods, to live a structured, regimented existence. She accelerated away, her stomach tightening at the notion of such mundanity.

This gray industrial landscape was so familiar to Juliette that she navigated her way among it with little need for concentration, her truck purring and rattling underneath the pink and blue gradients of the twilight sky. As her mind wandered from the road, memories of her weekend flashed through her thoughts. She was transported back to the ice cream parlor, where she'd allowed a spoonful of her frozen yogurt sundae to spill down onto her T-shirt, a successful attempt at manipulating Shelby into cracking a reluctant smile. Then there was the hike the pair had shared up through the dusty pine forest and into the hills so they could walk off a few of the innumerable calories they'd consumed at breakfast. Juliette could almost taste the still, warm air that lingered among the trees at this time of year, tiny flies hovering in swarms, the sandy earth littered with fallen pine cones and needles. She smiled as she thought back to the tranquility of the moment she'd shared with Shelby at their favorite spot up in the hills, a location the pair would visit regularly to sit underneath the tangled branches of a tall oak tree so they could take in the views of the town below.

Juliette recalled mentioning to Shelby the way in which the hilltop surroundings made her feel a little closer to her own mother, Shelby's grandmother.

"Seriously, you can be a real weirdo sometimes," Shelby had replied. "So what are you trying to say? You think you're closer to heaven up here, or something?"

"It's more than that," Juliette said, taking an extended breath to fill her lungs with the highly-oxygenated woodland air. "Maybe I'll explain it all to you someday."

"You're always treating me like a kid," Shelby complained. "It's the same whenever I dare to ask about my dad, what he was like or how you even met him."

"You should really enjoy being a kid while you can," Juliette said. "When you get to my age, you'll see life's got a habit of punching you in the face."

Shelby screwed up her face and toyed with the dusty earth where she sat. She tore at the patchy grass and watched as the blades were carried from her open fingers on the breeze. With her palm outstretched, she began to notice several droplets of water making their way through the branches of the oak tree, pattering at her skin. "You've got to be kidding me," she said.

Juliette laughed at her daughter's dismay. The pair scooted closer toward the center of the tree, taking shelter under the dense foliage above.

"What's so funny?" Shelby asked. "You do realize we're gonna get soaked, right?"

Juliette put her arm around Shelby and pulled her closer. "Come on, lighten up, Doll," she said, rubbing the goose-pimpled skin of her daughter's lower back to keep her warm. "This rain is just Grandma's way of teasing us." She watched Shelby's eyes flutter as the raindrops made their way through the leaves and fell onto the lenses of the teenager's spectacles. "Come on, Momma," Juliette called out into the sky, "is this really the worst you can do?"

Shelby rested her head on Juliette's shoulder. "Why did I have to end up with such a crazy mom?" she sighed.

"I'm not all that bad, am I?" Juliette asked. She pulled her daughter closer still and felt her body slacken as she finally submitted, her stubborn mood dissipating at last.

In the midst of this brief embrace, all that existed beyond seemed to pale into insignificance. It was as though all the noise in Juliette's world was muted. Gone was the constant pressure to conform to Earl's expectations, the never-ending desire to improve and hone every aspect of her fighting abilities, the relentless ache it all drove into her, stifling the clarity of her thoughts. All of it faded away until the only things that mattered were Shelby's spindly arms wrapped around Juliette's neck, the silken strands of Shelby's hair dancing on the breeze and teasing the side of Juliette's face. As they separated, both mother and daughter sunk back onto the grass, their elbows and forearms supporting their reclining bodies.

"You know you're all I've got, don't you?" Juliette said.

"I know," Shelby replied, drawing patterns with the raindrops that had settled on the surface of her stomach.

"And pretty soon, some hot young boy is gonna come along and steal you away from me. And you'll be all obsessed with him, and I won't even get so much as a hello out of you anymore."

"You're so embarrassing," Shelby said.

"I'm serious, it's just a matter of time. I've got to make the most of you while I can."

"Don't be silly. We're always gonna have each other. You know it's always gonna be this way, just you and me versus everyone else, right?"

"Of course it is, Doll. Just you and me."

"You promise?"

"I promise." The pair leaned toward each other, their eyes slowly closing as their bodies came together again.

Juliette shook her head to wake herself from the recollection. She swung her truck into the parking lot of a steel-clad warehouse unit and pulled up alongside the only other vehicle in sight, Earl's bottle-green Mustang. She took a moment to marvel at the pristine emerald paintwork of her brother's car as it basked in the first light of the morning. An infinity of minute metallic flecks glistened over every inch of the vehicle's curvaceous body. She glanced around at the cluttered interior of her own vehicle. A burn of annoyance ran through her as she imagined Earl scrutinizing the mess, his judgmental eyes darting over the unopened mail heaving from the door pockets.

As Juliette climbed down from her truck and wrestled a swollen duffle bag from the passenger seat, she saw—through the open doors of the entrance foyer—her brother was conversing with somebody out of sight.

"Hey, Tommy, you missed a spot over here," Earl said, signaling to a muddy imprint of a sneaker sole.

Tommy walked on his knees, paying great attention to detail as he swept the carpeted section of the foyer with a dustpan and brush. "Think that's most of it, Coach," he said, sweeping up what he believed to be the last of the dirt.

"It's done when I say so," Earl replied. "How many times have I told you guys not to trample this mess in here after you've been out on your runs?" Earl was leaning against a semi-hexagonal counter, the front side of which was painted with a wire-grid to symbolize the patterned walls of an MMA cage. Earl sipped from a mug of coffee as he watched Tommy shuffling about on his knees like an amputee.

Juliette made her way into the foyer and dropped her heavy duffle bag onto the carpeted floor to signal her entrance. "See you're working hard as usual, Earl," she said.

"What's this I see so early in the morning?" Earl asked. "Surely it's gotta be some sort of a mirage?"

Tommy laughed at Earl's joke as if it was his duty to do so.

"What are you doing out of bed at this hour?" Earl asked. "What's the matter, you couldn't sleep or something?"

Juliette shrugged, trying to appear casual about what she was going to say, knowing that her words were going to have an effect on her brother. "Maybe I changed my mind," she said.

Earl took a long sip of his coffee as he paused to consider his sister's words. "Hey, Tommy," he said, "why don't you go sweep up in the gym? Me and Jules need to talk business."

"But, Coach, you know I'm a businessman," Tommy pleaded. "Maybe I should stick around." The fact he was on his knees made him look as though he was begging.

Earl shot his assistant a heavy-browed glare that told the young man in no uncertain terms he was not invited to partake in the conversation that would follow.

Tommy climbed to his feet obediently, and hurried into the gym.

"Just so we're clear," Earl said, "what exactly is it that you've changed your mind about?"

"The kid's coming in at eight," Juliette replied, forcing nonchalance into her voice, watching from the side of her eyes for Earl's reaction.

Earl's heavy features lifted as if his entire face was waking from a slumber.

"You can put your hard-on away," Juliette said. "I'm not making any promises, okay?"

"All I'm asking is that you give this a try. It's like I always say, the little bird has got to fall out of the tree a couple of times before it can learn to fly." Earl landed his right fist into his left palm to illustrate his point.

Juliette's eyes wandered upward as she considered his statement. "I'm sure there's a message in there somewhere," she said.

"So, why the sudden change of heart?" Earl stepped outside to empty the last of his coffee with a flick of his wrist. "You finally realized your big brother knows what's best for you?"

Juliette sighed. "Can't be taking these punches forever, can I? Might end up with a face like yours."

"Nothing wrong with a few scars here and there," Earl said, checking his reflection in the windows of the foyer. "Glad you came to your senses, anyway. Now, are you gonna take off your sunglasses? Let me take a look at those bruises?"

"Give me a break. I've already been through all this with Shelby."

"Suppose she's been giving you hell for missing her show, right?"

"We worked it out. We always do. That's how it is when all you've got is each other."

"Sure," Earl nodded, staring blankly toward the floor, struggling with this particular point of conversation.

"But thanks," Juliette said, breaking the uncomfortable silence, "for taking Shelby to the mall and whatever. Can't say much for your taste in clothes, but you know, thanks for looking out for her and all."

"You know how much it means to me, spending quality time with her. Whatever little I can do."

Juliette noticed Earl's eyes were glazing over as if they were welling with emotion. As the siblings struggled for the right words, a third voice interspersed. "Aw, what is this, couple's therapy or something?"

Amiyah's distinctive silhouette lingered in the doorway, a dark shape backlit by the morning sun. Juliette immediately recognized the wide hips, narrow waist, and slender limbs. The close fit of the young woman's sportswear defined her outline so vividly she may as well have been naked.

"So, you couldn't find anything better to do after all?" Juliette asked, gazing at the willowy figure just beyond the threshold to the foyer, unable to make out the details of the young woman due to the harsh back-lighting.

"Well, it looks like someone needs to give you a little help brushing up on your footwork, sugar," Amiyah replied. "And your head movement, judging by the state of you."

"You got your hands full with this one, Jules," Earl said with a grin settling onto his lips.

Juliette detected a faint scent of combustion on the air. She glanced at Amiyah's hands and saw the glowing end of a rolled-up cigarette extending from between the young woman's spidery fingers. "You're a smoker?" Juliette asked, turning to her brother as if the gift he'd presented her with was faulty.

Amiyah raised the stubby roll up to her mouth, pouted her lips over its end and drew a deep breath. "What of it?" she asked, her voice straining as she held the smoke within her lungs.

"If you run out of gas in the cage, kid," Earl said, "you're gonna be in some serious trouble." He folded his arms together and leaned back against the counter to watch the conflict unfold, his shoulders gently bobbing with laughter.

Amiyah took another drag. She exhaled long and hard, her head oscillating as she filled the air with a fog of cigarette smoke. "Relax, I got cardio," she said, her face partially obscured by the mist.

"Well, nobody likes training with cigarette smokers," Juliette said. "When you roll with them on the mat, and they're breathing all over you—"

"—You gotta be able to take me down first," Amiyah interrupted. "Before you can roll with me, that is."

"Are you kidding me? I'd have you flat on your back in two seconds."

"Been a while since I had an offer like that," Amiyah said, arching one eyebrow suggestively.

"Come on now, ladies. You're supposed to be training partners, not opponents."

"That's cute, but are we gonna do this or what," Amiyah asked, flicking her cigarette end out of the door. "Because I certainly didn't come all the way down here at this time of the morning just to converse."

Juliette stepped a little closer toward Amiyah and began to look her over as if conducting a military inspection. The dull scent of cigarette smoke strafed at Juliette's nostrils as she surveyed Amiya's choice of attire, her garish running shoes, her day-glow leggings, her close-fitting tank top, and the little backpack slung over her shoulders. Her hair was tied in a loose bundle of plaits that sat on top of her head; her skin was natural and free of the heavy makeup she'd worn the last time Juliette had seen her. The pattern of freckles splayed across her cheeks was more clearly visible now. Her dark, unyielding eyes flashed judgmentally at Juliette's uniformly black sportswear, a colorless ensemble that appeared to have been selected primarily for efficiency and functionality.

"You do realize it's not a fashion show, don't you?" Juliette said. She began to circle Amiyah, studying the young woman like some kind of an obstacle that needed to be overcome.

Amiyah's hands rose to her hips. She tilted her chin upward, taking on the stance of a high fashion model striking a pose, feigning attitude for the camera. She remained entirely motionless, determined to stand her ground in the midst of Juliette's examination.

Early looked on intently, clearly enjoying the tension between the two women.

Juliette continued to circle; she was behind Amiya now. She peered over the top of her sunglasses, surveying the young woman from her feet upward. Her eyes paused as they arrived at the small of Amiyah's back. She marveled at the way it swept inward so dramatically, curling back out toward the pert mound of her ass. Juliette tried to look away, to continue with her inspection, but she was drawn back to Amiyah's heart-shaped posterior, the way it seemed to stand so erect, such a beguiling combination of rotund plumpness and solid definition that it was confusing for the eye to behold. The tight fabric of Amiyah's leggings flaunted her form so brazenly, it almost seemed inappropriate for a public place, so hard to ignore that it bordered on offensive. Juliette felt a wave of heat pass through her, aggravation perhaps at the fact she couldn't help but admire the young woman's appearance. She didn't quite understand her annoyance. She wondered if it was jealousy or something else, this strange compulsion to study and assess every inch of another woman's anatomy.

"Are we done yet?" Amiyah asked.

"Just checking everything's in order," Juliette replied.

"Gotta check the merchandise before you buy," Earl added, taking out a handkerchief to dry his salivating lips.

"What more do you want to see?" Amiyah said. "You gonna ask me to take my clothes off next or what?"

"You already did that for me, honey, remember?"

Earl rattled out a throaty laugh and Amiyah's face tightened with frustration. "So are we gonna hit the gym or not?" She flexed her arms into the air, preparing her body for physical exertion.

Earl's squinted eyes disguised the direction of his gaze, but Juliette was certain he'd be ogling the young woman's body, her hip bones jutting forth against the waistband of her leggings, the smooth triangle of her crotch tucked neatly between her thighs. Juliette couldn't allow her focus to linger on any particular area for too long, fearing her intrigue might be detected. "So, you say you got cardio, huh?" she asked.

"You've seen me dance, haven't you? I can go on like that all night if I need to."

"Well, let's go then," Juliette said, making her way toward the open doors of the foyer.

"Think you might be a little confused, old lady," Amiyah said. "Surely the gym's that way?"

"What's the hurry? If you've got so much cardio, how about you and me go for a little run first? Just a couple of miles or so to loosen up, nothing too strenuous. If you think you can keep up with an old-timer like me, that is."

"I guess we'll see about that," Amiyah said, shrugging the backpack from her shoulders, tossing it into Earl's arms. "Hold onto this for me, sugar. I'm about to teach your little sister just how old she really is."

"Good luck with that," Earl replied, grinning enough to imply he was confident in his sister's abilities.

Both women attempted to exit the foyer at the same time. They faced each other, trapped in the doorway, unable to pass through without making physical contact. Juliette's posture was rigid, her upper body leaning backward, her hands clasped at her chest in a defensive boxing guard.

Amiyah's body language was quite the opposite, her arms hanging loosely by her sides. "Age before beauty," she said, signaling with an outstretched hand for Juliette to proceed.

"Maybe you should go first," Juliette insisted. "You'll probably need the head start."

"Beauty before the beast then, I guess," Amiyah replied. The young woman made her way onto the tarmac of the parking lot, where she began to limber up, shaking out her spindly limbs, clutching her knees one after the other to her chest and then leaning forward over each leg in turn.

Juliette stretched her arms up into the air, attempting to straighten her back and loosen her joints so she could move with the same effortless fluidity as her younger companion. Something clicked within her back and she released a groan of discomfort, her aging body refusing to cooperate.

"You okay there, Grandma?"

"I'm fine," Juliette replied. "Nothing a little run won't sort out, I'm sure."

"You're looking kind of rigid to me, sugar. When was the last time somebody gave you a proper massage, anyway? You know, I'm actually pretty good with my hands myself."

"I've been doing this long enough to know what my own body needs, thanks."

"Suit yourself," Amiyah said, her face straightening at Juliette's rejection. "Just don't complain to me when you've got no flexibility." Amiyah spun around, placed her feet together and bent forward, reaching down so her body was completely parallel to her legs.

Juliette felt a rush of jealousy as she watched the young woman contort her body. Amiyah's pose stretched the fabric of her leggings so thinly Juliette felt the need to avert her gaze. "I can do that," Juliette said. "Just maybe not the day after a three-round war with The Ox, that's all."

"Sure you can, Grandma," Amiyah replied, straightening herself out.

"Less of the Grandma, okay, kid? Let's see how old you think I am when we get a couple of miles down the road, huh?" With that, Juliette turned and stepped away from the young woman. She flexed her back a final time and swung her arms in circular motions. Her movements were somewhat ungainly as her feet shuffled awkwardly beneath her, carrying her away into what would eventually become a steady running gait.

"I guess that means we're leaving then," Amiyah called out as she hurried to follow.

"Try to match my pace," Juliette said, looking over her shoulder as far as her impliable neck would allow, her whole upper body twisting rather than just her head.

"Think I'll just about manage, thanks," Amiyah said, quickly catching up with Juliette.

The pair made their way out of the parking lot onto the sidewalk, their feet pounding against the hard surface below. Juliette felt the solidity of the concrete ricocheting up through her weary legs. Her thighs and shins were stiff and heavy with exhaustion. A dull ache lingered in her lower back, hindering the fluidity of her strides. She was determined to work through the pain, to run it off, to put on a display of stamina and endurance. A passing truck sounded its horn and an arm that hung limply from the driver's window suddenly became erect. Juliette raised a hand above her head, gesturing an exaggerated hello back at the vehicle's occupant. She made sure to flail her arm with enough vigor to ensure Amiyah would notice the exchange.

It was around the third time of this sequence occurring that Amiyah reluctantly acknowledged the greeting gestures. "I see you're something of a local celebrity then, are you?"

"You know how it is," Juliette said. "You pick up a few fans over the years."

Amiyah rolled her eyes. "Where are we heading, anyway?" she asked through heavy breaths.

"If you stop talking for a minute, you might actually be able to control your breathing."

"I've got plenty of gas left," Amiyah gasped, struggling to speak and run at the same time.

"Didn't anybody ever teach you how to breathe?"

"Is this the part where you go all kung fu master on me?"

"Why don't you quit the wisecracks for a second and focus on your breathing? If you can't even breathe properly, how are you gonna take in enough oxygen to fuel your body in a fight?"

The pair continued through the concrete labyrinth of factories and warehouse buildings, running side by side on the road whenever the sidewalk narrowed, their stampede against the tarmac almost synchronized. The cool morning air that filled Juliette's lungs was laden with a mire of industrial notes, a faint chemical taste that seemed to grate on the back of her throat. She coughed and spat to clear her airways.

"Charming," Amiyah said.

"You're the one struggling for breath," Juliette replied. "Some fresh air in those smoker's lungs is what you need." She diverted the young woman into a field of sandy earth and led the way along a trail worn through sparse patches of tall pale grass. The rolling shriek of a red-tailed hawk echoed about the open scrubland. Juliette glanced upward, hoping to watch the bird's splayed silhouette drifting on the breeze, but the dazzling glare of the morning sun forced her to look away. The pair exited the field by passing underneath the barren steal framework of a disused advertising hoarding, a vast rectangular grid laid out over the pale blue backdrop of the panoramic sky.

"Hey, give me a second, will you?" Amiyah called out.

Juliette turned to see the young woman hunched over, her hands on her knees, her chest heaving as though she was struggling for air.

"I got a cramp," Amiyah said, punching at her calves to provide evidence for her claim.

"Looks like you ran out of gas to me, kid. What happened to all that cardio you said you had?"

"I got plenty left in the tank, it's just you took off before I even got a chance to warm up properly, that's all." Amiyah was up on a bank of knee-high meadow grass which ran underneath the metal framework of the empty advertising hoarding.

Juliette had already passed the bank of grass and made her way down through a track that led to the overgrown remnants of an old train line. "Breathe, kid," Juliette called out. "Try to relax." She scrambled back up onto the bank of grass. "Come on, take some deep breaths with me."

"Give me a break for a second, will you? What's the hurry, anyway?

Can't we just stop a moment to appreciate the views out here?"

"Try asking your opponent for a break in the middle of a round, see how that works out for you."

"I said I got a cramp, okay?"

"Cramp doesn't stop you fighting. Let's see if you can defend a takedown now, shall we?"

"Just hold on a second," Amiyah gasped.

"Come on, stand up, let's see this takedown defense of yours."

Without further notice, Juliette charged forward, ducking as she drew closer to the young woman. Amiyah released a huff of breath as Juliette made impact. Juliette grabbed Amiyah around the middle and drove her backward until she collided with a steel girder at the base of the hoarding.

"I wasn't even ready," Amiyah said, her voice straining as she fought to stay upright against the vertical girder.

"You think your opponent's gonna ask if you're ready?" Juliette was bent over, her arms wrapped around Amiyah's waist in an effort to wrestle her to the ground. Juliette struggled to establish a firm grip, her hands sliding over the sleek fabric of the young woman's sportswear. She moved her hands cautiously, unsure of where to place them, her palm shifting from the underside of a thigh to the fleshy mound over the back of a hip.

Amiyah widened her stance and lowered her center of gravity. "Give up, already," she groaned.

Juliette attempted to clasp her hands together behind Amiyah, knowing this would give her better leverage to complete the maneuver.

"Come on, give up, old lady. There's no way you're getting me down."

Juliette paused to conserve energy and consider her options. She was impressed with Amiyah's defense, but there was no way she could allow somebody so young to get the better of her. "The thing is," Juliette began, still pressing Amiyah up against the steel girder, "there's one important factor you seem to have overlooked."

"And what might that be?"

"I'm not scared of pulling you into my guard." Juliette adjusted her weight and dropped to her back among the soft cushioning of the meadow grass, pulling Amiyah down on top of her.

"Sure, you might have got me down," Amiyah said, "but now you're on the bottom. If this was a real fight, I'd be raining elbows down into your face right now, and you know it."

"Go ahead," Juliette said, grabbing hold of Amiyah's forearms, "elbow me now."

Amiyah fought to yank her arms free.

"Just relax," Juliette said. "In about five seconds, I'm going to grab hold of your wrist to control you, scoot my hips out from underneath you, and scissor my legs to roll you over, okay?" Amiyah barely had the chance to look confused before Juliette carried out the actions she'd described, effortlessly transitioning from the bottom and rolling Amiyah onto her back in one swift movement. Juliette slid one leg across Amiyah's body, straddling the young woman and kneeling over her in the dominant mount position. "That's called a scissor sweep," Juliette explained, pinning Amiyah's arms to the flattened grass. "Maybe I'll teach it to you sometime."

Amiyah was strewn out on her back beneath Juliette, making no effort to free herself. "Now you've got me where you want me," she said, "what exactly are you going to do to me?"

Juliette looked down at the young woman's limp body, her chest heaving with exhaustion through her tank top, beads of sweat glistening in the shallow groove of her cleavage.

"It's just me and you here, sugar," Amiyah said. "So what are you waiting for?" Her voice was soft, little more than a whisper.

Juliette felt the gentle breeze against her skin. The semi-rural surroundings were almost completely silent save for the chiming of birdsong and the rustle of the undergrowth. She was frozen with uncertainty, unable to process her thoughts amidst the serenity of the moment. She watched the young woman's throat straining and heaving in time with her inhalations, her body writhing in slow motion, her torso twisting among the grass. Amiyah's dark eyes slowly closed, her plump lips formed a pout. The young woman's face told of sensations of pleasure, as though she was enjoying being held down. Juliette was confused, unsure of how to react.

Amiyah's lips broke into a smile, and then a laugh. She bucked her hips, her body jolted from the ground. Juliette was caught off guard and lifted into the air. Amiyah slipped out from underneath and sprung to her feet. "I got you!" she said, clapping her hands together and laughing wildly.

Juliette sat among the tall grass with her arms resting on her knees. She hung her head, fearing her embarrassment might be showing on her face. "Why don't you quit fooling around?" she said. "This isn't a game to me."

"Oh come on now, you're just mad you couldn't keep me down."

"You distracted me and you know it."

"Must have been something to be distracted over then, huh? What was it that got your attention, exactly?"

"Give me a break, will you?"

Amiyah sat down next to Juliette and placed a hand on her shoulder. "Come on, lighten up. I was just playing around."

Juliette shrugged Amiyah's hand away, frustrated and confused by the fact she'd been so easily seduced by the young woman's charms.

Amiyah began to laugh again and placed a hand over her mouth in a half-hearted attempt to contain her amusement.

"What's so funny now?"

"Your top," Amiyah snorted, "it's inside out."

Juliette looked down at the long-sleeved rash vest she was wearing. "Who says it's inside out?"

"Um, maybe it's the fact the seams and the label are both on the outside."

"I already told you it's not a fashion show, didn't I?"

Amiyah stared open-mouthed, waiting for Juliette to take some kind of action.

"What?" Juliette snapped, doubly aggravated by how undeniably flawless the young woman's face looked even while adorned with such a mocking expression.

"Well, aren't you gonna sort your vest out?"

"It can wait," Juliette said. "I'll do it when I get back."

"Just take it off, what's the matter? There's nobody here. Come on, I'll even turn around if you're shy."

"Look, it's not that, okay?"

"What's the problem then?"

"If you must know, I think I might have pulled something in my back when I took you down."

"Must really suck to be so ancient," Amiyah said, her voice trembling as she struggled to hold back her laughter.

"I got a few miles on the clock, kid, that's all. It'll straighten itself out in a day or so, it always does."

"Come here," Amiyah said, standing up over Juliette. "Let me help you out of that thing." She reached down and tugged at the hem of Juliette's rash vest. "Lift your arms up, come on."

Juliette climbed to her feet and attempted to raise her arms. Her aching body jolted when her hands reached shoulder height. "Careful," she said, wincing with pain.

"Stop making a fuss," Amiyah said, pulling Juliette's rash vest up over her head, stripping her down to her sports bra. "Woah, hot bruises you've got there, sugar."

"You should be a comedian, really," Juliette said, turning to hide the blemishes on her back.

"Who says I was being sarcastic?"

"Well, thanks, I guess," Juliette said. She clutched her rash vest over her chest, suddenly feeling self-conscious under Amiyah's gaze.

"Can I see?" The young woman asked, her eyes darting curiously over Juliette's skin.

"So what, you like bruises, or something?"

Amiyah paused, dropped her head to one side, and gazed up into the sky as if she was pondering the best means to express herself.

Juliette realized this was probably the first time she'd seen Amiyah lost in thought, sparing a moment to consider her words instead of immediately answering back with a witty remark.

"Well, let me see now," Amiyah began, still gazing skyward, her voice softer in tone and somewhat slower in pace than usual, "personally, the way I look at bruises is they're kind of like art, I guess."

Juliette spat out a short burst of laughter. "What are you talking about, art?" she said, determined to ridicule the young woman in the same way she, herself had been ridiculed.

"You know how it is?" Amiyah said, unperturbed by the older woman's amusement, her voice still soft and slow. "It's like, after you fight somebody, you stand back, you look at the damage you've inflicted and you try to take it all in. The way I see it, my opponent's body, their face, and all of their skin, that's my blank canvas. And I paint my artwork on top of it, with my fists, my elbows, and my feet. And then, after I'm done, the color and the pattern of their bruises, the blood all over their face, that's kind of like my masterpiece, you know?"

Juliette swallowed loudly, a little lost for words. As much as she'd wanted to be amused by Amiyah's appreciation for bruises, she couldn't help but stare back at the young woman silently, fascinated by this unexpected glimpse into the workings of her mind.

"Why are you looking at me that way?" Amiyah asked. "All wide-eyed. You think I'm crazy?"

"No, it's not that. It's, I don't know, I guess I just never really heard it put that way, that's all."

Amiyah scanned the dark lenses of Juliette's glasses. It seemed like this was the first time the pair had actually locked eyes in any kind of meaningful way. Juliette felt there was a moment of connection between them, a moment where they understood each other in a way only two fighters could.

Amiyah smiled, and then released a few breaths of laughter. She looked away, as if the sharing of eye contact was too intense. "So did I pass my test anyway?" she asked.

"What test?"

"My test to train with you, of course."

"Every day is a test, kid. That's how it is when you're a fighter. How about you come back tomorrow and we'll see how you get on? Think you can find your way back to the gym for your bag?"

"You mean, on my own? Why, where are you going?"

"To school," Juliette said, signaling in the direction of the abandoned train tracks. "My daughter forgot her lunch money."

"You never told me you had a kid," Amiyah said, her gaze somewhat stern, almost accusatory.

"Why would I?" Juliette asked.

"I bet she's hot, anyway."

"She's fourteen."

"A fighter?"

"A ballerina, actually."

"So, how about her daddy, is he around?"

"It's complicated," Juliette said, kicking at the earth around her feet.

"Sorry, I shouldn't have—"

"—Look, I gotta go, anyway, I got a yoga class when I get back."

"You go to yoga classes?"

Juliette stared blankly at the young woman, unsure of why this would seem so strange.

"I guess that explains how you manage to stay in shape, huh?"

"So, you're not calling me 'Grandma' anymore then?"

"Not now that I've seen you without your shirt on, sugar."

"Oh, right, well, I try to eat the right things and whatever," Juliette said, her cheeks reddening as she pulled on her vest. "I'm gonna write you up a diet plan as well, okay?"

"A diet? You trying to say I'm fat now?"

"Don't be silly, your body's perfect," Juliette replied a little too quickly, blurting her words out with the speed of a knee-jerk reaction. She frowned at her own clumsiness, glancing anywhere but toward Amiyah. "It's just, I mean, you need the right fuel, for cardio and recovery, and whatever."

"Sure," Amiyah said, her lips twitching with amusement at Juliette's verbal fumbling. "So why did I come all the way down here anyway, if you only had like a half hour to spare?"

"If I'm honest, I didn't think you'd actually turn up," Juliette said. "Besides, this was just an audition, remember? I guess I'll see you tomorrow." With that, she turned and scrambled her way down the grassy bank that led toward the skeletal remains of the overgrown train track, its rust-mottled rails almost entirely consumed by the undergrowth.

"Wasn't too bad for a first date, was it, sugar?" Amiyah called out.

The comment stopped Juliette in her tracks as though she'd run out of slack on a restraint she was bound by. She turned back to reprimand Amiyah, but saw the young woman had already departed. Juliette watched Amiyah disappear among the dry yellow brush like some kind of a shadowy feline, kicking a fog of dust up from the parched earth in her wake.

CHAPTER 7

Earl lumbered toward Juliette from the opposite side of the gymnasium. The front of his rash vest was sodden with sweat, revealing the details of his upper body as though he were competing in a wet T-shirt contest. His stomach bulged through the tight vest, a swollen mass heaving beneath his toned pectorals. He walked with an exhausted stoop, carrying his rotund midriff around like some sort of excess baggage that he might offload upon arrival at his destination.

Earl's brow was heavy with aggravation as he made his way across the mats, sidestepping several pairs of sparring athletes as if he were effortlessly weaving through traffic. "Keep your hands up, Red," he said to one of the young men in passing. As Earl approached Juliette, he nodded toward the corner of the gym where Amiyah was throwing kicks into a heavy-bag, causing the weighted leather sack to jolt back and forth on its chain. "What the hell is that kid wearing over there?" he asked.

Juliette couldn't tell whether her brother was offended or enthralled by Amiyah's choice of attire: a pair of black leggings which appeared to have been crafted from some kind of rubberized material. The tight, shiny fabric gave the illusion Amiyah was wearing nothing on her bottom half but a coat of high-gloss paint.

"How can she expect the guys to take her seriously when she's dressed like that?" Earl growled under his breath, not wanting to draw attention in the crowded gym.

"She can wear whatever she likes as far as I'm concerned," Juliette replied. "Wouldn't bother me if she walked in here naked."

"Oh, I bet you wouldn't mind that at all, would you?"

"What's that supposed to mean?"

"Nothing. Just keep an eye on her. I don't want this place turning into some kind of a strip club, okay?"

Tommy had taken hold of the heavy-bag, and was pushing his weight up behind it, providing a solid level of resistance for Amiyah to kick against.

"Nice of you to let somebody else play with your new toy," Earl said with a sardonic smile before departing to make his way back across the mats.

Tommy took a step back and scratched at his chin as Amiyah performed a kick for him in slow motion. He approached the young woman from behind, pressed his lean frame right up against hers, and took hold of her prominent hips. Using her hip bones as handles, he rotated her body ninety degrees to demonstrate the fact she needed to turn further with each strike in order to achieve a greater level of torque.

Juliette noticed the way Amiyah seemed to be laughing childishly, toying with her ponytail of braided hair and flicking it from her shoulders as she watched Tommy perform a powerful kick of his own. Amiyah gasped and clapped at the heavy-bag swinging in a wide circle as Tommy's shin made impact.

"Okay, I think that's enough work on your striking for one day," Juliette said, arriving beside the heavy-bags.

"But I was just getting into it," Amiyah replied.

"It's okay, really," Tommy said, eager to keep the peace. "We can come back to it another time."

"But I thought we were gonna start working some punches—"

"—Fine, do whatever you want," Juliette snapped, her outburst causing several of the other martial arts practitioners to pause and look over.

"Okay, relax, sugar," Amiyah said. "You're the boss. Whatever you say."

"Forget it," Juliette said. "Nobody ever listens to me, anyway." With that, she turned and stormed across the mats, shaking her head in disbelief as she disappeared into the women's locker room. Juliette tried to control her breathing, inhaling slowly as she wedged her feet into her running shoes. She threw on her sunglasses, picked up her leather duffel bag, and pushed open the fire exit door, not wanting to go back through the gym to gain access to the parking lot. In her haste, she tripped and stumbled on her untied laces, barely maintaining her balance for a few steps before she gave up and purposely crash-landed onto a steel bench just beyond the entrance foyer.

She sat for a moment, still trying to focus on her breathing. A rage burned inside of her, prompting her to take some kind of action, to smash something, to get into her truck and drive off at high speed. Fleeting memories of her day passed through her thoughts. It was all a jumble — Amiyah arriving in her rubber pants, the guys in the gym unable to take their eyes off her, Juliette feeling protective. "Stick with me kid," she'd said with a wink.

Amiyah smiled, her whole face seemed to glow with appreciation at Juliette's gesture. Then there was the moment Cody walked in. Cody, the aggressive little character who was covered from head to toe in tattoos, the ink creeping up his neck and onto his face as though he'd tried to make himself look as menacing as possible to compensate for his diminutive stature.

"What the heck is she doing here?" Cody asked.

"You two are going to shake hands," Juliette proclaimed in front of the entire gym full of people, including her brother. Cody protested. Amiyah checked her nails, indifferently.

"It's either that or you can both get out," Juliette said.

Amiyah and Cody resisted, but Earl backed his sister as always. "Do as she says," Earl commanded, sounding like the voice of authority, the head of his tribe.

When Amiyah and Cody finally locked hands, Juliette even dared to push things a little further. "Now hug it out," she said. Despite her current state of fury, she almost laughed as she recalled the uncertain, wide-eyed look on Cody's face as he was told to embrace the young woman who'd humiliated him in front of his training partners a couple of weeks previously. "I'm just kidding, you don't have to go that far," Juliette said, and the whole gym erupted with laughter.

Juliette had spent the entire afternoon with Amiyah, rolling jiu-jitsu with her on the mats while the males of the gym stole intrigued sideways glances. She'd strapped on full body pads so Amiyah could show off her punching and kicking abilities. Juliette had winced at every blow she'd received, her body still tender from her fight with The Ox. And then, after all of this, when things seemed to be going so well, the moment Juliette had taken a break to rest for just five minutes, Amiyah had gone off with Tommy, laughing and joking, tossing her hair and flirting the way a girl does with someone she's attracted to, instead of setting all that aside and behaving like a focused, professional athlete the way Juliette had wanted her to. And to add insult to injury, there was Earl's comment, "Nice of you to let somebody else play with your new toy," he'd said, criticizing Juliette for monopolizing Amiyah and not allowing anybody else the opportunity to train with her. He was telling Juliette she was doing it wrong as usual, and on her first day as a coach as well, when she was just trying to find her way, unsure of the correct way to proceed.

Juliette inhaled deeply, her breathing slowly coming back under control, her temper rebalancing at last. "Your new toy," she repeated, shaking her head. But she couldn't deny the fact Amiyah was kind of like her new plaything, a novelty she wanted all to herself, something to be excited about among all the hardship and struggle of her existence, all the striving to make ends meet to provide for her daughter. The prospect of training Amiyah had finally shown Juliette there could be some kind of brief respite from the constant focus on her own fighting career. She struggled with the thought of anybody taking that glimmer of hope away from her. She panicked when she saw how naturally Tommy interacted with the young woman, his experience as a coach under Earl's tutelage clearly evident.

Juliette leaned forward on the bench to tie her shoelaces. When she came back up the sun was in her eyes, and she saw — like a faint and distant mirage through the glare — Amiyah coming toward her on a bicycle, a low-slung, rust-covered BMX that looked like something straight out of Juliette's childhood. "Is there a twelve-year-old looking for his bike somewhere?" she asked.

Amiyah skidded the bike to a halt. "It's vintage," she said. "And, I'm into older things. You of all people should know that by now, sugar."

"You oughta go back inside," Juliette said. "You got a lot of work to do."

"Don't you wanna get out of here for a while?" Amiyah said, narrowing her eyes to observe the sullen woman before her.

Juliette had sunken so low in spirit that her initial instinct was to immediately reject the offer. She glanced up at the young woman straddling the saddle in her glossy black leggings. The rubbery material reflected the sunlight like the sleek body of an automobile passing underneath streetlights at night. Amiyah's thumbs rested in the waistband of her leg-wear, weighing the fabric down to reveal the vague grooves of her pelvic muscles. Fortunately for Juliette, her sunglasses hid the direction of her gaze. You didn't get sights like this around Earl's gym very often. The young woman was like some unexpected rarity, unique among the endless supply of male athletes Juliette was used to training with.

"Well, what's it to be?" Amiyah persisted. "You wanna sit here all day, or what?"

"I don't think we're gonna get very far on that old bike of yours."

"So where's your ride at?" Amiyah asked, glancing around the parking lot.

Juliette got up off the bench and walked over to her steed. She threw her duffle bag over her shoulder and swung it down into the open cargo bed at the back of the truck.

"This is your ride?" Amiyah asked, leaning back to capture the entirety of the vehicle within her frame of vision.

"It's not exactly a Ferrari, but the old girl gets me around." Juliette swept a hand over the body of her truck as though she was affectionately stroking a beloved pet.

"You know, you can figure a lot out from the type of car a person drives," Amiyah said.

"What, like maybe they couldn't come up with the money for anything else?"

Amiyah hung her head to one side. Her eyes blurred out of focus as she pondered the best way to express herself. "Let me put it like this," she began. "Do you think, maybe this big old truck over here might just be some kind of a physical representation, a manifestation, if you will, of the type of person you feel you truly are on the inside?"

"You've lost me."

"Well, if I'm honest, the beat-up old thing kind of looks like a humongous black guy to me. It seems obvious that's how you really see yourself. As a big, black heavyweight champion. A 265-pound monster with a big old dick swinging between his thighs. Not some scrawny little white woman who can barely even make bantamweight."

"What are you, a shrink now?" Juliette asked, climbing up into the driver's seat and shaking her head incredulously. "Hurry up and throw your little tricycle in the back there," she said, watching Amiyah struggling with her BMX in the rearview mirror. As Amiyah pulled herself up into the cab, Juliette lowered her window a small amount. "You'll have to excuse me if I'm not exactly smelling all that fragrant right now. Been breaking my back in the gym all day taking care of you."

Amiyah breathed in through her nostrils. "There's nothing quite like the scent of fresh sweat," she said. "It's kind of intoxicating, don't you think?"

"I guess that's one way of looking at it."

"So, why did you storm out of the gym back there, anyway?"

Juliette crunched the truck into drive. The sound of the vehicle's straining engine echoed her feelings toward the young woman's question quite precisely. "I guess I needed some air. I've kind of got a lot going on at the moment."

"Tell me about it, sugar. We already established the fact I'm a psychiatrist, didn't we?"

"I get a little stressed with Earl trying to criticize my every move, my coaching techniques and whatever."

"Why do you even listen to him anyway?"

"It's a family thing. You might understand if you had an older brother."

"I've got four of them, thanks. How else do you think I turned out like this?"

Juliette steered the truck out of the parking lot and into the main road. "Also, word on the street is, I hear The Ox is asking for a rematch. Says I got lucky with the triangle choke."

"So, you're going to fight her again?"

"If it turns out that's the fight people wanna see, then I guess I don't have a lot of options, do I?"

Amiyah took an extended pause before she dared to ask her next question. "So what's the problem? You scared to fight her again or something?"

"It's not about being scared, kid. You'll figure that out when you've been doing this as long as I have. Fighting somebody who's spent most of their career on steroids is never gonna be much fun. Especially when you gotta fight them twice in a row."

Amiyah's silence suggested she was contemplating Juliette's

explanation; whether she actually believed it was another matter altogether.

As Juliette guided the truck through the industrial zone, the sun was getting low and intense, its morose afternoon glow becoming focused and sharp, a piercing light in the rearview mirror. Amiyah never asked where they were going, she just commented that Juliette had better get her back home in time for her shift at The Pink Tunnel.

"Okay, Cinderella," Juliette said.

The landscape passing outside the truck's windows slowly morphed from the gray monotony of the industrial zone into a lush green wilderness. Tall evergreens encased the road on either side, the sunlight flashing sporadically through their branches and over their peaks. Juliette slowed the truck and exited the main road, driving onto a track that was cast into darkness by the overshadowing canopy of trees. The truck was traveling uphill now, rumbling over the firm, uneven earth beneath its wheels.

"Steady, girl," Juliette said to her steed.

"You talk to your truck?"

Juliette stared blankly at Amiyah, as if comforting the vehicle was a perfectly normal thing to do. She brought the truck to a stop in front of a wooden gate that was locked up with a tangled chain. The track appeared to continue uphill beyond the gate, extending into the distance, where it grew increasingly narrower among the encroaching foliage.

"No access," Amiyah said, squinting at a faded sign that hung from the gate.

"You can blame my mother for that," Juliette said.

"Why? What's Old Momma Diaz got to do with all this?"

"It's a long story." They climbed down from the truck and Juliette pulled the cover over their bags and the bicycle in the back.

"Well, this is romantic," Amiyah said, peering around into the dense woodland that surrounded them.

"Nice place for a second date, huh?" Juliette quipped.

Amiyah's face lit up with a smile. "Now you're getting it," she said.

Juliette was overcome with an instantaneous burning sensation, a rush of adrenaline that left her feeling weak. She couldn't believe she'd allowed herself to joke this way, to play by Amiyah's rules. It felt so dangerous, completely alien, but she hadn't experienced this sort of a thrill since she'd stepped into the cage with Oksana. Juliette paused for a few beats to settle her nerves and then led the way toward the locked gate.

"It says no access," Amiyah pointed out.

"It means by car. We have to go on foot from here," Juliette explained before effortlessly climbing over the shoulder-high gait.

"Fair enough," Amiyah replied, pulling herself up and then somersaulting over the tall gate, determined to scale the barrier more athletically than her older companion.

"Guess I'll see you at the top," Juliette said, refusing to be outdone. She broke into a fast walking pace, practically jogging along the track.

"Not exactly my idea of a date, trekking up a hill," Amiyah replied, as she followed behind with a slouched, unenthused posture.

A while later, Juliette was sitting alone—in her beloved spot— among the patchy grass that sprouted beneath the tall oak tree. The earth below the branches was scattered with a gravel-like mixture of twigs and acorns that had been shaken out of the branches by the wind. The tree was perched a short distance from the edge of a steep drop which overlooked a ravine containing a fast-flowing river. On a calm day you could hear the water rushing below even though the river was well out of sight unless you got right up on the ledge, an activity Juliette would never allow either herself or her daughter to partake in.

Juliette heard movement among the leaves behind her where the branches of the crooked oak tree hung almost to the ground. "We call this the umbrella tree," she said, sensing Amiyah's presence. "I mean me and Shelby, my daughter. Because of the way the branches come down at the back and then open up at the front. You see, it kind of looks like an umbrella resting at an angle, if you sort of stand back and look at it the right way, and tilt your head, and blur your eyes."

"Yes, I think I get the idea," Amiyah said, coming down with a thump beside Juliette, struggling to speak due to her shortness of breath.

Juliette looked out beyond the ledge, over the canopy of trees that extended beyond the other side of the ravine and faded into the distance, where glimpses of the town looked like sections of a model village crafted in miniature scale. A blanket of cloud hovered on the horizon like foam on top of a wave. The sun was getting low, its base merging with the horizon in a trick of the light. "You should breathe in some of this fresh air," Juliette said. "Repair some of the damage you've done to your lungs. You know, you really oughta quit the smoking."

"Not much else to do in a house full of strippers."

"Then you need to quit the stripping as well."

"You gonna pay me a wage, are you?" Amiyah said, her tone sharpening as if she were offended by the way Juliette had commented on her profession. "You know, we're really not all that different, you and me," she said.

"Oh, really? How do you figure that out?"

"The way I see it, Caesar's got us both busting our asses for him one way or the other, hasn't he?"

Juliette thought for a moment. "Well, maybe if you stick with me, kid, we'll be able to figure a way out of this mess together."

Amiyah smiled and Juliette felt a warmth inside, a sense they'd shared a glimmer of mutual understanding, a realization they both had more or less the same goal in mind, a desire to better their lives via their chosen art form, the art of stepping into a cage and going to war with another human being.

"You come up here a lot?" Amiyah asked.

"Every couple of days," Juliette replied. "This place is kind of special to me."

"How so? You have your first kiss up here or something?"

"It's where my mother died, actually."

"I'm sorry, I didn't mean to—"

"—It's okay, she went over the edge there in her car," Juliette said flatly. "That's why the track's all closed off. Earl says they shut it out of respect, but I'm pretty sure it's more of a safety thing."

"When did it, I mean, how did it happen?"

"Happened around fifteen years ago. Little while before Shelby was born. Toxicology report said my mom was probably drunk, which wasn't exactly a surprise. So we don't know if she did it on purpose, or, maybe it was just an accident."

"Damn. Must have been real tough for you and Earl."

"My mom was pretty messed up toward the end. She drank a lot, suffered with depression and bipolar. So I guess we'll never really know the truth of what happened up here."

"And what about your dad? Where's he at?"

Juliette took a deep breath before answering. "Everyone in this shitty little town likes to think my dad was some kind of a hero, just because he fought for some heavyweight title or something. But the truth is, he walked out on us when we were kids, left us with our asshole stepdad even though he knew exactly what that drunk was doing to my mom, the way he used to throw her around. And where was my dad, the supposed tough guy? Nowhere. He let us down, all of us, and I can never forget that, any of it."

"I'm sorry, Jules, I never realized it was that bad," Amiyah said, placing a hand on Juliette's shoulder.

"You know, any time someone tries to tell me that martial arts is violent," Juliette continued, "I say to them, 'You don't even know what real violence is until you've had to call the cops to stop your stepdad from beating your mom half to death.' There's no violence in MMA, or in the cage, and don't ever let anybody tell you any different. What we do is just sport, it's competing, that's all."

"That's some pretty deep stuff to be talking about, right there."

"Well, you asked," Juliette said, shrugging her shoulder free from the young woman's hand. "So, what makes you want to get involved in fighting anyway, kid? Why in the world would you want to mess up that pretty little face of yours?"

"I want to be successful," Amiyah said, sitting up tall and straightening her back. "To feel like I'm actually worth something for once."

"You think fighting is gonna do that for you?"

"Well, I don't have anything else, do I?" Amiyah said, hanging her head dejectedly. "My mom never really wanted me around when I was younger. So I went to live with my grandpa. He's the only one who, shall we say, tolerated me, the way I was."

"He still around?"

Amiyah shook her head. "I was the one who found him when he went. Found him right in the middle of a heart attack, all laid out on the kitchen floor, gasping for air like a fish trying to get back in the water."

Juliette rotated her stiff neck, turning halfway toward Amiyah.

"Of course, I wanted to call 9-1-1 and whatever," Amiyah continued, "but Grandpa didn't want it. Just asked me to hold his hand like he knew it was his time to go. And while I'm clutching his hand and looking into his wide, frightened eyes, and he's gasping for breath, and his grip on mine is getting tighter and tighter, I remember thinking to myself, I mean, I remember feeling I'm not even worthy of being the person who gets to see this old man die. He was ninety years of age, served his country in the military half his life, had six kids, stayed married to my grandma until she went and died on him. Everybody in my family worshipped him like he was some kind of a god, the leader of our tribe. And I was the one who got to be with him at that important time, the moment he went. I just didn't feel I was good enough to be there, like I didn't deserve it, like it should have been somebody else."

Juliette noticed — in her peripheral vision — Amiyah's hands moving about her face as if the young woman were wiping tears from her eyes.

"You see, that's why I can't only be a stripper forever. I gotta be worth something, Jules. You understand?"

"I guess that makes sense," Juliette said, turning fully to look through her sunglasses toward Amiyah.

"A moment ago," Amiyah said, "you asked me why I would wanna mess up this pretty face of mine."

"So, what's your point?"

"Well, do you really think I'm, you know, pretty?" Amiyah looked into Juliette's dark glasses, a separate vision of the setting sun reflected on each lens.

"Why do you even care what I think?" Juliette asked, noticing Amiyah's tearful eyes were wide and unsure, her lips quivering with emotion. "Do you want me to think you're pretty?"

"Maybe," Amiyah said, her head hanging bashfully to one side.

Juliette was suddenly aware of the mounting force of her own heartbeat, the pressure of her blood pulsating in every part of her body. "Why on earth would a young girl like you want some beat-up old-timer like me to think you was pretty?"

"Come on, don't torture me. Why do you think?"

Juliette removed her sunglasses, presenting Amiyah with the reality of the bruising around her eyes. "I want you to explain it to me," she said. The breeze blowing across the hilltop seemed to gain momentum, rushing through the branches of the oak tree as if the tense energy between the two women had spilled out into their surroundings. "Tell me what you want from me," Juliette said.

"You don't want to know, trust me," Amiyah replied.

"I'm sick of all this playing around," Juliette said. "All of the innuendo, the cryptic clues. Just tell me, dammit. Tell me exactly what it is that you want."

"Fine," Amiyah replied, raising her voice a little. "If you really insist on knowing, I wanna pull off that damn sports bra of yours and take a look at those tits I can see all pushed up together as if they're bursting to escape." She shook her head, seemingly annoyed with her own outburst. "You happy now?"

Juliette's heart was beating hard and fast at the revelation, like a bullet of adrenaline had been fired into her.

"What, you want me to go on?"

Juliette was speechless.

"And then, I want to kiss those lips of yours, so hard," Amiyah continued, "so hard, that you're trying to hold me off of you, because you're scared of how good it all feels."

The branches of the tree seemed to be rotating around Juliette. She felt light-headed, short of oxygen.

"And then I want to taste you, all of you. Is that what you wanted to hear? Because, how much more do you want me to spell it out, Jules?"

Juliette felt a cold shiver run up her spine and linger over her entire body.

"Well, come on, say something," Amiyah said. "You pushed me."

"Just give me a minute, kid," Juliette said, focusing her eyes on the muddy earth beneath her, desperate for some kind of distraction from the bizarre situation she'd found herself in.

Amiyah scooted right up next to her. "I'm sorry," she said, "I didn't mean to upset you."

"It's okay, just, give me a minute, please."

"But I know you want it as well, Jules," Amiyah said, whispering softly now. "I want to feel the warmth of your body, your skin against mine. Tell me you want it as well."

Juliette had lost the ability to speak; maybe it was shock, maybe she just didn't know how to respond.

Amiyah leaned closer still. "Tell me you want it," she whispered, her lips hovering over Juliette's.

The women were breathing stuttered breaths into each other's mouths. Juliette had never felt so intensely confused, so compelled to act, but so overwhelmingly terrified at the same time. She felt a tingle on her lips, Amiyah's mouth skimming her own. Without even thinking, she raised a hand and placed her outstretched palm in the center of Amiyah's chest. "I'm not gay," she said, pushing the young woman away. She closed her eyes, unable to face Amiyah's reaction.

"Well, you could have fooled me," Amiyah said, "taking me off so we're alone. Bringing me out here to the middle of nowhere and telling me I'm pretty. What did you expect me to think?"

Juliette opened her eyes and saw the young woman was hurrying away from her, disappearing through the hanging branches of the oak tree. "Amiyah, wait. Don't be like that," Juliette called out, and she climbed to her feet so quickly she was reminded of her injuries. Amiyah was gone and suddenly it was raining. Juliette had been so distracted, she didn't even know when the rain had started to fall. It was coming down fast through the overhead branches and Juliette knew Amiyah would be getting drenched on her way down the track. "What have I done, Momma?" Juliette called out into the sky, her arms splayed at her sides. "Why do I have to ruin everything all the time?"

The sky answered with a rumble of thunder and Juliette took off through the branches of the tree. She called out to Amiyah, but the young woman was nowhere to be seen. Juliette's running shoes slid across the wet mud of the track, her feet failing to maintain purchase on the slick downhill terrain and then getting stuck where the rain had turned the earth to a bog. Her progress was hindered to the point of frustration. She imagined Amiyah hopping from foot to foot along the track, her youthful agility and her anger carrying her at great speed. Juliette took out her cell phone and called the young woman's number, knowing there would be no answer. The rain beat down against her face. Her thoughts were a frantic mess. How would she explain any of this to Earl?

When Juliette got back to her truck, she half expected Amiyah to be waiting beside it, taking shelter underneath the cover of surrounding trees. But as she arrived at the end of the track, she found the clearing beyond the locked gate was starkly empty save for the aging vehicle waiting in the downpour like a faithful old horse. Juliette looked under the cover in the cargo bed, but Amiyah's backpack and bicycle were gone. She climbed up into her truck and started the engine. The wheels span in the mud as she pulled away. She drove slowly through the rain. The wipers struggled to keep the water off the glass even on the maximum speed setting. Juliette scanned the shoulder at either side of the road. The windshield fogged up and Juliette wiped at it with her sleeve. "Come on, old girl, help me out," she said. Everything seemed to be going wrong. She breathed a long sigh of frustration as she finally accepted, Amiyah was gone.

CHAPTER 8

A mist of condensation obscured the mirrored wall above the bathroom sink. The air in the little apartment was thick with humidity. Juliette preferred it when the mirror was misted this way, like a soft-focus filter had been cast over her reflection, taking the edge off the graphic brutality of her facial injuries. The swelling to her face was subsiding now, reduced to a highwayman's mask of bruising around her eyes. Her lips had deflated, returning to their usual shape, but the dull ache still lingered in her lower back, a constant reminder of her brawl with The Ox.

As Juliette emerged from the bathroom — with her wet body and sodden hair wrapped up in separate towels — she turned to her left and entered her bedroom, the doorway to which was directly opposite that of her daughter's room. Juliette proceeded to dry herself off as though she was operating on autopilot. Her thoughts were occupied solely by recollections of the events which had taken place earlier that day beneath the branches of the umbrella tree. She couldn't stop thinking about Amiyah's candid declaration of her feelings, the young woman's face coming toward her own, the words she'd uttered in response. "I'm not gay," she recalled herself saying over and over, until the phrase had no meaning at all. The words crippled Juliette with a burn of nerves every time she mentally replayed them.

Juliette dressed herself and then surveyed her outfit in the full-length mirror across the room. She was clad entirely in black, wearing tight jeans, a V-neck T-shirt, and leather biker boots. She wasn't sure why she'd chosen to throw on her satin Diablo MMA jacket with the devil's face embroidered on the back. Maybe it was because the garment made her feel the support of her brother. Maybe she'd convinced herself that what she was about to do was for the benefit of her whole team. She appeared to be clothed in preparation for some kind of underhanded nocturnal activity, as if she were about to sneak out into the night, moving unseen among the shadows, operating stealthily as a cat burglar or a getaway driver. She checked her reflection from all angles and then raised her clenched fists, adopting a boxer's stance. She threw out her hands, bobbed her head from side to side, and rolled her shoulders. "Still got it, Jules," she said, "still got it."

A short hallway led from the two bedrooms and the bathroom at the back of the modest apartment to an open-plan kitchen and lounge area at the front. As Juliette made her way into the kitchen, she saw—across the countertop separating the room from the lounge—Shelby laid out on the couch, her limp body and splayed limbs making her look barely alive, her narrowed eyes and the lenses of her spectacles reflecting the multicolored glow of the TV screen.

"I've gotta go out for a while, Doll," Juliette called out.

Shelby's head spun toward her mother. "You're going out?" the teenager said, as if Juliette had just announced she was about to leave the country. "Where on earth are you going?" Shelby asked, getting up on her elbows.

"It's just a work thing with some of the guys from the gym."

"What guys? And why are you all dressed up?" Shelby peered over her glasses, looking more like the parent than the child.

"I won't be too late. But don't wait up for me."

"Hang on, are you going on a date or something?"

"Don't be silly. I already told you, it's just a work thing. I gotta go, and don't go crazy with the snacks, okay?"

"But I thought you wanted a massage tonight, for your back?"

Shelby looked up at her mother with the eyes of a puppy who hadn't been walked for several days.

"We'll do it tomorrow. I promise." Juliette leaned down to kiss her daughter goodbye, but as their mouths met, Shelby's lips did not form a willing pout.

"Bye then, I guess," the teenager said, disapprovingly.

Juliette exited the front door and locked it behind her as she made her way onto the exterior landing. People had always commented — almost in a derogatory manner — on the way the building looked more like a motel than an apartment block, a feature Juliette had tried to pass off as a novelty to a discerning twelve-year-old Shelby when they'd moved in a few years previously. Juliette descended the stairwell, climbed into her truck, and drove through the night with her radio on mute. Her thoughts were focused solely on the task ahead as though she was preparing herself mentally for an opponent she was about to face in the cage. Juliette drove to the outskirts of town, where tightly packed rows of wooden-clad houses and apartment blocks gave way to a sparse landscape of large metallic and glass-based structures suited more to the needs of commerce and industry. She passed a vast truck stop with endless lay-bys stretching out parallel to the roads, where truckers would park their vehicles for the night and pull curtains closed over their cab windows.

When the darkness of night descended on this part of town, the industrial activity would grind almost to a complete halt. The large retail outlets would close their doors, and the landscape would transform to a silent ghost town. As Juliette drove along the deserted streets, every now and then the spotlight glow of a street lamp would reveal the curious sight of a sex worker touting for business. The scantily clad, shivering women stared back from the roadside, their eyes haunted with an unsettling mix of sadness and allure. This was the part of town in which the businesses that nobody wanted operating on their doorsteps had been forced to ply their trades. Caesar's strip club, The Pink Tunnel, was one of several such establishments dotted throughout the industrial zone, most of which served the drivers making use of the sprawling truck stop as they passed through the town to continue onto their final destinations.

Juliette pulled up among the handful of vehicles currently occupying the club's parking lot. A neon sign mounted on a tall post displayed a series of concentric archways which lit up one after the other to give the effect you were being led into the depths of a tunnel. Above the illuminated arches, the club's name was splayed out in italics, the letters flashing on and off in vibrant pink. The neon sign and a pink canopy above the entrance were the only features distinguishing the club from the warehouses and industrial units that surrounded it on every side.

Juliette checked herself in the rearview mirror, covering the blemished skin around her eyes with her sunglasses. She could hear the music rumbling from within the club, a faint pulsation coming through the walls. The muffled sound acted as a foreboding indication of all that lurked inside. Juliette thought about her brother, about her daughter back at home, about the fact she was operating secretly without their knowledge. She climbed out of her truck. She hadn't been certain up until this point whether she would have ended up driving straight past the club, or whether she would have been able to muster the courage to park her vehicle and go through with it all. She was operating on instinct, the way she did when she fought, and now she was here outside The Pink Tunnel and she was actually going in.

"You here to see Caesar, Jules?" the bearded monster of a door supervisor asked with a voice so deep it made him seem like some inhuman gatekeeper on Juliette's mythical quest. "He's in the back if you want me to call him."

"I'm good, thanks," Juliette replied. "Just here to see a friend."

"Ain't that what they all say?" the door supervisor said, unhooking a rope barrier to let Juliette through.

As the doors swung open, the full force of the music hit Juliette, making her abundantly aware she was leaving one realm of reality and entering another. She stepped into a dark foyer where she noticed Dolores' white-blonde lampshade of hair glowing behind the window of a booth that was used to collect entrance fees and take jackets from customers. Dolores didn't even bother to look up from the little window in the booth; she just waved a hand for Juliette to proceed without paying the fee.

Juliette passed through a beaded curtain into the main portion of the club. The long, rectangular space — bathed in a neon magenta glow — looked practically empty compared to the last time she'd visited. She glanced around at the clientele within her immediate field of vision. A wiry-limbed man in a cowboy hat was seated before the bar, his slouched posture and jocular interactions with the barman suggested he probably came here every other night. A bespectacled little man in a corporate-looking suit was at a nearby table, sandwiched between a duo of underwear-clad strippers like a defenseless fly tangled up in the leaves of a carnivorous plant. There was a trio of customers occupying three of the stools that were positioned in front of the stage. The men conversed casually as they waited for the next dancer to emerge onto the catwalk. Juliette felt exposed as she entered the sparsely occupied room, but she was determined to put all of that aside, committed to succeeding in her mission. The heads of every other customer turned with perfect synchronicity as she made her way to the bar and ordered herself a beer.

"You dancing tonight, sweet pea?" the wiry-limbed cowboy asked in Juliette's direction. The hair jutting forth from underneath the man's hat was silvering with age. The sallow features of his mustached face were all red and demonic under the lights of the club. He looked as though he was chewing tobacco, rolling a wad of it around over his jagged little teeth.

Juliette ignored the cowboy's advances. She glanced around anxiously, aware that Amiyah might emerge from some dark alcove at any second.

"Well? What is it, you dancing or not?" the cowboy persisted, his sunken eyes peering out from the shadow of his hat. He climbed onto the stool next to Juliette's, swinging his leg over as if mounting a horse. He smelt the way tobacco tastes, musty and unwashed.

Juliette swigged from her beer, uninterested, aware this individual was just a minor inconvenience to her mission, a bump in the road that she needed to pass over to proceed.

"How about you and me watch a private dance together?" the cowboy suggested. His voice at such close proximity was a gruff whisper, like a bizarre vocal track accompanying the bass-heavy drone from the club speakers. "These girls will let you do whatever you want if the price is right," he said through his vicious little teeth.

Juliette watched him fingering the condensation on his glass of something-or-other on the rocks. She struggled to hold off the thought of smashing the drink into the man's face. She pictured little pieces of broken glass jutting from the loose skin of his neck, the terror in his eyes as his gabardine shirt slowly turned a deep shade of red.

"What's the matter, cat got your tongue?" the cowboy asked. "You're not one of the man-hating variety of lesbians, are you? Or maybe you're just rude."

Juliette felt her nails piercing into the flesh of her palms as her hands tightened into fists.

The cowboy was on his feet now, right up next to Juliette. "I'm talking to you, girlie."

Juliette's beer bottle was tucked between her legs on the stool. She took hold of it with an upside down grip, clutching its neck like the handle of a bat. She thought to herself for just a brief moment: perhaps if she started a fight, she might be able to get herself thrown out of the place. Maybe that would be her ticket out of all this, like tapping out of a submission hold early instead of risking getting your limb broken or being choked unconscious. Then she could go home, get into bed in the room opposite her daughter's and forget all about this whole mess.

Suddenly, the cowboy was moving away. A giant bear claw of a hand was upon his shoulder, a black fist clutching a wad of his shirt. "Easy now, Rodeo," a drawl of a voice said to the cowboy. "Sit yourself down before Jules here takes your damn head clean off." Caesar squeezed himself in front of Juliette, eclipsing the cowboy from her line of sight. Juliette released her grip on the beer bottle and took a deep breath in preparation for this latest obstacle.

"So what is it, Jules?" Caesar asked. "You had one little dance in here and now you can't stay away?"

"Just having a quiet drink, that's all."

"Isn't that what they all say?" Caesar suggested, with a sentiment echoing that of the door supervisor. The silken shirt draped over Caesar's spherical mass was tested at the seams as he hoisted himself onto the stool next to Juliette's. His bald, neckless head shone gloss red under the neon lights, looking almost as though it had been polished. "We need to sign some papers for your rematch with The Ox," he said, and then with the same causal air of assumption, he waved the barman to fetch him a drink. "We'll do the fight in three months or so," Caesar said, pulling a dish of nuts toward him on the bar. "That gives us plenty of time for the buildup."

"Who says I'm even gonna be fighting Oksana again?"

"So tell me, Jules, what other fights do you think are out there for you right now?" Caesar asked, shoveling a handful of nuts into this mouth.

"Maybe I'm done with looking for fights. Maybe it's time I start looking for something else to do with my life."

Caesar choked with laughter and thumped at his chest to clear his throat. "Oh, is that right?" he said. "You seriously think you're gonna be able to kick the habit of a lifetime just like that? Cold turkey, huh? You're not done yet, Jules. Trust me, you don't just quit fighting on a whim. Not when it's in your blood."

"Yeah, well, we'll see about that," Juliette said, guzzling her beer, feigning confidence in her own conviction.

"I'll talk to Earl," Caesar said. "We always manage to work it out one way or the other. He knows what's good for you."

"It's my life, not my brother's."

Caesar shook his head, disregarding Juliette's opinion. "Oh, and I know all about you and Mimi as well," he said.

"Who's Mimi?"

"Amiyah, of course. Mimi's her stage name, her stripper name. I hear you and your brother have been coaching her at Diablo's."

"What of it?"

"Just remember, she belongs to me," Caesar said, fixing Juliette with a look she'd only witnessed previously in stare downs across the cage. "Any money you make off of her goes through me. As long as you understand that, we're good."

"She in here tonight?" Juliette asked.

Caesar slid himself down from his stool. As he turned to leave, he raised his glass and signaled toward the catwalk-shaped stage running along the opposite wall of the club. He clicked his fingers through the air like a puppet-master who had full control over every aspect of the place.

The strobe light blazed into action. The club flashed white. Amiyah emerged onto the catwalk from behind a scarlet curtain. The young woman looked magnificent up on the stage, her toned body moving in freeze-frame through the strobe lighting, her muscular legs flexing as she strode about on tall heels, her athletic physique clad in strappy latex underwear like she was some kind of a wild beast trussed up in a harness or reins. Amiyah worked the audience for tips, prowling the catwalk on her knees, thrusting her head back so the braids of her hair whipped across her back. She stalked around like a cat on all fours, kneeling in front of each onlooker in turn so they could deposit bills into the waistband of her glossy underwear.

Amiyah's performance hit Juliette like a punch to the solar plexus.

She was left breathless, mesmerized by the expertise and sensuality of the young woman's movements. Juliette hadn't felt such a chill of awe run through her body since the last time she'd seen her brother fight or her daughter perform ballet.

Their eyes met across the room and Amiyah's face straightened. Her movements slowed as though she'd been distracted by Juliette's presence. Juliette averted her gaze, fearing she'd been caught in an act of voyeurism. The trio of stage-front onlookers waved their dollar bills, spurring Amiyah to focus on her dance moves. She seemed to regain her momentum, the seductive pout returning to her lips.

Juliette tried to look anywhere except the stage, but her eyes were drawn to Amiyah's again. The young woman's body seized up and her dark eyes intensified as she struggled to maintain focus. She shook her head and gave up, snatching handfuls of bills from the catwalk before turning to depart.

Juliette got up off her stool but Amiyah was gone, retreating backstage just as quickly as she'd appeared, the scarlet curtain flailing being her. Juliette hurried toward the catwalk. "Amiyah, wait," she called out, attempting to project her voice over the music.

"You can't go back there," a member of the security staff said, his hands splayed to form a barrier.

"But I just need to speak to her," Juliette pleaded.

"Come on, calm down. Take a seat." The security staffer took Juliette by the shoulders and turned her back toward the bar.

"Okay, relax," Juliette said, shrugging herself free. "I'm fine, okay? I just wanted to talk to her." Juliette felt the eyes of every other person in the room upon her. She downed the rest of her beer, trembling with frustration. She glanced around, noticing the place appeared to have been caught in a freeze-frame, the faces of the other patrons looking toward her with blank expressions.

"Don't you worry, sweet pea," the cowboy said, "I'll dance with you." Juliette felt the man's fingers clamping around her waist. He pulled her closer and breathed his warm, whisky-infused breath over her neck. "Come on, girlie, loosen up," he whispered into her ear, pressing his body against hers.

Without even thinking, Juliette reached behind herself and looped one arm around the man's neck. She pressed her butt up into his stomach and leaned forward, tossing him over her hip, swinging his lanky body over her own so that he came somersaulting down into a tangled heap of arms and legs on the floor, his cowboy hat spinning off his head like a Frisbee. The man sat upright on the floor clutching the small of his back. His wrinkled face was all screwed up with pain. Juliette had noticed how rigid his lean body felt as he'd gone over, like a rotten branch that was more likely to fracture than bend. She thought — for just a split second — about the damage she might have done to his aging bones. She came down to her knees and threaded her arms under the man's shoulders so she could help him back to his feet.

Suddenly, another pair of arms were around Juliette's waist, pulling her body into the tightening grip of a bear hug. She felt herself being lifted up off the ground, her dangling feet trying desperately to gain some kind of traction. She fought to free herself, noticing the arms tied up around her stomach were covered by dark woolen sleeves, the type which belonged to the coats worn by the security staff.

"Calm down," the security staffer said. "Don't make this any harder than it needs to be."

Juliette struggled for a while, looking like an unruly child being carried away by its father. She quickly realized she'd be no match for her mountainous assailant, and besides, she understood that what she'd done probably meant it was time she should leave anyway. She resigned herself to her fate, her lifeless body hanging limp from the solid grip of the man's arms. All she felt now was a surge of intense embarrassment for the few seconds it took the security staffer to transport her to the exit. As she floated toward the beaded curtain of the foyer, she knew Dolores would be waiting on the other side and that she would be watching a lot more intently than when Juliette had made her entrance.

The beaded strings of the curtain pelted over Juliette's face as she was carried through them, and just as she'd anticipated, Dolores' darkly-penciled eyes peered out from beneath her white-blonde bob of hair. Juliette resisted the urge to struggle, realizing any kind of protest of her current predicament would only make her appear more pathetic than she already did. She could see Dolores' red-painted lips were curled up with glee. Juliette closed her eyes and cursed her lack of self-control, the fact she'd let her temper get the better of her so easily. Seconds later, she was spilling out onto the sidewalk, struggling to stay upright as she was thrust out of the man's arms. She stumbled out into the night and sucked in a deep breath as though she'd just resurfaced from being held underwater.

"You okay, Jules?" the bearded door supervisor asked, looking to his colleague—the one who had been manhandling Juliette—for an explanation.

"I just need a minute," Juliette said. She placed her hands on her lower back and twisted her upper body this way and that to straighten herself out. She listened for a few seconds as the men squabbled over the events that had just taken place within the club. She decided to take advantage of their distraction, and slipped away from the pair so she could retreat to her vehicle and make her escape. As she staggered back to her truck, she noticed a faint mist was rising up from behind a fence at the back of the parking lot. The evening breeze that wafted by was tainted with a vague hint of cigarette smoke. Juliette wandered toward the fence, blending with the shadows in her stealthy outfit, checking over her shoulder to make sure the door supervisors hadn't seen where she was going.

She squeezed her slender body through a narrow opening in a pair of gates. Her movements triggered an automatic security light, its blinding glare forcing her to squint. She shielded her eyes with one hand, and there, with her bangles and jewelry shining in the darkness, was Amiyah, perched upon a doorstep next to a row of dumpsters, looking forlorn as though she'd thrown herself out in the trash. The young woman was shivering, huddling for warmth in a puffball fur coat, sucking on a cigarette which extended from the tips of her black-painted fingernails.

"I thought I told you to quit?"

Amiyah took a long indulgent drag from her cigarette.

"I gotta admit, kid, you're one hell of a dancer," Juliette said. "I mean, really, you are."

Amiyah rolled her eyes. Her teeth were chattering. Her bare legs emerged from her fur coat indicating she probably had nothing on underneath the beastly garment except for the underwear she'd worn on stage.

"You wanna go somewhere we can talk?" Juliette asked.

"Who says I'm even talking to you, sugar?"

"Then don't talk. Maybe we can just, I don't know, hang out."

"Sounds like a blast."

"Look, I didn't mean to offend you earlier, okay? You just took me by surprise, that's all. I thought we made a good team, you and me at the gym. But if you don't wanna sort this thing out, then I guess you can keep dancing for these creeps in here every night. Do you really wanna be Mimi the stripper forever? Or do you wanna be Amiyah, the professional mixed martial artist? Like I said, you're a good dancer, there's no doubt about that, but I'm pretty sure you realize you're an even better fighter."

Amiyah blew a trail of smoke up into the air and flicked her cigarette end off among the dumpsters, where it exploded with a little firework-like burst of embers. "Go wait out front for ten minutes," she said. "If I don't show up, that means either I changed my mind or Caesar won't let me out, and you might as well get back in that old truck of yours and go home, okay?"

"I'll be waiting," Juliette replied, straightening her face to show her sincerity. "Don't you worry, I'll be waiting.

CHAPTER 9

Juliette glanced at the digital clock on her dash. She'd been waiting for nine of the allotted ten minutes already, but still, there was no sign of Amiyah. It was raining again. The water beating down on the roof of the truck sounded like raindrops falling on the canopy of a tent. Juliette looked out through the waterfall cascading over her windshield, surveying the club as though she were staking the place out. The scene framed within the bounds of the windshield was like some melancholy work of modern art, the illuminated sign up on its tall post casting a hue of hot-pink over the otherwise colorless industrial building below, the fuchsia glow of the lettering bleeding down through the rain like the paint of a neon watercolor. The bearded doorman cast a tall shadow over the sidewalk as he sheltered underneath the entrance canopy, sucking on a cigarette as though he thought the smoke would keep him warm.

Juliette watched the glowing digits on the clock transform as the tenth minute expired. She exhaled long and hard, a sigh of both frustration and relief in equal measures. She pictured herself turning the key in the ignition, the truck hocking up mucus from its throat as it rumbled to life. Her hand moved from her lap to the key and back again as she struggled with her indecision. She realized how easy it would be to drive straight out of the parking lot, knowing she'd fulfilled her part of the deal. She'd made her apology, waited the full ten minutes, this was on Amiyah now. Besides, Juliette realized she didn't even have a plan of action for the eventuality of Amiyah walking out of the club anyway.

The white noise of the rain swelled in the background like the fuzz of an untuned radio. Juliette tried to align her thoughts to that notion, focusing on the sound of the downpour, clearing her mind of her anxieties. She closed her eyes and sank back into the bench seat. In the blank nothingness of her thoughts, she saw Amiyah's eyes coming toward her out of the darkness. She pictured the band of freckles peppering the young woman's cheeks, the playful smile that always seemed to be dancing about her lips as she rolled wads of gum around in her mouth. Juliette's mind was awash with a muddle of half-asleep imaginings as she began to fade out of consciousness. A blast of cold air rushed into the truck and she awoke with a shiver. The rain was louder now. The passenger door was wide open.

"Thought you'd be long gone by now, sugar," Amiyah said, climbing up into the cab.

Juliette sat up straight and gripped hold of the steering wheel. "I was just about to leave, actually."

Amiyah parted the lapels of her fur coat to show her body was still strapped up in the latex underwear she'd worn on stage. "You'd have waited all night for this and you know it," she said, swiveling her hips within the downy fur.

Juliette pulled the garment back into place with the speed of a reflex reaction. "Are you out of your mind?" she said. "The doorman's just over there."

"Relax, will you? I'm just having a little fun. Why've you always gotta be so uptight all the time?"

The air in the truck was thick with the scents of Amiyah's perfumes, body lotions, and moisturizers, the atmosphere flavored by her semi-nakedness.

"What took you so long, anyway?" Juliette asked. She wound her window down a little and stole a breath of the cool air from outside to keep her head clear.

"I'm here now, aren't I?"

The collar of Amiyah's coat hung open revealing the bronze skin of her chest underneath the shiny straps of her bra. The bulk of the fur coat accentuated the slightness of her athletic frame. Juliette scanned the truck for something else to focus on. Amiyah's erratic, unpredictable behavior filled Juliette with a burn of nervousness. She found herself trying to prepare for whatever the young woman was going to do next, the same way she would attempt to predict her opponent's maneuvers in a fight so she'd be ready to counteract with an appropriate technique of her own.

"So, are we getting out of here, or what?" Amiyah asked with a raised eyebrow.

Juliette felt her nerves stirring further as she wondered what the young woman had in mind. "Well, where do you suppose we should go?" she asked, shrugging her shoulders in the hope she might appear unfazed.

"Paradise," Amiyah replied, jangling a large wooden key fob from an outstretched finger.

Juliette watched the key fob dancing about on its chain until it swung to a rest. The fob was engraved with the words "Paradise Gardens" next to a little carved outline of two palm trees. "A motel?" Juliette asked. "Are you out of your mind?"

Amiyah stepped out of the truck into the rain. "Come on, sugar," she said, "I'll behave, I promise." She passed in front of the windshield, rushing by in her heels, wobbling off balance every now and then as though she were walking along a tightrope.

"Where are you going?" Juliette called out as she climbed down from her seat. Amiyah seemed so wild and untamed, Juliette struggled to keep up with the spontaneity of the young woman. Amiyah paused, turned back and stretched out a hand, her upturned palm inviting Juliette into all the sinister possibilities that lay beyond the mass of that fur coat. Juliette knew if she accepted, this would be like crossing an invisible line, one there might be no turning back from.

"You wanna stay out here in the rain forever?" Amiyah asked.

Juliette inhaled deeply. The force of the rain against her face prompted her to make haste with her decision. She slipped her hand into Amiyah's and instantly felt the young woman's grip tightening as she finally got her own way. Amiyah led Juliette across the parking lot, splashing through puddles on her stilt-like heels. The door supervisor was watching them over the cigarette he held to his mouth. He knew Juliette by name, and she was certain he knew Earl as well. Word could get around. It all felt so dangerous.

They passed alongside the fence Juliette had slipped through earlier. They were behind the club now, waiting for cars to pass so they could cross a road. The male faces in the passing vehicles turned to look at them, probably assuming the pair were touting for business. As they waited—holding hands in the rain—Amiyah turned and smiled, running her thumb back and forth over the skin of Juliette's knuckles. Juliette assumed it was a friendly gesture, but still, the display of affection from another woman made her feel uncomfortable. She loosened her palm, trying to release her grip, but Amiyah snatched her hand closer and led the way through a break in the traffic. They ducked into a shadowy passage that ran between another pair of units, sticking close to the buildings to avoid the rain. They reemerged under the glow of the streetlights and stumbled into another half-filled parking lot. Juliette squinted through the downpour, attempting to survey the building before her. It was a pastel-colored, multi-floored structure with landings running along each level. The flickering, illuminated sign suspended above the reception lobby matched the design on Amiyah's key fob.

"Welcome to The Paradise Gardens," Amiyah said, sweeping a hand through the air in the style of a gameshow hostess revealing a prize. "Caesar keeps a few rooms in here on standby," she explained. "For the girls who like to go that extra mile with their clients, if you get what I'm saying. But that's not me, of course," she added with haste.

"You sure about that?" Juliette asked. "Seems like you're pretty well acquainted with the place."

"Okay, so, I might have peed in some guy's mouth here this one time," Amiyah confessed, rolling her eyes.

"Come again?"

"Look, don't judge me, the money was good, okay?"

As they passed underneath the porch that stretched out in front of the lobby, Juliette glanced at a collection of potted palm trees, the only remotely garden-like features of the exterior decor. She noticed the hard, cracked soil in the plant pots, the way the dry earth seemed to be strangling the trees, their sagging leaves asphyxiated under a layer of industrial dust. In the half-lit depths of the lobby, a young man with hair that looked as if it was seldom washed and skin that looked as if it rarely saw daylight was sitting behind a counter, openly watching what looked like a pornographic movie on a wall-mounted television. His pale, expressionless face was lit up by the melancholy glow of the screen.

"We've really gotta get you out of this place, kid," Juliette said.

"I'm working on it, okay?" Amiyah replied, and she squeezed Juliette's hand a little tighter to emphasize her point.

They passed the lobby, continuing until they arrived at the door of the room on the building's furthest corner. Amiyah released Juliette's hand at last and worked her key in the lock.

"I probably shouldn't stay all that long," Juliette said, "what with Shelby being at home on her own, and all."

Amiyah held a finger to her lips before taking up both of Juliette's hands and encouraging her into the room. Juliette resisted a little to show her apprehension, to make one final half-hearted attempt at avoiding the inevitably uncomfortable scenario that awaited beyond the threshold before her. Amiyah fumbled blindly for the light switch as though she had a vague memory of its location. Seconds later, the half-light glimmer of a single bulb shone from the ceiling, not quite illuminating the little room into its corners. There was a double bed pressed against one wall, a small armchair at its side. A painting of a tropical landscape hung over a dresser, a reference to the type of exotic wilderness the motel's name alluded to. Amiyah locked the door and Juliette flinched at the sound of the key.

"Relax, sugar. Take a seat."

Juliette sat down in the armchair. It was a half-backed thing that looked to be a relic from the 1970s. Its unergonomic shape reminded Juliette of her back injury, forcing her to sit bolt-upright. The atmosphere in the room was stagnant and undisturbed, but with faint citric undertones of sanitary products from whenever the place had last been cleaned. Juliette glanced around at the tired, uninspiring decor, wondering what kind of bizarre and debauched scenes Caesar's clients had inflicted upon this unassuming little motel over the years.

Amiyah hovered about the dresser at the foot of the bed. She kicked off her heels and emptied her pockets of keys, cigarettes, a roll of bills. The young woman exhaled a huff of breath, sighing casually as if she'd just arrived home after a long day of work and was finally able to relax. Juliette was anything but relaxed, gripping the armrests of her chair like somebody on a roller coaster about to go over the edge.

Amiyah flashed her eyes at Juliette's Diablo MMA jacket. "Why did you show up in your team colors, anyway?" she asked. "You here on official business, or what?"

"I guess that's what we're here for, isn't it?" Juliette replied, attempting to sound professional while shifting in her seat to find a comfortable position.

"Why don't you sit over on the bed? That old chair won't do your back much good. You should probably hang that jacket out to dry in the bathroom as well."

"I'm good, thanks. Can we just talk?"

Amiyah stood asymmetrically with one hand resting over a hip. She was looking down at Juliette as though she found the older woman's nervousness entirely ridiculous. "Don't be such a child. Come on, it's hot in here. Make yourself at home and take the jacket off."

"Well, if it's so hot, why don't you take your own jacket off?" Juliette spluttered in response, an awkward attempt at matching Amiyah's imperturbable demeanor.

Juliette's question seemed to catch the young woman off guard, stopping her in her tracks. She almost laughed as she responded. "Do you want me to take it off?"

Juliette shrugged, unsure of how to answer.

"Well, that's not exactly a no, now is it? And why would you possibly want me to take my coat off?"

Juliette remained silent, trying to avoid Amiyah's penetrating gaze.

"You see, the thing is," Amiyah began, "you know very well that all I've got on under this faux fur is my underwear. In fact, I'm basically half-naked under here. So if I remove the coat, you're going to be able to see pretty much everything. Is that really what you want?"

"Damn it, kid," Juliette growled. "What are you trying to do to me?" She leaned forward over her knees with her head in her hands, exhausted by the younger woman's behavior.

"It's okay, sugar," Amiyah said, coming down before the little armchair, resting a hand on Juliette's knee. "Just relax. We're gonna work this out, okay? Just you and me." She walked to the window and pulled the curtains closed. "You see? Nobody but the two of us is going to know what happens in this room. So, come on, calm down." She sat on the bed and patted at the mattress beside her.

Juliette took a deep breath. She got up, removed her sodden jacket and tossed it over the back of the low-slung armchair. She felt overly aware of the movements of her limbs, unsure of her outfit under the scrutiny of the younger woman, suspicious that Amiyah would be judging her dress-sense and her physique. She sat down on the edge of the bed, her hands clinging to the mattress at her sides, her body and facial expression both overly rigid as she tried to conceal her inner panic.

Her heart was racing and her head was spinning.

Amiyah reached up to sweep Juliette's hair out of her face. Juliette recoiled with the speed of a boxer avoiding a jab.

"Settle down, will you? I just wanna take these sunglasses off so I can actually see your eyes."

Juliette felt exposed, unmasked without her glasses.

"Sit back," Amiyah said, directing Juliette to fully mount the bed and recline against the headboard.

"I really don't know if this is such a good idea, kid."

Amiyah held an outstretched finger over Juliette's lips. "Look, I know you like to think you're the strong, silent type and all. But your eyes tell me everything I need to know. You see, the thing is, I've been paying real close attention, and what I've noticed is, you kind of seem to like looking at me."

"What are you talking about?" Juliette said with a burst of nervous laughter.

"It's okay, if that's your thing. I get it. I mean, you're pretty obsessed with our sport, aren't you? So, it's really no surprise that you like to look at the bodies of other athletes. Just from a strictly technical point of view, of course. I mean, some people are into race cars, and they like to look at all kinds of vehicles and whatever. You're into MMA, so you like to admire the physiques of other fighters, right?"

"I guess that's one way of putting it."

"If that's the case, then why don't you take this opportunity to really look at me?"

Juliette was silent again.

"You've got me here all alone," Amiyah continued, "why don't you make the most of it and look at me all you want? You can study my body from every conceivable angle. Position me any way you like. Take in every muscle, every last detail. There's no harm in just looking, surely?"

"Well, I don't know about that, kid. Sounds a little strange to me."

"Okay, so how about if I just take off my coat, and then you can see how you feel?" Amiyah walked to the foot of the bed and turned to face Juliette. "Now, you're sitting comfortably, the door's locked, the curtains are closed. The world isn't about to end, now is it? So, are you ready?" She read Juliette's silence as an affirmative response and slowly began to part the lapels of her fur coat under the gentle glow of the single bulb. Juliette's breaths grew heavier at the sight of the shiny black bra pushing the young woman's breasts together, holding them so tightly against her body they bulged over the latex and appeared larger than they actually were.

The mental fog clouding Juliette's thoughts grew thicker as she watched Amiyah lowering the coat from her shoulders. Juliette was mesmerized, unable to take her eyes off the spectacle before her. She wasn't even trying now. She'd finally submitted to her fascination with the young woman's appearance, exhausted by her own resistance to it all. And now, she was practically collapsed out on the bed, unable to move, unashamedly feasting on the display of flesh that was being presented to her, like it was some kind of powerful narcotic that was holding her spellbound.

Amiyah dropped her coat to the floor. Juliette looked from the young woman's vaguely-muscular stomach to her latex-encased crotch. Amiyah was paying close attention to the direction of Juliette's gaze. "Do you want me to turn around?"

Juliette nodded, somewhat involuntarily, unable to suppress her intrigue.

Amiyah laughed a little and turned her back on her captivated prey.

Juliette followed the multiple straps of Amiyah's bra as they zigzagged down to the small of her back. Her rubberized briefs glimmered under the light, exaggerating the curvature of her ass. The sleek fabric encased only the upper half of each buttock, so that the lower portions heaved out from underneath the latex.

"So, tell me, how do you want me to pose?" Amiyah asked, looking back over her shoulder. "Unless you want me to put my coat back on, of course, and then we can just forget the whole thing—"

"—Stand up on your toes," Juliette interrupted.

"My toes?"

"Yes. Stay in that position, but come up off your heels so I can take a look at your calf muscles."

"Like this?" Amiyah asked, stretching up so her legs tensed and strained to hold her in place. "Now what?"

"Lift your arms up above your head, so I can see the definition over your shoulder blades."

As Amiyah raised her arms into the air, the muscles in her back shifted and contracted underneath her skin.

"Now bend over at the waist, slowly," Juliette dared to say, struggling to hold her voice from trembling. Something awakened inside her as she uttered the words, an internal wild fire that blazed through her body so forcefully it made her clench up with fear.

Amiyah leaned forward over the dresser. The central seam of her underwear was pulled up further between her legs, emphasizing the shape and form of everything the latex garment concealed. "Are you looking at my ass?"

"I just want to see the definition in your thighs."

"If you say so." Amiyah tugged at the hems of her underwear so the shiny fabric rode up deeper between her buttocks. "So, do you like what you see?"

"You got a great body, kid. That's for sure. Maybe we can run through some yoga positions together, see if there's any areas that need loosening up."

"But don't you wanna get a closer look," Amiyah asked, turning to face Juliette, crawling cat-like toward her on the bed. As the young woman approached, Juliette's stomach was hot and tight with nerves. She felt a sense of urgency within, compelling her to put a stop to of all

128

of this, to get up off of the bed, to tell Amiyah she'd got the wrong idea. But, before Juliette could act, Amiyah had straddled her, and was kneeling over her lap as though she'd achieved the dominant mount position in an MMA bout. Juliette's hands were on Amiyah's thighs now, holding the young woman away.

"Do you want me to stop?"

"No. It's just, you gotta understand, this is all a little weird for me."

"But, surely you can get a real good look at me from here, sugar."

The cords of Amiyah's braided hair hung about Juliette's face. She was reminded of the way Amiyah smelled: vanilla or cinnamon, something evocative of a body lotion or moisturizer, but with faint, foreboding undertones of cigarette smoke, making her seem like some kind of a poisonous flower, beautiful to behold but dangerous to touch or to consume.

"It's one thing to look at me, Jules, but don't you want to see how I feel? You can put your hands anywhere you like."

"Okay I'm tapping out," Juliette said. "Maybe I should go back over in the armchair for now."

"But I just wanna stay here and be close to you for a while. I haven't been held by anyone in so long. Is it okay with you if we just stay here a little while and talk? Just like this, with our bodies close together?"

"I guess, if that's what you want," Juliette replied, unsure of where she should place her hands on the body of the young woman who was kneeling over her lap.

"Does it feel okay, being this close to another girl," Amiyah whispered into Juliette's ear. "Do you like it?"

Juliette shrugged, uncertain of the answer herself.

"Because any time you want me to stop, just say so, and —"

" —Just keep going, okay?" Juliette said, closing her eyes as tightly as she could. "I don't know what the hell is happening right now, but I guess we're gonna find out, aren't we?"

Amiyah laughed at her older companion's discomfort. "Well, okay then, but can I see your body now, Jules? Why don't you take your shirt off for a while?"

"My shirt?" Juliette replied, forcing a laugh. "But, I don't have anything on underneath."

"That really doesn't bother me at all." Amiyah tugged at the hem of the older woman's shirt, lifting the garment up over her head and discarding it on the bed. Amiyah pulled Juliette's naked torso to her own and Juliette felt—against her own skin—the soft portions of the young woman's warm flesh that were bulging from between the contrastingly cold straps of her underwear. Their bodies seemed to fit together so naturally, but still, being so close to another woman felt unsettling to Juliette, as though she was trying to hold the opposing sides of two great magnets together and the whole time there was some unseen force, an invisible boundary between them that was injecting doubt and confusion into Juliette's thoughts. Time seemed to pass at a torturously slow pace. Juliette wanted desperately to separate, but was too afraid of her own nakedness to let go. In the midst of her confusion, she felt the young woman fumbling an arm down in-between their interlocked bodies.

Amiyah moved her face among the wisps of Juliette's hair and began to breathe into her ear. "Does it bother you, if I, you know?" she said, flashing her eyes in a downward direction.

Juliette glanced down in the half-light to see Amiyah was holding onto her own crotch, running her fingers over the shiny surface of her underwear. "Oh, right, well no, I mean, I guess not," Juliette said, more than a little startled by the young woman's actions.

Amiyah released herself from the embrace and sat back over Juliette's thighs to admire her exposed torso. Juliette's modest breasts— little more than domed pectoral muscles—sat firm and taught upon her chest. Amiyah raised a hand to her mouth, gathered a small amount of saliva on her fingertips, and then, unabashed, reached down into her underwear and began to work her fingers back and forth. She looked deep into Juliette's eyes for a while and then at her naked chest as she continued to pleasure herself. Her breaths became stuttered and irregular, almost a whimper. Juliette held her arms over her chest, unsure of how her aging body would appear to the younger woman.

"Don't be shy," Amiyah breathed, "you look amazing."

"You sure about that?"

"I'm serious."

Juliette dropped her arms to her sides and shook her head at the ridiculousness of it all.

Amiyah leaned further forward. "I want to kiss you so bad," she whispered.

The words hit Juliette like ice against her spine. Amiyah brought her hand close to Juliette's face. She could see the wetness glistening over the young woman's fingertips, could smell the familiar, tangy scent of female sex on the air.

Amiyah closed her eyes and plunged her fingers into her own mouth, either to taste herself, to gather more saliva, or both. She loosened a zipper on the front of her underwear and slid her hand back inside. Her mouth hovered over Juliette's. "Do you want to kiss me?" she asked.

Juliette could smell the scent of sex on Amiyah's lips now, could almost taste it. Her head was foggy, as though the fumes of an intoxicant were flavoring the atmosphere. She felt the warmth of Amiyah's body against her own. The rainfall was pattering against the window. The white noise drowned out all distractions, forcing Juliette to succumb to the young woman's seduction.

"Kiss me, please," Amiyah begged, her lips brushing against Juliette's. "Undo me," she said, and she twisted her upper body and swept her braids aside to present Juliette with the buckles of her harness-like bra. "Come on, I want to show you."

Juliette hesitated but was spurred on by the distant glimmer of rejection in Amiyah's eyes. She unfastened the straps in several places and Amiyah pulled the lingerie away from her body. Her breasts — without the support of the bra — were only marginally larger then Juliette's, although their shape was more classically feminine, pointed and streamlined. Amiyah leaned forward so the tips of her nipples skimmed over Juliette's pale skin. Juliette shivered and exhaled stammered breaths. It felt so wrong and forbidden.

Amiyah took hold of Juliette's wrist and guided her hand downward until her palm found its way onto the surface of Amiyah's underwear. Juliette could feel the movement of the young woman's fingers through the smooth, rubberized fabric.

"Fuck me, please," Amiyah said in one short exhalation.

Juliette couldn't be sure if she was aiding the movement of Amiyah's fingers, or if she was just a passive bystander, baring witness to the young woman pleasuring herself. Juliette's fingers read — like brail — the frantic rhythm of Amiyah's masturbation. Fluctuations of pace and pressure told of the varying degrees of ecstasy she was inflicting upon herself. Juliette looked down at Amiyah's pointed breasts vibrating with every jolt of her arm. Amiyah's eyes were closed, her mouth open, her facial expression indistinguishable from agony and ecstasy.

Juliette felt strangely privileged, honored to be witnessing such a deeply personal act. She watched Amiyah's plump lips, noticing the way they shifted constantly like the subtle, ever-changing flickers of a flame, a flame fueled by euphoria. Juliette wanted to place her lips against Amiyah's, to read with her own mouth, the pleasure the young woman was experiencing, the same way Juliette was reading it with her fingers. She leaned toward Amiyah, feeling as though she was about to leap from the edge of some great precipice. Juliette closed her eyes and halted her breathing, but as her mouth arrived a hair's width from its target, Amiyah exhaled a few words. "I'm gonna come," she whispered in a single breath, forcing her crotch against Juliette's hand. Amiyah's body shook and convulsed. Her eyes tightened and her body solidified, as if the pleasure was so intense she was trying to fight against it.

Juliette was unsure of how to react in such an alien situation. She found herself placing a kiss on the young woman's forehead to comfort her through the ordeal. Eventually, Amiyah's body slackened and her head came to rest on Juliette's shoulder. She was breathing heavily now, recovering from the exertion of it all. As Juliette held her young companion's trembling body to her own, she felt a strange glow somewhere deep inside, as if the intimacy they'd shared must have created a bond between them. It hadn't exactly been full sex, but surely it must have meant something. She knew they'd crossed the boundary of mere friendship alone and had moved onto something else, something she didn't quite understand. Juliette was at least certain she felt connected to Amiyah, in a way she hadn't been connected to anyone for a long time. She smiled inwardly, her fingertips trailing across the young woman's skin in the half-light.

"It's such a shame you're not gay," Amiyah said.

The comment instantly deflated Juliette's swell of inner happiness. The words sounded so dismissive, implying Juliette had played no part. "Yeah, right, I guess," she replied, with a sort of awkward laugh.

Amiyah slipped away, lying flat on the bed with one arm covering her chest. She fastened her zipper back into place, drawing a line under any notion of intimacy, highlighting the fact the pair really were just friends after all. "The things I would have done to you," she said, gazing up at the ceiling as though her mind was running wild. "You don't even want to know, trust me."

Juliette pulled her shirt back on, suddenly feeling cold and exposed in the midst of her confusion about whatever it was that had just happened.

"Don't you wanna lie down for a while?" Amiyah asked. "Do you ever loosen up? Or are you like this with everyone?"

Juliette tried to act casually. She stretched out on the bed with her back against the mattress. As soon as she was horizontal, the young woman moved in, resting her head on Juliette's chest as though it was the most natural thing to do. Juliette's body stiffened again. She tried to relax, but the closeness was unsettling, even after everything that had just occurred between them.

Amiyah's breathing was slow and heavy. Her body twitched in places as it began to shut down. Juliette cleared a few of Amiyah's braids from her face, eager to observe her at rest. She felt her nerves fire up as she considered the implications of harboring the desire to look at Amiyah in this way. And then, without even thinking, she leaned in and kissed the young woman among the plaits of her hair. Maybe she did it just to see how it would feel, to see if she could make any sense of all this, to be absolutely sure she wouldn't feel anything as her nostrils were filled with the scent of whatever sweet-smelling products the young woman used on her hair. She breathed in long and hard, attempting to inhale as much as she could.

Juliette's head fell back onto the pillow. She sighed with frustration as she tried to untangle her emotions. She was struggling to focus her thoughts, sedated by the warmth of another body, drained of energy by the bizarre situation she'd found herself in. As she faded from consciousness, her mind was flooded with surreal dream-like visions, her brother and daughter walking further and further away from her until they disappeared into complete darkness, driven away into oblivion by Juliette's betrayal of them.

It felt like only seconds had passed when Juliette awoke with a startle. The mattress was moving beneath her, jostled by her companion spinning off the bed and onto her feet in one swift motion. "What's wrong?" Juliette asked. "Where are you going?"

"I gotta get back to work," Amiyah said, snatching up her belongings from all over the room. The bobbing points of her bee-sting breasts added an air of comedy to her frantic movements.

"Why, what's the hurry?"

"If I'm late, Caesar won't let me dance for a week. That means I don't earn any money and that means I can't afford to pay off my debt to him."

"What debt?"

"It's complicated," Amiyah replied, swinging her fur coat on over her naked torso.

Juliette got up on her elbows. "Do you really want to go back to that place? Surely there's gotta be another job out there for you, kid."

"Caesar and I have a deal. The type I can't get out of all that easily, you know?"

"Yeah, well, we'll see about that."

"Oh, and what are you gonna do, sugar? Come riding in there on a horse and save me?"

"Me and Caesar go way back. I'll talk to him."

Amiyah checked her hair in a mirror that was propped up on the dresser. "Whatever you say, Jules. It's not quite that simple, I'm afraid. But look, I gotta go. Just shut the door behind you and it will lock itself. I'll see you around, okay?"

"Hey, Amiyah," Juliette called out.

"What, Jules? I'm kind of in a hurry."

"I just wanted to say, I guess I kind of had a good time tonight. That's all."

Amiyah stood in the open doorway with the rain beating down behind her. She looked like some kind of superhero up on her tall heels, her muscular legs extending into the tousles of her coat, her face painted a somber shade of gray by the moonlight. She raised a hand to her lips, blew a kiss, and disappeared into the night.

135

CHAPTER 10

Residents occupying the upper levels of Juliette's apartment block were required — throughout the nocturnal hours — to employ a specific technique when passing through any of the gated entrances that secured each of the building's external stairwells. Juliette had been awoken on countless occasions by one of the various wrought iron gates swinging on its unoiled hinges, its metallic shriek echoing through the night air like the cry of a wild animal. Juliette took hold of the gate at the base of her stairwell and guided it to a gentle close, knowing only too well how the rusted thing loved to slam itself shut, sending vibrations throughout the entire building to let everybody know of her arrival. She had no desire to give any of her neighbors cause to complain, but even more foreboding than that prospect was the idea she might rouse her slumbering daughter and find herself suffering the teenager's relentless inquisition.

Juliette was still trying to come to terms with whatever it was that had just taken place between herself and Amiyah. Her thoughts were still decorated with the dimly-lit interior of that little motel room. With every breath she took she could taste the vanilla-infused scent of Amiyah's skin and she was forced to recall the unsettling, intoxicating warmth of the whole encounter. Juliette could ruminate over her emotions all she wanted, but she was unable to deny the strange buzz of optimism that had taken hold of her. It was a feeling she was barely acquainted with, a type of positivity she'd only known previously from gaining victories over opponents, or from scoring a rare scrap of praise from her brother. And now, in her current enthralled state, she didn't want to give anybody the opportunity to dampen her mood.

As Juliette climbed the steel-grate staircase, she trod cautiously at the outer edge of each step, avoiding the unsupported center-points so her feet wouldn't drum out the rhythm of her ascent. Entering her apartment, she handled the front door with a similar level of expertise, skillfully lifting the hardwood slab of a door just a tiny amount as she eased it back in into its ill-fitting frame. Juliette moved slowly into her open-plan lounge, paying close attention to every noise among the darkness: the hum of the aging fridge, water dripping from the loose kitchen faucet, the steady ticking of a clock on the wall. In the still of night, even the rustle of her satin jacket was amplified to sound like the abrasive grating of glass-paper. She twisted her key in the lock and the remainder of the bunch tumbled over itself, clattering and jangling as though she'd just unfurled a giant steel chain. "Fuck," she whispered through gritted teeth, her whole body seizing up as she listened for movement. Then, just as she released her breath and turned to make her way across the lounge, she heard the heart-stopping squeak of the springs in her old couch informing her of Shelby's location in the unlit room.

"Did you have a good time?" Shelby's half-awake voice croaked out from the darkness.

"Why aren't you in bed?" Juliette asked, flicking a light switch, the illumination causing Shelby to squint and grimace through her spectacles.

"Well, come on then, how was your date?" Shelby persisted.

"Don't be smart. When was the last time I ever went on a date?" Juliette sat down at the far end of the old couch, the surface of which was strewn with a fleece blanket to cover up the patches of upholstery that were either faded, stained, or worn down to the point of being threadbare. As Juliette pulled off her leather boots, Shelby was upon her in seconds, climbing behind her on the couch. The teenager wrapped her pajama encased legs around Juliette's body, and threaded her nimble arms around Juliette's neck.

"So, where exactly did you go wearing your tightest jeans and the cologne I brought you for your birthday?" Shelby moved in and kissed her mother on the neck. She paused there for a while and inhaled, as if hoping to pick up some scent that would give her an idea of what her mother had been up to.

"I told you it was a work thing, didn't I?" Juliette said, shrugging to unleash herself from her daughter.

"The thing I find strange," Shelby whispered right into Juliette's ear, "is the fact Uncle Earl told me he didn't know absolutely anything about this so-called 'work thing' you keep talking about." Her menacing words were juxtaposed with the comforting sensation of her face nestling into Juliette's hair. "Don't you think that's strange?" Shelby asked.

"And why would you have been talking to Uncle Earl about it?"

"He rang to speak to you," Shelby said, her tone indicating she was confident of having her mother in checkmate.

Juliette shot up from the couch. "What is it with you two?" she said. "Both of you always talking about how you want me to quit fighting. But the second I try to do something about it, you won't even give me so much as an inch of space to work it out." She came down with a thump into an adjacent armchair, and sank back into the lifeless cushions beneath her.

Shelby followed her like a relentless cat demanding attention from its owner. It almost seemed like Shelby was staking claim to her mother's affections, as though she had some vague intuition that Juliette's attention was focused elsewhere, toward some other person. The teenager climbed onto her mother and knelt over her lap in the creaking armchair.

Juliette sank further into the cushioning, uncomfortable with the close contact after all she'd just been through. "Do you have to interfere in absolutely everything I do?"

Shelby sat up tall and tied her sleep-tangled hair into a ponytail, holding her spine rigid the whole time with the type of upright posture only achievable by somebody trained in the art of ballet.

Juliette knew that Shelby was stretching out her lithe little body in an exaggerated manner for attention, but as always, Juliette was unable to resist the teenager's manipulation. The sight of her daughter posing with such effortless grace could appease even the most turbulent of Juliette's rages. "Look, you're just gonna have to trust me on this, okay, Doll?"

Shelby came down to rest her head on her mother's shoulder. "So what is it then?" she asked solemnly. "You got a new job or something? Come on, Mom, we always tell each other everything, don't we?"

"I wouldn't exactly call it a job. It's just, I guess I've kinda been training somebody, one on one. Like a coach, you know?"

"So that's it? You're gonna start coaching now?" Shelby's tired eyes widened with intrigue. "And who is he then, this guy you've been training?"

"It's, well, it's a girl, actually," Juliette explained reluctantly. "And tonight, I went to the shitty little bar she works at on the other side of town to see if we could figure things out, away from Uncle Earl. You know how he has to interfere with everything I do."

"Then why all the sneaking around if that's all you're doing? Why do you have to be so secretive about everything?" Shelby looked directly into Juliette's eyes, preparing to pass judgment on her mother's response.

"In case it didn't work out, I guess," Juliette shrugged, feigning innocence.

"And, has it? Worked out?"

"I'm working on it. So you're gonna have to give me a chance to do this my way. But let me tell you, Doll, I'm determined to make a go of this for us. For our future. No matter what it takes, I'm gonna see this thing through. I'm not gonna mess this opportunity up, okay?"

"I'm just happy you're not gonna be fighting anymore," Shelby said, and she slid a hand behind her mother's neck and placed a kissed upon her lips.

Juliette sat back into the armchair, closed her eyes and allowed Shelby's body to merge into her own. As soon as everything was okay between them, Juliette felt an unburdening, as though the pressure to work through her feelings toward Amiyah had been relieved somewhat, even if only for a little while.

***

Juliette had been craning her neck to study the clock mounted high on the wall of the gymnasium so regularly throughout her morning warm-up, she feared her teammates may have noticed her distraction. She'd met Earl's watchful gaze from across the mats on several occasions as he conversed with the other attendees of the early workout session. Juliette was certain her brother would be able to read the extent of her woes, thus enabling him to calculate much of what had occurred the previous evening.

It was Tommy who first dared to pose the obvious question, his eyes narrowed into an apprehensive squint, his voice marred with nerves. "Is Amiyah coming in today, or...?" he asked, standing over Juliette as she sat at the edge of the mats, pulling her upper body down toward her outstretched legs.

"I guess we'll see," Juliette replied. "I'm not doing this Earl's way, not planning on being too military with the kid, you know?"

Tommy's query seemed to draw the attention of everybody close enough to hear him speak. The question had been hanging in the air of the gym for the entire morning, with all of the athletes wondering the same thing like they shared a kind of collective consciousness. Juliette noticed the eyes of the other fighters shifting away from her as soon as she looked in their direction. The fighters went back to whatever they'd been doing before Tommy had asked his question, pretending they hadn't been eager to hear Juliette's response. They all knew exactly how much was at stake, that Juliette's retirement from fighting was dependent on the success of this particular venture. The team of martial artists who operated out of Diablo MMA were a closely-knit community, a warrior tribe with a hierarchy or pecking order based upon their individual levels of skill and experience. Juliette sat right at the top of this power structure alongside her brother, Earl, a position which afforded her a certain level of respect and admiration from those beneath her.

The truth was, Juliette didn't know the answer to Tommy's question herself. She had no idea whether Amiyah would be attending the session or not. Her thoughts were riddled with uncertainty, as though she'd been discarded after a one-night stand. She wondered if Amiyah had gotten everything she wanted from their relationship during their rendezvous the previous evening. Maybe Juliette's unwillingness to fully participate had left the young woman feeling exasperated, believing their relationship had ultimately been taken as far as it could go.

Juliette sensed her brother approaching. His unmistakably heavy footsteps sent little tremors reverberating through the surface of the mats, alerting her to his presence. "Strictly cardio for you today, Jules," he said in passing. "Way too soon for you to be sparring. You can come and watch these kids going at it with me. Give us your two cents worth. We'll make a coach out of you yet. Amiyah or no Amiyah." He shot his sister a wink of encouragement, telling her it was okay to be struggling with her student at such an early stage of proceedings.

Juliette was reminded of what a masterful leader Earl was, the way he could relieve the tension in the atmosphere with one simple comment, how effortlessly he could lift the morale of his students. His reassuring gesture filled Juliette with a glow of gratitude, a brief moment of respite from the pressure she'd mounted upon herself.

With each day that passed, Juliette studied her reflection in the mirror, watching as the mask of bruising faded from around her eyes. When the time came, she clipped the stitches from her brow and plucked the thread from her skin as if the medical procedure was a standard part of her daily skin-care routine. The discolored flesh of her face slowly turned from a dark and angry purple to a subtle flush of red that was barely distinguishable from the rest of her pale skin tone. She took note of the days flicking over on the clock in the gym until an entire week had passed and still there was no sign of Amiyah. It wasn't until the eighth day that things finally came to a head and Juliette was, at last, able to muster the strength to pull herself from the abyss of self-doubt she'd been wallowing in.

At around lunchtime, exhausted both from her workout and by the knot of anxiety that was tangled up in her stomach, Juliette decided to exit the gym for a brief intermission away from the endless groans of exertion, the relentless thumping of bodies crashing against mats, the ceaseless drone of her brother barking out his instructions. She settled down on the bench just beyond the entrance lobby, closed her eyes and tilted her head back to bathe her face in the soothing warmth of the midday sun. Just as she began to enjoy the sensation of the breeze against the exposed skin of her arms and shoulders, the tranquility of her solitude was interrupted by the growl of an approaching vehicle. The sound of loose tarmac crunching beneath tires gave a vague indication of the automobile's vast scale. She opened her eyes, and her fears were confirmed as she caught sight of a bulbous white SUV bounding into the parking lot like an overexcited dog. Margot sat up tall in the driver's seat, her upper body leaning close to the windshield as though it took a great deal of effort and concentration for her to pilot the ungainly vehicle. Margot's head swung about and her mouth gaped open as she wailed along to the muffled country music emanating from the SUV's interior.

"What the hell is she so happy about all of a sudden?" Juliette mumbled under her breath.

The door to the SUV swung open and Margot climbed down from the driver's seat clad in high heels, close-fitting jeans, and a silk blouse. She had a little scarf tied around her neck like something out of the 1950s, and her coppery hair was, as always, impeccably styled into loose waves which tumbled around her shoulders. Whenever Margot came to see Earl at work, Juliette was put in mind of a convict's wife donning her most flattering outfit to visit her husband in jail. Juliette had wondered previously if it was Earl—hoping to impress his younger teammates—who insisted Margot should make such an effort with her appearance. Upon further consideration, Juliette decided it would have most likely been Margot herself who opted to dress this way, probably in an effort to highlight Juliette's own sartorial inadequacies. Margot reached back into her car and gathered up a tall paper cup of coffee.

"That's a lot of waking up you've got in that cup right there," Juliette said. "You planning on hitting the gym with us or what?"

"Well, it's very important to stay hydrated," Margot replied, implying Juliette—the professional martial artist—knew nothing about health and fitness.

"Caffeine's a diuretic, actually," Juliette said, refusing to be outdone.

"Oh, don't be silly, there's no caffeine in this, sweetie," Margot said. "I can't be drinking too much of that at the moment." She patted at her stomach and then blushed slightly as though she'd revealed a little too much information about some medical condition she was suffering from.

"Why on earth wouldn't you be able to drink caffeine all of a sudden?"

Margot flailed a hand dismissively "Oh, never mind," she said. "And where's that husband of mine, anyway?" she asked, quickly changing the subject.

"He's inside," Juliette said with a nod toward the gym. "I'll take you through." Margot followed Juliette through the glass-walled entrance lobby into the main body of the gym. "Careful not to step on the mats in those heels," Juliette said.

"I think I get that by now, thank you," Margot replied. The other fighters paused and nodded to greet Margot as she passed. Margot flashed them coy smiles in return, reveling in the attention she was receiving. The piercing, floral scent of her perfume wafted throughout the open-plan space, an alien aroma in the sweaty, testosterone-filled gym. "Now then, Juliette," Margot said, "I must ask, where is this brilliant new student of yours? I'm absolutely dying to meet her. Earl tells me you're thinking about retiring from fighting altogether." Margot raised her voice a little, fully aware of her growing audience. "And I must say, I think that's tremendous news." The activity in the gym seemed to have ground to a halt, punching bags swung to a standstill on their chains and the shuffle of feet over mats died down almost to complete silence. "So where is she?" Margot asked, glancing around in an exaggerated manner. "Don't tell me you've scared her off already?"

Juliette's heart was beating rapidly within her chest. She wasn't sure if this was due to her nerves or a mounting fury at being cast into the spotlight by her sister-in-law. The skin of her face tingled both hot and cold all at once. She felt the eyes of every other gym-goer upon her. She couldn't process her thoughts to answer calmly while struggling with a rage like this inside herself. She could have just as easily thrown a swift uppercut straight into Margot's porcelain smile. As Juliette contemplated the fragility of her sister-in-law's jawbone, a door halfway along the side wall of the gymnasium was thrown open.

"Amiyah's not in today, sweet-cheeks," Earl said, clambering over a pile of dismantled exercise equipment as he emerged from the depths of a storeroom. "We're breaking her in gradually," he said. "She's a little untamed, shall we say? Isn't that right, Jules?"

"I guess," Juliette confirmed, inwardly cursing herself for the fact she had to be rescued like a child by her brother.

Earl flashed his eyes around the gym and everybody went back to work. "Jules hasn't quite got the hang of this whole coaching thing yet, have you, Sis? You can't seem to get your head around the idea that in order to coach somebody, you've actually gotta get them to come to the gym in the first place." Earl shook his head, laughing to himself the way parents laugh at the infantile behavior of their children.

Margot bit down on her bottom lip to contain her amusement. "I'm sure you'll get the hang of it eventually, won't you, sweetie?"

Juliette felt their derision sweeping over her in waves, filling her with a burn of embarrassment and shame. Their eyes—narrowed with contempt—seemed to look at Juliette as though she was a small, insignificant, and troublesome little girl who couldn't help but wet herself repeatedly, when she was far too old to be doing such a thing. They looked at her for a while, smirking and grinning, and then, without any form of a goodbye or parting gesture, they turned on the spot and left, continuing with their conversation as if Juliette had never been included in it to begin with.

"Don't worry, sweetie," Margot said to Earl, clinging to his side as they departed. "Try and remember, not everybody's a natural at this the way you are."

Earl turned back and glanced over his shoulder. "Oh, and, Jules," he said, "if you want to make yourself useful, I just dug out the mop and bucket. The men's locker room could do with a once-over, whenever you get a minute."

Juliette opened her mouth to protest, but in the absence of her student, she couldn't find any valid reason to suggest she should be doing anything to the contrary.

"Let's take this in my office?" Earl said to his wife.

Juliette stood and watched as the pair of them climbed a staircase to a small mezzanine level situated above the locker rooms. Earl glanced back toward his sister a final time before entering his office at the top of the stairs. As Juliette looked into her brother's eyes—his pupils darkened by his heavy brow—she could read everything he felt toward her, the disappointment that had been cast into him by her pathetic attempts at coaching Amiyah, the sheer level of his disapproval, almost as though he pitied her. And then, Earl closed the door, locking both himself and his wife into their own private world, a world in which Juliette played no part. She was instantly reminded she wasn't the most important person in her brother's life anymore, and apart from her daughter, she had no important person of her own. She stood at the center-point of the gym, on a walkway that ran between the cardio equipment and the matted area. Although there was activity all around her, people conversing and interacting with one another, Juliette suddenly came to realize she didn't have a deep or personal relationship with any single individual on her team. Regardless of the large number of bodies scattered about the place, Juliette felt totally isolated, as though she might as well have been among a crowd of complete strangers. She longed for a human connection; she felt a pang of hunger for it deep inside.

Juliette's eyes were drawn to a little hatch-like window positioned high up on the wall, a pane of glass nestled inconspicuously among an endless collage of promotional posters and fight memorabilia. On the other side of the window was the interior space of Earl's office. The little hatch was a kind of observation point from which Earl could monitor the entire floor space of the gymnasium, from the double-doored entrance at one end to the caged enclosure set up at the other. Juliette could see—through the window—that Earl was gesticulating wildly, and that he was especially animated in his conversation with his wife. Margot was bobbing up and down on her toes, her hands gleefully clutched together at her chest. Juliette wondered what piece of news or good fortune the pair could possibly be discussing in this exuberant manner. The fact she hadn't been informed left her feeling excluded, like

146

an unworthy child who was far too immature and unimportant to be consulted on the kind of matters adults concerned themselves with.

Juliette hurried into the women's locker room and came down on her knees before a wooden bench where her duffel bag sat slumped in a heap, looking old and weary from its countless years of loyal service. She unzipped her bag and rummaged through her clothing until she located her cell phone. She tapped at the screen of her phone and scrolled through a list of names until she arrived at Amiyah's contact details. Her index finger hovered over the telephone icon next to the young woman's name. She wanted so badly to make the call, but there was some invisible force holding her back. Her mind was filled with a vision of Amiyah's dark, unflinching eyes and she unwittingly recalled the way it had felt when their unclothed bodies had been pressed together in that little motel room. She slumped back against the wall and slid down onto the floor, her defeated body trembling with frustration. "What the fuck is wrong with you?" she said repeatedly, her eyes glossing over with tears. She brought the end of her cell phone up into her forehead, thumping herself over and over in an effort to relieve some of her mental anguish with a dose of more tangible, physical pain.

As her limbs dropped to the floor with exhaustion, the door before her creaked open and the commotion seeping in from the main portion of the gym grew louder. Juliette scrambled to her feet, her head turning this way and that as she frantically scanned the place for something to busy herself with. A set of tentacle-like fingers crept around the edge of the door and held it ajar. Juliette instantly recognized the bony digits, the dark skin, and the uncertain movements.

"You in there, Jules," Tommy called out from the other side of the door.

"Come on in, kid. It's okay," Juliette replied.

As Tommy eased himself through the narrowly opened door, he kept his eyes tightly closed, seemingly terrified of what he might see.

"You can open your eyes," Juliette said, just about mustering the energy to laugh at the young man's awkward demeanor. "It's just me in here."

Tommy glanced around suspiciously, his lean body rigid with unease.

Juliette sat down on the bench with a slouched posture similar to that of her duffel bag. "So, what's up?" she asked.

"Came to give you this," Tommy said. His hushed voice gave the impression he didn't want anyone else to hear what he had to say. He reached out toward Juliette with his palm facing downward, his hand loosely clenched into a fist, concealing something unseen. Juliette studied the young man's features to gauge his intentions, but his wide eyes — although flashing encouragingly — were somewhat unreadable. He nodded enthusiastically, prompting Juliette to hurry up and accept whatever it was he was offering. Juliette stretched out her open palm so that it hovered beneath Tommy's. She felt him deposit the item into her hand. It was light, almost weightless, and it rustled slightly as Juliette brought it toward herself for inspection. Juliette saw she was holding a small, scrunched-up ball of paper that was creased enough to indicate Tommy had been carrying it around in his pocket for some time. She unfolded the scrap of paper to reveal a few lines of loose handwriting.

"What's it supposed to say?" she asked, squinting at the note.

Tommy sat down on the bench, his long body separated from Juliette's by the duffel bag that was sandwiched between them. "That's where she lives," Tommy said with a quiet but eager tone. "It's just down the road from my momma's place."

"This is Amiyah's address?"

"It's the stripper house," Tommy explained. "I see the girls from Caesar's club going in there all the time. They've got this yappy little dog that's always out in the front yard upsetting the neighbors. Not that I'm trying to interfere, of course," he said, raising his hands defensively. "Thought you might want to know, that's all."

"Well, thanks, I guess. But, I really don't know what's going on

148

anymore. Things don't exactly seem to be working out all that well between us right now, you know? I mean, I'm not even sure if I'm actually cut out for this whole coaching thing."

Tommy toyed with the zipper of Juliette's bag as he struggled to find the confidence to express his thoughts. "Come on, Jules," he said, sounding like he was trying to utilize all the skills he'd learned as an aspiring coach, "surely you can't just quit like that, before you've even got started." He glanced sideways at Juliette, wary of her reaction.

"It ain't that simple, kid," Juliette sighed. "And why do you care so much anyway? You like her or something? Because, let me tell you, I don't exactly think you're her type."

Tommy straightened his face at Juliette's misreading of his intentions. "Just thought she deserved a second chance, that's all."

"There's some pretty messed up stuff going on between us. You probably wouldn't understand."

"Can't be any worse than when Earl first took me under his wing, surely?"

"You mean when he caught you trying to rob this place?"

"Yeah," Tommy replied with a nervous laugh. "I can remember the first time I met Earl like it was yesterday. When he came in and busted me with that bag of money, and he said to me, 'Look, kid, you got two options. You can take off with a couple hundred bucks, or you can come back in the morning and maybe I'll teach you how to fight.' And then look what happened."

"Yeah, you ran off with the cash, didn't you?"

"But, I came straight back with it the next day," Tommy said, eager to correct Juliette.

"Sure, I guess you did."

"And if Earl hadn't given me that second chance, where do you think I'd be right now? Probably dead or locked up like most of my friends are."

Juliette nodded to admit he had a point.

"People think Earl's hard on me, but the thing they gotta realize is, I never really had any kind of a father figure. I've never really had that kind of discipline in my life before."

"Okay, Tommy, I get your point. You're gonna have me all emotional if you keep talking like this."

"And, you can ask my momma if you want. See if she thinks Earl's too hard on me."

"Earl's not as bad as people like to make out, I'll give you that."

"Look, Jules, I don't exactly know the people Amiyah used to run with before she moved here, but I do know of them. And I can tell you, they're bad news. She must have come here for a good reason, if it meant taking her clothes off for a living."

"You know, you're a smart kid," Juliette said. "You got a lot going for you. And even though Earl's tough on you sometimes, you know he thinks of you as family, right?"

"I don't know about all that," Tommy said, hanging his head with embarrassment.

"I mean it, kid. Training you probably helped Earl just as much as it helped you. Whipping you into shape gave him something to focus on. He was about ready to give all this up until he found you, his little sidekick. You really think he'd let any of these other guys help out with cornering me?"

Tommy shrugged, too emotional to answer.

Juliette watched him drying his eyes on his T-shirt, and then pretending to mop perspiration from his forehead to cover up the truth of his actions. "Damn, it's hot in here," Tommy said, just in case Juliette had any doubt over why he was wiping his face.

"Now go on and get out of here before you get me all welled up," Juliette said, landing a playful jab on Tommy's shoulder. "I gotta take a shower before I go. Can't turn up on Amiyah's doorstep looking like this now, can I?"

"I knew you'd come around," Tommy said, with a smile that showed in every muscle of his face.

CHAPTER 11

Juliette lowered the volume of her truck stereo so she could focus on navigating her way through the unfamiliar neighborhood. A mist of cloud cover hung in the air, filtering the glow of the sun, dispersing its light evenly in muted hues across the suburban landscape. The lack of sunlight seemed to further exacerbate the morose, grayscale color palette of the houses at either side of the road. Juliette slowed her truck to a crawl and glanced over her dark glasses, checking the street names on every corner she passed. She noticed the increasing number of houses with plywood boards covering their windows, overgrown yards in which the flora seemed to be taking over, the wild unpruned bushes and trees reclaiming the land, swallowing up the vacant properties that would have once stood dominant over them.

"Damn it," Juliette said, swinging her truck into a sharp turn as she finally matched a street sign to the scrap of paper laid out on her dash. The truck's wheels shrieked against the tarmac until Juliette got the vehicle back under control. She placed a hand on the dash and apologized to her aging steed. "Now, where the hell are you, Amiyah?" she said, narrowing her gaze to survey her surroundings. The road ahead was lined with a procession of tattered little wood-paneled houses, each of them set back from the sidewalk behind a chain-link fence as though the whole neighborhood was locked up in a network of adjoining cages. Suddenly, the buildings on one side of the road gave way to a block's worth of open parkland, a grassy area that was sparsely furnished with a scattering of low-lying trees, a collection of decaying swing sets, and half dismantled play apparatus daubed with illegible graffiti scrawls. Juliette steered around the edge of the park, studying the door numbers of properties through the passenger side window until she pulled up in front of a row of houses directly opposite a fenced off ball court. The snarl of the truck seemed to antagonize a nearby, out of sight dog, causing the incensed beast to bark and howl with ear-piercing ferocity. "Doesn't exactly sound very small to me," Juliette mumbled to herself, remembering Tommy's description of the animal.

Juliette craned her neck to assess her reflection in the rearview mirror. She tightened her ponytail and swept a few stray locks into place over the permanently inflated skin of her cauliflower ears. She pouted her lips, admiring the sight of them now that they'd returned to their usual shape. Finally, she was beginning to resemble something she considered vaguely presentable. As Juliette climbed down from her truck, a basketball was thumping against the ground across the street.

"Hey, *mamacita*, why don't you shut that fucking thing up?" a voice called out from beyond the wire fence of the ball court.

Juliette turned to see a duo of players on the court, a pair of young men with contrasting physiques, one fat, one thin, both with similarly close-shaven heads. In a matter of seconds, Juliette ran her eyes over the two men, quickly assessing the level of threat they posed, both individually and as a pair.

"I got money riding on this game, *chiquita*," the larger of the double act called out. The man looked as though he would struggle to get down to the heavyweight limit if he ever decided to compete as a fighter. His doughy body was draped in a garish team shirt which hung over him like a kaftan. The other, comparatively scrawny young man was bare-chested, his boxer shorts creeping out from the waistband of his jeans, a seamless collage of colorless tattoos covering most of his torso.

Juliette looked the men over, deciding who she would need to take out first if any kind of confrontation were to arise. She considered herself to be something of an expert in the art of unarmed combat, but right now, outnumbered two to one, she wasn't naive enough to believe she was invincible. With this in mind, she reached back into her truck and rummaged under the driver's seat until she felt the cold steel of a wheel wrench. She took out the wrench, tucked its long handle into the waistband of her jeans, and pulled her T-shirt over its head.

"Are you lost, or something?" a female voice called out from the house closest to Juliette's truck. The woman's soft, slow voice was barely audible over the incessant barking of the dog. Juliette was struggling to concentrate through the aural assault, trying to pay attention to the laughter from the ball court so she could be certain the players were still focused on their game and not on her. "Can I help you?" the woman persisted. She was standing out on the porch of the house wearing a floor-length nightdress, gently rocking a crying baby in her arms. Juliette assumed this fair-skinned young woman with a contrastingly Rastafarian hairstyle was most likely another dancer from Caesar's club.

"I'm looking for Amiyah," Juliette answered loudly enough to be heard over the wailing baby and the barking dog. She approached the gate in front of the house and saw there were a number of wood panels fixed to the inside of the chain-link fence, probably to keep the dog from seeing anything on the sidewalk that would set it off. The crazed animal was a few feet from the fence, straining at the full extension of a long chain that was anchored somewhere around the steps of the house. The stout, muscular beast appeared to be of the pit bull breed or similar, its loosely-striped, brindle coat closely resembling the fur of some exotic wildcat.

"What's that you say?" the dreadlocked woman asked calmly over the screaming baby, the barking dog, and the bouncing ball, seemingly immune to all of the chaos around her.

"I said, is Amiyah there?" Juliette asked a second time, barely able to conceal the aggravation in her voice.

The woman shrugged and frowned excessively enough to imply she had no idea who Juliette was referring to. And then, with her flowing nightdress concealing her feet, she glided across the porch with her baby in her arms until she disappeared into the house and shuttered the door closed behind her.

Juliette noticed a distinct change in the rhythm of the ball beating against the hard surface of the court. There were three loud and very separate bounces, each one getting closer until Juliette saw the basketball roll up against the fence of the house. Her heart rate increased as she watched the ball come to a standstill by her feet. She looked back at the wire fence surrounding the court and quickly realized the structure was far too tall for the ball to have escaped accidentally. The two contrastingly-built ball-players were right up against the fence like a pair of caged animals desperate to escape. Juliette lifted the ball above her head and hurled it back with all of her strength, aware that a half-hearted throw would make her appear weak and vulnerable.

"*Órale*, you got some crazy skills, lady," the fat man said as the ball scaled the fence and landed in the center of the court. "You wanna come play with us, or what?"

The thin man began to bark and growl along with the dog, throwing his head back and howling wildly into the sky. He pressed his heavily-inked torso against the fence, opened his mouth wide, and poked his tongue through the wires, growling and panting until saliva spilled from his mouth and trailed from his chin. A chill ran through Juliette as she watched the man's unsettling behavior.

The fat man took his thinner companion by the shoulders and attempted to pry him away from the fence. "Relax, *cabrón*," he said, "let's play some ball."

All the while, the dog was getting more and more incensed by the commotion, barking and yanking on its chain, sounding as though it might break free at any second.

"Hey, get out of here, dumb and dumber," another voice called out from the direction of the house. Juliette turned to see Amiyah coming down from the porch wearing a silk kimono robe, with her hair tied up in a loose knot on top of her head. "Why don't you two mind your own damn business?" Amiyah said to the men on the court. "Or maybe I'll let Angel here off his chain, and then we'll get to see just how fast the pair of you can run."

"Why don't you take that robe off for us, *mujerzuela*?" the fat man replied. "I got some dollar bills here for you."

"I'll be at The Tunnel all night if you got the balls," Amiyah said. "I'll be waiting."

"*No hay bronca*," the fat man replied, followed by, "No problem," just to clarify the meaning of the phrase.

The thin man continued to pant like a dog, a thick column of drool hanging from his bottom lip and spilling onto his chest.

"Sorry about the neighbors, sugar," Amiyah said, arriving just beyond the chain-link fence surrounding the yard.

The way in which Amiyah's blood-red kimono clung to her upper body aggravated Juliette and prompted her to avert her gaze. The silken fabric—embossed by the tips of the young woman's nipples—forced Juliette to recall everything she'd witnessed during their last encounter at The Paradise Gardens.

"Shush now, Angel. That's a good boy," Amiyah said, her palm gliding over the dog's head.

Juliette watched the gentle sweeping motion of Amiyah's hand and a flurry of heat passed through her stomach. "Why's he have a girl's name, anyway?" she asked.

"You think animals conform to the same gender stereotypes as humans do?"

"I guess I never really gave it that much thought."

"If you wanna come in here and tell him he's got a girl's name, then by all means, be my guest. Besides, that's exactly what he is, our guardian angel, aren't you, boy?" Amiyah crouched to pet the dog and ruffle the loose flesh behind his ears. The scarlet kimono crept further up her thighs as she lowered herself toward the ground.

Juliette closed her eyes and took a deep breath. "So, where have you been anyway?" she asked, folding her arms across her chest. "It's been over a week."

"Is that really any way to greet me after all this time?" Amiyah asked in return. "Whatever happened to absence makes the heart grow fonder?" She stepped closer to the fence and stretched her arms out to offer a welcoming embrace.

Juliette glanced over each shoulder to see if anybody was watching. It was an involuntary response to Amiyah's actions, one Juliette was barely even conscious of. Her eyes were drawn to the triangle of flesh that was exposed by the plunging neckline of Amiyah's robe. She shuffled toward the fence and into the young woman's open arms, unwittingly entranced by all she could see.

Amiyah pulled Juliette closer until they were cheek to cheek. "I've really missed you, sugar," she whispered, her lips hovering against the side of Juliette's face and then skimming further down toward her neck.

Juliette tapped on Amiyah's back to submit from the embrace. "Alright, come on now," she said, "that's enough."

"I'm just glad to see you, that's all," Amiyah said as they separated from one another. "So, how did you know where to find me, anyway?"

"Word gets around, I guess," Juliette replied. "Couldn't get you on the phone, so thought I'd better come on down here to see if you were still interested in training with us."

"Why the dramatics?" Amiyah asked. "It's only been like a week, hasn't it?"

"Well, I kind of think it's gonna take more than one session a week if you wanna be serious about all of this."

"Maybe I've been a little busy, you know? I do work all night, straight up hustling for hours, crawling around up on that stage. You think it's easy for me to get out of bed after that, come all the way over to the gym, bust my ass training, and then come back here and get myself ready to go to work all over again? Because let me tell you, Jules, it's really not all that easy."

Juliette kicked at the dusty sidewalk beneath her feet, looking like a child who'd just received something of a telling off. "Well, you're awake now aren't you?" she said. "Unless you wanna stay here and listen to that baby crying all day."

Amiyah sighed a long breath and rolled her eyes. "So, what's it worth?" she said. "You see, if you want me to come all the way over to the gym as soon as I get out of bed, I'm afraid you're gonna have to make it worth my while."

Juliette realized she was going to have to bargain hard to get her own way, but she couldn't bear to go back and face her brother empty-handed. "Look, no promises, okay," she began, "but how about if you come train with me this afternoon, and if things go well, then maybe, and I do mean maybe, we could think about hanging out for a while afterwards."

Amiyah's freckled cheeks twitched and quivered enough to indicate she was trying to stop her enthusiasm from showing on her face.

"So, do we have a deal?" Juliette said, offering her open palm to seal the agreement.

"I suppose so," Amiyah said, feigning disinterest as she took up Juliette's hand to shake on the matter.

"Remember, I said no promises, okay?"

"Whatever," Amiyah said. "Just give me ten minutes to get dressed, will you? You wanna come inside, or what?"

Juliette glanced at the dog at Amiyah's side, his panting mouth hanging open in what looked like a wide smile, a column of drool dangling from either side of his jaws. "I think I'll wait in the truck, thanks."

"Suit yourself," Amiyah replied. And with that, she blew a kiss in Juliette's direction and turned back toward the house.

***

As Juliette sat in her truck waiting for Amiyah to reemerge, she glanced at the dull, colorless exterior of the house and wondered if somebody had actually chosen to paint it such a muddy shade of gray or if the wood had faded this way through a general lack of maintenance. She noticed the paint flaking from the clapboards, dark grime obscuring the windows, patches of green moss over the asphalt roof. "Nice to see Caesar's taking care of his girls," she said, shaking her head and laughing incredulously until something else drew her attention, causing her to sit up tall and alert. The basketball was bouncing in her direction again, thumping against the road until it ricocheted about under the truck. Juliette adjusted the rearview mirror so she was able to see the basketball court without rotating her head. She thought about exiting the vehicle to retrieve the ball, but decided to stay in her seat when she saw — in her rearview mirror — the duo of players were already outside the confines of the wire fence looking like a pair of wild animals who had somehow managed to escape their cage. Juliette watched the heavier-built of the two men leading the way, the slimmer, bare-chested man following a few steps behind. She wondered why it would possibly require two people to retrieve a ball, a ball that should never have made its way out of the court in the first place. She ran her hand over the head of the wrench that was still tucked in the waistband of her jeans. The cold steel of its handle was a reassuring presence against the inside of her thigh.

Seconds later, the fatter of the two men was right up beside the truck, his wide torso — clad in a bright sports shirt — filling most of the passenger side window. He knocked at the glass with a gold ring that was squeezed over his little finger, and then he bent over so that his oversized head was neatly framed within the bounds of the window. Juliette looked into the man's doughy face. His features appeared disproportionately small, lost among the vast expanse of his shaven head. He made a loose, circling motion with his hand, and Juliette leant over to wind the window lever, lowering the glass just enough to hear the man's voice.

"Excuse me, *señorita*," the fat man said with an exaggerated smile forced onto his narrow slit of a mouth. "I was wondering if it would be okay for *mi hermanito* over here to take a look underneath your truck for our ball?"

Juliette surveyed each of the men, suspicious of their intentions. The fat man continued to peer in through the window, his face straining to hold his smile in place, channels of sweat running from his temples. The thinner man—who up until this point had only communicated via the language of barking—lingered awkwardly in the background, glancing over each shoulder in turn as though it was his duty to stand watch. Juliette's mind raced as she tried to figure out their plan so she would be ready to counteract. She glanced at the bunch of keys hanging from the ignition, and at the door handles pushed inward to the lock position. She knew if her old truck cooperated, she would be able to put her foot down and get out of there in seconds.

"Well, *señorita*, can we get our ball back, or not?" the fat man asked again, his discolored teeth showing through his fraudulent smile.

"Help yourself," Juliette replied with a shrug.

"*Muchas gracias*," the fat man said. He signaled to his companion with a nod and the thinner man hurried to the rear end of the truck.

Juliette struggled to pay attention to the movements of both individuals. The fat man kept his eyes on Juliette the whole time as if he were trying to distract her, his face tightening further as his demented smile intensified. "Can I help you with something else?" Juliette asked.

"Well, now that you ask," the fat man said, "both myself and *mi carnal* over here were actually kind of curious about one thing in particular."

"And what might that be?" Juliette watched—in the rearview mirror—the thinner man disappearing from her line of vision as he squatted to retrieve the ball.

"I hope you understand that I don't mean to cause you any

offense," the fat man said, placing a hand over his heart to express his sincerity. "But, the thing I wanted to ask you was…" He paused and moved his wide face closer to the glass, his tiny eyes darting all over Juliette.

"What is it?" Juliette asked. "What do you want?"

"Would you happen to be the fighter they call Jules Diamond Diaz?"

Juliette exhaled a breath of relief as she came to understand why the men had come over in the first place. "That I am," she replied, and she released her grip on the wrench at last.

"I told you, Hernández," the fat man called out to his companion. "The thing you gotta understand, Jules Diamond Diaz, is you was all disguised behind those big old sunglasses of yours, like you was Clark Kent instead of Superman, or Bruce Wayne instead of Batman. If you understand what I'm saying?"

"I guess that kind of makes sense."

"Let me tell you something," the fat man said, placing his hand over his heart again, "I saw your fight with The Ox on the Internet. What you did to that girl, that was some cold-hearted, *sicario*-type shit you pulled off in there. The way Oksana's eyes came right up out of their sockets when she was gasping for air, that right there is going to become the stuff of legends."

"Well, thanks," Juliette replied, blushing slightly at the praise she'd received. "That's a real compliment."

"When's the rematch gonna be happening?" the fat man asked. "Can you get me and my brother here some tickets?"

"Oh, well, nothing's really been agreed as yet."

"Are you for real? But surely Oksana's the only fight that makes sense for you right now."

Juliette drew a sharp breath through her teeth as she considered the man's words. "I guess we'll see how things play out," she said, noncommittally.

"*Sí, seguro,*" the man said, confirming he understood Juliette's point of view. He nodded his head in agreement, but at the same time, his eyes looked down at the floor and his brow tightened up into a frown of disappointment, an expression Juliette was used to seeing on the face of her brother. She knew exactly what her fans expected of her, and the burden of fulfilling their demands was a weight she carried around at all times.

"Now, if it wouldn't be too much to ask," the man said, "would you mind if we took a photograph with you? Something for us to remember this moment by."

"I don't know about all that," Juliette said. "I'm not really the posing type."

The man held his hands together as if he were praying. "For my *familia* back home," he said.

Juliette glanced in the rearview mirror to see the thinner man was sniffing the ball he'd retrieved from under the truck as though he feared it may have been contaminated somehow. "If I get out of this vehicle," Juliette said, "is your friend over there gonna behave himself?"

"Don't worry about my brother. He's just a little, how do you say...?" The fat man trailed off, swiveling a finger about his temple to explain the other man's erratic behavior.

"Well, as you asked so nicely," Juliette said, "I guess I could make an exception. Just this one time."

"*Excelente,*" the man said, fumbling in his pocket for his phone.

Juliette climbed down from her truck and made her way over to the sidewalk. The fat man held his cell phone away from his body and angled the screen back toward him and Juliette. The thin man crouched down in front of them both and held his hands up with several fingers extended in a way Juliette didn't understand.

"Quit it with the gang signs, Hernández," the fat man said, slapping at his brother's wrists.

Juliette glanced anywhere she could to avoid looking directly at the

161

phone's camera lens. "Are we done yet?" she asked.

The thin man took off with the basketball again, unable to stand still for more than a few seconds at a time. As Juliette watched him slapping the ball around in the road, she noticed, among the faint sheen of stubble covering his head, a long, crescent-shaped line of scar tissue that made it look like somebody had taken an axe to his skull. "What's up with your brother?" Juliette asked the fat man.

"He grew up living the crazy life," the man explained. "*La vida loca.*"

"You mean, he was in a gang?"

"Of course, look at his tattoos," the man said. "And when he didn't follow orders, they turned on him just like that." He clicked his chubby fingers through the air to illustrate his point.

"I guess that would kind of explain the scar then," Juliette said, tugging at the hem of her T-shirt to make sure it was fully covering the head of the wrench.

"Those punks wanted him to take the rap for something he never even did. Kid would have been looking at twenty-five years to life."

As Juliette listened to the man's story, she saw from the corner of her eye Amiyah coming out of the house in her sportswear. The sight of the young woman up on the porch in her leggings distracted Juliette from focusing on the man's words. She knew that Amiyah was fully aware of the fact she was being watched, that she was performing up on that porch the same way she performed on stage at The Pink Tunnel. It wasn't any kind of an accident when Amiyah swept her hair from her shoulders, flicking her braids through the air so they spread out over her back. Neither was it mere happenstance when, turning to close the door, she paused and reached down to sweep some nonexistent piece of dirt or debris from the fabric that was stretched so tightly over her derrière. Her fingers lingered against that particular part of her anatomy for a little too long, in a manner that suggested she was attempting to draw attention to the region. Juliette knew she was being manipulated, but as much as she tried to fight against her fascination with Amiyah's appearance, she found herself falling further and further under the young woman's spell.

"And here we are, two years after he woke up from his coma," the fat man continued.

"Oh, right, carry on," Juliette said, having forgotten the man was even speaking to her. She studied the thin man for a while as he bounced the ball against the road, noticing the way his eyes seemed to be focused somewhere in the distance at all times, as if he was constantly tuned out from his surroundings. She turned to watch Amiyah coming down from the porch, the breeze blowing against her loose sweatshirt to reveal a vague relief of her slender body and the conical mounds of her breasts. The two visions were in stark contrast to each other. There was Amiyah, so utterly perfect, with all the promise of having her whole life and her career as a fighter stretched out in front of her. And then, there was Hernández, the young man with his unsightly scar carved into his head, his brain functioning in a way that meant he was unable to communicate with those around him.

"But, it's like I always used to tell my little brother," the fat man said, "if you insist on dancing with the devil, sooner or later you're gonna get burned." He focused his gaze right into the lenses of Juliette's sunglasses. "You understand what I'm saying?"

Juliette nodded her head, her eyes following Amiyah's approach the whole time.

"Who said you could talk to my friend?" Amiyah asked as she came out of the yard onto the sidewalk.

"How does a little *puta* like you come to know a fighter like Jules Diamond Diaz?" the fat man asked in return.

"She's my coach," Amiyah replied. "Isn't that right, Jules?"

The proclamation sounded so strange to Juliette's ears. Her initial instinct was to correct the young woman, to offer an alternative explanation of their relationship. It was the first time she'd ever been referred to in this way, as somebody's coach, a title she usually associated with her brother, as if he was—in some sense—superior to her. Juliette tried to hold her face straight, not wanting to give in to the overwhelming sense of pride that was pulling her lips up into a smile. "I guess that's right. I'm her coach," she agreed, eventually.

Amiyah raised her eyebrows at the fat man. "So next time you wanna call me a whore, just remember, I'm actually doing something with my life. I'm gonna be getting out of this place soon. And you'll be stuck right here playing ball all day with your stupid little brother."

"Hey, come on," Juliette said, "there's no need for that."

"Can we please just get the hell out of this place?" Amiyah asked, swinging her backpack up and over into the bed of the truck. She snatched the basketball away from the thinner of the two men and tossed it over the fence into her yard. The dog went straight for the ball, clanking and rattling on his chain as he darted this way and that.

"*Chingada madre*," the fat man said.

"Good luck getting your ball back, tough guy," Amiyah said, climbing up into the passenger side of the truck.

The thin man threw his head back and began to howl along with the dog.

Juliette joined Amiyah in the truck to escape the ensuing chaos. "Don't you think maybe that was a little excessive?" she asked.

"You're not the one who has to listen to that thing bouncing around all day."

Juliette twisted her key in the ignition and the old truck came to life with a throaty roar. "You realize that kid's got brain damage, right?" she said, pulling the truck away from the curb and taking off down the street.

"He probably got more or less what he deserves," Amiyah replied. "How many people do you think he's messed up in the past? Whatever it was that happened to him, I'm pretty sure that's what they call street justice. You'd understand that if you were from where I'm from."

"That's some cold-hearted thinking, right there," Juliette said. "How many people do you think I messed up in the cage throughout my career? Would it be justice if I got hurt in my next fight and ended up the same way as that kid back there?"

"Don't talk silly, you know that's not what I was saying."

Juliette brought her truck to a rest at the edge of the park. She switched her engine off and rested her head against the steering wheel, causing the horn to blast out an aural representation of the frustration she was feeling within.

"Hey, come on, what's up?" Amiyah said, taking Juliette by the shoulder to pry her up off the wheel.

Juliette sat back in her seat, her body slouched with exhaustion. "I'm serious," she said. "Are you absolutely sure you even want to get yourself into this whole fighting thing?"

"What are you talking about? Of course I do."

"You realize that could be you, right? What happened to that kid back there, you risk that every single time you step into the cage."

"I'm not stupid. I know what I'm getting myself into."

"Listen, kid, let me explain it like this. Remember how it was when you started going through puberty?"

"Analogies aren't exactly your strong point, are they?"

"Just hear me out," Juliette insisted. "You know how your body changes when you get to a certain age? You grow hips and tits and all the rest of that stuff. Well, some girls did anyway," she said, glancing down at her own body with a dissatisfied expression on her face.

"So, what's your point?"

"When you become a fighter, when you start training every day, your body kind of goes through a whole new set of changes. It hardens up, you know? And then there's the damage you're gonna do to your face as well. Is that really what you want?"

"You've lost me," Amiyah said, turning her hands over to check her nails.

"Look at the definition in my arms." Juliette flexed her triceps as she held onto the steering wheel. "My cauliflower ears. The scar tissue all over my eyes. I'm a monster, kid. Not many guys are into girls who look like this."

"Funnily enough, I don't really care what guys think about the way I look."

"The point is," Juliette said, "I kind of like your face the way it is, okay?"

Amiyah dropped her head to one side and looked back at Juliette with a smile that was so sympathetic it was almost patronizing, as if to suggest the older woman's concerns were completely neurotic. "Come here," Amiyah said, wrapping her arms around Juliette. "I know what I'm getting myself into, okay?"

As their bodies came together, Juliette felt a warmth igniting somewhere deep inside. She submitted further into the young woman's arms, unable to resist the narcotic effects of being held so gently. "I just don't wanna be responsible for you getting hurt," Juliette said. "Seeing that kid back there brought it all home to me. I guess I never expected to be training somebody I actually care about, you know?"

"What do you mean, somebody you care about?" Amiyah laughed.

Juliette felt—over the top of her T-shirt—Amiyah's hand skimming back and forth across her chest, causing her nipples to harden against the weightless fabric. "You know what I mean," Juliette said.

"So why don't you tell me how you feel?" Amiyah said, sliding her hand up inside Juliette's shirt. "What exactly is it that's going on between us?"

Juliette shivered with every movement of the young woman's hand. "Fuck, kid, what have you done to me?" she said, paralyzed by the sensation of Amiyah's fingers trailing over her nipples. Amiyah's hand swept further down, across Juliette's stomach and on toward the waistband of her jeans. Juliette snatched hold of the young woman's wrist, suddenly waking from her hypnosis.

"I'm sorry," Amiyah said. "I thought you wanted me to."

Juliette slumped back into her seat and stared out into the windswept trees that were scattered over the expanse of open parkland. "Just give me some time to figure it out," she said. "To get my head around it all."

"I think I'm okay with that," Amiyah said. "If that's what you need."

They sat quietly for a while, both of them contemplating the line which had almost been crossed. Eager to break the silence, Juliette reached under her T-shirt, pulled out the wheel wrench and dropped it into her lap.

"What the hell were you gonna do with that?" Amiyah asked. "Change their tires?"

"Give me a break, kid. I hadn't exactly guessed they were members of my fan club."

"They won't be if you hit them over the head with that thing."

They laughed together and Juliette started her truck, resigning herself to the fact the younger woman found her behavior almost entirely ridiculous.

CHAPTER 12

"Are we gonna have to start thinking about finding you a new student, or what?" Earl asked, arriving at the base of the staircase that led down from his office.

"You'd love that, wouldn't you?" Juliette replied. "If I'd messed this up already. I'm sure you'd take great pleasure in telling me exactly where I went wrong and how you would have gone about it all."

"Why've you always gotta think the worst of me? Did it ever occur to you that maybe I'm just trying to help you out?"

"Did it ever occur to you," Juliette replied, "that maybe you should back off for once and give me a chance to do this my own way?"

Earl took Juliette by the arm and led her into the storeroom so they could converse more privately, away from the eyes and ears of the other athletes. "How many times have you actually had her in here, once?" he asked. "I think it's fair to start evaluating the situation, don't you? I don't think you're taking this whole coaching thing very seriously. If it's not for you, then why don't you just say so? Not everyone's cut out to be a mentor. Maybe you should stick to teaching kids jiu-jitsu on a Sunday morning if you think you're gonna be satisfied stepping down from being a world-class, championship-level martial artist and walking into that kind of a life. Or, maybe you should get a part-time job in one of the factories around here. Plenty of work going for somebody at a loose end if you can't cope with teaching someone how to become a real fighter. You see, that takes hard work. You gotta be a special kind of person to be able to spot somebody's strengths, and then to be able to sharpen those skills to their full potential, sculpt that individual into the best possible version of themselves. Look at Tommy; that kid could barely tie his shoelaces when he first walked in here. And now, not only is he shaping up to be a serious welterweight contender, he's a pretty useful assistant coach as well. You think that was easy? Why's it so hard for you to figure out? You've seen how I work with him, haven't you?"

"You mean, the way you treat him like he's a piece of dirt?"

Earl narrowed his eyes and shook his head at Juliette. "You just don't get it at all, do you?" he said, removing a towel from his shoulder to pat the sweat from his hairline. "Why do you think I'm so bothered about all this?"

"Because you love to criticize everything I do?"

"Because I can see what a great opportunity this is for us. For you and me. Fighters like this don't just come along every day, Jules. If you blow this, some other gym is gonna snatch this kid up and you're gonna have to watch her career taking off, wishing it was you in her corner. How do you think that's gonna make you feel?"

"Are you done yet?"

"You know what, maybe I am. Maybe I should just let you do whatever the hell you want and throw your life away."

"You're such a fucking drama queen," Juliette uttered under her breath. She raised her chin and looked past her brother, signaling with a casual nod to something behind him.

Earl leaned out of the storeroom to survey the main body of the gym. The coarse skin of his face slackened as the frustration that had been holding his features so tightly gave way to disbelief. His mouth hung open as he watched Amiyah stepping out of the women's locker room with her gangly frame shrink-wrapped in a skintight rash vest and a similarly close-fitting pair of shorts. "Are you fucking kidding me?" Earl said, seizing Juliette behind the neck, pulling her head to his chest. "That's what I'm talking about."

Juliette couldn't hold the smile from her face, aware this was the closest thing to an apology she would get from her brother.

Amiyah walked timidly on her long, fawn-like limbs, looking as though she'd just been born into this bizarre world of trained killers. She hovered around the locker rooms, not quite sure of her surroundings, not knowing which way to turn or which part of the gym she should head off to first. She reached behind herself and plucked the tight fabric of her shorts from between her buttocks, stealing furtive glances at the other athletes to see if any of them had noticed her presence.

"Now, isn't that quite the picture," Earl said, throwing one arm over Juliette's shoulders and pulling her to his side. "Just look at her over there. That's everything I wanted for you, kid."

Earl's enthusiasm filled Juliette with such an overwhelming sense of relief she almost felt the need to sit down. She saw Tommy was clapping his hand into Amiyah's, bringing his shoulder to hers, welcoming her back into the gym. Cody walked over to Amiyah, his posture straight and rigid to exaggerate his stature, his features unreadable as he looked the young woman up and down.

Earl tightened his grip on Juliette. "Here we go again," he said.

Cody and Amiyah locked eyes, each of them pausing to gauge the other's intentions. The fighters around them exchanged apprehensive glances, preparing themselves to intervene. Cody looked deep into Amiyah's eyes for a while and then nodded his head as though he'd seen right into her very soul and had witnessed her unyielding warrior spirit. He stretched his splayed palm out toward her, and after what seemed like an intentionally drawn-out period of inaction, Amiyah accepted the young man's hand and pulled him into a forgiving embrace. The bodies of the other fighters slackened with relief. They jostled about and laughed together; a few of them even applauded.

"Isn't that just a beautiful thing?" Earl said, watching the scene unfold on the other side of the gym. "Almost brings a tear to my eye. That's everything I love about martial arts right there, the level of respect it brings."

"Oh, really?" Juliette said. "Then maybe you should start respecting me a bit more."

"Come on, Jules. Can we not just enjoy this moment together? Look at what I found for you. Look what you've got there." Earl spoke as though he was referring to an extravagant gift he'd given to his sister, as if Amiyah was some exquisite, shiny new object: a bicycle, a car, or a pony.

Juliette wanted to be mad at Earl, wanted so badly to be frustrated with him for the lecture he'd subjected her to only moments earlier, but she couldn't help giving herself over to the moment, her big brother presenting her with this magnificent gift. She could feel the weight of Earl's arm around her shoulder, encasing her in the warmth of his love. She hated the fact she was so susceptible to it all, rendered defenseless by any faint glimmer of affection in her brother's eyes. She had no significant other, no parent to spoil her, and she knew this was the closest she would ever come to experiencing anything remotely like that. It was such a rare occurrence that it filled her with an almost childish sense of joy.

"That's all yours," Earl said. "Isn't she just perfect?"

"Yeah, she is," Juliette said, with a note of laughter in her voice. "She's perfect." Somewhere, deep inside of Juliette, lurked a vague knowledge that Amiyah belonged to her, not only as a student, but in another more profound way, a way she didn't quite understand. This strange sense of ownership filled her with a swell of pride as she watched Amiyah interacting with the other fighters, laughing and exchanging pleasantries, stretching and contorting her slender body in preparation for the afternoon workout. Juliette's eyes were drawn to the undersized pair of shorts Amiyah had chosen to wear, the fabric of which was pulled up so closely between the young woman's thighs it revealed, in somewhat explicit detail, the plump folds and contours of everything the garment concealed. Juliette marveled at the way Amiyah was displaying this most intimate part of her anatomy so shamelessly in a gym full of male fighters, forcing them to deal with the full force of her physical perfection, confronting them with their own pathetic weakness and vulnerability to the power of the female form.

Earl was paying close attention to the direction of Juliette's gaze, his head cocked to one side contemplatively, a slanted half-smile on his lips.

Juliette averted her eyes, looking anywhere but toward Amiyah, wondering if Earl had detected her fascination with the young woman. She felt a rush of excitement at the notion of being caught this way. It thrilled her to think her brother had almost found her out, had come so close to uncovering her secret. She felt her cheeks flushing as he studied her. It was an embarrassment she enjoyed, a shame she reveled in.

Earl withdrew his arm from around Juliette's shoulder and took a few steps away from her to get a better view of Amiyah and the other fighters. "She really is something, isn't she?" he said. "But don't you go squandering this," he added. "Don't take her for granted now, will you?"

"I won't," Juliette replied. Her swell of pride intensified as she watched her brother's narrowed eyes studying Amiyah's every move. She began to consider — for just a brief moment — the sense of shock Earl would feel if he ever came to discover the true nature of her relationship with Amiyah, if he ever learned of the things they'd done together. She reached behind herself and slipped a hand into the back of her jeans. She took hold of the cold flesh of her ass and then allowed her palm to venture deeper, toward the warmth that emanated from the central furrow. Her hand lingered beneath the veil of her underwear, her fingers wandering dangerously between her buttocks until her whole body tingled with exhilaration. Her heart fluttered at the realization she was exploring herself so publicly. She readjusted her underwear and stood up tall to regain her composure, struggling to resist the urge to pleasure herself further.

"So, you want to find out what she can do, or what?" Earl asked.

"Sure, why not," Juliette said, resting her hand over her top lip in an attempt to appreciate any faint hint of her own scent that might have been transferred to the skin of her fingers. Her thoughts became muddled with arousal as she breathed in the subtle, comforting aroma.

***

Earl tossed a pair of boxing gloves to Amiyah. "Strap these on, kid," he said. "And let me introduce you to this young man over here." He ushered an individual fighter to emerge from the huddle of bodies gathered before them. "This is Ghost," Earl explained, and a narrowly-built, bald-headed young man stepped forward from among the crowd. The man's scalp was so shiny and barren it looked as though no single strand of hair could ever have grown upon it. His skin was white to the point of being translucent, the blue threads of his veins visible in places through his pallid flesh. His elongated head was adorned with prominent features: bulging eyes, a proboscis nose, and razor-sharp cheekbones.

"How did he get a name like Ghost, then?" Amiyah asked, to several rumbles of laughter from the other fighters.

"Hilarious," Earl grumbled. "Ghost here is gonna be your sparring partner for the afternoon."

"You okay with that?" Juliette asked.

"Why wouldn't I be?" Amiyah replied.

Ghost shook his limbs out and threw his head from side to side in rapid motion as though he considered his body to be such a high-performance instrument it needed to be kept limber and tuned to perfection at all times. Amiyah stared back at the man, unimpressed by his peacocking.

"Come on, kid. Let me wrap those hands up," Juliette said. She took Amiyah by the wrist, led her into the women's locker room, and sat her down on one of the wooden benches.

"I'm perfectly capable of wrapping my own hands, you know? Why did you insist on bringing me all the way in here to do this?"

173

"Why do you think? So we can talk tactics, of course."

"What tactics? We're just sparring aren't we?"

"This is a competitive gym, kid. You better get used to that. Why do you think Earl's picked another southpaw to fight you?"

Amiyah's eyes drifted as she pondered the question.

"Because he doesn't want a lefty like you confusing one of his right-handed fighters, that's why. Trust me, I know Earl well enough. He wants to put you in your place, break you down before he builds you back up. Doesn't want you getting too big for your boots. He's picked that kid out there to put a beating on you. Might sound rough, but that's how he is." Juliette took out two narrow reels of cotton fabric from her duffel bag and sat down beside Amiyah on the bench.

"I have got my own hand wraps, thanks," Amiyah said.

"We're gonna strap you up properly," Juliette said. "These are brand-new. Now, come on, give me your hand."

Amiyah held her left hand face down in front of herself. Juliette began to unreel the two-inch-wide fabric, hooking a little elasticated loop that was attached to its end over Amiyah's thumb. Juliette wound the fabric around Amiyah's wrist three times, back around her thumb once, and then around her entire palm once before layering it back and forth across her knuckles.

"Not too much, I do actually want him to feel my fist, you know?"

"Can't have you breaking your hand on his bony face," Juliette replied. She continued working the band of fabric, looping it over the young woman's palm and between each of her fingers in turn. She finished by wrapping it over Amiyah's knuckles twice more and then finally once more around her slender wrist, fastening the fabric in place with a strip of Velcro that was stitched to its underside.

"How about we raise the stakes a little?" Amiyah said, arching an eyebrow suggestively.

"You're already fighting a man. Isn't that enough for you?" Juliette started the binding process on Amiyah's other hand.

174

"All I'm saying is," Amiyah began, "you remember our deal, right? I come and train, and then maybe we can hang out afterward. Well, how about if I come out of this sparring session on top, we agree to turn that maybe into a definitely?"

Juliette paused. "And, what does hanging out involve, exactly?"

"I don't know, spending some time together so we can actually get to know each other. Whatever you like to do when you're not training."

"All I do is train," Juliette replied, her eyes focused intently on the length of fabric she was manipulating into place. "I don't have time for much else. Been a while since I've hung out."

"I'm sure we can think of something to do. That's if I win, of course."

"Ghost's been fighting a lot longer than you have," Juliette said, fastening the Velcro on the hand-wrap. "If you can hold your own in there, that's good enough for me. That will earn you the respect of everyone in the gym."

"That might be good enough for you, Jules, but not me. Didn't you see the way Ghost looked at me? He looked straight past me, the same way half the guys I take my clothes off for look at me, as if I'm nothing, as if I'm worthless. I wanna mess this guy up for even having the nerve to step in there with me in the first place. That's the kind of respect I'm talking about."

"Yeah, well, we'll see about that. Just look after yourself in there, okay? I don't want you messing up this face of yours." As Juliette spoke, she was compelled to reach up and place a hand over the young woman's cheek, curious as to whether the skin of her face could possibly feel as flawless as it looked.

Amiyah closed her eyes, "Your touch makes me shiver," she whispered.

Juliette traced the outline of Amiyah's quivering mouth. She fought the urge to push her thumb deep into the warmth of the orifice, to penetrate the young woman's mouth, to watch her lips close down and suck the digit further in. She struggled to keep her mind on the task that lay ahead. She shook her head to clear it and withdrew her hand, watching as a cord of saliva trailed and then broke off between the tip of her thumb and Amiyah's lips. "Let's try and stay focused, shall we?" Juliette said. "Or you're gonna wind up getting yourself hurt."

Amiyah pawed the moisture from her mouth and sprung up off the bench. "Don't be silly, I'll be fine," she said. "But, maybe I could use a little extra motivation to keep me going in there."

"Not sure I even wanna know what that means," Juliette said.

Amiyah unzipped her backpack and searched among her clothes. "Here we go," she said, removing a small, darkly-colored ball of tangled fabric. "Take these," she said, and she extended her arm so the wad of black fabric unfurled and hung from her fingers.

Juliette studied the small piece of clothing that was being presented to her. "Is that underwear?" she asked. "What in the world do you want me to do with those?"

"Put them on, of course," Amiyah said, as if it was obvious.

Juliette opened her mouth to speak, but was stunned into silence by the young woman's suggestion.

"Come on, don't be such a square. It'll bring me good luck."

"How exactly d'you figure that out?"

"Because you see, I'll know, the whole time I'm fighting, that you're wearing my underwear, and it will be our little secret, just yours and mine. And then we'll be more connected to each other, in a way nobody else understands."

"You're so messed up," Juliette said, putting her head in her hands.

"You do want me to win, don't you?"

"I guess, but..."

"Well, go and put them on then," Amiyah said and she dropped the underwear into Juliette's lap. "If I win, not only do we get to hang out, but you'll be wearing those as well."

The door of the locker room creaked open a few degrees. Juliette panicked, bundling the underwear up inside her hands.

"Are you girls still doing your makeup in there, or what?" Earl asked from beyond the locker room door.

"Two minutes," Juliette replied.

"Well, don't you go bailing on us," Earl said, and then, closing the door he added, "Don't you worry, Ghosty's gonna be real gentle with you in there."

Amiyah gestured in the direction of the bathroom stalls. "Quickly," she mouthed, waving a hand to direct Juliette.

Juliette stood up from the bench holding the black lace underwear stretched out in front of her. She shook her head as she inspected the intricate floral pattern of the sheer fabric. Amiyah was nodding and waving her off encouragingly. Juliette drew a sharp breath through her teeth and made her way into the bathroom stall, unhooking her belt buckle and popping the buttons of her fly.

CHAPTER 13

Juliette held the locker room door open so Amiyah could make her entrance. The heads of the other fighters swung around in perfect synchronicity as the young woman skipped with sprightly steps from the doorway. She punched her fists out in a pair of sixteen-ounce boxing gloves, the balloon-like proportions of which made her spindly arms appear almost comically thin. Juliette had insisted Amiyah should wear a specifically closed-face headguard, a padded helmet that encased most of her facial features.

Earl and Ghost were waiting over in the caged enclosure at the far end of the gymnasium. The wire-fenced structure, elevated from the ground at a height of around four feet, consisted of eight equally sized walls, an homage to the type of octagonal enclosures used at the highest level of the sport. Earl had always insisted on this particular configuration, believing it would encourage his students to aspire to compete among the upper echelons of mixed martial arts.

Amiyah bounced from foot to foot as she made her way through the cluster of fighters gathered before the cage. As Juliette followed a few steps behind, she noticed the sardonic expressions on the faces among the crowd. She could see the doubt and the ridicule in their eyes as they looked Amiyah over, measuring her petite frame and her wiry limbs. Juliette knew the fighters would be making their own judgments about her young student's capabilities, deciding in an instant that she wouldn't stand a chance against Ghost, and that Ghost would most likely have to go easy on her to make this bout in any way competitive.

Amiyah seemed oblivious to all of this as she skipped a path through the crowd, her expressionless face indicating just how intensely focused she was on the task at hand. She was paying little attention to the fighters nudging each other and exchanging knowing glances as she passed. Juliette was in total awe of Amiyah's stoic demeanor, her unyielding determination. And it was in this very moment—as she watched the young woman soaring above all the arrogant bravado of the male athletes—that Juliette finally realized and accepted just how much she wanted Amiyah to be hers, to be hers completely, in whatever sense Amiyah wanted to belong to her. Juliette's insides were aflame with an overwhelming sense of panic as her feelings toward her young student began to make sense.

"Nice of you to grace us with your presence," Earl said, as Amiyah ran up a little set of steps and entered the cage via an open gate in the wire fence.

Juliette stepped up onto a stool so she could lean over the top of the cage to get a better view.

"Don't you get hurt in there, Ghosty," one of the onlookers said, and Ghost laughed, his pointed face sinking backward, his cleft chin disappearing into his neck.

"Stop messing around, Ghost, and put your headguard on," Earl demanded.

Ghost held his hands splayed at his sides, as if to ask why he would possibly need that level of protection, and then he pointed one of his boxing gloves at Amiyah to further emphasize his point.

"Come on now, Ghosty," Earl said, "you not worried about that pretty little face of yours?" The audience howled with laughter like a wild mob excitedly awaiting a public execution. Earl knew exactly how to get his teammates worked up, how to build the tension so he could make a real event out of a simple sparring session like this. "All right, calm down already," Earl said, and the laughter faded. "Now, is everybody ready?"

The crowd mumbled in confirmation.

Earl cleared his throat several times over. "Okay then, fighting out of the blue corner," he began, with a hand stretched out toward Ghost, "with a record of eight wins and one loss, a loss he suffered because he wouldn't listen to what his coach was telling him, we've got Callum, The Irish Ghost, O'Leary."

The crowd clapped out an obligatory applause.

"And, fighting out of the red corner, with a record of four wins and no losses, it's Amiyah, Mimi, Amoré. You'll go a long way with a name like that, kid," Earl added.

A wolf whistle shrieked out from somewhere close by and Juliette scowled into the audience to seek out the perpetrator.

"Okay, let's square this off," Earl said, directing the two fighters to join him in the center of the cage.

Ghost strutted over, his pale legs emerging from the diaper-like padding of a groin guard. His body was bandy and angular compared to the solid physiques possessed by many of the other athletes on the team, but opposite Amiyah's slight frame, he looked wide and foreboding, his shoulders spherical with muscle through the rash vest that was clinging to his torso.

"This is strictly MMA boxing, okay?" Earl explained. "No takedowns, no kicking, and no knees. We'll do two five-minute rounds. Tommy's gonna be the ref to stop you two from tearing each other apart." It was never discussed or mentioned in any way, but everybody seemed to understand how this was going to work, that Juliette was going to be cornering Amiyah, and Earl was going to be working the corner of her opponent, Ghost.

The sparring partners stood opposite each other in the center of the cage, their faces uncomfortably close to one another's, and both of their expressions purposefully void of any display of emotions, each party eager to prove just how little they feared the prospect of going into battle. Earl looked into each of their faces in turn, studying their features for any indication of uncertainty. He'd been in the same position as both of these individuals so many times throughout his career as a fighter, he knew exactly what to look out for, all of those little clues an untrained eye might overlook: a fighter fidgeting needlessly with their equipment, avoiding eye contact with their opponent, blinking excessively, or paying too much attention to the referee.

Juliette was also looking for these subtle indications of self-doubt from her elevated position on the stool. She looked for them in Amiyah's body language because she wanted so badly for her to be okay, to believe in herself, and not to be afraid. She saw that Ghost was looking down into Amiyah's eyes with his mouth turned up into a smirk, his lips bulging under the pressure of his mouthguard making his features appear even more unsightly than they already were.

Amiyah kissed the air in front of her lips and blew the gesture away into the face of her opponent. The crowd whooped and howled as Earl separated the combatants and directed them into their respective corners.

"It's all yours from here, Tommy," Earl said, flashing his young assistant a glower that told him exactly how much trouble he'd be in if he messed this up.

The look Earl gave Tommy only served to remind Juliette exactly how much was at stake, and how real the possibility was that Amiyah might actually get hurt. She suddenly noticed how tightly she'd been gripping the tubular padding that ran along the top of the cage walls. As Amiyah came back into their corner, her wide, inquisitive eyes shone out of her headguard as though she was awaiting some kind of instructions or advice. The weight of the responsibility caught Juliette off guard, and she glanced around for anybody else who might be able to offer the young woman a few words of encouragement. She quickly realized there was nobody by her side to offer assistance and she understood the burden of tuition fell on her shoulders alone. Her heart was thumping hard and fast as she came down off the stool to speak with Amiyah through the wire fence. Juliette could feel the eyes of the other fighters watching her, all of them waiting to see how she would choose to direct her student. Her natural instinct in this situation was to look over to her brother for guidance, but in doing so, she saw he was talking to his own fighter, his fists firing out from his body as he demonstrated a specific technique.

Tommy called out to ask if everybody was ready, and with no game plan of her own, Juliette felt like she was already behind in the fight. Amiyah's dark eyes seemed wider than ever now, glistening with a kind of fearful look of abandonment. Juliette had no doubt that the young woman's pleading eyes would haunt her thoughts relentlessly in the days to come, and that they would keep her awake at night the same way Earl's glare of disappointment always did. Amiyah turned to face her opponent and Juliette called her back. "Hold on, will you?" she said, "just give me a minute."

"I gotta go, Jules," Amiyah insisted.

Juliette had been coached by her brother for so long, it was easy for her to decipher the precise words of instruction he was delivering to his fighter just by studying the movements of his fists thrusting out from his hips. "Listen to me, kid," Juliette said. "He's telling Ghost to take it to your body. Probably thinks that's where he's got the best chance of hurting you. He's gonna try and push you up against the cage and put his head right in the middle of your chest so he can unload on your ribs. Stay on the outside and circle to your left, away from the power in his left hand. Don't get cornered in there. Stay loose and keep touching him with the jab. You understand?"

Amiyah's eyes drifted as she pondered Juliette's advice. "I work better on the inside," she said. "Plus, he's got a reach advantage. I gotta get in close and rough him up a little, you know?"

"But you're quicker than him, use your footwork," Juliette attempted to explain, but it was too late, Amiyah had already departed and had taken up her position across the cage from her opponent.

"Let's get this show started," Earl said. "We haven't got all day."

Tommy hurried obediently to the center of the cage. "Okay, let's fight," he said, taking a step back to get out of the way.

Ghost came forward with his hands held high about his face. He walked flat-footed, plodding about in a Muay Thai stance. He stalked Amiyah relentlessly, his constant pressure causing her to back away into the corners of the cage.

"Don't let him cut you off like that," Juliette called out.

Amiyah was light on her feet. She bounced on her toes with her chin tucked defensively into her lead shoulder.

"Come on, Ghost, let's go," a voice cried out from among the crowd. Juliette understood why her teammates' loyalties would lie with Ghost, the person they trained with every day. But she got a sense the other athletes were eager to reassert their male dominance over the female fighter who'd defeated one of their comrades a few weeks previously.

Ghost threw a flurry of jabs out into the air, attempting to keep Amiyah—the smaller fighter—at bay. His reach advantage was immediately apparent, his long limbs firing out repeatedly to create a defensive barrier. Amiyah ducked and weaved from side to side, searching constantly for the right angle to make her advance so she could bring herself within striking range.

"Stay on the outside," Juliette said. "Be patient."

Amiyah refused to head her coach's words. She charged toward her opponent and ate a solid punch to the face as she rushed in. Ghost seized the opportunity to get hold of his startled prey. He wrapped his gloves around the back of Amiyah's headguard, tying her up in a Muay Thai clinch.

"Get out of there," Juliette said, "don't wrestle with him."

Ghost held onto Amiyah's head and walked her to the edge of the cage, pressing her up against the wire fence. Amiyah's body stiffened as she struggled to break free from the clinch. Ghost continued to have his way with her, muscling her this way and that. He tossed her head aside and her body followed, swinging down toward the ground so she ended up in a tangled heap on the mat. The crowd erupted with savage bursts of laughter.

"Come on, Tommy," Juliette protested. "I thought this was a boxing match."

"Let them fight," Earl said, indifferently. "This is MMA boxing, not traditional."

Amiyah clambered back to her feet, biting down on her mouthguard with frustration. She glanced down to check herself over and readjust her shorts. Noticing her distraction, Ghost charged forward and landed a looping left hand directly to the side of her head, a powerful blow that caused her to stumble sideways into the fence until she lost her footing altogether and wound up back on the floor. The audience gasped with disbelief.

"Is this a joke?" Juliette said. "She wasn't even ready."

"Defend yourself at all times," Earl said, quoting the advice referees give fighters at the start of every bout.

The rest of the round played out in much the same way. Amiyah came forward repeatedly, attempting to get past Ghost's jab so that she might be able to land some kind of offense of her own. Ghost grappled with Amiyah at every opportunity. He pinned her up against the fence and slammed his fists into her midsection the way Earl had instructed. Juliette hung her head on multiple occasions, unable to watch the punishment her fighter was suffering. She wanted so badly to scale the fence, to climb into the cage so she could protect Amiyah by taking up the fight herself. Ghost's face bore a twisted grin of amusement the whole time. Juliette knew he would be taking great pleasure in displaying his superior skills to both his coach and his teammates.

Earl's slouched posture indicated he was confident everything was going exactly as he'd planned. Even though it was Amiyah and Ghost who were competing within the cage, Juliette understood the real contest was taking place between her and Earl. She knew her brother would be judging her coaching abilities, and that he would want her to do well, but not so well that her fighter was able to defeat his own. It often seemed every minute of Juliette's life was fraught with a constant struggle to predict Earl's specific expectations of her, and then to strive endlessly to satisfy his every whim.

"Ten seconds," Earl barked.

Ghost got hold of Amiyah again as the round came to a close. He spun her around, and with a hand on the back of her neck, he bent her over at the waist and thrust his hips toward her in a somewhat lewd gesture. She floundered forward, ending the round face down in the center of the mat. The crowd was silent, the onlookers holding back their jeers as if they pitied Amiyah for the mauling she'd received.

Earl caught Juliette by the shoulder as she rushed into the cage. "We're just breaking her in, Jules," he said. "She's a tough kid. She needs this."

Juliette shrugged herself free from her brother's grip and hurried to place her stool down against the wire fence. "What the hell was that?" she asked. "Do you enjoy getting punched in the face, or what?"

Amiyah collapsed down onto the stool, gasping for air.

Juliette got down on one knee. "Why didn't you stick to the game plan in there?"

"Give me a chance, will you?" Amiyah's said, spitting her mouthguard into her glove. "I was just wearing him out, that's all."

"That's bullshit, kid. This is a two-round fight. You can't be taking a round off like that."

"You know I'm a hustler. Gotta make him think this is easy. That's just how I work."

Juliette set her teeth as she considered the young woman's words. She was certain Amiyah was making excuses for her substandard performance. "If you don't start listening to me, then we might as well quit right now. If you can't even follow simple instructions, you're never gonna make it as a fighter."

"I heard everything you said, Jules. Stay on the outside and pick him apart, right? Don't you get it? That'll be the last thing he's expecting now. You gotta start trusting me if we're gonna work as a team."

"Time's up, let's go," Tommy said, clapping his hands together.

Juliette saw that Ghost was already up on his feet, breathing effortlessly as though he'd barely even broken a sweat. She ran her eyes over Amiyah, noticing the way her chest was heaving back and forth with every breath. Juliette knew they were a round behind. She had to find a way to ignite the fire of urgency within her fighter. "Look, just keep your focus on the prize, okay?" Juliette said, and she lifted her T-shirt just enough to reveal the frilled waistband of the underwear Amiyah had asked her to put on emerging over the top of her jeans.

Amiyah's breathing slowed to a steady pace; her features settled into a tranquil reverence.

"Don't let me down in there, kid," Juliette said, and the pair of them locked eyes for a moment in which they seemed to understand one another without the need for communication.

"You quitting on us, or what?" Earl said.

"Mess him up for me, please," Juliette said.

Amiyah pawed her mouthguard back into place and thumped her gloves together several times. She let out a roar to psyche herself up, her body tensing and straining enough to show all the sinews within her limbs. Juliette exited the wire fence and Earl closed the gate behind her. Tommy ushered in the start of the second round and the two fighters proceeded to circle each other in the center of the cage. Ghost pumped out his jab as though he expected the round to play out exactly the same way as the first, but this time, Amiyah did not rush forward. She kept herself just out of range, yet close enough to make Ghost believe she was still within striking distance.

Juliette felt a faint burn of optimism as she began to suspect Amiyah might have been telling the truth, and maybe she had spent the first round lulling her opponent into a false sense of security. Every time Ghost's jab fired out, Amiyah got out of the way, leaning back or to the side a fraction of a second faster than his glove could catch her. Juliette looked over to Earl and saw he was standing up straight and alert. She knew her brother well enough to understand the shift in his posture meant he'd already detected the change in Amiyah's tactics.

Amiyah toyed with her opponent like a matador, tempting him in and then dancing away until his pale face turned red with frustration. He began to swing his punches wildly, leaving himself open to the counterattack. Amiyah forced him to chase her, made him step further forward with every swing until she finally made her move. When Ghost's fist was at its maximum extension, she skipped in toward him and thrust her left hand into his face so fast, his head whipped back and sent a mist of saliva and snot spraying over the front row of the crowd.

"Damn, kid," Juliette said, unable to conceal her delight.

"Get your fucking hands up, Ghost," Earl barked. "Stop messing around in there."

Ghost shook his head to clear it and wrinkled his brow with determination. Amiyah danced away from him, forced him to come toward her, and then she stepped in with the right-hand jab over and over. And whenever Ghost raised his gloves to defend his face, Amiyah would land a blow to his midsection, stepping forward off her back foot, bringing all of her weight up through her body and transferring it into the force of the punch.

"That's beautiful," Juliette called out. "Use your footwork and keep touching him with the jab just like I told you." She wanted to make it clear to everyone that this was her game plan Amiyah was implementing inside the cage. She knew Earl would have to be impressed, even if his lifeless facial features suggested otherwise.

Ghost's vexation was showing on his face. He chased Amiyah down and shouldered her into the fence. He held her there against the cage, and kicked her feet out from under her so she crashed down onto the mat.

"Come on, get up," Juliette said. "Just keep doing what you're doing. Let him get frustrated if that's what he wants."

The narrow portion of Amiyah's face that could be seen through her headguard was taut with anger as she climbed back to her feet. "I'm gonna teach this little bitch a lesson," she said to Juliette through the fence.

"Don't do anything stupid. You got this."

Earl's face had come alive with a devilish grin that suggested he'd detected Amiyah's fury and couldn't wait to see what kind of brutal acts she was capable of. "Thirty seconds left, Tommy," he said. "Square them off."

As the action in the cage resumed, the series of events that transpired seemed to unfold in slow motion, almost as if Juliette could have scaled the fence to intervene at any moment. At the same time, it all happened so fast, with any chance of victory for Amiyah disappearing in an instant. The young woman spun toward Ghost, rotating her body a full 360 degrees. As she came back around to face him, she lifted one arm and landed the point of her elbow directly in the center of his face. Juliette closed her eyes as the blow connected, unable to watch Amiyah's reckless act of retaliation. The audience gasped in perfect harmony at the hollow sound of bone against bone. The force of the spinning elbow sent Ghost stumbling backward. His beak-like nose exploded all over his face, covering his pale skin with a splatter of vibrant red. He sat down on the floor with his flattened nose leaking blood all over the mat. Amiyah raised her arms above her head and ran a few victory laps around the circumference of the cage.

The onlookers exchanged sideways glances, none of them quite sure of how they should react.

Earl looked deep into Juliette's eyes as he announced his ruling, "Winner by disqualification, Ghost," he said.

Amiyah continued to circle her fallen opponent without a care for the fact she'd lost. The wide smile beaming from among her headguard indicated she was confident she'd won the respect of everyone in the gym.

CHAPTER 14

A cool breeze startled Juliette as she emerged from the gym into the fading light of late afternoon. The bracing air swept through the T-shirt she was wearing, filling the weightless fabric like a sail, reminding her of her nakedness underneath the loose-fitting garment. She paused before reaching her truck, dropped her swollen duffel bag to the floor and threw on her Diablo MMA jacket. As she fastened the zipper, her right arm was snatched away, her bicep encircled by the tightening force of a firm and powerful grip. She knew who her assailant would be without needing to turn and verify her suspicions.

Earl pulled Juliette close to his barrel chest. His thick fingers clamped down so tightly over her upper arm it seemed he wanted to inflict a small dose of pain, just enough to let Juliette know how he felt about Amiyah defeating the fighter he'd been cornering, just enough to show he was still the boss. Earl's features were taut and unreadable as always, but Juliette knew him well enough to recognize the muscles twitching and spasming beneath the leathery skin of his face, his gnarled flesh trembling to indicate the discontent that stirred within him. Juliette awaited her chastisement with a hint of a smile hovering about her lips. She drew a strange sense of satisfaction from the realization she'd been able to ignite such a fury within her brother. She was certain he'd be trying to fathom a way to criticize everything she'd done in her coaching of Amiyah. At the same time, she knew he would be unable to deny the sheer brilliance of the young woman's performance.

"That kid was fucking awesome in there," Earl said, eventually, the words spilling out of his mouth like a climax. He loosened his constriction of Juliette's arm, but kept hold of her enough to show he wasn't finished with her, enough to make sure she paid close attention to what he was about to say. "I think we might actually have a champion on our hands there," he whispered through his teeth. "You do realize that, don't you?"

"I know," Juliette said, straining to hold any indication of her excitement from showing on her face.

"Don't you dare go screwing this up on me," Earl said. "You hang on to her for dear life, do you understand me? Don't you go doing anything that's gonna jeopardize this opportunity for us."

"Okay, I get it."

Earl let go of Juliette's arm and tossed it aside. "Embarrassing me in there like that," he said, shaking his head as he turned to walk away.

Juliette saw, in the final glimpse of her brother's face, that his features were relaxed and buoyant as if the pressure weighing them down had been relieved to some degree. In that moment, she understood Earl was happy with her, and he was turning away to hide it, far too proud to let his acquiescence show.

Amiyah spilled out of the gym and made her way into the parking lot. "What the hell was that all about?" she asked.

"Where did you get that jacket from?" Juliette asked in return, noticing the oversized Diablo MMA jacket hanging over Amiyah's shoulders, making her look like a miniature version of her usual self.

Amiyah turned a full circle on the spot. "Don't you think it suits me?" she asked.

"Who gave that to you?" Juliette persisted.

"Relax, it's Tommy's. He said I could borrow it. Come on, sugar, you're not jealous, are you?"

"Don't be smart," Juliette said.

"So, how are we gonna celebrate anyway?" Amiyah asked. "Because I seem to remember we had a deal. And let's face it, we both know I won in there, don't we? And now look at me, all dressed up with nowhere to go."

Juliette tried to look away, but she couldn't resist peering from the corners of her eyes to admire the short black dress Amiyah was wearing underneath her jacket. Amiyah had paired the simple, close-fitting garment with contrastingly garish running shoes, a style choice which made little sense to Juliette, one she would never possess either the courage or the inclination to attempt herself. Despite her bemusement, Juliette couldn't help appreciating the creativity of Amiyah's dress sense, the brightly colored running shoes lending an almost sportswear-like quality to the otherwise chic and sophisticated dress. Amiyah dropped the oversized satin jacket to the crooks of her elbows, revealing the full shape of her silhouette, the curves of which were emphasized by the dress that was stretched so tightly over her body. Juliette glanced at the blades of Amiyah's hip bones, the outline of her pelvis, her glossy thighs shining under the street lights. "Put your coat back on, and let's get out of here," Juliette said, noticing a few of the other fighters coming out of the entrance foyer.

Amiyah jumped up into the passenger side of Juliette's truck with the same level of energy she'd displayed throughout her sparring session with Ghost. "So, what's the plan?" she asked.

"What are you asking me for? This was your idea, wasn't it?" Juliette replied, already worn out by the young woman's enthusiasm.

"Why do you have to be so damn serious all the time?" Amiyah said. "Lighten up, will you? Can't you see I'm buzzing over here? I did just win a pretty tough fight, you know?"

Juliette sucked in a deep breath, bracing herself for what she was about to say. She knew there was little chance her words were going to be well received, but she was unable to hold back from blurting out her thoughts. "Why did you have to go and blow it in there like that?" she said, exhaling at last.

"What the hell are you talking about? I made that little bully look like a total amateur, and you know it."

"You've seriously gotta get a hold on that temper of yours," Juliette said. "You were probably way ahead in there, but you had to go and overreact, didn't you? You lashed out with that spinning elbow when you should have just risen above it all and kept doing exactly what you were doing."

"That's absolute bullshit, Jules. He deserved everything I threw at him. He was the one who wanted to play rough, not me."

"Martial arts is all about self-control and discipline," Juliette said. "Not revenge and retaliation."

"It's also about respect," Amiyah said. "And I'm pretty sure that asshole respects me now."

"You've got so much to learn," Juliette said. "Look, it's like this," she began, and then she paused to consider the best way to convey her thoughts. She watched Amiyah shifting in her seat, pulling her dress down over her thighs as though she was beginning to regret her choice of attire. The young woman's eyes were sad, like those of a child who'd been told off excessively, when all she'd done was try her best. Juliette opened her mouth to speak several times, but with each attempt she caught herself, realizing just how much she would sound like her brother if she were to continue. "Let's just forget it," she said, defeatedly. "I'll admit it, you did good in there, okay?"

"Are you serious?" Amiyah said, her dark eyes sparkling with optimism. She threw her arms around Juliette's shoulders to pull her into an embrace.

Juliette pushed the young woman away and glanced around to check if anybody was close enough to see into the truck.

"What's the matter?" Amiyah asked, sitting forward and parting her legs in a way that seemed intentionally antagonistic.

Juliette rubbed the heel of her hand into her eyes, trying to avert her gaze from the white triangle of underwear tucked at the crux of Amiyah's thighs. The vision simultaneously thrilled and terrified Juliette in equal measures. Her heart was thumping so hard, she thought Amiyah might actually be able to hear it pounding through her chest. She twisted her key in the ignition and stepped on the gas pedal so forcefully, the truck came to life with a roar.

"Where are we going?" Amiyah asked with a hint of laughter in her voice that suggested the ferocity of the truck's engine had excited her.

"We'll figure it out," Juliette said, trying to play it cool. As she steered her vehicle toward the exit, she noticed Earl and a handful of the other fighters glancing up from their conversations. They peered into the truck curiously, nudging one another and sniggering, undoubtedly making the kind of jokes and innuendos only a gathering of men would be able to appreciate. Juliette couldn't help but smile as she watched their jealous eyes disappearing in the rearview mirror. She looked down at Amiyah's golden-brown legs coming out of her dress and extending into the depths of the footwell.

"You should probably focus on the road," Amiyah said. She folded her legs together slowly, her purposefully drawn-out movements acting as a stark reminder of what she did for a living. "You know somewhere we could get a drink around here?" she asked.

"Bars aren't really my scene, kid."

"Well, I'm certainly not going back up that hill to sit underneath the damn octopus tree."

"I think you might mean the umbrella tree."

"Whatever," Amiyah said, with a roll of her eyes. "So what exactly is it you do for fun around here, anyway?"

"I like to sit in my truck and think."

Amiyah burst out laughing. "You're joking, right?"

Juliette stared blankly at the young woman.

Amiyah shook her head bewilderedly, her mouth hanging open in disbelief. "Can we at least have some music on in here?" she said, and she reached forward to adjust the volume of the stereo. The aging speakers began to rattle out the lamenting tones of a string section, a chorus of violins whining in perfect unison. A male voice moaned out lyrics with a dusky, soulful timbre. Amiyah closed her eyes, sat back in her seat, and silently mouthed along to the music. Juliette was endlessly captivated by the way the young woman could lose herself in the moment so easily. She was fascinated by Amiyah's carefree nature, her ability to enjoy life without the restraints of pandering to other people's expectations.

As Juliette guided her truck along the road—exiting the colorless industrial zone via a densely tree-lined highway—she realized just how much it soothed her woes to look upon Amiyah, to study the constellations of freckles scattered across her cheeks, or the plump folds of her lips swollen like ripe fruit begging to be consumed. Juliette timed her sideways glances to coincide with the intermittent flashes of each street lamp. The rhythmic bursts of warm light shone over Amiyah's features, her face appearing handsome and boyish one second and then elegant and fragile the next. She was an endlessly unfathomable conundrum, one that Juliette loved to agonize over.

Amiyah began to rock back and forth in her seat. She looked out through her window, her head darting rapidly as if she were searching for something among the dark, tangled woodland at the side of the road.

"You okay over there?" Juliette asked.

"Can we pull over?" Amiyah replied. "I really gotta pee."

"Are you kidding me? Why didn't you go back at the gym?"

"Sorry, Mom. I guess I didn't need to go back then. Can you just pull over?"

"What are you, twelve?" Juliette said. She slowed the truck and strained her eyes through the windshield. "I think there's a rest area up ahead," she said, nodding into the distance.

"Well, hurry up. Unless you want me to go all over your truck."

Juliette pulled off the road onto a dusty track that cut through the trees. The track looped back on itself, running parallel to the main road, leading to a clearing that was sparsely lit by a series of illuminated guideposts. There were a few picnic tables scattered about the place, a notice board with a map displaying hiking trails, and a pale concrete structure which Juliette assumed housed the restrooms. She parked and wound her window down. "Washrooms locked at 6 p.m.," she said, reading from a sign fastened to the notice board.

Amiyah threw her door open to climb out of the truck. "I guess I'd better look out for rattlesnakes then," she said.

"Wait a second," Juliette said, catching the young woman by the wrist.

"What is it? I'm about ready to burst."

Juliette hesitated. She hung her head as she struggled to find a way of expressing her thoughts. "Look, just forget it," she said, "it doesn't matter."

"Spit it out, will you, Jules. This isn't exactly the time to be shy."

"It's just, I was kind of thinking..." Juliette gritted her teeth. "No seriously, forget I said anything. I was just being dumb as usual, I guess."

Amiyah's body hunched down into an angry shape. "Juliette, if you don't fucking tell me what you were gonna say, right now, I'm gonna go ahead and pee all over your goddamn truck. Do you understand me?"

"Okay, okay. I was just going to ask..." Juliette shook her head at the absurdity of what she was about to say. "Well, I thought it might be nice if, I dunno, if maybe I could kind of watch."

"I fucking knew it," Amiyah said, her eyes practically doubling in size.

"Knew what?" Juliette said, defensively.

"That you were a freak, of course."

Juliette felt the blood drain from her face in an instant. "I'm sorry, I shouldn't have said anything. It was a stupid idea, really."

"Are you kidding me? Let's do it."

"What? You mean, you don't think it's weird?"

"I'm a stripper, Jules. That barely even registers on the scale of freaky shit I've been asked to do. So, come on, what are you waiting for? Let's go."

"Are you sure about this?" Juliette asked, but Amiyah was already out of the truck, her running shoes crunching over the graveled earth with every step. As Juliette climbed down from her seat, every sound was amplified by the still evening air that lingered among the trees.

"Well, come on then," Amiyah said, taking Juliette by the hand. The young woman's face was alive with a playful grin as she led the way toward the picnic tables. She tilted her head to one side, surveying the area and considering her plan of action. "Okay, sit right here," she said, and she directed Juliette to a bench beside one of the tables. Amiyah backed up toward the truck. She hoisted herself up onto the hood and sat with her legs hanging over the grill so that her sneakers rested against the mirrored surface of the bumper. She reached up into her dress and shimmied her hips back and forth, pulling her underwear down over her legs and dropping them by her side. The discarded underwear drew Juliette's eyes in the darkness, a white scrap of tangled fabric strewn out over the shiny black steel of the hood, a symbol of Amiyah's nakedness emphasizing the magnitude of everything that was about to occur.

"We don't really have to do this," Juliette said, shielding her eyes with one hand.

"Then don't watch," Amiyah said. "It's not like anybody's forcing you, is it? But I hope you realize I'm not gonna be able to hold this in forever, sugar. So you'd better make your mind up one way or the other."

Juliette lowered her hand, resigning to her curiosity.

Amiyah was smiling from ear to ear, clearly pleased she'd got her own way. She parted her legs with all the expertise of a stripper, watching Juliette's eyes for their reaction the whole time. Juliette's gaze was intentionally unfocused, her line of vision centered loosely in the general direction of her truck, where the abstract shape of the young woman was moving about up on the hood. Amiyah tugged at her dress and pulled it up over her navel, exposing further horrifying expanses of her grotesquely youthful flesh. She looked back over the roof of the truck to make sure they were completely alone, and then she released her dress from each shoulder, lowering the tight garment so the peaks of her breasts sprung free into the night air. The dress was reduced to little more than a band of fabric wrapped like a bandage around her waist.

Juliette squinted through the darkness. Every second of observation was like stepping deeper into ice-cold water. She was practically hyperventilating, unable to think straight due to the lack of oxygen reaching her brain. She somehow found the courage to run her eyes down over the subtle paunch of Amiyah's stomach, and then, venturing further still, she glanced down between the young woman's thighs, where her naked skin seemed to continue endlessly, stretching right to the hairless mound of her mons pubis, the plump little buttocks of her labia, and the dark, foreboding cleft that sat neatly tucked at their center. Juliette clasped at her throat as she struggled to catch her breath. Amiyah was laughing quietly the whole time, fully aware of the torture she was inflicting. The smooth flesh of her crotch shimmered under the light of the moon, her genitalia appearing muscular and defined. The complete absence of hair was jarring to Juliette's eyes, shocking and fascinating all at the same time. Amiyah parted her legs further, shamelessly revealing the shape and form of everything within, and Juliette threw her head back, overwhelmed by all she could see.

Amiyah lifted her hips. "It's coming," she said, her voice straining with exertion. Seconds later, a flurry of clear liquid sprung out from between her thighs, sprayed over the hood, and then settled into a steady projectile stream that arched out onto the graveled earth.

Juliette clutched at her lap as she watched the liquid jetting forth, barely able to resist the urge to pleasure herself. Amiyah groaned as she forced it all out. The torrent stopped and started, dribbling for a while and then becoming steady again. Every time Juliette thought the ordeal was over, the stream would reemerge, as if Amiyah were intentionally teasing with its varying momentum. Eventually, the flow of liquid ceased and Juliette's body slumped with relief. A fog of steam rose up between them, mist emanating from the puddle that had accumulated on the stony ground.

"Come here," Amiyah said, and she beckoned Juliette with the movement of one finger.

"Why, what for?" Juliette was defeated, barely able to get up off the bench after everything she'd witnessed.

Amiyah gathered her underwear and scrunched it into a ball. "So you can dry me off, of course," she said, smiling devilishly through the fog.

"You're kidding me, right?"

"You know you want to."

Juliette wandered over to her truck, feigning reluctance with a slouched, unenthused gait. She took hold of the tangled ball of fabric and patted it timidly between the young woman's thighs.

Amiyah took Juliette's hand to guide it. "Keep going," she demanded.

Juliette closed her eyes, unable to bear witness to what she was doing.

"I think that's enough," Amiyah said. She snatched the underwear back and tossed it away in the direction of an open-topped garbage can. She slid down off the hood and landed on the graveled earth with her naked body pressed right up against Juliette's. "Don't you want to kiss me yet?" she asked.

Juliette answered with a shrug.

"Why not?" Amiyah asked with an exaggerated frown. "Don't you want to see how I taste? What are you so afraid of?"

Juliette took a moment to breathe in the scent of the young woman's nakedness. "Maybe I'm afraid of how much I'll like it," she confessed.

Amiyah shivered at the revelation. "Just close your eyes," she whispered. "It won't hurt, I promise."

Juliette closed her eyes and waited anxiously.

"Just one thing I have to ask," Amiyah began. "Before we do this, I need to know, is it really just my body that interests you?"

"What do you mean?" Juliette asked, struggling to process the young woman's question in the midst of such a strange situation.

"I mean, what else could you possibly want from me? What exactly is it that you like about me so much?"

It amazed Juliette that someone who acted so brazenly with their own body would need to seek reassurance in this way. She saw a glint of insecurity shining from the dark pools of the young woman's eyes, so she held onto her a little tighter, overcome with a desire to reassure her, to look after her and to make her feel worthwhile.

"Well, to start off with," Juliette said, "I guess there's your determination, and your spirit. And, I suppose I kind of like the unique way you tend to look at things and analyze them. I've noticed that. Oh, and then I guess there's your sarcasm as well, even though you seem to laugh at pretty much everything I do. And the way you don't seem to care what anybody else thinks about you. I like that as well. Is that enough, or do you want me to go on?"

Amiyah didn't answer; she took Juliette behind the neck and pulled her in so their lips finally met. Juliette resisted instinctively, disgusted by how wrong it felt to kiss another woman. She tried to pull away at first, but soon gave in to the warmth of Amiyah's tongue sliding over her own. As she gave herself over, her brain was flooded with waves of extraordinary pleasure, as though a powerful charge of electricity was running right through her body. She couldn't get enough of how rebellious it felt to suck back and forth on Amiyah's tongue, to bite down on her lips, to explore the inside of her mouth. As they continued to kiss, Juliette began to appreciate the dichotomous power of being simultaneously disgusted and driven wild with lust all at the same time. She broke away to catch her breath like a swimmer surfacing for air.

"It's okay, just relax," Amiyah said, kissing Juliette on the face and neck.

Their mouths came together again and Juliette's subconscious conjured up a vision of Earl's judgmental eyes squinting out of the darkness, Shelby's face all screwed up with confusion. Instead of deterring Juliette, these woes only served to make her crime all the more enthralling. She kissed Amiyah harder, devouring all she could. The trees surrounding them danced on the breeze, their branches rustling wildly as if they'd been shaken up by the force of Juliette's arousal.

Amiyah reached down and began to fumble with the fly of Juliette's jeans. She tugged at the waistband, yanking it down over the cheeks of Juliette's ass. The young woman paused in the midst of her frenzy, sparing a few seconds to take in the sight of her own black underwear disappearing between Juliette's contrastingly pale buttocks. "I need to suck you off," she said, and she lowered herself down to her knees. It was all happening too fast for Juliette. She tried to pull her jeans back into place, not quite comfortable with this level of exposure, but suddenly Amiyah let go and became frozen there on the ground, kneeling motionless now that something else had caught her attention.

"What's wrong?" Juliette asked, noticing the sudden shift in her companion's behavior.

Amiyah held an outstretched finger over her lips. She got back to her feet and broke away from Juliette, distracted by something among the trees. She walked to the center of the clearing wearing nothing but the strip of fabric twisted around her midriff. She stood without a care of her nakedness, the brown skin of her body turning pale under the light of the moon. "I think I heard something," she said, and she cocked her head this way and that, listening attentively for something unseen. A pair of white lights came flashing through the darkness, a vehicle's headlamps flickering as they passed behind distant branches and trees. Seconds later, the sound of an engine accompanied the lights, its growl becoming louder as the vehicle approached along the track. Amiyah adjusted her dress and tiptoed back toward Juliette. "Let's get the hell out of here and go back to mine," she said, flashing her eyes suggestively.

Juliette paused to consider Amiyah's proposition.

"Come on," Amiyah said, "there's nobody home. We can listen to some music and fix something to eat. It's my night off."

The approaching vehicle swung past the guideposts and came to rest opposite Juliette's truck. The automobile's headlights shone from the other side of the clearing, blinding Juliette as she tried to figure out her next move. She waited for the lights to shut off, but they continued to cast their spotlight glare right into her face. The driver's door swung open and the silhouette of a man emerged, visible only as a dark outline thanks to the vibrancy of the vehicle's lights. The man ignited a cigarette and leaned back against the body of his car casually enough to suggest he was planning on staying there for quite a while.

"Why the hell doesn't this asshole turn his lights off?" Juliette asked. She reached into her truck, sounded her horn and flashed her headlights several times.

"Relax," Amiyah said. "Let's just get out of here."

The man stepped away from his car and threw his unspent cigarette down on the gravel.

"Who does this fool think he is?" Juliette said.

"Look, can we not spoil this moment?" Amiyah said, taking her older companion by the forearm.

Juliette yanked her arm free and rolled up the sleeves of her jacket. "We were here first," she said, and she took a few steps in the direction of the other car. As she made her way over to the stranger's vehicle, the passenger door swung open and a second individual emerged, stopping Juliette dead in her tracks. Seconds later, one of the rear side-doors was flung open as well, and shortly after that, the fourth and final door opened up to complete the entire set. "Okay, let's get the hell out of here," Juliette said, hurrying back toward her truck. The women clambered up into the cockpit, laughing together as they locked their doors and fastened their seat belts. Juliette twisted her key in the ignition and the engine spluttered but failed to come to life. "Holy shit," she said, fixing Amiyah with a wide-eyed look of terror.

"You gotta be messing with me," Amiyah said. "Try it again."

The quartet of shadowy figures staggered about in the glare of the headlights. Their bodies appeared warped and elongated, menacing like phantoms thanks to the harsh backlighting. They chattered and called out profanities as they began to wander over, their competing voices echoing unintelligibly through the still night air.

"Start the fucking truck, Jules."

"Just give her a minute."

"What the fuck? Hurry up, will you?"

"Just calm down, okay. You gotta give the battery a chance to wake up."

"Well, how the fuck long does that take?"

Something hit the front of the truck. There was a smash and a spray of liquid all at once, the sound of exploding glass, a bottle thrown by one of the men. Juliette closed her eyes to sharpen her focus. She twisted her key and stepped on the gas simultaneously, timing her movements with the exact synchronicity required to resuscitate her vehicle. The engine stirred angrily as it awoke from its slumber. Juliette slammed her foot down and the truck skidded away, spraying gravel about in its wake.

"Fucking hell, Jules." Amiyah twisted around in her seat to watch the men giving chase until they were out of sight behind the trees.

The narrow escape filled Juliette with a surge of adrenaline. She leaned over and pressed her lips against Amiyah's, eager to taste her again now that line had finally been crossed. The vehicle rumbled over uneven ground as it wandered close to the edge of the track.

"Watch where you're going," Amiyah said, breaking away from Juliette's grip. "You're determined to get us killed one way or the other."

Juliette laughed as she steadied her truck, pleased she'd actually been able to provoke a sense of panic in her younger companion.

"You're fucking crazy," Amiyah said, folding her arms and crossing her legs.

Juliette strained to contain her amusement. The sight of Amiyah's body folded up this way had a novel quality all of its own. As Juliette brought the truck back onto the main road, she reached over and pried Amiyah's arms apart so she could take the young woman's hand in her own. A reluctant smile crept onto Amiyah's lips as her eyes met Juliette's in the darkness.

CHAPTER 15

"I thought you told me nobody was gonna be around?" Juliette said, noticing the illuminated windows of Amiyah's house.

"I'm pretty sure they should all be at work by now," Amiyah said. Her face was fraught with confusion as she climbed down from the truck. She pulled at the hem of her dress as if the prospect of encountering other people had made her conscious of her lack of underwear. She gathered her backpack and led the way toward her front door with the same straight-faced look of determination she'd displayed on her way into the fight with Ghost. The dog was all over Amiyah as she entered the narrow hallway. The excited animal leaped up at the young woman and burrowed his face between her thighs, looking as though he was eagerly seeking her naked crotch.

"Hey, Angel," Amiyah said, crouching briefly to greet the playful dog.

"Let him out, will you? He's been driving me crazy," a female voice called out from somewhere deep within the house.

"Why aren't you at work, Celeste?" Amiyah replied.

A woman draped in a shapeless nightdress emerged into the hallway cradling a swaddled baby in her arms. "Is something up with your phone again, Mimi?" the woman asked, her drawn-out voice almost a whine.

"I've been at the gym all afternoon," Amiyah said. "Funnily enough, I don't keep the damn thing strapped to the side of my head."

Juliette recognized the woman's dreadlocked hair from her last visit to the house. A pungent odor lingered in the hallway rendering the air thick and unpleasant to breathe. With every inhalation, Juliette tried to distinguish whether the atmosphere had been tainted by the baby's food or by the equally repulsive stench of its excrement.

"I like your matching jackets," Celeste said with a lilt Juliette interpreted as sarcasm. Celeste's moth-colored nightdress reminded Juliette of just how asexual a woman could look.

"Why are you still here?" Amiyah asked, bluntly.

"I've been trying to call you all day," Celeste said. Her high-pitched voice suggested she was used to communicating with infants.

"And what's Solstice doing here, anyway?" Amiyah asked.

"Who's Solstice?" Juliette scoffed, unable to conceal the fact she found the moniker somewhat amusing.

"This is my little Solstice Moonbeam, right here," Celeste said, kissing her baby on the head, and nuzzling her face into his. "And, who do we have here, Mimi? Is this your new girlfriend?"

Amiyah paused and glanced back toward Juliette. She chewed on her bottom lip for a while, clearly struggling with some kind of indecision. "This is Jules," she said, eventually. And then, stumbling over her words a little, she added, "And yes, she's my girlfriend."

Juliette's whole body clenched up as she heard herself being introduced this way.

"Isn't his dad supposed to have him tonight?" Amiyah asked, with a nod toward the baby.

"Daddy got called into work, didn't he, Moonbeam?" Celeste said to her child. "That's why we've been trying to call Auntie Mimi all afternoon, isn't it, little man? So that Mommy can swap her shifts around."

"Are you kidding me? This is my first night off in weeks."

"Oh, come on now. Don't be like that. How many times have I covered for you in the past?"

"No way," Amiyah said, shaking her head profusely. "We've got plans."

"But, I already told Uncle Caesar you'd do it."

"Why the fuck would you have gone and done that?"

"Hey, come on," Juliette interjected. "No cursing in front of the child."

"Why not? It can't understand me."

"Look, calm down, Mimi," Celeste said, bobbing rhythmically to soothe her baby. "There's no need for tantrums now, is there? I'll cover for you next time, I promise."

"You're a fucking joke," Amiyah said. "Always expecting everyone to work around you and your stinking little brat. You think it's our fault you decided to crap that thing out?"

The baby started wailing the second Amiyah raised her voice. Juliette closed her eyes and winced as the ear-piercing cries reverberated around the narrow hallway.

Celeste's face straightened. "You selfish little dyke," she said, with a calmness not quite befitting the vulgarity of her words. "Maybe you oughta think about all the times we've had to cover your rent, and the trouble you would have gotten into if you hadn't been able to keep up your repayments to Caesar." She shifted her eyes toward Juliette as if checking whether she had prior knowledge of said payments.

"For fuck's sake," Amiyah growled. She pushed past Celeste and stomped her way up the uncarpeted staircase.

"So, you'll do it then?" Celeste called after her.

"I don't really have much choice, do I?" Amiyah said as she disappeared over the top of the stairs and slammed a door shut somewhere along the landing.

"Such a nice girl you've got yourself there," Celeste said to Juliette with a smile that appeared both sympathetic and sarcastic in equal measures.

"Sorry about the language, and all," Juliette said. Her back was pressed up against the wall as if she were trying to get as far away from the situation as possible.

Celeste stared straight at Juliette, looking her over curiously. "I didn't mean to call her a dyke," she said. "It was just a heat-of-the-moment thing, you know? I don't have a problem with lesbians, really I don't. I mean, if little Solstice here turns out to be gay, that's absolutely fine with me."

"Okay then," Juliette said, uncomfortable with the topic of her sexuality. "I think I'd better go see where Amiyah's got to." She edged past the mother and child, holding her breath the whole time to avoid the indistinguishable stench emanating from the pair. She ascended the creaking staircase and spotted Amiyah coming out of a bathroom wearing her scarlet kimono robe. The young woman's shoulders were hunched with rage as she stormed across the landing. Juliette followed her through the warren-like house, turning corners and climbing additional little staircases until they reached a room at the back of the property. As they entered the room, the smell of soiled diapers was quickly replaced with an equally overpowering yet considerably less offensive blend of aromas. Juliette could almost taste the beauty products in the air, as though a scented candle was burning somewhere out of sight. These were the kinds of fragrances she associated with people she thought of as real girls and women, not atypically androgynous characters such as herself.

As Amiyah locked the door behind them, Juliette took a moment to survey her surroundings. The glow of a nearby streetlamp entered the dimly-lit room through a window that was covered only by a loosely-draped scarf, the floral-patterned fabric of which cast dramatic shadows over the surface of a double bed. The walls were adorned with magazine clippings, pinup-style photographs of female celebrities, and images of martial artists captured in the midst of battle or standing dominant over fallen opponents. It occurred to Juliette that she could have been in the bedroom of a teenager, the walls covered with collected tokens of Amiyah's youthful optimism and visual representations of all the wondrous things she aspired to.

Juliette felt like an intruder, as though she—in all of her world-weary maturity—had no right to be there, attempting to steal a part of this young girl's enthusiasm for life in the vague hope it might make her own mundane existence a little more tolerable. She caught sight of a collection of books on a shelf, *The Art of War* by Sun Tzu, *The Book of Five Rings* by Miyamoto Musashi, along with numerous volumes on the workings of the human mind. Despite her reservations, Juliette felt herself falling deeper under Amiyah's spell. Her attraction to the young woman was crossing the boundary of mere lust alone and hurtling into the territory of something infinitely more terrifying.

Amiyah screwed her dress into a ball and threw it down on the floor. "Fucking waste of time, putting that on." She swung a wardrobe open and began to empty its contents onto her bed, pulling one garment after the next from the hangers and discarding them into a tangled heap.

"Hey, come on, calm down," Juliette said.

Amiyah roared with frustration. She ruffled her hands through her hair and collapsed among the pile of clothes on her bed.

"Listen, we can hang out some other time," Juliette said. "Honestly, it's not the end of the world."

"You're not the one who's gotta work in that shithole of a club all night, are you?" Amiyah sounded more like a teenager with every word. "I fucking hate this place. It's so unfair," she said. "I've gotta get dressed. I should have been at work, like, half an hour ago."

"I'll take you in. It won't hurt if you're a little late. I'll talk to Caesar."

"I can't even think straight," Amiyah said, sweeping her clothes onto the floor. "That white-witch downstairs has got me so worked up."

"Just try to relax, okay? What is it you usually do when you're feeling like this?"

"If you weren't here, I'd go outside, right now, and I'd smoke myself a goddamn cigarette."

"Well, I can't allow that, I'm afraid," Juliette said. "So, we'll have to try something else." She took Amiyah by the hands, pulled her up off the bed and led her to a couch in the corner of the room. "Remember, I do have a teenage daughter," Juliette said. "And believe me, Shelby has her moments."

"I'm not fourteen, Jules."

Juliette sat at one end of the couch and guided Amiyah to come down beside her. "Lie down and put your head in my lap," she said.

"I don't have time for this."

"Just lie down and be quiet for once, will you?"

"Okay, Mom," Amiyah said, rolling her eyes. She stretched out on her back and rested her head over Juliette's thighs.

Juliette placed her cold palm against the heat of the young woman's forehead, the surface of which had been thoroughly broiled by her temper. "Close your eyes and relax," she said, running her hand over Amiyah's forehead and on into the weightless cords of her plaited hair.

Amiyah closed her eyes and released a long breath as her rage finally began to subside. Juliette looked down at the heart-stopping vision of Amiyah's face resting within her lap. She wondered for a moment whether she herself could ever have looked half as young and unspoiled as the young girl she was holding in her arms, whether her own battle-hardened skin had been—at any point in her past—so thoroughly unblemished as this, so free of creases and furrows, so ironed-out and held taut with youthful vitality. Amiyah's infantile flesh made Juliette overly aware of her own advancing years, making her feel like a worn-out old creature, a haggard monster undeserving of the young girl before her. She held Amiyah's head tenderly, cherishing it like a precious object. She studied every detail of the girl's features with her fingers, running the back of her hand over the sides of Amiyah's cheeks, and further down to her sinewy neck. She tried to expel the tension from Amiyah's features, paying close attention to her breaths, every respiration a telling indicator of her serenity.

"Shelby's so lucky to have you as a mother," Amiyah said.

With each stroke, Juliette's hand wandered further across Amiyah's chest and down toward the lapels of her robe. Juliette's fingertips ventured beneath the silken garment and then quickly withdrew as though shocked by some powerful electrical current. "Sorry," she said, "I didn't mean to..."

"It's okay," Amiyah said, her wide, vulnerable eyes looking up into Juliette's. "You can touch me, if you want to."

Juliette allowed her trembling hand to slide back into the robe. She shivered as she felt the skin within, the flesh more silken than the garment that lay over it. Her palm grazed over the mound of a breast, her hand finding the textured head of a nipple, causing it to rise up and harden further. Juliette felt a warmth between her legs, a massaging sensation that resonated deep within her crotch even though no hand was caressing her there. She couldn't allow herself to be so easily seduced. Her mind raced, searching desperately for any kind of distraction. "Just one thing I need to know," she began, remembering something which had been playing on her mind. "What did Celeste mean exactly when she mentioned the repayments you're making to Caesar?"

"It's nothing," Amiyah said, dismissively, her forehead tightening with anguish.

"Surely, it must have meant something for her to have brought it up."

"Look, I fucked up and Caesar bailed me out, okay? So, now I gotta pay him back what I owe, that's all."

"Well, how much are we talking about here?"

"Enough to keep me working in his club for a while, let's just put it that way. But please, can we talk about this some other time?"

"But, this sounds kind of serious. How much do you owe?"

"I really don't need a lecture right now, Jules. Can we change the subject?" Amiyah unfastened the belt of her robe and allowed the garment to slide open over her skin.

The sight of the young woman's body instantly distracted Juliette from her line of questioning. She marveled at the landscape of flesh laid out before her, Amiyah's hipbones jutting forth into the air, her ribcage swelling and receding with every breath, her breasts appearing smaller and more erect now that she was lying on her back. Juliette was afraid to touch any part of the anatomical arrangement. She was perfectly happy to simply observe and would have gladly spent the entire evening admiring this juvenile body, slowly devouring every inch of it with her eyes. "And, why did you tell Celeste I was your, well, that I was your girlfriend?"

Amiyah raised a hand to cover her face with embarrassment. "It just came out that way, okay? That new-age cunt downstairs likes to think I don't have a single thing in the world; that I'm just some stupid little kid. She thinks she's so important, always parading about with her shit-factory of a baby like it's some kind of a trophy. I just wanted to make her see I actually have something in life, that's all. I'm sorry if I exaggerated, okay?"

Juliette traced Amiyah's lips with her thumb. "I understand," she said.

"But, you know, Jules, the thing is, I would kind of like it if I could be your girl." Amiyah was still covering her eyes, afraid of whatever reaction her words might provoke.

"Be careful what you wish for, kid. There's things about me you probably wouldn't like."

"Such as?"

"Things about my past. Stuff you wouldn't understand."

"But, don't you want me to be your girl?" Amiyah asked. She reached up and took Juliette by the hand. Without uttering another word, she guided Juliette's fingers down onto the hairless mound of her mons pubis.

Juliette could sense the burgeoning wetness of her own arousal. She tried to fight against it, embarrassed by her own excitement.

211

"Touch me, Jules, please," Amiyah whispered, lifting her hips to press herself into Juliette's hand. "I need it."

Juliette held onto the plump folds of the young woman's crotch, her middle finger resting neatly in the central groove. She wanted to savor the magic of this first touch, drawing the moment out for as long as she could. Amiyah showed no such patience or restraint, parting her legs so that Juliette's hand found the wetness within. The young woman moaned and her body twisted with ecstasy. She sat up and looked right into Juliette's face as though staring her down before a fight in the cage, as if something momentous was about to happen between them and Amiyah wanted to see if Juliette was ready to accept the challenge. She took hold of Juliette's hand and made her taste the slick moisture on her own fingertips, spreading it all over Juliette's lips and all around her mouth like some kind of an initiation process. She moved in and their mouths met. It seemed Amiyah was eager to taste herself on Juliette's lips. The young woman sat back and nodded her head, confirming she believed Juliette to be ready for all that was about to occur.

Amiyah got up off the couch, climbed out of her open robe and took Juliette by the hand. As she led the way toward the bed, the muscle-tone in every part of her body was highlighted by the glow of the streetlamps shining in through the window. Her back tensed up and then released with every step; the looser flesh of her buttocks heaved over her thighs. Juliette gazed into the dark crease at the center of Amiyah's tear-drop derrière. She'd never felt such a sense of impending terror, not during a single walk-out to any of the fights she'd been in throughout her career. She'd never known an opponent quite like this, had never been so overwhelmed with nervous energy.

As they arrived at the bed, Juliette took the young woman by her neck and encouraged her head down toward the mattress. Amiyah wound up on her knees with her head resting on the pillow and her ass up in the air. Juliette took a step back to take in the view. It came as no surprise to her that every last part of Amiyah was so perfectly formed.

Even the most intimate regions of her anatomy captivated Juliette with their mouthwatering allure, like some fantastically obscene dessert begging to be devoured. Juliette's features hung heavy with awe. She came down on her knees, and then moving slowly as if entranced, she leaned in and kissed Amiyah between her legs from behind. As she sucked Amiyah's labia into her mouth, Juliette's own crotch was throbbing with pleasure, causing her conscious thoughts to dissolve into euphoria. All of her fears were quickly forgotten as she feasted on the pulp of the young woman's succulent fruit.

She felt Amiyah bucking away and then coming back as if repeatedly stricken with unbearable pain. Juliette pushed her tongue deeper into the moist flesh, eagerly gorging on the slick nectar within. She noticed—in the midst of her lust—how the sweet, sharp taste was similar to her own, but with a unique, distinguishing tang, a flavor that was entirely specific to her lover. She sucked at the fleshy nub of Amiyah's clitoral hood, eager to taste the very essence of the girl.

Amiyah buried her face deep into her pillow, hoping to muffle the clarity of her moans. It thrilled Juliette to imagine the dreadlocked woman would be listening attentively somewhere below, a puzzled expression emblazoned across her face as she tried to imagine the scandalous acts that were being committed upstairs. Juliette ran her tongue up between the cheeks of Amiyah's ass, compelled to taste the deepest, most unchartered regions of her skin. She bit at the flesh of each buttock and then returned to the warmth of the center point, making out with the tight orifice as though it were a mouth, tracing the grooved circumference with her lips, and then forcing her tongue further inside until Amiyah's breaths grew labored with agony.

When Juliette finally broke away, Amiyah sat up in a daze, cursing about how good it had felt. She kissed Juliette on the mouth more vigorously than before, eager once again to taste herself on Juliette's lips. "Seems a little unfair that I'm the one who always winds up naked," Amiyah said, lying back on her elbows, preparing to watch Juliette undress.

Juliette sat on the edge of the bed, ashamed of the fact she was still fully clothed, but unable to find the confidence to shed any of her garments.

"Please," Amiyah begged, "I haven't got long. I wanna feel your skin against mine."

Juliette stood up and began to disrobe. She stripped down to her underwear as quickly as she could, hanging her head with shame the whole time. "Happy now?" she said, trembling like a child shivering at the edge of a pool, unable to find the courage to jump into the water.

Amiyah stared longingly at the black lace of her own underwear covering Juliette's pale skin. "Take them off," she said.

Juliette glanced at the floor as she struggled with her nerves.

Amiyah guided Juliette to join her on the bed. "Lay down," she said, "and lift up your hips." She peeled the underwear off and discarded it out of sight.

The air felt especially cold against the moist skin between Juliette's thighs. She covered herself with a hand in her lap, conscious of the fact she wasn't quite as hair-free as her lover.

"It's okay, just let go," Amiyah said, pulling Juliette's hand aside so that every part of her was on display.

Juliette tried to focus on her breathing, barely able to cope with the exhilaration of being exposed this way. She closed her eyes and clutched handfuls of the bedding beneath her. And then she felt it, the warmth of Amiyah's tongue sliding over her innermost skin, through the central crease and up over her clitoris in one swift motion that seemed to trail on forever, delivering pleasure so great, her body shuddered and spasmed. Amiyah's eyes were narrowed with concentration, like those of an expert focused on their craft. She encased Juliette's most erogenous zone with her mouth, taking in all that she could, working her tongue inside and then circling it over Juliette's clit. Juliette felt the pleasure mounting dangerously within. She pushed the young woman away, not wanting this experience to be over so quickly.

Amiyah crawled up beside her and their naked bodies became entangled into one mass of slithering flesh, their individual limbs distinguishable only by the contrasting tones of their skin. They pressed their wet crotches together and slid over each other's thighs, filling the air with the warm smell of sex. Juliette's fingers found the damp center-point of Amiyah's ass, and she eased a single digit in among the tight grip of the hole. She couldn't resist the urge to penetrate the part of Amiyah she'd spent so long admiring from afar. They kissed frantically, covering each other's faces with saliva, smelling the scent of sex on each other's skin. With their fingers moving inside of one another, their bodies became synchronized, writhing in perfect time, each of them adjusting the speed and pressure of their touch in order to maintain a harmonious equilibrium in the race toward climax.

"I want you to bite me when you come," Juliette said through heavy breaths, "and the mark will remind me of how good this all felt."

The suggestion seemed to push Amiyah over the edge and she clamped her teeth down into Juliette's shoulder. Juliette felt with her fingers, the flesh inside of Amiyah pulsating, contracting, and then relaxing over and over. The intensity of these sensations sent Juliette past the point of no return. The ecstasy surged uncontrollably inside of her, rendering her defenseless to its insurmountable power. She feared giving in to the malevolent sensation as though it was an extreme urge to urinate right there in the bed. When she finally submitted, the sense of relief was like an explosion going off in the pit of her stomach, pulverizing her body so that it could dissolve into Amiyah's. Every nerve ending was shrouded with a profound sense of warmth, numbing Juliette's body and fogging her mind so that no conscious thought could exist, and all that remained was a feeling of oneness with her lover.

CHAPTER 16

Juliette stood alone at the bar, entranced by the pattern of bass tones rumbling up through her boots, resonating in every part of her body. The neon lights of the club bathed her surroundings in varying shades of red, casting a scarlet filter over all she could see, saturating the walls and furnishings with every hue from blush pink to burnt mahogany. Semi-naked bodies writhed about in her peripheral vision, rose-tinted flesh gently undulating like perpetually burning flames. The faces of the male patrons leered motionless, their blood-red eyes hypnotized by the dancers' graceful movements. Juliette paid little attention to the activity around her, as though she was blocking out the commotion of jeering spectators in the midst of a fight. She was focused solely on completing her mission, her eyes fixed on the shadowy booths at the back of the club.

A broad figure emerged from the darkness, a beastly doorman whose slow movements were synchronized to the steady drone of the bass. As the man drew closer, Juliette quickly identified his bearded face, recognizing him to be the same acquaintance of Earl's who'd been working the door on her last visit to the club. A wave of heat swept through Juliette as the familiar doorman came toward her.

"You ready, Jules?" the doorman said, his low voice booming from the dense foliage of his facial hair.

Juliette followed the man's hulking frame into the depths of the club. They passed through shadowy annexes, entering a door marked, "no admittance," and continuing on into a maze of narrow corridors. "You still training?" Juliette asked, trying to get a sense of how much regular contact the man had with her brother. "Haven't seen you at Diablo's in a long time."

"You know how it is, Caesar likes to keep me busy," the doorman answered, his wide body filling much of the hallway like a rubber bung stuffed into the neck of a bottle.

Juliette paused in front of an open door and stared curiously into a room occupied by several barely-dressed women. She watched the dancers adjusting their stage-wear, arranging tiny scraps of fabric over the naked flesh of their bodies, chatting and laughing as they perfected their makeup in illuminated mirrors. Juliette felt a surge of adrenaline rising within. The spectacle of these athletically built women readying themselves for battle triggered flashbacks to her own laborious pre-fight preparations. She could have just as easily been backstage at some vast arena, waiting anxiously for her call to walk out to the cage. Her mind shifted into fight mode. A sickening nervousness gripped her, making her feel like something terrible was about to happen, as though some impending doom awaited in the form of an opponent.

"Let's go," the doorman said. "Don't wanna keep the big man waiting, do we?"

Juliette was reminded that her opponent on this occasion was Caesar, and that her bout with him would soon take place somewhere deep in the belly of the club. She breathed slowly to steady her nerves. She thought of Amiyah, her motivation in all of this, and her mind was flooded with the warmth of everything they'd done together. If she could come to terms with the implications of their last encounter, could face up to the magnitude of her feelings for the young woman, she knew Caesar would be no match for her. Suddenly, the prospect of negotiating with the man filled her with no fear at all.

The doorman was getting away from Juliette. She hurried along the corridor to catch up with him, not wanting to get left behind in the depths of the maze. They descended a staircase which brought them down to a level previously unknown to Juliette, a network of tunnels running beneath the main body of the club. Darkness and near-silence engulfed them as they plunged further downward. The walls were lined with endless channels of rattling pipes and hanging ribbons of electrical wires. A pungent fog lingered all around them, a cloud of smoke carrying with it the unmistakable, earthy scent of marijuana. Juliette felt the intoxicating mist beating at the back of her throat, filling her lungs with potent fumes. Time seemed to slow down. Her movements became delayed, lapsing out of synchronicity with her thoughts.

"That's Caesar's office, right over there," the doorman said, and he signaled to a faint outline of a doorway glowing at the end of the dark passageway.

A distant whining sound emanated from beyond the sealed door, increasing in volume and clarity as the pair drew nearer to the source. Juliette listened carefully, deciphering the sound to be the grandiose chords of classical music. In stark contrast to these intricately arranged melodies, a single ear-piercing clap rang out through the air, a resounding slap of flesh against flesh. Moments later, a female voice squealed out and then erupted into a flurry of shrill laughter.

The doorman's eyes were heavy with sympathy as though he was taking great pity on Juliette for all that awaited her. He closed one of his enormous hands into a fist and beat the side of it over the cast-iron surface of the door, drumming out a loud and distinctive rhythm, a secret code that was required to gain entrance. The vault-like doorway clanked and rattled as its innumerable locks and bolts unfastened in sequence. The doorman flashed his eyes to wish Juliette luck, and without further comment, he nodded once and left, satisfied he'd delivered Juliette to her final destination.

Juliette pushed all of her weight up against the heavy door, wondering what kind of underworld activities Caesar had got himself involved with to require this level of protection. As the door slowly opened, the marijuana smoke grew thicker and the music louder. When Juliette's eyes finally adjusted to the dense atmosphere, she found herself peering into a room that was so elaborately decorated, it wouldn't have looked out of place tucked away in an alcove of a sprawling historic mansion. As Juliette made her way over the threshold, the skin of her face was warmed by the crackling heat of an open fire. The walls were adorned into their furthest corners with an array of ornately-framed fight memorabilia, a collection of championship-level belts, and a collage of promotional posters, much of which depicted Caesar when he was both considerably younger and more athletically built.

"Take a seat, Jules. Don't be shy," Caesar's drawling voice slurred out over the soaring crescendos of the music.

Juliette squinted through the mist, focusing on the central portion of the room her eyes had been trying to avoid, and right there — behind a large hardwood desk — was Caesar, his rotund, neckless body slouched lethargically in a high-backed throne of a chair.

"Come on in and join the party," Caesar said, sweeping a bejeweled hand through the mist in slow-motion.

Juliette surveyed the surface of the desk, and realized Dolores was laid out in front of the man, stretched out on her back like some kind of a slumbering pet, her bandy limbs splayed among a scattering of ashtrays and smoking paraphernalia.

Dolores got up on her elbows. Her actions appeared stunted, as if she was moving under water. "Hey, Jules," she said, her heavily-penciled eyes glazed with intoxication, her claw-like hands resting over her chest, close enough to her breasts to make Juliette feel uncomfortable.

"Am I interrupting something here?" Juliette asked.

Caesar billowed a thick stream of smoke out into the already potent atmosphere. "Just sit down," he said. "Dolores won't bite. Not unless you ask her to."

The heat from the open fire was suffocating, causing Juliette to gasp for oxygen in the subterranean lair. She struggled to focus on her movements as she crossed the room, walking unsteadily until she came down onto one of two chairs opposite Caesar. She couldn't help but notice the fact that Dolores was dressed entirely in white, her scrawny legs emerging from a pleated skirt, her similarly-wizened arms jutting from the capped sleeves of a polo shirt. "What's with the tennis outfit?" Juliette asked.

Dolores threw her head back and squealed with laughter.

"It's kind of my thing," Caesar said, his swollen body bobbing with amusement.

"Oh really, you play?" Juliette asked.

"Let's just say, I appreciate the uniforms."

"Fair enough," Juliette replied, certain she was high on the fumes of whatever Caesar was smoking.

"Come on, make yourself at home," Caesar said. "Take a hit with me." He removed the lid from a small filigree dish to reveal its white, crystalline contents. He lifted Dolores' shirt, exposing her malnourished stomach, the colorless flesh of which was so empty, it was almost concaved. He spooned out a helping of the white granules from the dish and tipped them onto the surface of Dolores' belly.

Juliette shuffled evasively in her chair.

"Don't be such a square," Dolores said.

Caesar extended the smallest digit of one hand to reveal a fingernail that was both longer and more pointed than any of his others. He used the unclipped nail to slice the powder he'd laid out on Dolores' stomach into a neat little line. As he leaned forward, his huge body—tightly packed into a silken shirt—bulged over the surface of the desk. Juliette waited for Caesar to snort the powder through a rolled-up bank note or some other form of makeshift tube, but instead, he stuck out his bloated slug of a tongue and lapped up the trail of powder from Dolores' stomach with a single sweep of his bald head, leaving a glistening smudge of saliva behind in his wake. Caesar worked the powder around in his mouth, savoring its taste. He closed his eyes, tilted his head back, and swallowed loudly, practically gargling the substance as it went down his throat.

"Damn Caesar, I kind of expected better of you," Juliette said.

"Relax, it's sugar," Caesar said. "Do I look like a junky to you? I'm on a diet. This is my one pleasure. Indulge me, will you?"

Dolores smirked at Juliette's confusion.

"That shit will probably kill you faster than drugs will, anyway," Juliette said.

Caesar wedged a joint between his lips, squinted his eyes with concentration, and turned Dolores onto her stomach, his thick-fingered hands arranging the woman's emaciated body with ease. He tossed the pleated fabric of Dolores' skirt up over her back, revealing the meager cheeks of her ass and the narrow strip of underwear tucked up between them.

"What the hell?" Juliette said, her eyes darting to avoid the spectacle.

Dolores was giggling the whole time, seemingly unfazed by her involuntary exposure.

Caesar spooned out another helping of sugar onto one of Dolores' pallid buttocks and deftly sliced the shimmering crystals into a perfect line with his fingernail. "Your turn, Jules," he said.

"You gotta be kidding me, right?"

"Don't insult me. Think of it as an offering, from me to you. Something to sweeten the air a little before we talk business."

Juliette allowed her eyes to wander over the gift that was being presented to her. She inspected Dolores' exposed derrière with a sort of suspicious curiosity, as though fearing she was about to be poisoned. Dolores' buttocks were hollow at their sides, somewhat deflated due to a lack of fat content. Juliette was unable to avert her gaze, intrigued and repelled in equal measures, somehow drawn to the brazen display of naked flesh no matter how much it disgusted her. She leaned in toward the offering, the clarity of her judgment clouded by the intoxicating marijuana fumes.

"Come on, take a hit," Dolores hissed through her teeth.

Caesar's eyes were wide and intense among the dark skin of his face. His shiny dome of a head was gently nodding, encouraging Juliette to do his bidding.

Dolores' pointed little tongue was circling her lips. "Do it," she said. "Just fucking do it."

Juliette glanced at the pale rump before her; at Caesar's bloodshot eyes bulging from their sockets. She realized how easy it would be to take a bite from the fruit that was being offered to her so freely. She'd already crossed the line with regards to being intimate with a member of the same sex. Surely the consumption of this single line of sugar would be nothing in comparison to the acts she'd already committed.

Caesar was almost trembling with anticipation, realizing Juliette was on the brink of taking the hit.

Juliette recognized the glee in his expression, the satisfaction it was giving him to know she was about to do his bidding. She understood — in that moment — there was more significance to the offering than the mere physical act it entailed. Caesar was trying to exert his power, to impose his will, to open the negotiations with Juliette playing by his rules, thus setting the tone for whatever discussions would follow. Juliette sat back in her chair, controlling her breathing to calm herself down. "I'm good, thanks," she said.

Both Caesar and Dolores seemed to exhale in unison, as though they'd been waiting with bated breath, teetering on the cusp of victory.

"Suit yourself," Dolores said, swiping the sugar from her skin and then sucking her fingers clean one after the other.

Caesar was grinning silently at Juliette, finally acknowledging her as a formidable opponent. "Why don't you go sit by the fire, pumpkin?" he said to Dolores. "Papa bear needs to talk business."

"You're always talking business. I thought we were actually gonna spend some time together this evening."

"Just go watch TV or something, okay?"

Dolores slid off the desk and walked barefoot across the room with the type of slouched posture Juliette was used to seeing her daughter adopt in the midst of a tantrum. Dolores switched on the television and curled herself up on an old wing-backed armchair that was positioned in front of the fire. She flicked through the stations, cursing every network in turn until she settled on a wildlife documentary. She nestled further into the chair, watching a pride of lionesses stalking buffalo through tall grass.

"So, let's talk," Caesar said. He reignited his joint and disappeared momentarily behind a thick cloud of smoke. "Tell me, Jules Diamond Diaz, why are you even here?"

"What, you're trying to tell me you haven't got it all figured out?"

"Cut the shit. What do you want?"

"I wanna buy her out, of course."

"You won the lottery or something?" Caesar scoffed, choking on the smoke of his joint. "Or did somebody die? Because, you must have come into some serious money to be talking like that."

"So, why don't you cut the shit, and tell me how much we're talking here?"

"Off the top of my head, I'd say she's gonna be dancing here for at least another couple years before she can pay me what she owes. That's if she works hard and focuses on her craft, of course."

"Damn, Caesar, two years? You know what kind of a difference that makes in a fighter's career."

"You think I'm running a charity here, or what? You think kindness and goodwill pays for all this? Everything you see here is antique. How much do you think it cost me to have that marble fireplace installed down here? I got a Jacuzzi hot tub out the back, a cinema screen, the whole set up. That's why I'm in business. So I can obtain the finest things this world has to offer. And you think I can just afford to throw money around? Well let me tell you, when I buy somebody else's debt, when I save them from owing money to the kind of people you really do not want to be owing money to, I expect that individual to pay me back, in full. And when they don't, I look inside of myself and I bring out the beast that stepped into the cage all those times and won all of these belts you can see up on the walls right here. You understand me, Jules?"

Juliette sighed with frustration. "I think I get the picture," she said. Her attention was drawn to the television screen in the corner of the room. A lioness snarled as it closed in on a loan buffalo and chased the horned beast through a shallow pool of water.

"Get it, girl," Dolores said, sitting forward in her chair to get a better view, her face scrunched up with glee.

"Of course, I'm sure we could always come to some kind of an arrangement," Caesar said, taking a long, hard drag to refuel himself before making his proposal. "The way I see it, I have something you want. So in return, how about you give me and everybody else exactly what it is that we all want?"

Juliette's posture deflated. "You're talking about me fighting The Ox again, aren't you?"

"It's the fight everybody wants to see, isn't it?"

"How much do you think you're gonna make off that fight, anyway?"

"It's not all about money. It's about being able to give people what they desire, being able to make deals happen. That's what gives you real power as a promoter. Take Mimi, for example. You think it makes financial sense for me to offer her any kind of a loan? Like I say, it's not all about the money. It's about having a hot piece of ass like her in my club. That's what keeps the customers coming back here every night. You understand?"

"You realize my next fight's probably gonna be my last, right? That's all I've got left, one good fight and I'm done. Do you really think I wanna spend my last outing giving somebody I already defeated the chance to get their revenge? Because that doesn't exactly sound very appealing to me."

Caesar took another drag as he considered his next move. "Thing is, when you turn down a fight like that, people start drawing their own conclusions. Even Shaolin's been going around telling anybody who'll listen you're running scared from The Ox."

"You think I care what that paper champion has to say? She's been picking and choosing fights her whole career. How else do you think she's hung on to that belt for so long?"

"Sounds like fighting talk to me."

"I wish," Juliette blurted without even thinking. Her statement seemed to affect the very atmosphere of the room. The soothing whir of the classical music, the wild beasts snarling from the television screen, all of it seemed to be muted now that the focus was on her proclamation alone. She felt a pang of embarrassment deep in the pit of her stomach as she contemplated the fact that she, an aging veteran who'd been considering the prospect of her own retirement, had just announced her desire to compete against the current reigning champion of her weight class. Much to Juliette's surprise, she could see by the squinted focus of Caesar's eyes that he was giving at least some level of consideration to her words, that he was making his calculations and ruminating over the possibility of a future bout between her and Shaolin. She waited for Caesar's response, his expressionless face looking her over from head to toe as he measured her and considered her worth. She felt exposed and vulnerable under the man's intense scrutiny, as though she might as well have been sitting there naked among the lavish decor of her surroundings, with Caesar's cold, glazed eyes inspecting every inch of her body.

"I ain't no miracle worker," Caesar said, after a torturously prolonged pause. "You've got a hell of a climb before you can get back to competing at that kind of a level."

"Well, you're gonna have to come up with something better than Oksana I'm afraid. Because that's just not gonna happen." Juliette turned to the television, noticing Dolores had slumped back into her chair with her arms folded over her chest, apparently disappointed with the turn of events in the wildlife documentary she was watching. The buffalo had somehow managed to evade the lions and was back among the safety of the herd. "Looks like nobody's getting what they wanted today, huh?" Juliette said with a nod toward the television screen.

Caesar picked his cell phone up off the desk. "We'll see about that," he said. The rectangular handset appeared almost miniature among the swollen digits of his hands. He began to compose a message, his stout, bejeweled fingers jabbing at the surface of the screen.

Juliette's nerves fired up as she wondered what kind of underhanded tactics he was about to employ.

Caesar settled his phone down on the desk. He sat back in his chair and looked at Juliette with his eyebrows raised, as if daring her to try and figure out his next move.

"Well, come on then," Juliette said, "put me out of my misery."

Caesar shook his head at Juliette, mocking her apparent lack of business acumen. "You see, the other side of the deal, I'm talking about Team Zen, of course, that's all tied up and ready to go. But on this side of the table, things are a little more, shall we say, complicated."

"Cut the riddles, and get to the point."

Caesar laughed again, taking great pleasure in Juliette's confusion. "The way I see it, we've got three people involved in this side of the deal. That's you, me, and a certain little lady, who right about now is probably shaking her ass somewhere upstairs. So the question is, how are we supposed to come to any kind of an agreement when we don't even have all of the concerned parties here to negotiate with?"

A chill ran through Juliette as she began to fathom Caesar's plan. "Just leave the kid out of this, okay?"

Caesar closed his eyes, sat back, and swayed along to the music, basking in the satisfaction of having Juliette up against the ropes. "She's already on her way down," he said.

"This is between you and me, Caesar, and you know it."

"Is that right?" Caesar said. "How do you suppose Mimi's gonna feel when she finds out that you, her so-called coach, had the chance to free her from all of this, but you simply weren't willing to make the required sacrifice."

"Are you trying to blackmail me?"

Caesar slammed a fist down onto his desk. "This is business," he said, leaning further forward. "She's a part of the transaction, isn't she? As far as I'm concerned, that makes her a business associate. So I would say it's kind of important for her to know the terms of the contract, wouldn't you?"

"Fine, whatever," Juliette said, trying to conceal the fire of anxiety that was burning within her.

Dolores was perched at the edge of the armchair. "Oh, this is gonna be so good," she said. "I oughta get myself some popcorn, really I should."

"Go wait out back, pumpkin," Caesar said. "Papa bear needs to focus on his game."

"No way. I'm not about to miss out on this."

"I said, go wait in the damn Jacuzzi. Papa needs to concentrate, and that ain't gonna happen if your little ass is wandering about the place looking like it just got off the tennis court. We're gonna be celebrating about five minutes from now. So, don't make me get serious with you, okay?"

Dolores got up off the chair with such little enthusiasm it looked as though she was being hoisted about by an invisible rope.

Caesar waved her away and then turned his gargantuan body back toward Juliette. "You should have known better than to have come down here trying to cut a deal with the devil himself."

Juliette was unable to respond due to the fury burning inside of her. She ran her eyes over the muddle of smoking paraphernalia spread out over the desk, focusing her attention on a large glass ashtray, a circular receptacle with a particularly substantial rim, the curved edge of which looked as though it would fill the hand quite ergonomically. She thought about how solid the ashtray would feel in the grip of her palm, how satisfying it would be to swing the glass disk through the air, its considerable weight carrying it forward with great force and momentum until she brought it crashing down into Caesar's bald sphere of a head. She couldn't help but smile as she imagined his hairless scalp cracking open like the shell of a boiled egg, his blood spilling out like yolk escaping from within.

"Something funny?" Caesar asked.

Juliette stared at the man silently, picturing his head giving way to the force of her blows, his fractured skull opening up to reveal the salmon-pink mush of his puréed brain matter. A series of loud bangs woke Juliette from her daydream. She sat up tall as a distinctive pattern of thuds reverberated from the doorway behind her. Caesar flicked a switch mounted on his desk and the locking mechanisms concealed within the door unfastened in sequence. As the door swung open, a blast of familiarly-scented air wafted into the room. Every muscle in Juliette's body seized up at once as she tasted her lover on the incoming breeze. She turned to watch the young woman crossing the room, noticing the way her upper body was wrapped up in her signature fur coat. Juliette's mind was haunted with a vision of everything that lurked beneath the beastly garment. She averted her gaze, conscious Caesar might detect her fascination and use it as extra leverage in the negotiations that would follow.

"What are you doing down here, Jules?" Amiyah asked as she came down into the chair next to Juliette's. "What's going on?"

Juliette studied the young woman's darkly-painted lips, unwittingly remembering how they'd felt against her own. She shifted awkwardly in her seat, unable to muster any words to justify her presence.

"Listen, Mimi," Caesar said, choking on the smoke of his joint as he laughed at Juliette's apparent discomfort. "Your coach over here came to me trying to buy you out of our little agreement. And, being the reasonable kind of a guy that I am, I said yes. Just as long as she agrees to give me something I want in return, of course."

Amiyah checked her nails and sighed as she contemplated the nature of her boss's demands.

Caesar had slumped further into his throne. His thick lips hung open to form a self-satisfied smile. Juliette knew he would be enjoying all the anticipation, the tense energy lingering in the atmosphere.

"Can someone please just tell me what the fuck is going on here?" Amiyah said.

"Look, I'll take the damn fight with Oksana, okay?" Juliette blurted out, not wanting to grant Caesar the pleasure of torturing her any further.

"So, that's it?" Amiyah said. "You think you're gonna play the hero and fight for my freedom? And then what? I'll just be indebted to you instead of him, won't I?"

"It's just one little fight," Juliette said with a shrug.

"I can fight my own battles, thank you," Amiyah said. She got up off her chair and pulled her coat tight over her chest. "I don't want any part of this sordid little deal. I got myself into this mess, so I'll find my own way out of it."

Caesar adjusted the crotch of his pants as though the sight of the women arguing had ignited a twinge of pleasure somewhere in the depths of his loins.

"Just sit down, kid," Juliette said. "Let's talk about this for a minute."

"I didn't ask for your help. You've got no right to be interfering like this."

"This is for both of us," Juliette attempted to explain, but it was too late, Amiyah was already making her way out of the extravagantly-furnished enclave.

Caesar reignited his joint, sucking hard so the tip of the thing flared up with a tall flame. "All I can say is, good luck coaching that one." He slouched back into his ornately-carved throne as if the whole matter had been of no real importance to him in the first place.

"Yeah, nice doing business with you, as always," Juliette said as she got up off the chair and hurried toward the exit. She felt unsteady on her feet thanks to her involuntary inhalation of the herbaceous smoke. She fought against the debilitating effects of the potent fumes, knowing Amiyah would be getting away from her and escaping back to the upper level of the club.

"Come back to me when you've talked her around," Caesar said. "You know there's always a deal to be done."

"Amiyah, wait," Juliette called out. "Don't be like this. I was just trying to help." She bounced off the walls of the narrow corridor as she ran to catch up with the young woman.

Amiyah slowed down but did not turn back, too enraged to face Juliette. "No more deals, okay," she said. "That's how I got here in the first place. I'm sick of always owing something to somebody. Whatever we've got between us, I don't want it to be about that. I don't want to owe you anything."

"But, like I said, it's just one fight." Juliette caught Amiyah by the hand. As their fingers became interlocked, Juliette felt the buzz of energy that seemed to surge through her every time they made physical contact. Even this simple touching of hands felt wrong and forbidden, a tantalizing reminder of the electrical charge that had passed between them when their naked bodies had been intertwined. "I don't want you to have to dance here anymore," she said.

"Don't ruin what we've got," Amiyah replied. "If you have to fight Oksana again, you'll end up resenting me for it. I know you will."

"But, I want to do it for you. For us," Juliette said, tightening her grip on the young woman's hand.

"I'm not going to let Caesar taint this. I'll work it out, okay. Trust me." Amiyah led Juliette along the gloomy passageway, checking over her shoulder to make sure nobody else was around. They turned a corner and entered a door that brought them into a small maintenance room, most of which was filled with a network of cylindrical air ducts. There was barely enough space for the pair to stand together among the thick metallic columns. They squeezed into a corner, laughing at the thrill of it all, trying to hold their faces straight so they were able to kiss. Amiyah ran a hand through Juliette's hair. She was gentle at first, but then she pulled at the locks, tugging Juliette's head back. "Open," she said and Juliette's lips parted, obediently. Amiyah smiled, pleased by the older woman's compliance, and then without any kind of warning, she spat into Juliette's open mouth, not just once, but several times over. Juliette swallowed her lover's saliva and then opened her mouth wide for more. Amiyah got down on her knees and pried open the fly of Juliette's jeans. "You're not fighting for me, Jules. Promise me that. Promise me you won't do any more deals with Caesar."

As Juliette looked down at the triangle of her own crotch disappearing toward Amiyah's face, she realized she would have agreed to anything the young woman desired.

CHAPTER 17

"Nice eyebrows," Amiyah said.

"Same," Shelby replied, returning the compliment.

Juliette lingered in the doorway, fumbling to pry her keys out of the rusted lock. She inhaled a deep breath to compose herself before entering her modest apartment where Shelby and Amiyah stood opposite one another, their motionless bodies separated by the countertop which cut a divide between the lounge and kitchen. Juliette made the necessary introductions, noticing the discernment on both of the young women's faces as they looked each other up and down.

Juliette wasn't quite sure why she'd decided to bring Amiyah into her home at such an early stage of their relationship. Maybe she wanted to get the introductions over and done with before the process turned into more of a big deal than it already was. Maybe this young woman had become such an important part of Juliette's life, she was unable to resist showing her off to Shelby, the person whose opinion she valued beyond anybody else's. Whatever her motivations had been, all three of them were occupying the same space now, and Juliette was listening to her daughter and her lover communicating in the colloquial language of young people, complimenting the shape and form of each other's eyebrows. The bizarre exchange reminded Juliette of just how old she was, and of the fact the other two people in the room probably had more in common with each other than she did with either of them.

"Amiyah's our new teammate at Diablo's," Juliette explained with haste. "And for the past couple weeks, I've kind of been coaching her, one on one, you know? So, I suppose you could say we've sort of got like a student and mentor thing going on. If you see what I mean?"

Shelby peered over her spectacles, perplexed by her mother's awkward demeanor. "So, is she staying for dinner, or what?" Shelby asked, flatly.

There was a moment of silence. Juliette was caught off guard by her daughter's question.

Amiyah pounced on the break in conversation, grasping the opportunity to accept Shelby's offer. "Sure, why not?" she said. "Sounds good to me."

"Oh, I don't know about all that," Juliette said. "I mean, we just came by to pick something up, that's all."

Shelby's eyes were focused intently on her mother, like those of a detective searching for clues in a suspect's behavior. "You came by to pick up what, exactly?" she asked.

Once again, Juliette struggled to come up with an appropriate answer.

"Underwear," Amiyah said. "Your mom asked if she could borrow some of mine the other day."

Shelby looked back and forth between her mother and Amiyah. "Why on earth did you borrow her underwear, Mom?"

"I, well, I guess I must have forgot my own."

"Okay, then," Shelby said, wincing with disapproval. "That sounds like a perfectly normal thing to do."

"So, we just came by to fetch those," Juliette explained. "And then I'm gonna run Amiyah home. She really needs to get back in time for work, don't you, kid?"

"But, you never bring anybody home. And I'm pretty sure I've made enough spaghetti for three."

"Maybe we could do it some other time," Juliette said. "We really oughta be on our way."

Amiyah breathed in to fill her nostrils with the appetizing aroma wafting over from the kitchen. "Thing is, I am kind of hungry," she said.

"I guess that means I'll have to set another place, then," Shelby said, grinning victoriously at her mother. She swept through the open-plan space, balancing a plate on her upturned palm, gliding with graceful strides towards a small square table that was positioned right in front of the window in the lounge.

Juliette turned to Amiyah and mouthed the words "what the fuck are you doing?" as Shelby breezed past them.

Amiyah rolled her eyes, ignoring Juliette's vexation. "Love the sweater," she said, flashing her eyes at the oversized knitted garment that was drowning Shelby's upper body.

Shelby paused and glanced down at her top, the baggy hem of which dangled about her naked thighs, making her legs look even thinner than they already were. "Thanks," she said, and she straightened her back like the ballerina she was.

"Don't you think you oughta go put on some proper clothes, Doll-face?" Juliette suggested.

"Well, you should have told me you were planning on bringing somebody home if you wanted me to get all dressed up."

"Don't go getting changed on my behalf, sugar," Amiyah said. "Your outfit looks perfectly fine to me."

Shelby thanked Amiyah with an exaggerated smile, grateful for the supportive gesture.

Juliette felt a pang of jealousy as she watched the youngsters interacting. She glanced at Shelby's sun-kissed legs coming out from underneath her top, and then at Amiyah's annoyingly taught buttocks bulging through her running trousers like some kind of permanently flexed muscles. Juliette turned her head ninety degrees to check her own reflection in an oblong mirror that was mounted vertically at her side. She sighed a breath of frustration, almost cursing out loud at the sight of her own tired shape, her dull hair scraped back into a ponytail, her ill-fitting T-shirt looking like a shapeless sack of creases hanging off her breastless torso.

"Why don't you two go sit down and relax?" Shelby said, sounding like a dutiful housewife. "Dinner will be served in ten minutes." The teenager flitted about among a thickening mist of steam, rummaging through cupboards and tending to the pans simmering on the stove, seemingly excited by the prospect of actually having a guest to cook a meal for.

Juliette sat at the head of the small table, purposely forming a central divide between the other two available spaces. The fourth and final side of the table was inaccessible due to the fact it was pushed up against the window, which looked out onto what Juliette liked to refer to as the balcony garden. In reality, this outdoor area was just a narrow walkway which led to the communal stairwell, but Juliette had dressed the space up with several planters and a bench seat to make it feel a little more homely.

Amiyah gazed out through the sheer drapes that hung over the window. "Kind of reminds me of a motel," she said.

"Oh, really? I honestly don't think I've ever heard that before," Juliette said, with a note of sarcasm in her voice.

"Well, it beats my place, any day," Amiyah replied.

Juliette reached across the table and placed a comforting hand over Amiyah's. She snatched her hand back when Shelby called out from the kitchen, asking what each of them wanted to drink. A while later, all three of them were seated around the small table, their plates piled high with spaghetti and meat sauce. Juliette exchanged a glance with her daughter, both of them noticing the way Amiyah was sucking down mouthfuls of pasta without taking a breath.

"Damn, this is good," Amiyah said, as though she hadn't eaten a decent, home-cooked meal in weeks.

"Thanks," Shelby laughed.

Juliette had barely touched her own meal. Her stomach was tight with nerves, scuppering her desire to eat. She felt the warmth of a hand resting over one of her thighs. The gesture filled her with a sense of reassurance for just a brief moment, until her brain computed the fact Amiyah was touching her in the presence of her daughter. She pushed Amiyah's hand away and the rickety old table was jostled enough to spill a little water out of each glass. Juliette wondered if Shelby had noticed what had gone on beneath the surface of the table. The light from the window reflected off the teenager's spectacles, hiding the direction of her gaze and shielding any clue her eyes would have otherwise revealed. The room seemed uncomfortably quiet all of a sudden, quiet enough for Juliette to hear her own heart thumping within her chest.

"So, where do you work?" Shelby asked, in an attempt to relieve the tense atmosphere of the cramped little lounge.

"I'm a stripper at Caesar's," Amiyah replied, without even looking up from her food.

Juliette dropped her fork down into her plate. "Come on, she's fourteen. Do you really think she needs that much information?"

"So, what do you suggest I tell her, then?" Amiyah asked. "You want me to lie about it, instead?"

"Yes, Mom, lying's bad, isn't it? And what's wrong with being a stripper, anyway?" Shelby looked over to Amiyah with a smile. "I guess that means we're both dancers then, doesn't it?"

Amiyah raised a hand to high-five Shelby across the table.

"But, we're working on getting you out of that hell hole, aren't we?" Juliette said.

"If you say so, Jules," Amiyah agreed.

"Yes, we are," Juliette insisted.

"We, is it now?" Shelby said. "What's with all this 'we'? Sounds a little odd if you ask me."

"I mean 'we' as in student and teacher, of course."

"If you say so, Jules," Amiyah said again with a roll of her eyes.

The room fell silent again as all three of them festered over what

236

had been said. "Did you get any dessert to go with this, Doll?" Juliette asked, unable to bear the tension any longer.

"Dessert makes you fat, remember?" Shelby said. "Isn't that what you always tell me?"

Amiyah looked Shelby over for a while. "If you want to grow any kind of an ass on that skinny little frame of yours, you're gonna have to start eating some serious dessert."

"Try telling that to my mom," Shelby said, dropping her shoulders with exasperation.

Juliette sighed and slumped back into her chair, realizing how hard it was going to be to deal with both of these young women at the same time. She checked her watch dramatically enough for everybody to notice. "Is that the time, already?" she said. "I guess we oughta be getting you on home now, hadn't we?" She made her excuses to leave the table so she could retreat to the bathroom and gather her thoughts. "You two play nicely now, won't you?" she said as she exited the lounge and hurried along the hallway. She didn't exactly like the idea of leaving the pair of them unattended, but she had to get away from them for a while, as though she was retreating to her corner for a break between the rounds of a fight. She needed some space to get her head around all of this, so she could try to make sense of the fact these two very different aspects of her life had somehow managed to come together. Her feelings toward Amiyah had quickly become her most preciously guarded secret, a secret she had—up until now—been able to exercise complete control over.

She spilled into the bathroom and wound up hunched over the countertop surrounding the sink. "Hold it together," she said, fixing herself with a reprimanding gaze in the mirror. After a few drawn-out breaths, she pulled her T-shirt over her head and dropped the garment onto the floor. She'd always enjoyed the way the harsh down-lighting of the bathroom exaggerated the definition of her upper body, the deep shadows carving out her abs and making her breasts look like pointed little pectoral muscles. She turned her hips about so the lighting brought out the grooves of her iliac furrows, the faint lines trailing into the waistband of her jeans acting as a reminder of just how hard she worked in the gym. She spent a while admiring her reflection, surveying all she had to offer Amiyah, hoping the flatteringly lit vision of her unclothed body would reassure her she was worthy of the young woman's affections. She held out her hands and was shocked by how badly they were shaking. The prospect of her daughter discovering the truth of her feelings toward Amiyah was infinitely more terrifying than any opponent she'd faced in the cage. She balled one of her trembling hands into a fist and jabbed at her stomach several times. "Come on, Jules," she said. "Round two. You've got this."

As Juliette reentered the lounge, she found Shelby and Amiyah sitting next to one another on the couch, eagerly comparing their fingernails while debating the benefits of some kind of manicure treatment Juliette had never even heard of.

"What are you two arguing about now?" she asked with a smile, enjoying the fact the two most significant people in her life appeared to be getting along.

Shelby stopped speaking and looked up towards her mother with an unreadable expression emblazoned across her face. The teenager's angelic features appeared amused and offended all at once. Her mouth was twisted up at one corner into a contemptuous grin. Her blue eyes were docile with aggravation, like two little portals offering a glimpse into her discontented mind.

Juliette didn't like the expression on Shelby's face at all. It made her think of Earl's disapproving eyes and the fact she could never seem to do anything right by him. "What is it, Doll?" Juliette asked. "Why are you looking at me that way?"

Shelby opened her mouth to speak, but when the words came out, her voice seemed to be detached from her face, out of synchronicity with her lips, as if the utterance itself was floating through the air, each individual syllable piercing Juliette's skin and burning her insides. The term "lovebirds" stood out as the most jarring part of the sentence Shelby fired off toward her mother. That expression alone almost knocked Juliette off her feet, made her lean back against the kitchen counter, draining all of the energy out of her body in an instant.

"What are you talking about?" Juliette asked, hoping she'd misheard or failed to comprehend the punchline of a joke.

"I said," Shelby began, "your girlfriend over here has been telling me how it was that you two little lovebirds met."

The words were even more affecting the second time around. "My what?" Juliette asked breathlessly.

"Oh come on, Mom, I figured it out as soon as you two walked in the front door. I'm really not as dumb as you like to think I am."

Amiyah held her hands up as if confessing to a crime. "Sorry," she said. "Shelby asked me what the deal was, so, I just kind of told her."

"Are you kidding me?" Juliette said. "I asked you to keep this between the two of us. What part of that didn't you understand?"

"Mom, relax, will you?"

Juliette hung her head, unable to make eye contact with anyone in the room. Her face was flushed with a mixture of anger and shame. "Amiyah, I think you should go wait outside for a while."

"I'm sorry," Amiyah said. "I guess I just didn't see any point lying about it."

"Go wait outside," Juliette said through gritted teeth.

Shelby shot up from the couch, her whole body stiffening with rage. "For fuck's sake, Mom. Why do you have to make such a big deal out of everything all the time?"

"Just sit down," Juliette said, still refusing to make eye contact with anyone else.

"No, I won't just sit down. I'm sick of you treating me like a child. You couldn't even be bothered to tell me you were a fucking lesbian. Your girlfriend had to tell me all by herself, because you think I'm too stupid to understand. Well, if it's such a big secret, then maybe I'll go wait outside so you can talk freely about whatever the hell you want."

Juliette was silenced by her daughter's outburst.

The teenager stuffed her feet into her boots and stomped across the lounge without even tying her laces. "I've had it with your bullshit," she said, slamming the front door behind her.

Amiyah leaned back into the couch, relaxing now all of the commotion was over. "That went surprisingly well," she said.

"Are you out of your goddam mind?" Juliette said, shaking her head in disbelief.

"You do realize you oughta be thanking me, don't you?"

Juliette couldn't believe how unflappable this young woman was, even in a situation as dramatic as this. "Thanking you?" she said. "What on earth would I be thanking you for?"

"Do you know how much I wish somebody would have told my family for me? So I didn't have go through it all myself?"

"Don't you even dare think about telling Earl," Juliette said, pointing a finger straight at Amiyah. "This is bad enough already."

"Are you really that ashamed of me?"

A thunderous bang went off somewhere in the distance, the reverberations shuddering up through the floor. Juliette instantly recognized the metallic chime of the cast iron gate slamming shut at the base of her stairwell. "Shelby?" she called out, before even reaching the front door. She hurried out toward the balcony garden, but quickly found the bench seat was empty.

"Now look what you've done," she said to Amiyah.

The young woman sat on the faded couch picking something out of her teeth with her fingernails. She took her time extracting bits of food from between her molars, making Juliette wait for her response. "As far as I can see," she began, "the only thing that's upset the poor kid is the fact you don't think she's ready to hear the truth."

Juliette's entire body was shaking with rage.

240

"Well, what are you waiting for?" Amiyah asked. "You'd better go after her, hadn't you?"

Juliette sat down on one of the dining chairs. She pulled on her running shoes, frowning straight toward Amiyah the whole time. "I'm not done with you yet," she said, before getting up and storming out of her apartment.

***

The rain forced Juliette to squint as she looked out over the rail of her landing. She was worried about Shelby being out in the downpour, knowing the teenager had nothing but her oversized sweater to huddle into for warmth. Juliette peered into the dark corners of the parking lot several floors below. She ran her eyes along the street, checking the sidewalk where it was lit up by streetlamps. The entire block appeared to be mostly deserted, as though the sudden change of weather had forced people to run for cover indoors. There was no movement on the streets other than the illuminated headlamps of a few cars crawling through gathering streams of rainwater.

An abstract shape darted like a fly in Juliette's peripheral vision, a tiny figure hurrying between a pair of distant buildings. Juliette quickly recognized the comical silhouette: a bulbous, sweater-clad upper body hovering over contrastingly spindly legs. Juliette called out to her daughter, but her voice was lost among the white-noise spray of the rain. She bounded down the steel-grate stairwell, leaping down the final few steps of each level until she burst out of the gated entrance and spilled into the parking lot. Moments later, she was weaving between rows of parked cars, giving chase in the direction she believed her daughter had been heading. She ran between the shelter of trees in an attempt to stay out of the rain. Despite her best efforts to seek cover, the downpour quickly made her wish she'd taken the time to throw on a jacket.

She hurtled along the path so frantically she almost didn't notice the sack-like shape that was bundled into the corner of a bus shelter. It was only after she'd passed the open-fronted structure that her mind's eye began to decipher the true nature of what she'd seen. She doubled back on herself without quite knowing why, walking into the glow of the backlit advertising panels that made up the walls of the bus shelter. She realized the object she'd initially believed to be nothing more than a bulging sack of garbage, was, in fact, the folded up body of her teenage daughter. Shelby was sitting on the floor at the back of the shelter with her knees pressed up against her chest and her sweater pulled down over her legs so that only the toecaps of her boots emerged from beneath the hem of the sodden garment.

Juliette got down onto the hard concrete floor and sat cross-legged next to Shelby. The two of them sat quietly for a while, looking out into the rain and listening to the steady flow of water trickling into storm drains. "What's up, Doll-face?" Juliette asked when she finally plucked up the courage to speak. "You waiting for a bus, or what?"

Shelby shivered under her sweater, determined to ignore her mother.

"So, where are you headed, anyway?" Juliette persisted.

"Just as far away from you as possible."

"I hope you brought some money for the bus then. Won't get very far without that."

"Maybe I'll just show the driver my tits and see how far that gets me."

"Probably about the end of the road, I should've thought."

Shelby punched her mother on the arm.

Juliette laughed at her own joke. "Come on, Doll, let's not fall out over this."

Shelby turtled up further into her sweater as if she were seeking to escape the awkward conversation.

Juliette wanted to climb into the sweater with her daughter, to hold her close among the warmth of the garment where the feeling of Shelby's body against her own would reassure her everything was okay. "Look, it's not exactly the easiest thing to do," Juliette explained, "talking to your child about this kind of thing."

"I'm not a child."

"You know what I mean."

Shelby exhaled a huff of aggravation. "Did you really think I hadn't figured out you were gay?"

Juliette swallowed painfully at the notion of being described this way. "Well, you must have known more than I did then."

"That's bullshit, Mom."

"I'm being serious," Juliette insisted. "What made you think I was, you know, into women?" She uttered the difficult words quietly, barely able to accept they were true.

"I've seen the way you look at girls. I'm not stupid."

"Then maybe it's me who's stupid, because I'm still trying to figure this out myself. I never thought I would end up dating a woman. Not in a million years, I didn't. But, I guess you can't pick and choose who you're attracted to in life, can you?"

Shelby looked straight ahead, refusing to engage.

Juliette broke down in tears as she finally gave in to the pressure of the situation. "I don't know what the hell is wrong with me," she said. "I didn't want to end up in this mess." She lifted her T-shirt to wipe the tears from her face. "I'm sorry, Doll. I messed up again, just like I always do."

Shelby shuffled closer to her mother and held onto her sobbing body. "You're not in a mess," she said. "Don't be so dramatic."

Juliette sniffed and snorted to hold back her tears.

Shelby was crying as well now, as if her mother's emotional state was contagious. "It's okay," she said. "This doesn't change anything between us."

"Of course it doesn't," Juliette said, wiping the tears from her daughter's eyes. "You know you're always gonna be the most important person in my life, don't you?"

"I know," Shelby said, and the pair of them embraced, holding each other close to show their sincerity.

Juliette was overwhelmed with a sense of relief, interpreting the sensation of Shelby's body against her own as complete acceptance of all that she was. She couldn't believe her secret was finally out. Her attraction to women had not only been exposed, it had been exposed to the person whose reaction she'd feared the most. She felt so vulnerable in her daughter's arms, having unwittingly revealed a part of her soul she hadn't quite come to terms with herself.

Shelby broke away and whispered into her mother's ear. "Now you've just gotta figure out how you're gonna explain all of this to Uncle Earl."

Juliette's body went limp in her daughter's arms. "I don't even wanna think about that right now," she said, closing her eyes with horror at the notion of her brother's reaction.

The two of them got up off the floor and straightened out their clothes. As Juliette turned Shelby about and dusted her down, a pair of headlights swung into the far end of the road. The blinding glare of the lights made it impossible to decipher the shape of the vehicle they belonged to, but the rattle of the automobile's engine was strangely familiar to Juliette's ears, like the distant voice of a friend she couldn't quite put a face to. She peered into the rain, watching closely as the vehicle's outline emerged through the downpour.

"What the hell?" she said. "Is that my truck?"

Her mouth hung open with confusion as her trusty steed approached along the highway like a loyal horse galloping to rescue them from the inclement weather. The beastly truck came to a standstill alongside the bus shelter. The vehicle's windows were beaded with rainwater, obscuring the view of whoever was inside. The driver's door swung open, and there at the wheel, with Juliette's sunglasses covering most of her face, was Amiyah. The young woman was casually slumped into the bench seat with one hand loosely resting over the steering wheel. "So, you wanna go get some dessert, or what?" she asked, peering over the lenses of Juliette's shades.

Juliette took her daughter by the hand and led her toward the vehicle. "Move over," she said, packing Shelby up into the cab. "I'm driving."

CHAPTER 18

Earl's tracksuit-clad body filled the doorway of the women's locker room like some kind of a makeshift blockade. Juliette felt cornered by her brother's presence, knowing she wouldn't be able to escape the locker room until he'd said his piece. She watched Earl arching his back as though he was limbering up for a particularly arduous confrontation. With every movement of his body, the solid definition of his shoulders heaved through the sheeny fabric of his track-jacket. Juliette couldn't help but marvel at the sheer scale of her brother's heavyweight physique. Maybe she was jealous of his imposing stature; maybe she was simply in awe of the man. Even at this advanced stage of his retirement—with his aging body a mere shadow of everything it once was—his broad shape still acted as a constant reminder of the innumerable years he'd spent as a fighter.

Juliette straddled the wooden bench in the center of the locker room. As Earl approached, she was unable to move, rendered motionless by the power of his presence. She was willing to accept whatever kind of lecture he was planning on subjecting her to, just as long as it meant she would be granted the rare pleasure of his undivided attention. The windows mounted high on the walls of the locker room were darkened thanks to the receding light of late afternoon. Juliette could hear the revving engines of the vehicles in the parking lot. The chorus of mechanical roars—swelling and then fading into the distance—signaled the departure of the other attendees to the afternoon workout session. Juliette rocked back and forth with the slats of the bench between her thighs, practically hypnotized by her brother's stalking gait. Only when Earl arrived before her did she finally stand up to meet him, not wanting to be caught in such a submissive position.

"Sit down," Earl said. "Relax for a minute, will you?"

"I'm good thanks," Juliette said. "What is it you wanna talk about anyway?" She threw her duffel bag down onto the bench with just enough force to communicate her lack of enthusiasm for any discussion that might follow.

"Where's your conjoined twin at?" Earl asked, glancing around to check if anybody was lurking among the opposing rows of shower cubicles and bathroom stalls.

"My what?"

"You know what I mean. You two are practically joined at the hip."

Juliette could only frown at her brother's comment, unsure of what he'd intended to imply.

"Relax, I'm just messing with you," Earl said. "So, come on, where is she?"

"She got a ride with some of the guys," Juliette explained. "She had to get back in time for work." The thought of Amiyah dancing half-naked in front of a crowd of drooling onlookers filled Juliette with a burn of inner turmoil, reminding her it was a situation she was desperate to resolve.

"You're trying to tell me you haven't managed to get her out of that place yet?"

"She does what she wants," Juliette shrugged, feigning indifference. "You know how she is." Juliette read her brother's dead eyes as a sign of his disapproval. She knew he'd be passing judgment on her failure to free Amiyah from the deal she'd gotten herself into with Caesar.

Earl paced around the bench, circling Juliette like a predator considering the best way to attack its prey. He looked to be deep in concentration, scratching at the back of his neck as if he had something of importance on his mind he was seeking to offload. "The kid's been making some real progress though, right?" he said, eventually.

"I guess so," Juliette replied, suspicious her brother was probing for some kind of information beyond the reaches of his question.

"She seems to be fitting in with the guys, as well," Earl added.

The mere mention of Amiyah had caused Juliette's mind to stray so far from the conversation, Earl may as well have been speaking to himself. Juliette's thoughts drifted back over the past few weeks she'd spent tutoring her new student. Each day, at around noon, Juliette had been filled with a glow of excitement as soon as she realized the time had come to carry out the newest part of her daily routine. She would climb into her truck and race across town, lowering her window so the incoming breeze would blast off the heat of whatever morning workout session she'd been taking part in. She'd have to remind herself not to speed as she hurtled toward the decaying part of town, where the houses were gray with neglect and the front yards looked like fenced-in quarantine pens. She usually arrived at her destination a little too early, barely able to wait for her young lover to get out of bed. Much to Juliette's frustration, Amiyah tended to rise at around lunchtime, sleeping in late due to the physical demands of her nocturnal occupation.

Juliette would rarely venture into the dankly scented stripper house, where both the dog and the baby would invariably be howling and crying in perfect harmony. On most days, she opted to kill a little time playing basketball with the shaven-headed brothers she'd befriended on her first venture into the depths of the impoverished neighborhood. When Amiyah's gangly limbs and erect bottom finally emerged onto the wooden steps of the house, Juliette would take a moment to admire her up there on the podium-like veranda. Amiyah's garish outfits—vastly differing from one day to the next—were like a procession of gifts Juliette got to unwrap with her eyes each time the young woman stepped out of that front door. And when Amiyah climbed up into the passenger side of the truck, the perfumed scent of her hair and body served as a reminder, every day, that Juliette had something brand-new and exciting in her life, something to look forward to each morning as soon as she woke up and got out of bed.

Earl cleared his throat loudly enough to regain his sister's attention. "I've been watching the two of you for a while now," he said. "And the thing is, there's something I've been meaning to ask, something about you and her."

Earl paused to take a breath and Juliette was weakened with nerves, certain he was going to ask about her relationship with Amiyah. "Well, what is it then?" she asked, impatiently. "What do you wanna know?"

Earl looked his sister over for a while. "Relax," he said. "What the hell's wrong with you at the moment?"

Juliette tried to readjust her stance, dropping her shoulders in an effort to appear blasé about the situation. "Just spit it out, will you?" she said.

"I wanted to ask if you thought she might be ready for a fight sometime soon."

"Is that it?" Juliette said, the tension disappearing from her posture in an instant.

"Why? What else did you think I was gonna ask?" Earl stared straight into his sister's eyes, hoping to glean some idea of what she was thinking.

"I just wondered when you was gonna get to the point," Juliette said, "that's all."

"Is that right?" Earl said. His voice trembled with amusement, leading Juliette to believe he was taking great pleasure in the process of extracting information. She was certain he was toying with her, like a cat torturing its prey before putting it out of its misery. "Of course, we'll have to find her the right opponent," Earl said. "Somebody local, one of the girls from Team Zen, maybe."

"Whatever," Juliette said. "You're the boss, after all."

"Look, there's no need to get all weird about this. I'm just trying to have a conversation here."

"I'm not getting weird. If you wanna put a fight together, then let's do it. Why's it gotta be such a big deal?"

Earl began to pace again as he considered his next move. "I know you're worried about the kid. That's only natural. I mean, obviously you've grown attached to her, haven't you?"

"What are you getting at, Earl?" Juliette asked, already growing weary of the interrogation.

"You've been spending so much time together. Surely you must have some kind of feelings for her by now?"

Juliette refused to answer, shooting her brother a look which told him she knew exactly what he was up to.

Earl was quiet for a moment as he reconsidered his strategy. "It's weird, you know?" he said. "Shelby really seems to talk about her a lot. In fact, I'd go as far as to say she's all I ever hear about."

"How is that weird? Amiyah comes over to our place all the time." Juliette pictured the young woman sitting on the faded couch in her lounge, skillfully twisting handfuls of Shelby's hair up into intricately-knotted plaits. She imagined Shelby perched on the edge of the couch with her eyes closed and her little face all serene with relaxation as she enjoyed the massaging sensation of Amiyah's hands weaving among the tangled locks of her flaxen mane. The thought of her daughter and her lover interacting this way acted as a natural sedative to Juliette's neurotic mind, and as the conversation went on, she was able to remain perfectly calm as she began to explain—to her discerning brother—the way in which Amiyah would come back to her apartment after training so that Shelby could prepare them all an evening meal to enjoy together. Juliette even managed to maintain her composure as she told Earl how Amiyah would come to sleep over on the rare days she took off work, and how the two of them would stay up analyzing fight videos on the Internet until the early hours of the next morning. What she opted not to disclose, however, was the fact she would usually be holding Amiyah in

250

her arms as they watched those very same videos, the two of them lying together on the couch, their splayed bodies intertwined beneath a blanket, Juliette's fingers trailing back and forth over the young woman's skin.

"Seems like Shelby's quite the little chef these days, huh?" Earl grumbled. "Now that you've got her fixing dinner, and all."

"She's baking as well now, actually," Juliette boasted, sensing the jealousy in her brother's voice. She went on to describe several of the various cakes and desserts her daughter liked to prepare in the tiny kitchen of their apartment. She made a point of explaining the fact there was usually an emphasis on gluten-free, dairy-free, and sugar-free recipes in an attempt to make the treats a little healthier. "You know how she likes to watch her figure," Juliette said.

Earl raised his eyebrows at the suggestion it would have been Shelby's idea to watch her weight.

As Juliette pondered the subject further, she chose not to recount to her older brother the tale of one particularly eventful evening when Shelby had gone off to bed early, leaving Juliette and Amiyah alone in the lounge, where the air was filled with the intoxicating aroma of freshly-baked chocolate cake. Throughout the course of that evening, each and every time Juliette had caught a chance sighting of Amiyah's athletically toned posterior swallowing up the seam of her leggings, she'd automatically sucked in a deep breath to inhale the dark scent of cacao that was flavoring the atmosphere. Juliette remembered how she'd wandered over to the rattling fridge in the corner of the kitchen, and then returned to the lounge a while later brandishing a large slice of homemade chocolate cake topped with buttercream frosting.

Amiyah sat up straight as soon as she caught sight of the tall wedge of sponge cake. "Shelby's gonna be so mad," Amiyah said. "When she finds out you took a slice without her permission, trust me, all hell is gonna break loose."

Juliette set her plate down and leaned in to kiss the young woman on the lips.

Amiyah pried herself away. "Seriously, what's with the cake?" she said, her voice tremulous with nervous laughter.

Juliette took her by the wrist and directed her to bend over the couch. Amiyah's body was submissively limp; her limbs falling into place obediently. Juliette peeled the young woman's leggings down over the taught sphere of her ass, freeing both rotund cheeks and plucking the thin cord of underwear from between them. Juliette's mouth hung loose with anticipation as her eyes feasted on the bronze peach of Amiyah's ass. The elegant curvature of each cheek shone out of the darkness, lit up by the ever-changing colors of the TV screen. Juliette took a long, hard breath to savor the chocolatey scent that was flavoring the air. Her senses were overwhelmed, her thoughts clouded with a warm rush of euphoria. She clawed off a handful of the cake, loading her fingers with a gloppy mess of sponge and cream. She applied the paste-like mixture to the parting at the center of Amiyah's derrière. The feeling of that deep, warm valley lurking beneath the cold cream was enough to drive Juliette wild with lust. She pressed the mush into the pit at the center of it all and Amiyah's body began to shiver and convulse.

Juliette couldn't resist any longer. She moved in and ran her tongue through the groove of Amiyah's ass. She filled her mouth with the sweet taste of her daughter's lovingly made dessert, pushing her tongue into Amiyah's asshole and swallowing all she could retrieve. She noticed Amiyah had reached down between her thighs to pleasure herself, her outstretched fingers moving in circular motions over her clitoris, her face buried deep in the blankets that were spread out over the couch. Juliette was fucking herself as well now, coming up for air every now and then, kissing Amiyah on the lips so their tongues twisted together, spreading the chocolate pulp inside each other's mouths. Juliette reloaded her hand with a second helping of the creamy dessert and eased her fingers into Amiyah's crotch.

"Fuck me, please," Amiyah begged.

252

"We gotta be quiet," Juliette said, terrified Shelby would hear them and emerge from her bedroom. She withdrew her fingers and pushed them into Amiyah's mouth. It thrilled her to think she might be caught at any moment, committing acts a teenager could never understand. It wasn't long before Juliette felt herself reaching the point of no return. As the pleasure took hold, she rubbed herself off to the sight of Amiyah's dark little asshole, and the half-lit vision of the young woman's buttocks smeared with traces of frosting.

Earl hunched down to bring his face level with his sister's. "Are you even listening to me?" he asked.

"Of course," Juliette replied, and she flailed the hem of her T-shirt, suddenly feeling the heat of the steam that hung in the air of the locker room.

"So, you're trying to tell me that's what you've been doing over at your place? You've been watching fights and baking cakes, have you?"

"Why, what else would we be doing?" Juliette said. She allowed her gaze to meet her brothers in a rare moment of eye contact. She held his gaze unflinchingly, daring him to suggest an alternative to her version of events.

Earl shook his head enough to show he hadn't quite accepted everything he was being told.

"We have a whale of a time together," Juliette said, enjoying her brother's apparent disbelief. "I guess we're kinda like a family, us three girls. A dysfunctional one, maybe. But a family, all the same."

"A family, huh?" Earl said, and the muscles tightened under the weathered skin of his face.

"Yes, Earl, a family," Juliette said. "Just the three of us. That's all we need." She was torturing her brother now, rubbing salt into his wounds. She knew how dangerous this game was, that he wouldn't tolerate being poked like this for long, but she was unable to resist the kick she got out of seeing him affected this way.

Earl took out a folded handkerchief and patted the sweat from his brow. "Fair enough," he said. "You wanna talk about family, huh? Is that what you're telling me? That the three of you are suddenly like some kind of a family unit? You, Shelby and this kid you've only known for a few weeks."

"I guess so," Juliette said. She could see the veins swelling in Earl's temples. She was wary of his reaction to her words, but the sense of fear thrilled her at the same time. His disgruntlement was like a drug she'd become addicted to over the years. If anger was the only reaction she could get out of him, was the only way she could be sure he cared, then she would gladly provoke his fury, no matter the consequences.

"Okay then," Earl said. "Let me tell you something about family. But if we're gonna do this, I really think you oughta be sitting down."

"I'm good, thanks," Juliette said, defiantly.

"Suit yourself," Earl said, turning his back on her. He steadied himself with his hands on the countertop that surrounded the wash basins. He took a while to psyche himself up for his announcement, and then, he looked at Juliette's reflection in the mirror, watching her face closely for her reaction. "Margot's pregnant," he said, blurting the words out with the speed of somebody trying to pull a knife out of a wound as quickly as they could.

As the revelation hit Juliette, she felt unsteady on her feet, like the floor was falling away and the walls were spinning around her. Despite her sudden loss of equilibrium, she was determined to remain standing, not wanting Earl to see she'd been affected by his announcement. "Well, congratulations, I guess," she just about managed to say, folding her arms across her chest, holding onto herself in consolation.

"And I'm sure you mean it, as well."

"Really, I'm happy for you. Why wouldn't I be?"

"You know why," Earl said, still watching his sister in the mirror.

Juliette joined Earl by the wash basins, hoping the act of talking to his reflection—one step removed from communicating with him face-to-face—would make the conversation a little less painful. "There was a time it would have bothered me," she explained. "But not now. Not with everything I've got in my life."

"And what is it you've got, exactly?"

"You know what I'm talking about."

"Maybe I do," Earl agreed. "But, I want to hear you say it."

"I can't, Earl. Please, it's too much."

"Come on, say it. How hard can it be?"

Juliette inhaled a long breath, held it in a while, and then finally, she let it all out. "We're together," she exhaled, hanging her head with exhaustion. When she eventually dared to glance up, Earl was looking back at her in the mirror with the same disapproving expression Shelby's face had displayed when she'd discovered the same piece of information.

"So, that's it?" Earl said "You're a lesbian now, are you?"

"Why do I have to be anything? It's not as simple as all that. It's about two people who are drawn to each other regardless of gender or anything else."

Earl emitted a grunt of laughter. "That all sounds very poetic, but if you're fucking another woman, I'm pretty sure that makes you a lesbian."

"For Christ's sake. Why do you have to be so coarse about everything all the time?"

"Because, let me get this straight, you are actually fucking her, aren't you?"

"That's none of your damn business."

"I think I've got a right to know. The kid is a student here, after all. And it was me who found her, not you. So, come on, are you sleeping with her or not?"

Juliette turned to face her brother. She squared right up to him, moving her face close to his. "You really want to know, don't you?" she said, getting closer and closer with every word. "You should be careful what you wish for, because I'm pretty sure you couldn't even handle the truth of it all."

Earl remained entirely motionless as his sister raised her voice and spoke directly into his face. "Try me," he said.

"Okay then, if you really wanna know, then yes, we fuck all the time. We do all the disgusting things two girls could possibly do together, things you couldn't even begin to imagine."

"Okay, Jules. Fair enough. I think I get the picture."

"What's the matter? You wanted to know, didn't you? So, I'm gonna tell you."

"I think I've heard enough, thanks."

"No. No, you haven't. You insisted. You pushed me and pushed me because you were so interested to find out. So, if you really want to know what two girls get up to, then let me explain—"

"—I said, that's enough," Earl snapped. He took Juliette by the shoulders and spun her away from him. He held her close to his body, restraining her like an unruly child.

Juliette drew a sharp intake of breath, shocked by her brother's actions. The warmth of his body against her own made her heartbeat intensify like a warning alarm going off in her chest. "I know you want to hear it," she said, refusing to pay any heed to her racing heart. "I know you do."

Earl tightened his grip on his sister. "Just give it to me then," he said, submissively.

Juliette closed her eyes and leaned into her brother's embrace. "You wouldn't believe how good she tastes." A shift in Earl's breathing pattern prompted Juliette to continue with her elaborations. "The thing you gotta understand is, I've pissed all over her in those showers, right there." Juliette's heart felt like it was going to explode as she made her revelations, but the thrill of confessing the truth was so intoxicating, she was unable to stop. "Have you got any idea how good it feels?" she continued. "The sense of relief when you let it all go, and you pee over the face of a girl who looks as good as she does?"

Earl wrapped his hand around his sister's throat in a half-hearted attempt to stem the flow of her words.

Juliette pressed her ass further into his groin. "We even rub off on the same vibrator together," she whispered, her voice straining due to her asphyxiation. "We put the throbbing head of that thing between our naked bodies and grind ourselves into it until we explode." She could feel Earl's arousal swelling through the thin veil of his track-pants. She pushed herself against it, slowly moving her hips up and down. "It feels so good to be naked with her," Juliette said, bending over the counter as far as Earl's restraint would allow. "She likes to sit on my face. That's her thing. She likes to look down into my eyes as she grinds her orgasm into my mouth. And, I love to suck her off as well. Honestly, I can't get enough of it." She glanced over her shoulder to observe the bulge of Earl's arousal heaving through his track-pants. She couldn't help but laugh with satisfaction as soon as she caught sight of it.

Earl reached down and lowered Juliette's leggings, pressing himself into the back of her underwear. "You're sick," he said. "You know that, right?"

"Yes, I'm sick, because you made me this way. With all the things we use to do together, what else did you expect?"

"What I wouldn't give to shove this into your little mouth right now to shut you the hell up."

"You wouldn't have the guts, Earl. The sheer guts. That's always been your problem. I would've given up everything to make it work between us, but you were too weak."

"Don't talk ridiculous."

"You're just like Dad. He was too weak to stay with us because he couldn't handle Mom."

Earl turned Juliette back towards him and took her by the chin. "We're not teenagers anymore, Jules."

Juliette rested a hand over the head of Earl's erection and studied its form with her fingertips. She felt it straining through his track-pants and twitching against her palm. Earl steadied himself on the washbasin, cursing under his breath. Juliette wondered why his body had suddenly gone limp, but then she felt the wetness of his semen seeping through his pants. It had only taken a few gentle strokes of his sister's hand to bring him to the point of orgasm, with years of pent-up frustration spilling out of him in an instant.

"I'm sorry," Juliette said, and she closed her eyes and took a few deep breaths to calm herself down. When she opened her eyes back up, she saw something strange in her peripheral vision, a long shard of darkness that immediately seemed out of place. She turned to focus on the object, but for some unknown reason, her brain refused to decipher exactly what it was. But then, when the apparition started to move, and then to speak, Juliette couldn't avoid the horrifying reality of the situation any longer.

"What the hell is going on?" Amiyah said, her rigid posture making it look as though she'd just been doused with ice-cold water.

"I thought you were getting a ride?" Juliette said. She separated from her brother until she was several feet away from him.

"I decided to wait," Amiyah said, with an emphasis on every single word.

"Didn't you ever hear of knocking?" Earl said. He spoke with no sense of alarm in his voice, apparently unfazed by Amiyah's intrusion.

"Shut up, Earl," Juliette snapped.

Amiyah sat down on one of the benches. She buried her head in her hands, and began to rock back and forth with distress. "This can't be happening," she said. "This seriously cannot be happening."

Juliette came down on her knees before the young woman. "It's okay, just listen to me, kid." She took Amiyah by the wrists to pry her hands away from her face. "Look at me, please."

Amiyah flinched away. "Don't fucking touch me," she said, her body vibrating with shock. The skin of her face had turned a bloodless shade of gray. Tears were streaming down her cheeks and into her trembling mouth.

"We were just fooling around," Earl said. "It's no big deal."

Juliette shot him a frown. She signaled with a nod of her head, ordering him to leave the room.

Amiyah got up from the bench. "No, it's okay Earl," she said. "You can stay right there. I'm the one who's leaving."

Juliette tried to catch her by the arms as she slipped away.

"Stay the fuck away from me," Amiyah said, clutching her hands to her chest. "You two can just go ahead and carry on with whatever the hell it was you were doing. And don't even think about coming after me." With that, she disappeared back into the main room of the gym, slamming the door so forcefully the resulting backdraft hit Juliette like a punch in the face.

Juliette's body turned cold and numb in an instant. The enormity of what had happened was too much for her to comprehend. She stood motionless, her eyes staring at nothing in particular, her arms hanging loosely at her sides. She hadn't felt so discombobulated since the last time she'd been knocked unconscious in a fight.

Earl was somewhere behind her now, repeatedly calling her name in an effort to break her out of the trance-like state she'd fallen into.

"What?" Juliette barked out eventually. "What the fuck do you want?"

"Jules, you need to get your shit together and listen to me. I'm pretty sure that's your goddamn truck running outside."

"What are you talking about?" Juliette said, but as she spoke, she was suddenly aware of the familiar splutter of her vehicle's engine. She rushed past Earl and shoved her way through the fire escape, bursting out into the cool night air, where she bore witness to the surreal vision of her own beloved automobile screeching out of the parking lot and roaring off into the distance. Her natural instinct—in the midst of her panic—was to turn to her brother for a solution, the same way she'd looked to him for guidance at every stage of her career. But as she spun around to face him, her mouth hung open silently, her brain unable to formulate a sentence.

"Just get in the car," Earl said, throwing Juliette the keys to his Mustang. "I'll go lock up. We gotta catch her."

CHAPTER 19

Earl shifted his car into drive and pulled out of the parking lot so fast Juliette was pinned back into her seat. "Where's she going?" Earl growled.

"Concentrate on the road, will you?" Juliette said, clinging onto her seat belt.

"Come on, damn it. Wake up, Jules. Where do you think she's going?"

"Just take me home, okay? She's got my keys."

"Is Shelby gonna be there?"

"I don't know. She's at ballet tonight. She's supposed to be getting a ride." Juliette shrugged her shoulders with a hopeless look on her face. "She might be back by now, I guess."

"Call her," Earl demanded, sounding every bit like the coach that he was. "Make something up to delay her."

"You seriously want me to call her right now and pretend everything's just fine and dandy?" Juliette spoke with a lethargic tone, like a teenager who'd been asked to perform household chores. "Well, what do you suppose I should tell her?"

Earl slammed his fist into the equine emblem mounted on the center of the steering wheel and the vehicle's horn blasted out his frustration. "I dunno, Juliette," he said, "just make something up, damn it. But I'm pretty sure you don't want her to be around when Amiyah gets back to your place and all hell is breaking loose, do you?"

Juliette sank into her seat with exhaustion. She took out her cell phone and attempted to call her daughter. Earl was speeding past every vehicle that got in his way, swerving into the left-hand lane to overtake. The narrow road they were traveling along was mostly unlit. In the black nothingness beyond the car's windows, there were no distractions to draw Juliette's attention, forcing her to focus on the magnitude of everything that had just occurred. With each new set of red taillights that appeared on the horizon, Juliette was filled with a wave of terror. She fretted over the possibility of an encounter with her own truck, knowing how painful it was going to be the next time she had to look into the eyes of her young lover. She couldn't erase the image of Amiyah's distinctive silhouette from her mind. The insides of her eyelids had been branded with the jagged outline of the young woman's body frozen rigid with shock in the corner of the locker room. "She's not answering," Juliette said, and she dropped her phone into her lap.

Earl leaned closer to the windshield. "Is that your hunk of junk up ahead?" he said, straining his eyes into the distance. "That's gotta be her."

"Just hold back, okay? It doesn't look anything like my truck."

The road widened into the mouth of a multi-lane junction. Juliette was willing the traffic lights ahead to remain in their current state, with the green signal illuminated, so that Earl would sail straight through the crossroads and the pair of them would be able to continue with their ominous pursuit. Despite her best prayers, the overhead lights came alive in what seemed like a conscious act of spite, turning first to a menacing shade of amber and then to an angry ball of red fire that meant Juliette would have to face up to everything she'd been hoping to avoid. The unidentified vehicle in front of their own skidded to a standstill beneath the red stoplight.

Earl slowed his car to a crawl. "Shit, it is her," he said. "Motherfucker," he added, coldly, as if the individual they were approaching was a complete stranger, an enemy even.

Juliette clung onto anything she could to brace herself as Earl pulled up alongside the stationary pick-up truck. Juliette knew every last blemish in the bodywork of her beloved steed. She couldn't deny the fact it was her own vehicle any longer. She could almost feel the music that was throbbing from within the commandeered automobile, as though Amiyah's fury was resonating out into the cool evening air. Amiyah didn't even turn to look down at Earl's low-slung mustang. She just stared straight ahead, determined to reach her destination.

"Fuck this," Earl said, and he threw his door open and climbed out into the road. Juliette reached over to catch him, but he was already gone, standing out on the tarmac with his feet spread apart like a boxer, his upper body bouncing back and forth as he attempted to yank open the passenger side door of the truck. He slammed the side of his heavyweight fist into the window, bowing the glass to its limit with each consecutive strike. "Get out of the damn truck," he shouted, but Amiyah refused to react.

Juliette climbed out to join him. "Calm down," she said, trying to pry her brother away from the vehicle. The truck's engine flared up repeatedly, like an angered bull pawing at the ground with its forefeet, threatening to bolt at any moment. And then, without further warning, the beastly pick-up truck took off, ripping itself free from Earl's grip on the door handle. As the truck slid away—with its black body shimmering under the streetlights like a great orca swimming beneath the light of the moon—it swerved in on Juliette and Earl, almost crushing them against the side of the Mustang. The split-second of relief Juliette felt as the truck narrowly passed them by was cut short when the huge thing plowed straight into the front wing of Earl's car. There was a horrible metallic shriek, the sound of a glancing blow dispelling any glimmer of doubt the two automobiles had made contact. Earl covered his eyes with his hands. He slumped down onto his knees, weakened with despair. As Amiyah roared off into the night, Juliette took hold of her brother's shoulders to comfort him for his loss. She couldn't muster any words to console him, so instead, she joined him in his silent mourning.

Earl stayed there for a while on his knees, quietly suppressing his rage. He glanced down at the floor, unable to accept the level of damage Amiyah had inflicted upon his prized possession. Eventually, he shrugged himself free of Juliette's embrace, placed his hands on the body of the car and pulled himself up to his feet. The glistening Mustang was scarred and deformed from its front wheel arch to its bumper. A streak of silver ran the entire length of the wing, a deep and jagged graze carved into the sparkling emerald paint job.

"We can get it fixed," Juliette said, nodding her head optimistically.

The look in Earl's eyes told Juliette that this was all her fault and that she would be thoroughly scolded for it at a more suitable time. "Just get in the fucking car," Earl said.

Juliette circled back to the passenger side and hurried into the wounded vehicle, not wanting to anger her brother any further. Earl fired up the Mustang's V8 engine and stepped on the accelerator before even releasing the brake. The raspy growl of the engine reminded Juliette of the vehicle's great power and of her brother's equally ferocious temper.

"Let's go get this little whore," Earl said, and he wheel-spun the Mustang out from underneath the traffic lights, paying no attention to whatever color they happened to be displaying.

"Just slow down, already," Juliette said. "You're gonna get us both killed."

Earl slammed through the gears, refusing to heed his sister's words, laughing quietly as he shot the Mustang along the road. His sinister chuckle sounded like that of a man who'd been pushed so far, he was past the past point of caring. "I still can't get my head around it all," he said, his lips curled up into a contemptuous grin.

"Around what?"

"The fact you've finally admitted you're a lesbian, of course," Earl said, and he ran his eyes up and down the length of his sister's body.

Juliette folded her arms, suddenly feeling self-conscious under her brother's judgmental gaze.

Earl shook his head and exhaled a breath of laughter. "Did you really think I hadn't noticed the way you're always looking at her?"

"Yes, I'm sure you had it all figured out, didn't you?"

"Don't get smart with me, kid." Earl stepped down on the accelerator as he spoke. "Maybe this was my plan all along. Maybe that's why I put the two of you together in the first place. Because I knew how it would all turn out."

"You're living in a fantasy, Earl. Not everything revolves around you." Juliette looked over to her brother, noticing the twisted grin on his face, a familiar expression of his that always seemed so belittling. She was determined to stand her ground over this and not be ridiculed for everything she'd confessed to. "You just can't stand the fact I've finally moved on and found someone else, can you? And now you've suddenly come to realize you've got no control over me anymore. The thing is, I can do whatever the hell I want with Amiyah. And believe me, I do."

Earl slammed the car into a sharp bend and Juliette was thrown about in her seat. "Somehow, I don't think you'll be doing much with her for a while now, will you?"

Juliette sucked in a long breath to control her anger. She looked out of her window, scanning the dark roadside for anything that might offer a distraction from her brother's words. The car's stereo was muted. Only the constant purr of the engine permeated the tense atmosphere of the vehicle's interior. The leather upholstery of the Mustang smelled as though it were fresh out of a showroom, even though the car was a classic of considerable vintage. Juliette begrudged the fact her brother kept his ride in such immaculate condition. She didn't think the spotless carpet of the footwells or the polished surfaces of the dash offered a fair representation of the man's multiple character flaws. Neither did she believe the vehicle's impeccable condition mirrored the extent to which Earl had allowed his own physique to fall into disrepair. She scowled at the walnut gear nob, the chrome dial surrounds, the emerald accents Earl had fitted here and there to match the Mustang's custom paint job.

As Juliette surveyed her surroundings, the entire cockpit was lit up by the glaring headlights of an eighteen-wheel truck coming straight at them from the opposite direction. Earl lowered his sun visor to shield his vision, and something tumbled out from behind the fold-down panel, a small sheet of paper which glided into Juliette's lap. There was just enough ambient lighting for her to decipher the image as she held it up for inspection. Earl saw it as well, from the corner of his eyes. There was a moment of silence as both siblings registered the ghostly black and white printout of the fetus that was growing inside Margot's womb. Juliette thought about all she stood to lose if she failed to work things out with Amiyah, and then about everything Earl had to look forward to now that his wife was expecting a child.

"You know Margot can never find out about this, right?" Earl said.

"Yes, because your life's so much more important than mine, isn't it?"

Earl crunched through the gears. "Why is she going to your place, anyway?" he asked.

"To get her clothes," Juliette said. "I do her laundry, okay?"

Earl broke into a fit of laughter. "You're washing her clothes already? You really have got it bad, haven't you?"

Juliette tried to keep a straight face, but eventually gave in and joined her brother in his amusement. They laughed together for a while, and Juliette was reminded of the unique connection they had always shared. Even in a situation as difficult as this, they somehow managed to find a way to work through the adversity together, the same way they'd soldiered on through all of Juliette's fights. Their eyes met for a second in the half-light and both of them understood, without the need for words, exactly how ridiculous the whole situation was, how bizarre their relationship had always been, and how unsettling it would seem to anybody who had the misfortune to learn of it.

Earl reached over and rested a hand on his sister's thigh. "Is it better than it was between you and me?" he asked. "I mean, when you're with her."

Juliette placed a hand over her brother's. She thought for a moment, trying to decide how much information she should relay to him, wondering whether she should intentionally hurt his feelings by describing how amazing it had felt each and every time she'd made love to Amiyah. "It's different," she said when she finally settled on the best way to answer.

"Different how?"

Juliette sighed at his persistence, but then noticed he seemed distracted somehow.

Earl craned his neck to look in the rearview mirror. "It's the cops," he said.

Juliette spun around in her seat to check through the rear windshield.

"Way back down the road," Earl said.

"Are you kidding me?"

"Why, was I speeding?"

"I told you to slow down."

"Just relax, okay?"

The car behind them set off a short blast of its siren.

"What are you doing?" Juliette said. "Pull over."

"We've gotta get back to yours," Earl said, and he tightened his grip on the steering wheel.

"Don't do it, Earl."

Earl looked over at his sister, looked in the rearview mirror one last time, then slammed the gearstick down a notch. Juliette was pinned into her seat once again as the Mustang shot away from the pursuing vehicle.

"Are you crazy?" Juliette said. "Pull the fuck over." The police car's siren was wailing consistently now. "I'm serious, stop the fucking car."

"Just be quiet and sit still."

As Earl fired the Mustang along the winding road, the lights of the town began to illuminate the grass shoulders all around them. They were passing under streetlights now, speeding along a tree-lined avenue with a uniform pattern of neatly-kept houses on either side. For a second amid all of the chaos, Juliette felt a wave of jealousy toward the inhabitants of the suburban neighborhood that surrounded her. As she peered into the immaculate front yards, she imagined the families occupying the houses would be living quiet and ordinary lives, doing all of the things normal people liked to do, preparing evening meals and settling down to watch their favorite television shows, not racing across town to intercept their gay lovers in a desperate bid to contain their darkest secrets. Juliette could see the police car in the distance behind them, its sirens flashing from blue to red among a blur of brilliant white light. Earl spun the Mustang into a sharp turn. Its wheels screeched over the tarmac as they entered a side street.

"What are you doing?" Juliette said. "This is a dead end."

Earl slammed on the breaks. "Get out," he said.

"What are you talking about?"

"Go on. I'll take the heat for this. You can run to your place from here."

"But, what about you?"

"Let's just hope the cops are MMA fans, huh? Seriously, get out of here, kid. Go and sort this mess out. Do what you gotta do." He reached across and opened the passenger-side door. "Go," he said, pushing Juliette out into the street.

She looked back into the car, thanking Earl with her eyes.

He winked at her, and then with a nod of his head, he told her to leave.

As she turned to flee, Earl called her name one last time. "We'll get her back," he said. "One way or another, we'll figure this out. We always do."

Juliette held onto her brother's words of encouragement as she took off into the night.

***

The light that shone from the front window of the little apartment, illuminating the spiky outlines of the plants that decorated the balcony area, had always seemed so comforting to Juliette. That familiar glow had so often acted as a welcome home beacon, alerting Juliette to the fact her daughter was going to be waiting for her somewhere inside. Whenever Juliette caught sight of that glowing window, a warmth would ignite in the pit of her stomach and she'd race up the spiraling flights of her stairwell, eager to be in the presence of her young daughter. But on this occasion, as Juliette ran into the parking lot of her building—breathing heavily with a mixture of panic and exhaustion—that glowing window stopped her dead in her tracks, sent a jolt of fear through her whole body, crippling her to the point where she wound up hunched over, gasping to take in enough oxygen to calm herself down.

She glanced up toward her landing, watching for movement behind the illuminated window, hoping to get some idea of who was in her apartment. She scanned the parking lot and spotted her truck in the far corner, its dark shape discarded haphazardly over the white lines of a bay. She hurried through the gate at the base of her stairwell and began the steep ascent toward her landing. Moments later, she was taking one last extended breath to brace herself for whatever kind of scenario might be lurking behind her front door. She listened for a while, half expecting to hear the commotion of raised voices, the thuds of heavy footfall, the frantic clatter of doors being thrown open and closed. She'd been almost certain her apartment was going to be positively humming with activity, but as she stood on the landing, lingering at the edge of the balcony garden, the cool air was silent save for the rustle of palm fronds scratching together on the breeze. When she finally plucked up the courage to creep into her lounge, the apartment felt unnervingly still, like a sleeping giant that might awaken at any second. Juliette moved slowly from foot to foot, not wanting to disturb the tranquility of the place in any way. As she turned to ease the warped front door back into its frame, she caught sight of Shelby sitting upright in the center of the couch, her slender body still drowned in her oversized varsity jacket as if she hadn't quite decided whether she was going to stay.

"She's gone," Shelby said, and as she spoke, her voice was completely devoid of warmth or affection. The teenager didn't even look up in the direction of her mother; she just stared into the middle distance, her eyes weighed down with disillusionment the same way Earl's eyes so often were.

Juliette tried to act casual, unsure of how much damage Amiyah had done. "Yeah, Doll, the thing is, I guess we kind of had a disagreement, you know?"

"I know," Shelby said, cutting her mother off abruptly. "I know."

"Oh, right. Well, what did she say, exactly?"

Shelby looked directly at her mother, torturing her with a prolonged silence before delivering the killer blow. "You mean, did she tell me about you and Uncle Earl?"

Juliette collapsed onto one of the fold-up chairs beside the dining table. The room closed in on her and fell away all at once. Her mind raced to compute the full implications of what had been said, as if she'd just woken up from a knockout punch and was struggling to realign her thoughts with reality.

Shelby got up off the couch and stood over the limp body of her mother splayed out over the dining chair. "What the fuck is going on, Mom?"

"Look, no cursing," Juliette said, trying desperately to hide her state of shock, the same way she would try to avoid letting an opponent know how badly she was hurt in a fight. "It was just a misunderstanding, okay?"

"Mom, if you don't tell me exactly what's going on, right now, I'm gonna pack my bags and leave. So either you start telling me the truth for once, or I'm out of here."

Juliette was unable to make eye contact with her daughter, knowing the teenager would be scrutinizing her every move. "We were just flirting, fooling around the way we always do."

"I said, don't lie to me."

"You know how close me and Uncle Earl are. Can't you see how that might look weird to somebody who doesn't understand, somebody who doesn't have that kind of a relationship with their brother?"

"Fuck off, Mom, don't treat me like an idiot."

"Hey, come on, there's no need for that."

"The poor girl was shaking," Shelby said. "She looked as though she'd just watched somebody fucking die. She could barely even speak, so don't feed me any of your bullshit. Do you understand?"

Juliette held her head in her hands as she came to realize the magnitude of the situation. She stole a glance through her fingers and saw Shelby's posture was all tight with rage, her jacket sleeves knotted up across her upper body.

"Look at me," Shelby demanded. "I said, look at me."

Juliette half-glanced up like an apologetic dog. "I can't," she said.

Shelby raised her chin and folded her arms more securely. "I'm going to ask you a question, and you've got one chance to tell me the truth."

"I really don't need this right now, Doll-face."

"Mom, have you ever slept with Uncle Earl?"

"What are you talking about?" Juliette mumbled, too exhausted to deal with the enormity of the question. She hung her head; there was no conviction in her voice.

"Are you fucking kidding me?" Shelby said, and she reached out to prop her mother up, hoping to see the truth in her face.

Juliette swept her daughter's hands away. "Give me a break, Doll. I said I don't need this right now, okay?"

Shelby was crying now, shaking her head in disbelief. "Please, tell me it's not true. It can't be."

The conversation was sweeping over Juliette like a wave, carrying her away to places she'd always hoped she would never have to visit. She was too exhausted to fight against the current of it all, so she allowed the emotional tide to batter her this way and that, the truth spilling out in ways she'd never dared to imagine. Juliette took hold of her sobbing daughter and tried to pull her close. "Come on, Doll-face," she said, "don't be like that." Juliette was crying as well, her hair sticking to the mixture of sweat and tears covering her face.

Shelby fell into her mother's arms, weakened by the enormity of the revelations.

"Shush, now," Juliette whispered, kissing the tear-sodden skin of her daughter's cheeks. "It's okay," she said, rocking the teenager back and forth like a baby. "It's all in the past. Me and Uncle Earl have put all of that behind us now. It was just a misunderstanding today. We'll work it all out, you'll see." They held onto each other for a while, and the warmth of their closeness brought Juliette a momentary sense of comfort in the midst of the emotional turmoil. But the more Juliette tried to hold on to her daughter, the more the teenager pulled away. And then Shelby's body slackened and slipped out of her mother's arms altogether.

"You're sick," Shelby said, and as she spoke, her eyes were dead again, deader than they had ever seemed before. "You know that, right? You're not normal."

Juliette felt a lump in her throat as if she were going to throw up.

"Do you hear me?" Shelby said. "You're sick."

"Okay, I get it," Juliette said, snorting back her tears. "Go ahead and blame me for all of this, just like your grandma and grandpa always did. They used to say it was all my fault as well. So whatever you want to throw at me, I'm used to it, okay? I've heard it all before. I'm a freak of nature as we know it. I understand that. I get the message loud and clear."

"Are you finished?" Shelby said.

Juliette exhaled a huff of frustration and ran her hands through her hair. They looked at each other silently now the conversation had reached a point of stalemate. Shelby sat down on the dining chair opposite her mother, the two of them facing each other across the table, their hostile body language mirroring one another's quite precisely. Although Juliette was unable to muster the courage to look up at her daughter, she felt the teenager's eyes on her the whole time, studying her like an abnormality.

"I'm sorry, Doll," she said, but as the words left her mouth she knew they wouldn't be enough.

"You're pathetic," Shelby said, and she bolted up from her chair, almost causing the rickety old table to collapse.

"Where are you going?" Juliette called out. "Can we at least talk about this?"

Shelby stormed out of the lounge and disappeared into her bedroom, slamming the door so forcefully Juliette feared her neighbors might complain. Juliette got up from her chair and paced about in the lounge. She looked herself over in the mirror to check if she really was the monster everybody believed her to be. She clenched her hands into fists and shadowboxed with her reflection. She had to remind herself of the fact she was — first and foremost — a fighter, a former champion, and not just some sexual deviant who'd slept with her own brother. She was an honorable martial artist, and all of the people who'd watched her compete over the years knew exactly how much she was capable of. Nobody could take that away from her, not Amiyah, not Earl, and not even Shelby.

As Juliette skipped over the carpet and threw her fists out into the air, she began to feel light-headed and nauseous, unsteady on her feet. She was unable to comprehend the level of damage that had been done to her life in a single evening. The realization she'd managed to drive both her lover and her daughter away filled her with nervous adrenalin, burning all of her energy until her limbs began to tremble. She sat on the floor with her back against the front door, guarding the exit in case her daughter attempted to escape. She watched the clock up on the wall, certain there would be less chance of Shelby trying to leave with every minute that passed. Her thoughts blurred out of focus to the constant hum of traffic passing outside. She struggled to stay awake for as long as she could, but her eyes soon began to close and her body slumped further toward the floor.

"Mom, what the hell are you doing on the floor?"

Juliette sat bolt upright, sucking in a trail of drool that had spilled out of her mouth during her slumber. Shelby was standing over her, clutching a backpack to her chest. "No way," Juliette said. "You're not going anywhere." She climbed to her feet and reached out to take the backpack from her daughter.

Shelby snatched the backpack away and slung it over her shoulder. "I'm going to stay at Grandpa's," she said.

"What, are you kidding me? You think I'm gonna let you stay out there with that asshole?"

"He's on his way to get me. I told him what happened."

"For Christ's sake, Doll, that's all I need." Juliette turned away and steadied herself on the back of a dining chair. "You can't do this to me," she said. "Please, don't leave me. You're all I've got left."

Shelby placed a hand on her mother's shoulder. "But I know you're not being honest with me. And I understand that you can't be. Grandpa will tell me what this is all about. We need some time apart, some time to figure things out."

"Why do I feel like I'm being dumped for the second time in one day?"

There was a beep from Shelby's phone indicating she'd received a message. "He's here," she said.

"Don't do this to me, Doll. I'm begging you."

"I'm sorry, Mom, I've gotta go. Grandpa's waiting."

Shelby closed the front door and Juliette's mind was blank. The teenager had taken everything that mattered from her mother's life including the ability to think straight. All that remained was an overwhelming sense of darkness. Juliette stayed there, hunched over the dining chair, until she could no longer stand. Then, she collapsed onto the couch, pulled a blanket over her weary body, and gazed into the darkness until she fell asleep.

CHAPTER 20

The coarse and tangled shrubs that carpeted the coastal scrubland appeared to be growing at a slanted angle thanks to the persistent winds that swept in off the ocean. The wind reminded Juliette of the fact she had — for some unknown reason — opted to wear a thin summer dress, the hem of which flailed about her knees as the breeze rushed up into the lightweight garment, cooling her body in a way that wasn't entirely unpleasant, but at the same time, made her abundantly aware of her uncharacteristic choice of attire. She patted at the lower half of the dress, trying to pin the fabric down against her thighs. She blew her lank, wind-tangled hair from her face and spat it out of her mouth. Everything about this wild landscape aggravated her — the sand on the breeze forcing her to squint, insects buzzing into her face from the undergrowth, the roar and crash of the ocean battering steep bluffs in the distance. It was all just noise, a distraction hindering the clarity of her thoughts like an opponent flicking their jab into her face while she was trying to formulate an offense of her own.

As she turned her back on the low-lying shrubs that spread out right to the point at which the land dropped off and gave way to the ocean, she looked up over the roof of her truck and saw a scattering of houses up in the hills, a collection of whitewashed dwellings spread out before a jagged wall of limestone cliffs. Juliette ran her eyes over the houses that were lined up in the distance, noticing the way they were all uniformly ultra-modern, blocky structures with asymmetric roofs, floor to ceiling windows, and white stucco walls. She was certain there had to be some kind of strict rules in place, guidelines that must be adhered to when building any type of property on this particular stretch of coastal land, as if somebody in a position of authority had decided the installation of these brutally minimalistic glass boxes was the most appropriate way to complement the rugged, natural beauty of this windswept wilderness. She rolled her eyes and shook her head at the pomposity of it all.

On her way back to the truck, she caught sight of her own reflection in the driver's side window. Her insides flared up with a kind of nervous embarrassment when she saw the flash of red lipstick she'd painted onto her battle-hardened face. She paused for a moment and took an extended breath to calm herself down. She looked back to the houses lined up at the foot of the limestone cliffs and her heartbeat began to resonate right up into her temples. As she climbed back inside her truck and met her own heavily-penciled gaze in the rearview mirror, she felt a sudden sense of awareness throbbing in every part of her body, an awareness that somewhere in one of those annoyingly perfect glass houses up on the hill, her latest opponent, her father, would be waiting on her arrival.

***

Juliette studied the gated entrance before her, looking for a way to gain access to her father's property. She'd visited this place so infrequently, she couldn't even remember how to communicate with the house that lay beyond these vast wooden doors. She waved a hand over the top of the gates, rattled them on their hinges, even thought about hoisting herself up to climb into the front yard. "For fuck's sake, Dad," she said, kicking the gates with one of her leather biker boots. She limped back and forth, cursing under her breath, reeling with pain from her assault on the immovable timber structures.

"What in the world are you doing, girl?" a male voice growled out from somewhere close by.

Juliette's body jolted with shock. She spun back toward the house so quickly she almost lost her balance. One of the gates was half open now, and standing right there in the shadow of the thing was the giant, square outline of Wild Billy Diaz, the old man Juliette had been so anxious about seeing for the past few months, ever since her daughter had walked out on her and come to stay in this sparsely populated part of town.

"You trying to start a fight with my damn property now, or what?" Billy Diaz said. His speech was drawn out as though his brain took a little longer than most people's did to formulate a sentence.

Juliette didn't answer her father; she just breathed hard to stifle the aggravation his sarcasm had injected into her. A pair of eyes—the same shape as those belonging to both her daughter and her brother—stared back at her from underneath the brim of her father's straw hat. She stood up straight and adjusted her dress, suddenly aware of the old man's penetrating gaze.

"You coming in or what?" he slurred out from the shadows, and as he turned and shuffled off through the gates, a small, wire-haired dog, no larger than an overgrown rat, came bounding out toward Juliette.

"Is that thing still alive?" Juliette said, hurrying to catch up with her father, the scraggy little dog yapping at her heels the whole time.

"Of course she is, she's a mongrel, ain't she? Just like her sister."

"Her sister?"

"Yeah, her sister. That's you, girl." He laughed and wheezed at his own joke until he coughed and spat on the gravel driveway. "Mongrels live forever, ain't that right, Champ," he said to the tiny dog, gathering the animal up in his monstrous arms. "That's why you're still fighting at such a ripe old age, Juliette."

"Damn, I'm not that old, Dad," Juliette said, flattening her windswept hair about her face. She watched her father walking back to the white-walled porch of the house, his thick arms and tree-trunk legs emerging from a patterned shirt and casual shorts. His outfit made him look as though he was on permanent vacation here in the twilight of his existence. He seemed almost as wide as he was tall, his substantial girth making him appear shorter than he actually was. And when he walked, he swung his broad shoulders through each stride, his distinctive gait making him look even wider still. The familiarity of the man's robust shape filled Juliette with an ache of nostalgia, a sense of longing for happier times.

The old man held open the pane of glass that was his front door, welcoming Juliette into his home. His war-wounded face was in the sunlight now, his boxer's features on full display. The white hair that was visible beneath the rim of his hat reminded Juliette of just how old he'd grown. He never looked this weathered in Juliette's thoughts of him. In her mind, he was too strong, too indestructible to age this way. She had to see him in the flesh to be aware of the fact he was only human like everyone else.

She took the door off him and was reminded of his distinctive smell, an ingrained, musty scent of masculinity that made her feel like she was a child again. She knew she had to be strong, to resist the fatherly power he had over her instead of giving in and succumbing to his dominant ways. She followed him into the hallway, raising a hand to shield her eyes from the sunlight beating down through the glass walls. She felt exposed by the harsh lighting, naked in her summer dress. One entire wall of the narrow hallway was mirrored all the way from floor to ceiling. She tried desperately to avoid the sight of her own reflection but couldn't help noticing from the side of her eyes the shape of her athletic physique, like a scrawny little man in a dress with muscular arms and defined legs but no breasts of any kind to speak of.

Her father paused in the center of a vast, sparsely furnished lounge, the walls of which were adorned with a collection of similarly vibrant expressionist paintings. "You on your way to the courthouse, or what?" he asked.

Juliette was perplexed by his remark, feeling like an infant who couldn't understand the humor of an adult.

"You gotta be going somewhere important, to be all dressed up like that."

Juliette felt her cheeks filling with blood. She shrugged her shoulders and pulled the hem of the dress down over her thighs.

The old man exhaled a breath of laughter at his daughter's apparent discomfort. "You look like a million bucks, kid," he said. "And the rest. Ain't that right, Champ," he said to the little dog he was cradling in his arms.

Juliette did all she could to hold the gratitude from showing on her face.

"What do you think of my latest piece, anyway?" he said, gesturing toward a large square canvas hanging over the fireplace. The artwork depicted a young woman's face in the gloomy shade of a tree, her skin dappled with patches of darkness and light as sunshine crept through the branches over her head.

"You painted this?" Juliette said, lowering her voice to disguise how in awe she was of the piece.

"These are all mine," her father said, and he glanced around to show he was referring to the paintings on every wall.

Juliette looked at the thick strokes of yellow and gold paint the old man had daubed over the canvas to illustrate the young woman's hair. She noted the serenity of the woman's eyes as they lingered on something in the distance, her fingertips resting among the plump folds of her glistening lips. The painting caused Juliette's eyes to well with tears, made her long for something that was absent from her life. "I'm guessing this is Shelby, right?" she said, and she began to look around at some of the other artworks, a little stung by this particular piece.

"So, come on then, let's have it, what do you think?"

"Yeah, it's nice, I guess," she said with a shrug.

"Well, you can't have it," he scoffed. "This one's mine. You'll get the kid back, sooner or later. And then I'll be out here, all on my own. So I'm keeping this piece of her, right here, so that I'll be able to remember the time we spent together."

"I understand," Juliette said. "It's beautiful," she added, unsure if she was referring to the painting or the words her father had spoken. She scratched at the back of her neck, uncomfortable with the level of praise she'd given him. And then she saw he was smirking, as though he'd achieved some minor victory over her. Standing there next to the huge man, Juliette realized just how comparatively tiny she was, and suddenly she felt like a little girl all over again. She straightened her posture, forcing herself to be strong.

"Look, is she going to school?" Juliette asked, eager to change the subject.

The old man frowned. "Where else do you think she is right now?"

"You know what I'm asking, Dad. Is she going to school, or what? I mean properly, every day."

"It takes me half a goddamn hour to drive out to that bus stop twice every day. So relax, she's going to school, alright?"

Juliette allowed herself to smile properly for once.

"Now, you want something to drink? Or, do you wanna stand here yapping like this all day?"

"Can I see where she sleeps?"

"You really think she'd appreciate you poking around in her room?"

"But I've gotta know that she's doing okay."

The old man shook his head disapprovingly.

Juliette knew from his silence he was at least giving some level of consideration to her request. "Please, Dad," she persisted.

He exhaled a breath of frustration and walked over to the base of a wooden staircase, the individual steps of which were suspended from an intricate wire framework. "Just don't touch anything, okay?" he said, and he motioned to a doorway at the top of the stairs. "Let's go fix us a drink, Champ," he said, lowering himself slowly enough to show his age until the dog leapt from his arms and skittered off across the wooden floor.

Juliette thanked him with a smile and climbed the suspended staircase. As she pushed through the bedroom door, the scent of her daughter almost swept her off her feet. A set of bifold doors that led out onto a balcony had been left half open and the wind was coming in from the sea, buffeting the white drapes and circulating the sweet aroma of Shelby's beauty products through the air. Juliette took a breath of it all and sat down among the unmade sheets that were strewn out over a double bed. She held one of the pillows up to her face and inhaled the bubblegum fragrance of her daughter's shampoo. She glanced around at Shelby's possessions scattered about the room as though this is where they had always belonged, her makeup spread out over the surface of a dresser, her clothes draped on the back of a chair, her underwear scrunched and tangled on the floor.

Beyond the glass doors leading to the balcony, the ocean stretched out to the horizon with all of its tranquil shades of blue laid out beneath the soft white fleece of the clouded sky. Juliette couldn't deny this place was like paradise in comparison to her own basic little apartment. It broke Juliette's heart to think of how much better Shelby's life must be out here with her grandfather. She shook her head to clear it, got up off the bed and made her way back down the suspended staircase.

"Come on in here," her father called out from somewhere beneath the stairs. She followed his voice through an open door that led into a double-width garage, the interior of which seemed a little darker than most of the other glass-walled rooms of the house.

"I prefer it in here," the old man grumbled. He was seated on one of two plastic patio chairs that were pulled up next to a matching table. The little dog was fast asleep, curled up in a basket by the old man's feet. "The rest of the house is a bit flashy for me," he said, screwing his face up into an expression that made Juliette think of her daughter.

"So why on earth did you buy the place, then?"

"I find the landscape inspiring," he said, "for my painting. Gotta keep my mind sharp somehow, right? With all the punches I took over the years."

As Juliette surveyed her surroundings—littered with objects collected from her father's life—she began to feel uneasy, as though she was inadvertently gaining a rare insight into the workings of the old man's mind. The walls were lined on all sides with cluttered shelving racks, a tattered punching bag hung from the rafters, a collection of paint-splattered easels stood haphazardly in one corner.

"Sit down, will you?" the old man said. "You're making the place look untidy."

"No, I kinda think it's all the junk that's doing that," Juliette said, sitting down on the chair opposite her father. The plastic was cold against the back of her thighs. She shifted awkwardly, folding and unfolding her legs as she attempted to find a comfortable position in the hard little chair.

"Relax, will you?" her father said. "Have a drink. Might help you loosen up for once." A pair of opened beer bottles stood together in the center of the table. The old man took hold of one and raised it to his mouth. Condensation glistened over the glass as he tilted the bottle and glugged hard on the beer. He let out a long "ahh" when he'd finished and wiped his mouth with the back of his hand.

Juliette didn't want to accept the offer of a drink, but the old man had made the whole process look so refreshing, she was unable to resist. She took hold of the remaining bottle timidly as though alcohol was something she was about to try for the very first time. She noticed her father was studying her actions with a fire of excitement simmering in his eyes. Determined to draw the moment out for as long as she could, she slid her fingers up the shaft of the bottle and then tightened her grip over its neck. She tried to act casually as she raised the bottle to her mouth and took its circular head between her lips. The cold liquid tingled over her tongue and made her shiver as it went down her throat.

"That's a good girl," the old man said.

Juliette half-laughed, exhausted by her own resistance to her father's charms.

The old man straightened his face as if he'd decided it was time to talk business. "So, what is it, Jules?" he said. "You spent half your life not knowing what you really was?"

"What are you talking about?"

"I'm talking about the fact it's taken you up until the ripe old age of thirty-five to figure out you're a lesbian, of course."

"Fuck, Dad," Juliette said, choking on her beer. "Jesus, I'm not a lesbian. You're as bad as Earl."

"Look, it's fine by me," he said. "I can't exactly say I blame you. I don't much like the idea of dealing with cocks and balls either, if I'm honest."

Juliette felt as though she was choking again. She thumped at her chest to catch her breath.

"And I gotta say, she's a pretty little thing you got yourself there as well. I saw her fight the other day. Watched it on the Internet with Shelby. Hell of an ass on the girl. I mean, great body for martial arts."

"Well, thanks, I guess," Juliette said. "But, we're not exactly together anymore."

"Oh, we'll get her back," her father said, and he sat up tall in his chair to show his sincerity. "Don't you worry about that. We'll figure it all out. You can't let one as cute as that slip through your fingers now, can you?"

Juliette curled her mouth up into a false smile, certain there was no hope of rectifying the situation with Amiyah.

"She's not a bad fighter, either, as it happens," the old man said. "The kid was effective when she was fighting at a distance, but what she really needs to do is work on her dirty boxing in the clinch."

Juliette tore at the label on her bottle as her father continued to analyze Amiyah's most recent performance. She didn't want to appear overly interested in anything the old man had to say, so she tried to act distracted and aloof, gazing vacantly at the half-filled bottle she was clutching in her hands. When she finally allowed herself a brief glance in his direction, she saw he was sitting bolt-upright in his chair, throwing his fists out every now and then to demonstrate the execution of various techniques. Juliette wasn't paying much attention to the precise details of her father's critique, but she'd become unwillingly mesmerized by the low, gravelly tone of his voice, as though he was whispering a soothing lullaby right into her ears.

One of the straps of Juliette's dress slipped from her shoulder and settled about her bicep. Although it made her nervous to do so, she allowed the fallen strap to remain exactly where it was. She wanted her father to see her this way, to notice her and to be interested in her. She felt an urge to show off her athletic body to the old man, because she'd looked at his paintings, and the way she saw it, her finely-tuned physique was the closest thing she had to any kind of artistic work. She wanted him to be impressed by it all, to compliment her on the level of discipline and commitment it must have taken to achieve such a high level of athleticism. She watched his mouth moving, and she remembered the way his stubble used to grate on the skin of her face when he held her close and kissed her goodnight. She wanted to climb into his lap and feel his powerful arms encasing her body. Then, she imagined, he would tell her it was all going to be okay, and he would kiss her on the forehead until she fell asleep right there in the warmth of his embrace.

"Have I lost Shelby, Dad?" Juliette said, interrupting her father's monologue.

"Don't talk stupid," the old man said, and he reached across to take Juliette's hands, but she recoiled when she felt his rough skin against her own.

"I miss her so much," Juliette was crying now. Something about being in the presence of her estranged father had weakened her.

"She'll come around. You'll see. You just gotta give her time. It's a lot for the kid to take in, all that stuff about you and Earl."

It pained Juliette to hear her father speak of her relationship with her brother. "Don't," she said, closing her eyes as tightly as she could, her eyeliner running in streams across her cheeks.

"I explained it the best I could," the old man said. "But you gotta realize, I don't much understand it all myself."

Juliette fixed her father with an accusatory glare. "How could you? You was never there."

He sat back in his chair as if his daughter's words had taken the wind out of him. He nodded in agreement, accepting his own shortcomings as a father. "I get that you and your brother always blamed me for walking out on you, but you know your mom didn't ever really want me around."

"Yeah, well, she's not here to speak for herself, is she?"

Her father took a swig of his beer to settle his nerves. Both of them glanced around the room, not wanting to make eye contact with one another after all that had been said. "Whatever happened to you when you was a kid," the old man said, "whatever you went through, that's what made you who you are today. And, although I might not get the chance to tell you all that often, I'm mighty proud of you, girl."

Juliette covered her eyes, trying desperately to hold back her tears. "So why don't you ever show up to any of my fights?" she said.

"You think I wanna see my little girl getting punched in the face?" He reached over, took one of Juliette's hands from her face and held onto it across the table whether she wanted him to or not.

"I'm not a little girl anymore, Dad."

"That's what you'll always be to me, my little Juliette."

She snatched her hand free of his grip. "I wanted to be your little girl, but you blew it. And I can never forget that." She looked at him through her tears and saw his eyes were glazing over. The realization her words had affected him this way filled her with a rush of satisfaction. She studied him for a while, enjoying the sight of his suffering, confident she had him defeated. She was certain that there was no coming back from this, that there was nothing more he could do or say other than to apologize endlessly and send her on her way.

The old man sat slumped in his chair like a boxer floored by a punch and out for the count. He looked down at the basket by his feet where his miniature dog was curled up asleep, completely oblivious to all the conflict going on around her. He smiled at the peaceful animal and then picked up his bottle to guzzle whatever was left of his beer. He let out another "ahh" and placed his hands on the flimsy plastic table, almost buckling it with his weight as he pushed himself up onto his feet.

"Right then, girl," he said, "let's sort this mess out."

Juliette looked at her father open-mouthed, horrified by his resilience. She watched him get up off the chair, straighten out his shirt, and push his straw hat further back over his hair. She was reminded of his great strength, his ability to overcome adversity, and in that moment, regardless of the fact she wanted him to be sad and defeated, he was acting like a hero, her indestructible father, the way she remembered him from early childhood. Juliette had tested him with her words, had thrown all she could at the old man, and here he was, getting back onto his feet and telling her he could sort everything out, the way she'd wanted him to her entire life.

"Now, let me show you something," he said, and he walked to the back of the garage, where a flat-screen television was mounted among the endless boxes stacked up on the storage racks.

Juliette hadn't even noticed the rectangular screen up until this point in time, but she watched eagerly as her father picked up a remote control handset and brought the television to life.

The old man squinted at the remote control, jabbing at individual buttons with his thick fingers while looking back and forth at the illuminated screen.

Juliette felt the need to intervene. "Do you want me to do it?" she said, reaching out to take over.

"Just you stay where you are," the old man said, and he slowly navigated through several onscreen menus until he brought up a list of video thumbnails. "Amiyah Amoré, post-fight interview," he read out, and the thumbnail he selected appeared to show two women standing side by side.

"Do we have to watch this?"

"Just quiet down a minute, will you?"

Juliette allowed her gaze to settle on the screen and her insides came alight with nerves. She closed her eyes, but the image of Amiyah standing next to her new coach had already been burnt into her thoughts. She blinked her eyes open, as though emerging into the blinding light of day, and right there, almost life-size on the widescreen television, was her ex-lover Amiyah standing next to the shaven-headed Shaolin, the head coach of Diablo MMA's rival gym, Team Zen.

Juliette breathed slowly to calm herself down. She crossed her legs together and hugged her body. Shaolin had thrown an arm around Amiyah's waist, most likely to offer the young woman support and encouragement, but Juliette read the embrace as a display of ownership, as if Shaolin was proudly claiming Amiyah as her own, holding onto her sweaty, glistening body like a magnificent trophy, a prize she would soon take back to her gym to put up on display among her growing collection of championship belts.

The women's mouths were moving intermittently, indicating they were answering questions from an off-screen audience of reporters. The old man pointed the remote control at the television to increase the volume and a single voice emerged from a gaggle of onlookers. "Amiyah, how much difference do you think your move over to Team Zen has made to your overall performance this evening?"

Amiyah smiled at her new coach before answering, and then she turned back to the camera so that her big brown eyes stared right out of the screen toward Juliette. "It made all the difference," she said, as if she knew Juliette would be watching.

"So, it's fair to say, you feel like you've found the right team now?" another reporter asked.

"I think it's safe to say I've found a match with Team Zen," Amiyah said. "And with my new coach, of course," she added, gazing into Shaolin's eyes in a way that turned Juliette's stomach.

"And if you don't mind me asking," the reporter continued, "why was it you decided to make the move from Diablo MMA in the first place?"

"Turn it off," Juliette said. "I can't watch this." Amiyah's appearance still affected Juliette the same way it always had. The sight of the young woman standing victoriously in her fight gear made Juliette wince at everything she'd lost. She felt as though she might throw up, sickened with a mixture of jealousy and lust.

The old man paused the footage. "Don't let this beat you," he said. "You're better than that. Just look at this bald-headed freak's hands all over her. Let that fire you up and motivate you to put this right."

"Don't, Dad."

"Are you really gonna let her take your woman off you like this? I thought you was made of stronger stuff, girl."

Juliette drew a long breath. "Just play it," she said, dropping her head to avoid the screen.

"The reason I left Diablo's was kind of personal," Amiyah explained. "I'm not really one to kiss and tell. Besides, I wanna focus on my future, and that's right here with Team Zen."

Shaolin planted a lingering kiss on Amiyah's face, rewarding the young woman for her words of praise.

"Look at the pair of them cavorting like teenagers," the old man said. "You think they might be, you know, together?"

"Don't be stupid." The thought of Amiyah being intimate with anyone else was too much for Juliette to bear.

The reporters shifted their focus toward Shaolin, eager to find out what she thought of her student's performance. Shaolin reached over to somebody off-screen from whom she retrieved her championship belt, a thick leather strap with several gold metallic discs fastened to its surface. She lifted the gleaming belt with both hands, handling it with great care and respect. She hoisted the belt up over one shoulder and stood up tall, quite separate from Amiyah, clearly preparing herself for the reporters to focus their attention on her alone.

"You gotta be fucking kidding me," Juliette said. Amiyah checked her nails and adjusted her hair, not knowing quite what to do now that the questions were being directed toward her coach. "Look at the poor kid standing there like a spare part," Juliette said. "This is supposed to be her interview, not that asshole's."

"Just listen, okay?" her father said.

"Shaolin, over here if you wouldn't mind," one of the reporters began. "I understand Amiyah's former coach was Jules Diamond Diaz."

"What of it?" Shaolin said with a dismissive grunt of laughter.

"I was wondering, is there going to be a rematch any time soon between Jules and your teammate, Oksana?"

Shaolin threw her shorn head back, closed her eyes, and laughed again. "Jules got lucky against Oksana the first time. She knows that, and she knows she's done fighting as well. She's too old to be getting in the cage with these hungry young lions. Isn't that right, Amiyah?"

Amiyah's eyes drifted as she pondered her coach's question. She opened her mouth to speak several times, but on each occasion, no words came out.

The young woman's silence tortured Juliette. She wanted her ex-lover to speak up in her defense, to show that some glimmer of affection still existed between them, no matter how small.

"It's clear that Jules is dodging The Ox," Shaolin continued. "We've offered her the fight, but she's running scared. She knows she can't beat Oksana a second time. Isn't that right, Amiyah?"

Amiyah tried to laugh the question off, seemingly reluctant to either confirm or deny her coach's claim.

"That's what she told you, wasn't it?" Shaolin asked, fixing her young student with a reprimanding gaze. "She knows she got lucky in the first fight, right?"

Amiyah tried to avoid making eye contact with the camera, clearly aware Juliette would see her response. "I guess that's more or less what she told me," Amiyah confirmed, eventually.

"Turn it off, I've seen enough," Juliette said, and her father paused the footage. She leaned forward over her thighs, burying her face in her lap. "I think I'm gonna throw up." She stayed there hunched over for a while as she waited for the room to stop spinning around her. "Why the hell did you have to show me that?" She came up for air and found her father had sat himself back down on the opposite side of the table.

The old man observed Juliette in her defeat, his eyes weighed down with that familiar look of disappointment.

"Why are you looking at me like that?"

He let out a long breath. "Are you really just gonna curl up and quit on me like this?"

Juliette shrugged her shoulders dramatically enough to show her father she was lost.

"These girls are acting like a gang of schoolyard bullies right now. And what did I always tell you to do when you was in school? Girl, if anyone starts giving you shit, you walk right up to the ring leader and you go ahead and punch that sucker square in the face."

"Yeah, I remember that advice getting me kicked out of school a few times."

"But, I bet those jerks didn't bother you anymore, did they?"

"I guess not," Juliette conceded.

"Well, who do you suppose is the ring leader in all of this?"

Juliette looked back toward the freeze-frame image on the television screen. Amiyah looked so devastatingly perfect in her fight gear, the contours of her toned arms and shoulders catching the light magnificently thanks to the sheen of perspiration glistening all over her skin. Despite the young woman's flawless appearance, she had undeniably been upstaged by her coach, a proud champion parading her belt for all to see. Shaolin had a distinctively upright way of standing that made her look ready for a fight at any moment, her feet splayed at shoulder width, her chest thrust forward, her bald head tilted back like she was constantly daring anybody to challenge her physical capabilities. Juliette's gaze lingered on Shaolin, and she began to make sense of everything her father had been alluding to.

"You gotta be kidding me, right?" Juliette said. "How would I even get a fight with somebody on her level?"

"Don't put yourself down, girl. You're a former champion. You just beat the number one prospect on her team. And what's more, she just happens to be coaching your ex-girlfriend. You think she needs any more motivation to take the fight?"

Juliette felt nauseous again as she considered the implications of her father's words. She opened her mouth to speak, hoping to utter something in protest of the old man's suggestion, but all that came out was, "I can't," and as she said the words, she understood exactly how pathetic they sounded.

"Pull yourself together, girl," her father said, and he took out a handkerchief to wipe the dark trails of eyeliner from Juliette's cheeks. When he'd finished, he placed his hands on the table and pushed himself up to his feet again. He walked over to the storage racks, rummaged in a cardboard box, and took out a swollen paper bag. He tossed the bag through the air so that it landed in the center of the table, almost knocking the empty beer bottles onto their sides.

"What the hell is this?" Juliette asked.

"Just go ahead and open it. I've had those things in here for years. Guess I've been waiting for the right moment to give them to you."

Juliette turned her head away from him, fearing her excitement might be showing on her face. "Since when have you ever given me anything?" she said.

"Just open it, okay?" The old man turned away as well, unable to deal with the emotional exchange.

Juliette opened the bag slowly enough to give the impression she had no real interest in its contents. Her jaw slackened with disbelief as a pair of fuchsia-pink boxing gloves tumbled out into her lap.

"It's not much," the old man said. "But, I picked out the colors all by myself."

Juliette was silent, her eyes transfixed by the gift her father had presented her with. The bright pink gloves had been customized with the letters of her last name embroidered in gold text across the wristbands. Juliette had always despised the color pink. The gloves were entirely ridiculous, the exact opposite of anything she would have chosen herself, but as she studied the garish leather and the gold embroidery, there was something strangely innocent about the choice of gift that made her question everything she'd ever thought to be true about her father. This simple offering seemed to represent the old man's character in a way that made Juliette feel cruel and unfair. Maybe he really was as clueless and naive as these bright pink boxing gloves would indicate him to be. Maybe it really hadn't been his fault when he'd walked out on Juliette's mother all those years ago. She couldn't allow herself to think that way, because if it was true, if he really was just a stupid old heavyweight boxer who'd been punched in the head a few too many times, that would mean Juliette had wasted her whole life being angry at him when she could have been upstairs sleeping in his spare room with the ocean outside the window, or having her portrait painted and hung over the fireplace, the way Shelby was.

"Well, come on, put an old man out of his misery. You like them or not?"

"They're...amazing," Juliette said, and she was immediately angry with herself for revealing her gratitude.

"Really? You like them?"

"Of course," she said, happy he'd given her anything at all.

"Well, what are you waiting for, girl? Put them on, and let's see how they fit."

"I don't know about that," Juliette said. "I should probably be going soon."

"What, you got somewhere else you need to be? Don't act like you don't have ten minutes to hit pads with your old dad."

Juliette sighed with frustration. She realized if she put her hands into the gloves, she would be doing her father's bidding and playing by his rules, when she'd been adamant she would do this all on her own terms. She wondered why he even wanted to train with her on this occasion anyway, when he'd never shown any kind of interest in doing so in the past. Maybe spending so much time with Shelby had shown the old man what he'd missed out on all these years he'd spent barely even speaking with his daughter. Maybe he realized just how much Juliette needed him in her life at this point in time. Whatever his motivations had been, Juliette found herself strangely compelled to pull on the bright pink boxing gloves he'd given to her.

"Get those on and get over here," the old man said. "You haven't got any time to waste. You've got a fight to be training for."

CHAPTER 21

"Can I get you anything else, ma'am?" the stout little waitress asked with an almost accusatory tone, as if to suggest Juliette had outstayed the length of welcome a single cup of coffee permitted.

"I'm good, thanks," Juliette replied. "Just waiting for a friend." She barely even managed to look up from her contemplation of the shallow liquid remnants in the bottom of her cup. She raised the cup to her mouth and tilted her head back, allowing the last mouthful of tepid coffee to trickle down her throat, its lukewarm temperature acting as a reminder of just how long she'd been waiting here in the booth at the back of the diner.

Most of the other patrons had chosen to occupy the tables at the front of the mom-and-pop establishment, where floor-to-ceiling windows provided views out over the mountainous terrain in the distance, the landscape beyond the freeway from which the eatery drew most of its business. Juliette had opted to sit as far as she could from everybody else, even if it meant her table was so close to the restrooms she was treated to the chemical scent of cleaning products every time somebody opened the door to use the facilities.

One of the waitresses guided a young family of four into a nearby booth. Juliette propped the collar of her leather jacket around her face and pushed her bug-eyed sunglasses up the bridge of her nose. She'd sunken so low in spirit throughout the past few months, she had no desire to converse with anyone who might happen to recognize her. She studied the family the waitress had positioned directly in her line of vision: a mother, a father, and two young children, a daughter and a son. They couldn't have been any more of a cliché. Juliette overheard snippets of their conversation, all spoken with an unfamiliar accent, and she decided the family must have been on vacation from some distant country. They might as well have been from another planet judging by how happy and carefree they all looked, a stark contrast to the way Juliette had been feeling of late. She tried to avert her gaze from the scene, but couldn't help noticing the little girl kneeling up on the bench-seat, her skinny legs emerging from her dress as she bent over the table to read from her father's menu. The idyllic vision of childhood filled Juliette with an ache for all she'd lost from her life.

She looked down at the coffee stains in the bottom of her cup. This was the type of mundane detail she had to focus on now to prevent herself from dwelling on all the misfortune she'd suffered in recent times. She glanced around at the decor of the place, noticing the waitresses were dressed like something out of the 1950s, the floor was tiled with a checkerboard pattern, the bench seats were upholstered with the same color leather as those in her truck. If she allowed her mind to wander from these distractions for any length of time, her thoughts would soon begin to focus on the fact Shelby was absent from her life. She would be overcome with a kind of chronic sadness, an abstract sense of longing for the part of her soul that had been torn away from her. The persistent sense of emptiness was like some kind of a callus on the roof of her mouth, a wound she couldn't stop probing with the tip of her tongue.

Juliette heard the bell ring over the entrance at the opposite end of the diner. Her nerves had fired up each time the door had swung open, and only when she'd seen it was a group of strangers wandering in on each of those occasions had her heartbeat begun to return to its normal pace. But now, with the door flung wide and the roar of passing cars wafting in, Juliette caught sight of an unmistakable streak of darkness lingering against the harsh backlighting of the sun, a terrifying slither of a person who strutted like a catwalk model into Juliette's peripheral vision. She glanced up through the dark lenses of her glasses and her heartbeat began to pound so hard, she felt as though she might actually pass out.

"You in disguise or something, sugar?" Amiyah asked, slurping on a wad of bubblegum as she spoke, her voice cold and mocking in tone, the same way it had been during Juliette's first encounter with her at The Pink Tunnel. And now, just like then, the young woman seemed to be little more than a stranger, an enigma standing at the edge of the table, casually checking her nails in a way that made Juliette feel she was too repulsive to even be looked upon.

"Sit down, kid," Juliette murmured, attempting to stop her nerves from resonating into her voice. Confident her sunglasses would hide the direction of her gaze, she allowed herself a brief inspection of Amiyah's clothing: a leather mini-skirt, an army surplus jacket, and a red beret, a choice of attire which made the young woman look as though she'd come dressed for some kind of conflict. As Amiyah slid into the vacant side of the booth, the motion of her bare legs and the shortness of her skirt forced Juliette to close her eyes and take a long breath. She was certain her ex-lover had dressed this way to torture her, but at the same time, she'd expected nothing less, understanding this kind of treatment was exactly what she deserved.

The same stoutly-built, snub-nosed waitress who'd served Juliette earlier came back to the table brandishing a notepad and pen. "What can I get you, sweetie?" she said.

Amiyah asked for a large coffee with several elaborate specifications. "She's paying," Amiyah said, nodding toward Juliette.

The waitress snorted out an ugly laugh and retreated back toward the service counter.

Amiyah's arrival had tainted the air with the dull stench of ingrained cigarettes. "Are you smoking again?" Juliette blurted out, unable to conceal her disapproval.

"That's none of your business," Amiyah replied, as if it were the kind of phrase she'd been waiting to use on her ex-lover for a long time.

"Fair enough," Juliette said, and all she could do was stare at the devastatingly perfect individual before her, safe in the knowledge her sunglasses would conceal the extent of her reverence. She was certain the young woman was even more beautiful than before, with her scarlet hat balanced at an angle on her head, her knotted braids tumbling down to frame her face, her dark eyes rolling with contempt. The mere sight of Amiyah's face was enough to get Juliette high, enough to numb all the pain of her life.

"Why am I here, Jules?" Amiyah sighed, folding her arms over her chest. "What do you want from me?"

Juliette was unable to answer, her concentration scrambled by her involuntary state of awe. She fumbled to remove something from her jacket pocket, an item that jangled and clanked until she brought it down onto the table. And then, with her hands concealing the object's form, she slid it across to Amiyah, before letting it go and watching the young woman's eyes for her reaction.

Amiyah screwed up her brow, and tilted her head to make sure she'd seen this thing right. She gathered the offering in one hand and held it up for inspection. "The Paradise Gardens?" she said, and from her outstretched fingers hung the item she'd been presented with, a single key on a wooden fob belonging to a room in the aforementioned motel.

Juliette looked at the key fob as well. The palm trees engraved over its wooden surface conjured up memories of happier times, but now, all these months later, the item had a new relevance, a purpose Juliette was going to have to explain.

"What am I supposed to do with this?" Amiyah asked.

"I bought you out," Juliette uttered in a single breath. She knew this scant explanation alone was not going to suffice, but with her heartbeat pounding so forcefully in her chest, these few words were the best she could do.

"What are you talking about?" Amiyah's eyes looked wide and uncharacteristically perturbed.

"I cut a deal with Caesar," Juliette explained, hanging her head in fear of the reaction her words might provoke.

Amiyah leaned further over the table and spoke with a quiet but forceful tone. "Juliette, you better tell me what the fuck is going on."

Juliette watched the young woman's mouth forming words and she realized she hadn't been in such close proximity to these darkly-painted lips since the last time she'd pressed her own mouth against them. She loosened her jacket and sat up straight in an attempt to focus her thoughts. "Like I said, I bought you out of your debt. And I got you a room at the motel as well. So you can stay there for a couple months, until you figure something out. It's a room with a kitchenette and all, so you can fix yourself something to eat. I know I promised I wouldn't cut any more deals with Caesar, but I figured I kind of owed you this much, for all that happened between us. So that's it, you're out, okay? You don't have to strip anymore." When Juliette finally dared to glance up, she saw Amiyah was staring back at her with an open-mouthed expression that lay somewhere between horror and disbelief. "It's my fee for taking the fight," Juliette explained.

"What fight?" Amiyah asked, throwing her hands about in a way that almost sent a nearby rack of condiments flying across the table.

"Okay, calm down," Juliette said, and she checked to see if anybody was looking in their direction. "What do you mean, what fight?"

"I mean, what fight are you talking about, Jules? How much clearer do I need to be?"

"Come on now," Juliette said, with a breath of laughter. "You're seriously trying to tell me you don't even know?"

Amiyah leaned further forward still, her dark eyes seeming blacker and more menacing than ever. "Don't fuck with me, Jules," she said. "I've got no idea what you're talking about."

Juliette took a moment to savor the young woman's agitation, taking great pleasure in the fact they were actually interacting, regardless of the nature of their conversation. "They honestly haven't told you?" she asked, dragging the moment out for as long as she could.

Amiyah thinned her lips and gritted her teeth, as if she were about to unleash all-out fury in Juliette's direction.

"Okay, okay," Juliette said. "If they really haven't even bothered to let you know, I guess I oughta fill you in." She leaned back so she could witness the entirety of Amiyah's reaction, and then she opened her mouth and uttered the words. "I'm fighting Shaolin," she said, and as the name left her lips, she felt a burn of embarrassment, fully aware of how ridiculous the revelation would sound.

The waitress appeared at their table with Amiyah's drink order and Juliette watched the pair interacting, waiting anxiously for the pleasantries to end. When the waitress left, Amiyah took a long, purposefully drawn-out sip of coffee, watching Juliette through the mist of steam rising out of the cup. She settled the cup back on the table, repositioned it a few times, and spun it around so the handle faced her precisely, clearly aware Juliette would be awaiting her response.

"She'll wipe you off the face of the earth," Amiyah said, eventually.

"You almost sound as if you care."

"How did you manage to get a fight like that, anyway?"

"I sold Caesar the backstory, and he made it happen. It's a hell of a tale, what happened between us."

"I'm guessing you left out the part about you fucking your own brother?"

Juliette closed her eyes behind her glasses, wincing at the young woman's words.

"So, with all that backstory," Amiyah said, "you finally decided to come out and tell the world you're gay, huh?"

"I got nothing left to lose," Juliette said with a shrug. "I lost everything that mattered the moment you told Shelby about me and Earl."

"You must really hate my guts," Amiyah said, with a satisfied smile creeping onto her lips.

Juliette wanted so badly to agree, but she'd been disarmed — as always — by how much she longed to have her ex-lover back in her life. "I could never hate you," she said, defeatedly.

Amiyah's sardonic smile grew wider. "Don't you think you at least owe me some kind of an explanation? It's not every day you discover something like that about a person, you know?"

"I know," Juliette said, fiddling with her empty cup as her anxiety increased.

"So, tell me," Amiyah persisted. "Tell me why it is you're attracted to your own brother?"

"Don't act as if you're any better than me," Juliette said. "I know how messed up you are. Remember that, okay? The things we used to do. The things you used to whisper into my ear when we were together. I know exactly who you are, Amiyah, and don't you forget that."

"That was just fantasy. Not real life. There's a difference."

Juliette glanced around again to check if anybody was paying attention to their conversation. "I thought it was all in the past," she said, her elbows resting on the table, her forefingers massaging her temples. "We might have had a thing when we were younger, but we knew it was wrong, of course we did. When you grow up in a house like ours, in a war zone, you pull together, you get close. And we got lost in that, somehow. We let it go too far. I thought I was over all of that nonsense, thought I'd finally moved on when I met you. But I guess the things we were doing together just put me back in that frame of mind, made me sick with lust all over again. I don't know how else to explain it, kid. If I could go back in time and change it all, I would." She reached across to take Amiyah's hands but the young woman recoiled as if touched by somebody with a contagious disease. "I'm sorry, okay?" Juliette said. "Tell me what I can do to put this right."

"It's too late for all that. I've moved on. We're ancient history."

The words hit Juliette harder than any punch she'd received in a fight. She took a moment to recover before speaking again. "Are you together?" she asked. "You and Shaolin?"

Amiyah choked on her coffee. "Is that why you're fighting her? Because you think we're together?"

"Either way, she's your new master, isn't she? And it's my job, as your former coach, to defend my honor, to slay your new master."

"You're pathetic."

"Do you really feel nothing for me at all? For the way we used to be?"

Amiyah ran her eyes over Juliette and laughed quietly to herself. "If you really want to know what I feel, the truth is, I hope you're wondering what I've got on underneath this skirt. I hope that tortures you, the fact you can never have me again."

"Don't," Juliette said. "Don't do this to me."

"And I hope you wonder who I'm sleeping with, and what we do together. I hope that keeps you awake at night, I really do."

Juliette tilted her head back to stop the tears that were welling in her eyes from spilling down her cheeks. "But, please, kid," she said, her lips trembling, "I think I might have been..." her voice trailed off.

"You thought what?" Amiyah demanded.

Juliette sniffed back her tears. "I mean, I think I might have been in love with you."

Amiyah shot up from the bench seat. "I haven't got time for this bullshit," she said, and she snatched the key fob from the table and slipped out of the booth, pulling her skirt down over her legs as she went.

"Amiyah, please," Juliette said, but the young woman was gone, storming off toward the other end of the diner with such haste, the heads of the other patrons followed her in unison.

Juliette was alone again, feeling as if everyone was watching for her next move. The young family in the nearby booth had spread a map out across the surface of their table. They were all studying the various locations on the map, probably plotting a route to their next destination. The children were up on their knees, trying to get a closer look at the places they might visit next. The parents were deep in concentration, carefully considering the infinite possibilities the map had presented them with. Juliette couldn't help but smile at the scene, despite the pang of jealousy it had driven into her. If she could never experience happiness quite like this, then she had to have something in her life, something of her own to make it all worthwhile.

***

Juliette's eyes took a few seconds to adjust as she emerged into the glaring light of day. She'd seen Amiyah take off in the direction of a gas station further along the freeway, so she started off on the same route, hoping she would encounter the young woman somewhere along the way. As she hurried from the diner, the scent of cigarette smoke stopped her in her tracks. She looked back over her shoulder, and right there, pacing around among a row of dumpsters was Amiyah, sucking on a roll up and silently mouthing curse words to herself, the movement of her lips spilling clouds of smoke out into the air.

"I'm sorry," Juliette said. "I didn't mean to upset you."

Amiyah took a long, hard drag from her cigarette, shaking her head in disgust the whole time. "Why did you always assume I wanted to quit stripping anyway?" she asked, and she blew a trail of smoke right into Juliette's face.

"But I thought you wanted to get away from that place?"

"Believe it or not, I actually like what I do. It was just you who could never accept that part of me when we were together."

Juliette paused for a moment, suddenly realizing she'd acted solely on her own assumptions. "Well, at least you can do it all on your own terms now, without having to pay Caesar back. That's gotta give you more time to focus on your training, surely?"

Amiyah took another drag, silenced by Juliette's reasoning.

"And answer me this," Juliette said. "Is Shaolin out here fighting to pay off your debt? I don't think so."

Amiyah sat down on the curb and folded her legs to conceal her underwear. She looked defeated there on the ground, exhausted by Juliette's persistence. "You must have a death wish," she said. "Asking for a fight like that at your age."

Juliette sat down next to the young woman and they watched the traffic passing over on the main road in front of the diner. "I've kinda got a plan," Juliette said. "I've seen a few holes in her game."

"Oh yeah, so what's your plan, a baseball bat? Because you're gonna need something, aren't you?"

"I'll figure it out. I always do."

"She's undefeated."

"But I've got experience."

"What you mean is, you're old."

"Thanks," Juliette said, and they laughed together for a while.

"It's been so long since I've seen that smile," Juliette said, running the back of her fingers against the underside of Amiyah's thigh.

The young woman's breathing intensified as she watched Juliette's hand trailing back and forth over her skin.

"We can figure this out," Juliette said. "I know we can make it work again." Her hand crept further up until it skimmed the hem of Amiyah's skirt.

Amiyah jerked away and scrambled to her feet. "Fuck, Jules," she said, shoving one of the dumpsters out of her way. "You just can't accept it's over, can you?"

Juliette took the young woman by the shoulders, attempting to contain her rage.

"Leave me the hell alone," Amiyah said, circling her arms wildly to break herself free. "You're sick. You're an absolute freak. That's all you'll ever be to me."

Juliette slumped back against the side wall of the diner, hugging herself and sobbing like the mess that she was.

Amiyah squared right up to her and stared deep into the lenses of her sunglasses. "You've really got it bad, haven't you? You just can't leave me alone. Or, do you just want to fuck everybody in your life? Maybe that's it."

"Come on, kid, there's no need for that." Juliette scanned her surroundings to check if anybody in the passing cars had noticed their altercation.

"So you really want me that bad, huh?" Amiyah reached up into her skirt, shifted her hips from side to side, and then, right there in the middle of the afternoon, she pulled her underwear down over her thighs and lifted her boots one at a time, stepping out of the string of fabric and scrunching it up into a ball.

"What in the world are you doing?" Juliette said, emitting a few breaths of nervous laughter, aware that only the cover of the dumpsters concealed the young woman's actions from the main road.

"Isn't this what you wanted?" Amiyah brought the ball of underwear up to Juliette's face. "Show me exactly how much of a freak you are."

Juliette was unable to move, frozen like a startled prey animal.

"Open your damn mouth. We both know you want this." Amiyah grabbed Juliette by the chin. "Open," she said.

Juliette allowed her jaw to slacken a little.

Amiyah pushed the ball of underwear into Juliette's mouth and rewarded herself with a smirk. She pressed her lips against Juliette's, and then broke away, laughing quietly. "Good luck with the fight, Jules," she said, before turning to depart, leaving Juliette alone with a mouthful of underwear.

Juliette was trembling. Tears were streaming over her cheeks. Her face was stretched out and distorted by all her bulging mouth contained.

The taste of cotton on her tongue flooded her mind with visions of all the places this knot of fabric had been pulled from. She hurried past the row of dumpsters and made her way into a small parking lot that was laid out behind the diner. Her truck stood alone in the far corner, parked well away from the main herd of vehicles, most of which appeared to have been lined up as close to the establishment as was physically possible. She climbed into her truck, struggling to keep her mouth closed in case anybody happened to be lurking in the stationary cars. She closed herself in, sucked hard on the fabric and her head began to spin.

She unbuttoned the fly of her jeans and slipped a hand beneath the waistband of her underwear, watching the windows of nearby cars for movement the whole time. With a newly acquired vision of her ex-lover fresh in her mind, she was a like a drug addict who'd just scored a hit of their preferred narcotic for the first time in months. Tears were running from behind her sunglasses as she relapsed into her addiction. And then, like a junkie at their lowest ebb, desperate to lift her spirits with some kind of a thrill, she tugged her jeans and underwear down from her hips, lowered both garments to her ankles, and spread her legs wide so she could openly pleasure herself right there in her truck. The cool atmosphere made her skin tingle and break out with goosebumps. The scent of her arousal drove her so wild with lust, she paid little regard to the fact she was masturbating in public. She lifted her T-shirt so she was completely exposed, almost hoping someone might see her like this and notice her despair.

Her lips strained to hold the underwear from spilling out of her mouth. Cords of drool dangled from her chin and trailed onto her breasts. Her pale body was slumped down in the cab, her heavy boots resting up on the dash, her hands working frantically to get to her to the point of ecstasy as quickly as possible. And as the pinnacle of it all drew near, she spat the sodden ball of underwear from her lips so it spilled down between her breasts, tumbled over her belly, and landed in a twisted heap between her thighs. She gathered the underwear up as the climax took hold, rubbing the fabric over her crotch and pushing it further inside herself with every wave of pleasure.

When the warmth of orgasm eventually receded from her body, her limbs collapsed all around her, feeling stiff and heavy now that her energy was spent. She stayed there for a while to recover, looking down at the damp underwear screwed up between her thighs like a discarded lover, unwanted now the act was over. With the unrelenting desire for Amiyah purged from her thoughts, all Juliette was left with was the sobering sight of her splayed body and the smell of sex hanging in the air. She realized—in this moment of post-masturbatory clarity—exactly how pathetic she was, and how badly her sexual deviancy had affected her life.

Juliette heard the muffled ringtone of her cell phone going off somewhere among her clothing. She rummaged in the pockets of her jacket and took out her handset. The screen was lit up with her brother's name and she knew he would be calling to ask why she wasn't at the gym training for her fight with Shaolin. She pulled her clothes back into place before accepting the call, fearing her brother might somehow detect her dishevelment from the tone of her voice. She removed her sunglasses to check herself in the rearview mirror, but all she could see reflected in her own tired eyes was the weight of all the hardship that was laid out in front of her.

CHAPTER 22

"Jules, it's almost time to make the walk," Earl called out from beyond the bathroom stall.

Juliette spat the last of her vomit into the toilet bowl. The back of her throat and the lining of her nostrils burned from all of the acidic bile she'd been regurgitating. Her body trembled all over, exhausted by the violent contractions of her stomach muscles. She tried to focus on her breathing. She knew this was no time to feel weak or afraid, but her nerves had always gotten the better of her this way. The sickness was just another part of her pre-fight routine, a ritual she'd endured so many times throughout her career.

Earl pushed the door open and helped his sister to her feet. "Did you get it all out?" he asked.

"I think so." Juliette stood shivering in her fight gear like a frightened child, her sallow skin glazed with sweat before she'd even made it out of the locker room.

"You know what else makes you throw up?" Earl asked. "Roller coasters," he said. "And they're a whole lot of fun as well. So let's get on this ride and enjoy it, kid."

Tommy entered the locker room and the roar of the crowd filtered in from the main arena. Juliette understood a large percentage of the audience would be waiting to watch her take a beating from the monster she was about to face in the cage.

"Is Shelby out there?" she asked, her voice sounding small and uncertain.

"I don't think she's coming," Earl said. "You need to forget about that and focus on your fight right now." He placed his forehead against Juliette's to deliver his final words of encouragement. "One last bank job," he said. "And we're out. We're going straight, right?"

"I guess so."

Earl waved his young assistant over to join them. "Come on, Tommy," he said, "you're a part of this family as well now. And as much as I hate to admit it, we need you out there, okay?"

Tommy hurried toward the siblings, almost sliding over on the wet floor in his haste, and the three of them formed a huddle in the center of the room.

"This is it, Jules," Earl said. "This is your moment to shine. Everything you've worked for your entire life has led you up to this point, right here. It doesn't matter if you win or lose. Just go out there and give her hell. That's all I'm asking of you. When Shaolin goes home tonight, I want her to know she was in a fight with Jules Diamond Diaz. I want her to feel it in every part of her body. You understand me?"

Juliette nodded her head, unable to speak due to the fact she was practically hyperventilating. She tried to focus on her brother's words, to enjoy the whole process the way he'd advised, but no matter how much she tried to relax, the fact Shelby was absent from her life made it seem her entire universe was out of balance. Shelby had always been Juliette's motivation to succeed, and right now, without the support of that driving force, she felt lost and alone, uncertain of her own capabilities, as if a vital part of her arsenal was missing at the time she needed it the most, when she was about to go into the toughest fight of her life.

"Focus, kid," Earl said, and he struck Juliette open-handed across the face. "You hear those voices out there? A lot of those people are here to see you. So, let's give them what they want, huh? Let's walk out there and show all these people exactly what we can do."

As Earl spoke, Juliette caught a glimpse of a strange and unfamiliar figure in the mirrors mounted over the wash basins. It took her a few beats to realize she was looking at her own reflection. Her hair had been braided and tied up out of her face. Her body was lean and muscular thanks to the grueling training schedule she'd endured over the past few months. She looked like an enhanced version of her usual self, a fearsome warrior ready to go into battle. Earl could offer all the encouragement he wanted, but it was the menacing glint in Juliette's own eyes that told her she had nothing left to lose. She glanced at Tommy and then at her brother one last time before she finally uttered the words both of her cornermen had been waiting to hear.

"Let's do this."

***

The stage lights that shone over the caged enclosure in the distance forced Juliette to look away. The lights seemed to burn brighter than they had in any of Juliette's previous bouts, their blinding glare reminding her of the fact this fight against a highly-decorated champion was the biggest challenge of her career. She squinted to focus on the walkway laid out before her, a narrow divide running through the shifting silhouettes of the crowd. The arena fell unnervingly quiet for a few seconds until the opening notes of Juliette's walk-out song resonated through the air like a battle cry heralding her arrival.

The chords of the guitar intro sent an electrifying chill through Juliette's body, and when the audience began to sing along, she was reminded of the euphoria their support could bring. The choice of song, as always, was "California Dreamin'," because as Earl had so often said, his sister was just a California girl chasing her dreams. Juliette fought to hold back her tears. She knew this might be the last time she would get to hear The Mamas & The Papas classic ringing out into the furthest corners of an arena.

Earl gave the nod to confirm the time had come to set off on the long walk toward the cage. The audience reached over the barriers to touch Juliette as she passed. The sensation of their fingertips skimming her arms and shoulders filled her with a sense of comfort, reassuring her she still had the adoration of her fans despite all she'd lost in her daughter and her lover.

Earl shot her a wink and mouthed the words, "Just enjoy it, kid."

She'd forgotten how good it felt to go into battle with her brother at her side. She realized—in this moment of clarity—exactly what made their relationship so special. It wasn't the intimacy they'd shared in the past; it was experiences like this that defined their unique bond. Margot would never understand how it felt to have Earl's support in a fight. This was something that belonged exclusively to Juliette, and only now did she finally appreciate the value of all the wild adventures she'd been on with her brother.

As they arrived at the cage, Juliette scanned the front rows of the audience for her daughter, but only found Caesar's spherical body and Dolores' white-blonde hair among the sea of faces staring back at her. Dolores drew a hand across her throat while Caesar bobbed with laughter and shook his head, confident he already knew precisely how the fight was going to play out.

Juliette's journey from the floor of the arena into the depths of the cage was mostly a blur, the officials checking her over and smearing Vaseline across her face to protect her from getting cut, her eyes darting over the crowd the whole time as she continued to search for Shelby. Moments later, Juliette was waiting up in the cage listening to her opponent's entrance music: some kind of monotonous Buddhist drumming that sounded more like the tolling of a death knell than a conventional song.

"Don't let it get to you, Jules," Earl said to his sister through the wire fence.

Juliette shrugged to ask what her brother was referring to, but then she saw it as well, Shaolin marching along the narrow pathway that cut a line through the crowd, with Amiyah and Oksana trailing a few steps behind, all three of them clad in matching rust-colored tracksuits as if they belonged to some sort of an army.

"You've gotta be kidding me?" Juliette said, understanding exactly why her opponent had selected this particular double-act to work her corner.

"Just ignore them, okay," Earl said. "Don't let it rile you up. You know that's what they want."

Regardless of Earl's advice, the crowd's rapturous applause forced Juliette to take notice of her opponent. The audience cheered so loudly, the entire building seemed to vibrate like a straining speaker. Juliette was certain most of the spectators were here to see Shaolin, a long-standing champion in this particular organization. Besides, many of those in attendance were probably too young to have ever heard of an aging veteran like Juliette, an old-timer whose career highlights took place long before the sport of mixed martial arts crossed over to the mainstream.

As Shaolin climbed the stairs into the cage and jogged a few warm-up laps around the circumference of the mat, she didn't even glance up in Juliette's direction, as if to suggest Juliette posed such a low level of threat, she was unworthy of being granted so much as a second of the champion's attention. Juliette took a deep breath to suppress her anger, not wanting her emotions to affect her performance. She tried to play Shaolin at her own game, ignoring the shaven-headed young woman as she circled past, but no matter how much Juliette tried to look away, she couldn't help noticing the veins swelling all over her opponent's limbs, the muscle-tone flexing in every part of her body. Juliette wondered if Amiyah's hands had ever explored the hardened flesh she was looking upon right now. Her insides burned at the thought of their naked bodies writhing together.

The ring announcer began to introduce each fighter in turn, calling out their names and detailing their statistics. Juliette was delirious with a mixture of nerves and adrenaline, unable to focus on anything the announcer had to say.

"We got this," Earl called out from over her shoulder. "Remember everything we trained for."

Juliette had pushed her body harder than ever in the buildup to this fight. She'd been so determined to succeed, she'd even gone to her father for help, visiting the old man on several occasions while Shelby was at school so she could sharpen her boxing skills and brush up on her footwork. She'd carried a punching bag—every few days—all the way up to her beloved spot in the hills, where she would hang the leather bag from the branches of the umbrella tree and practice the techniques her father had taught her, certain her mother would be watching from the heavens with tears of joy glazing her eyes and a wide smile stretched out across her face.

Juliette understood this was, in all likelihood, her last shot at gaining another championship belt. If she could just achieve this final victory over the head coach of Diablo MMA's rival team, it would be the perfect exclamation mark at the end of her career. Winning this fight would mean she could prove to herself and everyone else the countless years she'd dedicated to this sport had not been spent in vain. She had to show her daughter it had all been worthwhile. She had to be certain Earl wouldn't look at her for the rest of her life with that disapproving glare shooting from his eyes. In addition to all of this, she believed the harder she fought, the more Amiyah would know she was sorry, and then maybe there could be some slither of hope the two of them might somehow find a way to be together again.

Juliette held all of these notions in her mind as she squared up to Shaolin in the center of the cage. Juliette stared straight through her opponent, the mountain she had to climb over to get back to her lover. She finally allowed her gaze to settle on Amiyah's tracksuit-clad body through the diamond-grid wires of the fence. She was certain she saw fear in the young woman's dark eyes, and that look of trepidation made Juliette happy because she wanted her ex-lover to be afraid of everything that was about to happen.

"If you wanna touch gloves, then do it now," the referee said, but Juliette had no intentions of exchanging pleasantries with her rival, and judging by Shaolin's inaction it seemed she echoed this sentiment entirely. The referee directed both combatants back into their respective corners and the arena fell silent with anticipation. The complete absence of noise made Juliette feel as though nothing of importance existed beyond the cage walls and all that mattered was her fight to survive, to prevail in combat against the monster staring back at her from the other side of the mat.

When the referee signaled for the bout to begin, Juliette's mind had already shifted into fight mode. The animalistic part of her brain had taken control and she was acting on instincts alone, hyper-aware of every part of her immediate surroundings and every movement of her opponent's body. She advanced to the center of the mat, her limbs moving fluidly, her motions almost a dance. She saw her opponent's strikes coming toward her before they were thrown. Her years of experience meant she was able to preempt Shaolin's actions by expertly reading the smallest twitches of the muscles in her arms and legs. Juliette ducked and weaved, avoiding every shot with the same level of grace and poise her daughter displayed when performing as a ballerina on stage.

"Throw something, Jules," Earl cried. "Let your hands go."

Despite his relentless pleas, much of the round played out like a game of cat and mouse. Shaolin chased Juliette into the corners of the cage, and Juliette moved evasively, sliding away from kicks and lunging back to avoid punches. There was so little action between the fighters, the crowd began to voice their disapproval, and as the boos grew louder, Earl barked out his demands so ferociously his words lost all meaning, blending with the commotion of the audience until it sounded like everybody was roaring in disgust at Juliette's behavior.

When the air horn blasted to signal the end of the first round, Shaolin raised her arms into the air, confident the few punches she'd managed to land would be enough to put her ahead on the judges' scorecards.

Earl guided his sister onto the stool. "You gotta start doing something," he said. "You're not gonna win this by getting out of the way."

"Have you seen Shelby out there?" Juliette asked, oblivious to her brother's advice.

"The kid's not coming, damn it. You need to wake up and focus on the game plan. You just threw that round away. You've got four left to turn this around. That's twenty minutes out of the rest of your life. And then it's all over, there's no second chance."

Juliette took a bottle of water from Tommy and poured the liquid over her head to cool herself down. She couldn't decide which was the most unnerving prospect, the four rounds she had left to survive or the verbal battering she would receive from her brother if she didn't start performing to his expectations. "I got this," she said, and she climbed back to her feet before the break was over, eager to show her opponent she was ready to continue.

"Don't let me down, kid," Earl called out as the second round commenced.

Shaolin charged forward swinging her arms wildly, each consecutive strike an attempt to catch Juliette with a power-punch. The crowd gasped in unison. All of the spectators understood the fight would be over if any one of these haymakers were to land successfully.

Earl turned to his young assistant. "What the fuck is wrong with her, Tommy?"

"Coach, listen," Tommy replied, "we gotta slow Shaolin down and take some of the heat off those hands."

Earl drew a sharp breath. He knew his assistant was right, but faced with Juliette's lackluster performance, he couldn't think of any words of encouragement that might help her implement such a strategy.

As the fight went on, Shaolin grew increasingly frustrated. She altered her tactics and shot in for takedowns, running toward Juliette in repeated attempts at tackling her to the ground. In the final seconds of the round, the women began to grapple, and as the air horn fired off, Juliette lost her footing and wound up on the mat. Shaolin finally saw an opportunity to land a blow on her downed opponent who, up until now, had managed to avoid taking any significant damage. Juliette was on her hands and knees when the soccer kick landed with full force to the side of her face. Not a single member of the audience cheered at the sight of Juliette's lifeless body slumping to the mat, because every one of the spectators understood it was against the rules to kick a downed fighter to the head.

Earl clambered into the cage to be with his fallen sister. Tommy tried but was unable to stop the momentum of Earl's heavyweight body as he rolled over the top of the fence and swung down onto the mat. The referee ran over and pinned Earl against the fence. Oksana had vaulted in from her corner as well. Several suited officials hurried in to maintain order and keep everybody apart. As Juliette came around, half of her face felt like it was on fire. She sat up trying to figure out what was happening, and why she was suddenly surrounded by so much chaos.

Earl pushed the referee aside with the ease of an adult manhandling a child. "That was an illegal move," Earl barked in the direction of Shaolin's corner. "The fight's over."

Juliette hacked a mouthful of blood on to the mat. She checked her teeth with her tongue, certain a few of her molars were loose. The referee asked if she was able to continue with the fight, but her thoughts hadn't switched back on enough for her to understand the question. The officials ushered Oksana and Earl into their corners, leaving Juliette alone with her confusion.

The referee got down on one knee and repeated the question. "That was an illegal blow to the head," he said. "Are you able to continue?"

Juliette stared straight past him, studying Amiyah's body language to get a sense of whether she was concerned about what had happened.

Suddenly, a doctor was shining the light of a pen-torch directly into Juliette's eyes to check if her pupils reacted by constricting as they should.

"Seems okay to me," the doctor said to the referee.

Without a medical stoppage, Juliette knew the burden fell on her shoulders alone to decide whether she was able to go on with the fight. She now had the option of saying she was too hurt to continue, a decision that would render her the winner by default due to the fact her opponent would be disqualified.

Earl pulled her up onto the stool to recover. "Just take the belt, Jules," he whispered into her ear, encouraging her to accept the easy the way out. "Take the win bonus, kid. You need the money."

"That'll only line Caesar's pockets," Juliette replied.

"What the hell are you talking about?"

"I've given up my purse, okay?" Juliette explained. "I took the fight to pay off Amiyah's debt."

"You're out of your goddamn mind," Earl said. "Don't you dare go back out there. You've done enough already."

Shaolin thrust her arms into the air repeatedly, encouraging the crowd to boo Juliette for taking so much time to make up her mind.

The referee tapped at his watch. "I'm gonna need a decision," he said. "And no cornering," he added, but there was confusion as to whether Earl and Tommy should exit the cage due to the fact the round had already concluded.

Tommy placed a bag of ice against the back of Juliette's neck to cool her down. Juliette sat bolt upright as the frost made contact with her skin, but the words that came out of Tommy's mouth were far more startling than the sting of the ice. "Jules, I think your pops is here," the young man said.

Juliette tried to get up off the stool but Earl held her down by the shoulders. She pushed his hands away and leaned forward to see around him. Tommy was right; her father was shuffling through the crowd, battling to clear a path through the hordes of tightly-packed bodies on his approach toward the cage-side seats.

"Well, I'll be damned?" Earl said. "There really is a first time for everything."

Juliette felt a fire of urgency coursing through her veins. She didn't want her father to see her defeated like this the first time he showed up to one of her fights. "I gotta get back in there," she said.

"Just stay down," Earl growled through his teeth. "You were out cold."

As Billy Diaz's wide frame ambled closer to the cage, there appeared to be a pool of illumination shining all around him, as if somebody was pointing one of the stage lights directly at the old man. His weathered face and white hair flashed up on the giant screens that hung at either end of the arena and the crowd erupted with applause, eager to show their affection for the aging boxer.

"Who the hell does he think he is?" Earl said.

As Juliette studied the old man on one of the big screens, she saw something strange in the halo of light surrounding him. There was another body moving behind his, a smaller figure approaching the front rows with the same rate of progress he was. Earl was unable to hold Juliette back this time. She sprung to her feet and craned her neck for a better view. "She's here," Juliette said in a single breath. "She's really here."

Earl hung his head and closed his eyes, understanding exactly who his sister was referring to and what this meant for the continuation of the fight.

Shelby stepped out from behind her grandfather. The teenager looked so much older now than the last time Juliette had seen her. Maybe it was because she'd worn her best clothes and makeup to attend this event; maybe she really had blossomed from a child into a young woman since she'd walked out on her mother.

The referee shouldered his way past Tommy and Earl. "Do you

want me to stop this, or what?" he said.

Earl was shaking his head, imploring his sister not to go on.

Shelby's presence was like a shot of pure adrenaline, an antidote that woke Juliette from the tranquilizing effects of Shaolin's head-kick. Juliette gave a thumbs up signal up to the referee, and the audience cheered with more vigor than they had all evening.

"We're going straight into the break," the referee said. "You've got one minute."

Earl was sweating more profusely than Juliette, his cropped hair sparkling all over with perspiration. He stared into space, reeling from his sister's decision to continue.

Earl's silence prompted Tommy to speak up. "You gotta take her legs out, Jules," he said. "She's heavy on that front foot. Just kick it out every time you get a chance. That'll slow her down and stop her from stepping into those punches."

Juliette nodded her head in agreement and looked to her brother for his opinion.

Earl swept a towel across his forehead and emitted a few breaths of laughter, his fury placated by Juliette's display of grit and determination. "Tommy's right," Earl grumbled. "He's right." He reached out and took Tommy by the shoulder. "That's great coaching, kid," he said, finally acknowledging the young man as a worthy assistant.

"Thanks, Coach," Tommy said, and he glanced at the floor so the bulk of his Afro concealed the smile on his face.

"Why don't you two get a room?" Juliette said. "Now, if you don't mind, I've got some ass whooping to do."

Earl caught her by the wrist as she turned to leave. "You listen to Tommy, okay? Take her legs out from underneath her, or you're gonna get yourself knocked out in front of Shelby."

"That ain't gonna happen," Juliette said, pushing her mouthguard back into place. "Not today."

As the third round got underway, Shaolin rushed forward again, but this time Juliette was right there to meet her. They clashed in the center of the cage, exchanging a flurry of fists. The crowd went wild. This was the kind of frantic melee they'd been waiting to see all evening, the rivals throwing caution to the wind and trading blows at close range. Juliette caught Shaolin several times, but ate just as many punches in return. For just a split second in the midst of the carnage, Juliette was able to think clearly about what she was doing, her countless years of experience allowing her mind to operate rationally under such extreme conditions. Remembering the advice Tommy had offered, she twisted her hips and threw out a low kick, landing her foot directly to the side of her opponent's calf. Shaolin buckled for a second and backed away from the exchange, but Juliette refused to give the champion a break to recover, kicking her legs again and again.

"That's beautiful," Earl said.

Every time Shaolin came forward, Juliette punished her by whipping kicks out with both feet. She landed vicious switch kicks to Shaolin's thighs, calves, and ankles, almost sweeping her clean off her feet. Shaolin's face lit up with a wide, mouthguard-revealing smile, a clear sign she was trying to conceal how badly she'd been hurt by the blows. Her legs were a mess, reddened and gnarled with angry welts. As the third round came to a close, Shaolin hobbled back into her corner. The big screens brought up an image of her blemished flesh and the audience gasped with delight. Juliette nodded at Amiyah to tell her this was all being done in her name and the young woman turned and looked away, as if she understood the sacrifice Juliette was making and couldn't bear to look her in the eye.

Earl covered his sister's face with a towel. Juliette struggled to free herself from his clutches, but as she broke away from him, she saw the white towel was saturated with blood. She hadn't felt her face opening up during the exchange at the start of the round, but she understood now, she must have taken some form of damage. "How bad is it?" she asked, spitting her mouthguard into her hand.

"It'll heal up," Earl said. "You need to focus on your fight right now, not your face. Just keep doing what you're doing. Those leg kicks are gonna pay dividends as the fight goes on."

Shaolin appeared to be talking more than either of her cornerwomen. She snatched a bag of ice and held it against various parts of her own legs, chastising Amiyah for doing it incorrectly.

"That's what you call teamwork, right there," Earl said, gesturing toward his rival corner. "You're down two rounds to one, Jules," he said. "Let's even this out and get another one in the bag."

At the start of the fourth round, Shaolin was more aggressive than ever in her pursuit of a knockout, clearly realizing there was a good chance her injured legs weren't going to hold up until the end of the fight. Her desperation left her vulnerable to counterattacks, and her calves and thighs continued to take a beating every time she stepped into striking range. Despite her injuries, she was still a force to be reckoned with, and even though she was limping about the cage, she was able to catch Juliette with enough combinations to keep the spectators perched on the edges of the seats.

The cut on Juliette's forehead was leaking blood into her eyes and she was forced to throw punches blindly, hoping her strikes would keep her opponent away until the end of the round. Her right hand connected with some unseen part of Shaolin's shaven head, somewhere on the top of the woman's skull, where there was no significant covering of hair or flesh to offer any form of padding. A flash of pain ignited within Juliette's fist. Her palm felt as though it was swelling up, inflating inside her glove. She'd been doing this long enough to know her hand was broken, but she had to suppress the urge to react in any noticeable way. She couldn't allow such a debilitating injury to be detected by her opponent or by any member of her rival team.

The thrum of pain distracted Juliette from focusing on her defense. She dropped her hands in the closing seconds of the fourth round and

Shaolin struck like the apex predator she was, rushing in on Juliette and wrestling her to the mat. Shaolin lowered herself to speak into Juliette's ear. "You're done," she said. "Quit now and spare your daughter the misery of watching you take a beating." The fighters continued to tussle long after the air horn had sounded, forcing the referee to separate them and direct them into their corners for the break.

"That was a close round," Earl said. "I'm not gonna lie, she might be winning three rounds to one; you might have two each. But either way, we can't afford to let this go to the judges. You're gonna have to take her out."

Juliette shook her hand to silently communicate the fact it was broken, and Earl's brow grew heavy with frustration. His disillusionment knocked the wind right out of Juliette's lungs when she was already trying desperately to catch her breath. Struggling for the energy and the will to continue, she scoured the front rows, hoping to receive some scrap of support or encouragement from her family members. Much to Juliette's dismay, Shelby was burying her face into her grandfather's chest, unable to cope with the nightmarish spectacle of the gaping wound on her mother's head spattering blood all over the cage. Meanwhile, in the opposing corner, Amiyah's eyes had grown weary with sorrow, her body slouched defeatedly in a way Juliette had never seen it before.

Juliette felt alone and abandoned, as if everybody in her life had lost faith in her at a time when she needed them more than ever. She looked into the tired, broken faces of her loved ones, and she finally understood how much energy she'd wasted trying to please them. She knew they would never be satisfied, no matter how much she strived to do their bidding. She couldn't allow them to be her motivation anymore because they were far weaker than she was, and she understood that now. She was about to enter the final round of her life, and for the first time ever she was going to fight purely for herself; not to impress her ex-lover, her daughter, her brother, or her father, but to prove to herself she could accomplish more than any of them thought possible. Even though her hand was broken and ringing with pain, the wound on her head was gushing blood all over her face, she was going to earn the respect of every single person in the arena, no matter what it took for her to accomplish this goal.

"Five minutes for the rest of your life," Earl growled.

His voice might as well have been Juliette's own subconscious echoing about the inside of her head. As she got up to her feet, she felt like she was floating, her aching body carried into action by her determination to succeed. "Fuck all of you," she said under her breath as she turned to face her opponent.

Shaolin stared her down like a hungry animal who'd tasted the blood of its prey, but Juliette felt no sense of fear or discouragement. In fact, she was thankful for the opportunity to face such a formidable opponent, a worthy embodiment of all the darkness in her life. No matter the outcome—whether she was victorious or not—she knew her family was going to have to watch her go through the ordeal of this last round, and if that made them understand the pain of her existence in any significant way, that would be enough for her.

As the final round began, Juliette heard her daughter calling out from the audience. "Please, Mom, I love you," Shelby screamed, and those words affected Juliette more than any punch she'd received in the fight.

Noticing Juliette's distraction, Shaolin closed in for the kill. The fighters began to trade blows at close range, both of them understanding how dangerous it would be to allow the judges to determine who'd won. The five minutes that followed were the most brutal of Juliette's entire career. She walked through the storm of punches until her limbs, her face, and her hair were saturated with blood, making her look like the type of demonic creature her team's name alluded to. She waded forward, paying little regard to Shaolin's attacks, relentlessly kicking the champion to her calves and thighs, hoping her welted legs would eventually fail her and she would no longer be able to stand. In her pursuit of these kicks, she was punched to the ground over and over, but every time she went down, she fought tirelessly to scramble back to her feet. The audience exploded with appreciation for her tenacity. They chanted her name again and again, their synchronized cries fueling her with the energy she needed to go on.

With the bones of her most powerful weapon shattered into pieces, Juliette was forced to utilize other parts of her body. She swung her right elbow into Shaolin's face, and the glancing blow split the champion open across the bridge of her nose and sent her stumbling back against the fence. Shaolin swiped the blood from her wound and inspected it on the tips of her fingers. Incensed by the damage to her nose, she charged in for a takedown, but as she came forward, her steps were awkward and unsteady. Just as Earl had predicted, the kicks Juliette had been landing were finally paying off in the closing minute of the fight. Juliette rotated her hips as hard as she could to whip out a powerful kick. Shaolin was swept off her feet, her legs giving way so that she crashed down to the mat. Juliette collapsed onto her floored opponent, slid across her splayed body, and wound up straddling her in the mount position.

"Twenty seconds," Earl barked, his voice sounding horse and worn out.

Thick cords of blood and drool poured out of Juliette's mouth like entrails spilling from inside her, the dark liquid gushing down over Shaolin's face and body. The champion bucked and twisted to free herself from the bottom, but Juliette arched her back and adjusted her hips, effortlessly sitting dominant over her struggling adversary. Juliette looked through the wires of the fence, straight into Amiyah's eyes, and then, holding the young woman's gaze, Juliette began to slam her broken fist into Shaolin's face. An electrical charge ran through Juliette, a current that fueled her to commit acts of barbarity she knew would shock everybody in attendance, including her daughter and her father.

Juliette wanted them to see her behaving in this animalistic manner, because these acts of violence would communicate all of the things she could never bring herself to say.

Even though the blows were thrown to Shaolin's face, the pain was displayed on Juliette's own features. As she landed those punches over and over, the cold, unforgiving look in her eyes told everyone in the arena of all the torment she'd suffered throughout the countless years she'd been in love with her brother, the torture she'd endured during a lifetime of denying she was attracted to women, the emptiness that had been cast into her by the knowledge she would never be good enough for her daughter, and the unrest she lived with every day because she would never know the truth of what happened to her mother.

The air horn signaled the end of the fight and the referee threw his arms around Juliette to stop her bombardment. She was pulled away and wrestled to the ground, but she kept her eyes on her ex-lover the whole time, savoring the open-mouthed look of horror that was displayed on the young woman's face.

Earl rushed into the cage and began to mop the blood from his sister's face. "Put your hands in the air," he said. "Make it look like you know you won."

Juliette stared at him blankly. She wasn't willing to do his bidding anymore. After everything she'd just been through, she had no desire to please anybody else.

The referee took her by the hand and guided her to the center of the mat. He held on to Shaolin with his other hand and the three of them waited for the judges' decision. The two combatants stood side by side, separated only by the referee, their bodies drenched with blood, their chests heaving with exhaustion, their fates lying in the hands of the judges, a panel of adjudicators who'd been trying to keep track and make sense of the extreme acts of savagery that had played out before them.

Juliette was surprised by how little she felt as her defeat was announced. Even though Juliette had finished the fight on top, with her opponent barely able to stand, the judges decided the champion had done enough in the early rounds to win a split decision victory.

"And still," the announcer called out, "the bantamweight champion of the world, Shaolin!"

Juliette remained stoic, her face expressionless, her weary arms just about managing to clap out her applause. She was certain she'd done all that she could, had performed well enough against a formidable opponent to feel a sense of inner contentment for the rest of her life. The fact most of the onlookers were booing the judges' decision was enough to bolster Juliette with a rare sense of confidence in her own convictions. She held her head high, proud to be hanging up her gloves and retiring after the battle she'd just survived.

Shaolin slung her championship belt over one shoulder, squared up to Juliette, and began to look her over. Earl stepped towards them, ready to intervene, but after a brief pause, Shaolin dropped down to her knees and bowed her head at Juliette's feet. The cries from the audience shifted up a few octaves as they voiced their approval of the honorable gesture. Overcome with emotions, Juliette collapsed to her knees, her body hunched over to mirror the champion's.

Shaolin threw the gleaming belt she'd earned for this victory over Juliette's shoulder. "Please, accept this on behalf of my team," Shaolin said. "You've earned it."

"I can't," Juliette replied, her eyes brimming with tears.

"Just take it," Shaolin insisted, holding the belt in place over Juliette's shoulder. "Besides, I've got seven more at home."

As the women knelt opposite each other in the center of the cage, everybody in the building shared a mutual appreciation for the concept of respect. For the martial arts enthusiasts and practitioners in attendance, this was a spiritual experience that none of them would ever forget. This was the reason Juliette practiced her art, to share moments like this with her fans.

Even Caesar was giving a standing ovation. Dolores was tugging at his sleeve, trying to pull him back into his chair like a child embarrassed by their father's behavior.

Earl lifted Juliette up to her feet and tied the belt around her waist. Tears were streaming down his cheeks.

"I'm sorry," Juliette said. "I almost had her."

"Are you kidding me?" Earl said. "That was the greatest fucking thing I've ever seen. When people talk about this fight, they're gonna say you should have won, that you was robbed. They're gonna be talking about this forever. That's better than a victory to me."

"You mean that?" Juliette said, her swollen lips just about managing a smile.

"You're gonna be remembered as a legend, kid," Earl said. "The way you always deserved to be."

The cage was crowded with bodies: officials trying to maintain order, cameramen wielding their cumbersome apparatus, members of each team eager to celebrate with their comrades. Billy Diaz pried a path through the commotion and emerged into the clear space before his daughter. He stretched his palm out to Earl, and after pausing to get the measure of one another, both father and son shook hands for the first time in years.

"You did it, girl," the old man said, turning his attention to Juliette. "You showed us all what you're made of."

Juliette tried to wipe the blood from her face, conscious her father would be horrified by her disheveled appearance.

"Now, there's somebody here who wants to see you," the old man said, and he turned to form a divide through the tightly packed muddle of bodies.

Shelby charged out of the crowd almost bowling Juliette off her feet. They embraced so hard, they stumbled back into the camera equipment and bounced off the cage walls, their bodies tangled together, their lips meeting over and over.

"I'm so sorry, Mom," Shelby said.

"You've got nothing to apologize for, Doll-face."

"I wanna come home. I've missed you so much."

"I love you, Doll," Juliette said, holding her daughter's head and kissing her hair. "I love you."

Shaolin had already given her post-fight interview and was now hobbling out of the cage, her hunched body supported by her teammates, Amiyah and Oksana.

Earl took his sister by the wrist. "Come on, Jules," he said. "We gotta do your interview. It's your moment to shine. They wanna talk to you."

"Just give me a minute, okay?" Juliette said, watching as the three members of Team Zen struggled to make their way down the little set of steps that led onto the arena floor.

"It's time to say goodbye," Earl said. "Time to announce your retirement."

"Give her a minute, Uncle Earl," Shelby said, understanding precisely what her mother was watching and waiting for.

The orange tracksuits of Team Zen slowly disappeared from Juliette's line of vision, the trio swallowed up among the crowd of fans eager to congratulate Shaolin for her win. As Juliette watched Amiyah walking out of her life one final time, she felt her heart sinking harder than it had when her defeat was announced. She hung her head, unable to take any more punishment after the fight she'd endured.

Shelby gripped her mother's hand a little tighter, an encouraging squeeze that prompted Juliette to look up and squint into the distance. Just when it seemed all hope was fading, Amiyah hesitated, her body freezing as if gripped by some kind of indecision. And then, almost moving in freeze-frame slow motion, Amiyah turned, glanced over her shoulder and looked right into Juliette's eyes.

ABOUT THE AUTHOR

Based in the UK, Lanta Brown lives in a small house nestled among the trees at the edge of a Victorian park. When not writing, or working at her day job, she spends much of her free time tending to the needs of her house rabbit, a strange little being who lives at the top of the stairs.

I was compelled to write this book when I realized just how much hardship MMA practitioners go through to make it in the sport. Each one of those fighters has their own unique back story. This novel is my own imagining of one such tale.

www.lantabrown.com

Lightning Source UK Ltd.
Milton Keynes UK
UKHW041834150321
380411UK00001B/210